Baseball Fantastic

OUT OF THIS WORLD BOOKS

Aurora Awards:
An Anthology of Prize-Winning Science Fiction and Fantasy Stories
edited by Edo van Belkom

Arthur Ellis Awards:
An Anthology of Prize-Winning Crime Fiction
edited by Peter Sellers

Northern Dreamers:
Interviews with Famous Science Fiction, Fantasy & Horror Writers
Edo van Belkom

Death Drives a Semi: Horror Stories
Edo van Belkom

Out of This World:
Canadian Science Fiction & Fantasy Literature
edited by Andrea Paradis

Trapdoor To Heaven
Lesley Choyce

Baseball Fantastic

Stories edited with an introduction and contributions by

W.P. KINSELLA

The publisher gratefully acknowledges the
support of The Canada Council for the Arts
and the Book Publishing Industry Development
Program of the Department of Canadian Heritage.

ISBN 1-55082-268-3

Series Editor: Edo van Belkom
Design by Susan Hannah.
Copyedited by Mandy Chan.

Printed and bound in Canada by AGMV Marquis,
Cap-Saint-Ignace, Québec.

Published by Quarry Press Inc.,
PO Box 1061, Kingston, Ontario,
K7L 4Y5, Canada.
www.quarrypress.com.

CONTENTS

ACKNOWLEDGMENTS

Introduction copyright 1999 by W.P. Kinsella.

"Fred Noonan Flying Services" copyright 1999 by W.P. Kinsella.

"Zanduce at Second" from *The Hotel Eden and Other Stories*, copyright 1997 by Ron Carlson. Used by permission of W.W. Norton & Company, Inc.

"Judgment Call" by John Kessel, first appeared in *The Magazine of Fantasy and Science Fiction*, copyright 1987 by Mercury Press, Inc.

"Streak" by Andrew Weiner, first appeared in *Isaac Asimov's Science Fiction Magazine*, copyright 1992 by Davis Publications, Inc.

"In Boise" by Rick Wilber, first appeared in *Joltin' Joe: The Best of Joe DiMaggio*, copyright 1999 by Rick Wilber.

"Lost October" by David Sandner and Jacob Weisman, first appeared in *Pulp Eternity*, copyright 1999 by David Sandner and Jacob Weisman.

"Naked to the Invisible Eye" by George Alec Effinger, first appeared in *Isaac Asimov's Science Fiction Magazine*, copyright 1973 by Conde Nast Publications, Inc.

"The Vampire Shortstop" by Scott Nicholson, first appeared in *The Writers of the Future, Volume XV,* copyright 1999 by Scott Nicholson.

"Ted Williams Storms the Gates of Heaven" by Louis Phillips, first appeared in *Hot Corner*, copyright 1996 by Louis Phillips.

"Two Men On, Bases Empty" by Stefano Donati, first appeared in *Genre Tango*, copyright 1999 by Stefano Donati.

"Baseball Memories" by Edo van Belkom, first appeared in *Aethlon: The Journal of Sport Literature*, copyright 1989 by Edo van Belkom.

"The Winning Spirit" by Robert H. Beer, first appeared in *Eternity Online*, copyright 1998 by Robert H. Beer.

"Drayton's Ace" by L.K. Rogers, first appeared in *The Vampire's Crypt*, copyright 1997 by L.K. Rogers.

"Maxie Silas" by Augustine Funnell, first appeared in *The Magazine of Fantasy and Science Fiction*, copyright 1987 by Mercury Press, Inc.

"The Franchise" by John Kessel, first appeared in *Isaac Asimov's Science Fiction Magazine*, copyright 1993 by Davis Publications, Inc.

"Sunny Billy Day" from *Plan B For the Middle Class*, copyright 1992 by Ron Carlson. Used by permission of W.W. Norton & Company, Inc.

"The Indestructible Hadrian Wilks" copyright 1999 by W.P. Kinsella.

Introduction

W. P. KINSELLA

Twenty years ago I sat down to write a novel about a young Iowa corn farmer who hears a message from a disembodied voice that he interprets to mean he should build a baseball field in the middle of his cornfield, and that if he does, long-dead baseball greats will turn up to play on it. The novel was *Shoeless Joe* and it became the movie *Field of Dreams*. From its success I discovered that there was a market for fantastical baseball stories. I've since published three collections of stories, *The Thrill of the Grass, The Further Adventures of Slugger McBatt, and The Dixon Cornbelt League*, in which at least half of the stories are of a fantastical nature.

The one question I am invariably asked in every interview I do is, "Why do so many writers find baseball an appealing subject?" and consequently, "Why are so few books written about the other sports?"

I invariably answer that I feel baseball is conclusive to fiction writing because of its open-endedness. The other sports are twice enclosed, first because of rigid playing boundaries, second because of time limits. It doesn't matter how wonderful Wayne Gretzky was on ice, or Troy Aikman is on a football field, it is very difficult to write anything fantastical about those sports because they are twice enclosed. Baseball, on the other hand, knows no time limits, and on the true baseball field, the foul lines diverge forever, eventually, because of their sheer numbers, taking in most, or all of the universe. This complete openness makes for myth and for larger-than-life characters, two concepts that fantasy writers are always looking for.

Until I read the stories included in *Baseball Fantastic*, I did not realize that fantasy baseball tales had become a sub-genre of Fantasy. I grew up reading and being influenced by Ray Bradbury, and when I was a teenager, I read *Galaxy* and *Magazine of Fantasy and Science Fiction*, but it has been forty years since I've seriously read any fantasy. I was amazed at the quality of the stories submitted. I thrilled to the world-class tales by John Kessel and Ron Carlson, which are my favorites, but I'm sure you will find favorites of your own.

Fred Noonan Flying Services

W. P. KINSELLA

"Courage is the price that life extracts for granting peace. The soul that knows it not knows no release from little things."
— Amelia Earhart

"**E**mpty your pockets," Allison says.

"I'm not positive I want to do this," I say, as Allison gently turns me toward the plane, a single engine antique I'd guess was from the 1920s. While I rest my hands on the side, Allison, like a police officer, parts my feet, pats me down as if I were under arrest.

She extracts a business card from my shirt pocket, my wallet from one rear pocket, my money clip, bills and change from the other. My keys and comb, a pen, Kleenex, my bank book from my side pockets.

"Today's the day," Allison says.

"We're really going to . . ." I stammer.

"Don't you want to make love with me?" Allison asks, knowing full well the answer.

It's been three days since we've had sex. Allison has had 5:00 a.m. calls each morning. Her business is setting up photo shoots. Sometimes she is also the photographer.

I'd do anything for Allison. It is as if she has me under a spell of some kind. Conjured, my catcher, a Cajun from Bayou Jeune Fille, Louisiana would say. Her voice, low and sultry, is like mesmerizing music. She is my fantasy. Today, she wears a white sun dress with a few slashes of Aztec gold across the breasts and shoulders. Her Titian hair falls in waves to the middle of her back. Her cool blue eyes are the color of dawn.

"But, where's my uniform? We're doing a shoot, aren't we? 'Redbird Flying High'. You said that was what it would be called."

I'm babbling. I can't believe this is happening. When she finishes emptying my pockets, Allison discards the contents onto the tarmac at our feet. I think of my identification, credit cards, photos. All the years of my life casually tossed away, like ripping apart a stack of calendars.

"I told you whatever was necessary to get you here," she says, her voice a purr. She slips under my wide-spread arms, bobs up in front of me, between me and the plane, locks her arms around my neck, kisses me feverishly.

Though we've only known each other a short time, I am in love with Allison, thrillingly, magically in love, so much so that my senses seem more acute than I ever remember them. In restaurants I can gaze into Allison's eyes and hear conversations at other tables, smell the tantalizing food odors from nearby plates. Colors have a new intensity. In the on-deck circle I can pick her out in the stands twenty rows behind the Cardinals' dugout, tell at a glance what earrings she is wearing, read the smile on her lips as she watches me, her tongue peeking, massaging her bottom lip as it often does.

Allison works for the Cardinals' public relations firm. We met because early in the baseball year, the star players have to pose for photographs that are eventually turned into posters and given out to fans on various special promotion days during the season. Four Cardinal regulars, being the number 3, 4, 5, and 6 hitters in the line-up, the power of the order, were assigned to pose collectively. We met Allison at the ballpark at 9:00 a.m., an unheard of hour for a major league ballplayer to be up and alert, let alone dressed in an immaculate home uniform and ready to have make-up applied.

"I raised me a prize hog when I was in 4-H as a kid," said Foxy Rinehart, our home run hitter, who grew up on a dirt farm near Nevada, Missouri, "and after I washed him, perfumed him, and tied a blue ribbon around his neck, he wasn't no purtier than we are this morning." Foxy said this as Allison was powdering his forehead and nose. She had already made him apply some lip gloss to his large, pouty sweet potato of a lower lip that was always cracked and sunburned, looking like it was beginning to swell after a recent punch in the mouth.

"Soon as you boys are presentable I'll drive you out past Webster Groves to a big lumber yard; we'll meet the photographer there."

When she came to powder me, I was sitting on one of those blue metal folding chairs that are about as comfortable as ice. She nudged my knees apart and stepped in so close my nose was virtually between her breasts, her perfume was overpowering, expensive. I could feel heat radiating from her.

"Got to make you beautiful," she said.

"I'll reward you handsomely if you do," I said. "I'm thirty-one years old and no one's been able to come close so far."

Allison was wearing a rose-colored blouse. She was close to my age (thirty, I found out later). None of the other players on the shoot had turned twenty-five yet.

I had once owned a spice-colored shirt the same magnificent shades of yellow and red as Allison's hair.

"Maybe we'll settle for rugged," she said. "I'd need putty to fix you up properly, maybe even cement," and she laughed a deep, throaty laugh that was genuine, not the sad little tinkle a lot of women pass off for laughter. Her breasts bobbed in front of my face. She was wearing what I decided to think of as safari pants, khaki with about a dozen pockets on the thighs and below the knees. "Your nose has more pores than a pumice stone, and three bandits could hide behind it the way it's bent over."

"I used to be beautiful," I said, "until my face collided with a second baseman's knee a couple of seasons back. Doc said my nose looked like a zucchini that had been stepped on."

I stared up into Allison's eyes and was surprised to find a clear, almost iridescent blue — I expected hazel or green to match her hair.

We spent the whole day outdoors at a sawmill, amid the tangy odors of cedar and other cut lumber, the spongy ground layered with sawdust, a lathe operator set up in the foreground, supposedly turning a spoke of white lumber into a bat, while the four of us posed around him in different combinations, looking strong and rugged, some in batting stances, some holding the bat like a rifle, or cradling it like a baby. A sign behind us read CUSTOM LUMBER. There was a photographer, a wisp of a man with the body of a child and a windblown fringe of white hair. Allison arranged the poses for him, even snapped a few of the pictures herself.

"I hope you don't mind my saying so," she said directly to me, "but you look as though you're planning to kill worms instead of hit a baseball."

Then she repositioned me and the bat, leaving her hand on mine just an instant too long as she moved the bat up my shoulder. Placing her hands flat on my shoulders, she turned me a few degrees to the right; she left her hands there a long time, letting me feel the warmth filter through my uniform.

I scowled, trying to look at her as if she'd just poured a drink in my lap, but I couldn't quite bring it off.

"I've seen a few games in my day," she said. "When I was growing up, my dad and I had season tickets in K.C. Name the guy who let George Brett's fly ball drop for a hit so George could beat Hal McRae for the batting title?"

"He played left field for the Twins, and his name started with a Z."

"No points for a partial answer," said Allison, adjusting the angle of the bat, smoothing my uniform.

She hadn't flirted or acted even vaguely familiar with the other players. I wasn't surprised at the attention she paid me — I'm used to that kind of thing — but I was a little worried, for I found myself attracted to her. What concerned me was that many women are captivated by athletes, by famous people in general, often not by the person at all, but by the power they represent.

"Scott," Foxy Rinehart said to me one day, "the opportunities are endless. If a ballplayer on the road sleeps alone, he does so by choice."

I agree.

Wariness was one of the reasons I didn't make a move on Allison. All athletes, but especially married men, even semi-married men like myself, have to be careful of the women who make obvious overtures. Some women collect ballplayers the way boys collect baseball cards. Then there are the lunatic few hoping for a chance to file a paternity suit.

As Allison and I talked over a lunch of sandwiches and soft drinks at the sawmill, the other players never seemed younger to me. They horsed around, like the boys most of them were, talking music and nightclubs, girls and cars. The day was one of my rare off days in St. Louis. After the other players were dropped off, Allison and I went for dinner, where I found myself opening up to her more than I had with anyone in years.

"Ballplayers shouldn't marry," I heard myself saying, "or if they do, they shouldn't have kids. Once a baby comes along, the wife doesn't go on the road anymore, another child and she skips spring training. Then, when the oldest goes into kindergarten, the family stays home, wherever that may be, until school is out. That means they can't come to the city where you're playing until July, and if the city is like St. Louis where the summers are molten, the family stays home in the air-conditioned mansion. Half the guys on the team are in my situation. The season is long and lonely, and absence, as they say, does not make the heart grow fonder. The distances that are at first only miles become chasms of resentment on both sides. Everyone thinks they can handle the separations, almost none can."

"I know all about separation," said Allison. "I've got a guy, but he's always made it clear his career comes first. He a foreign correspondent with CBS. Now you see him, now you don't. I'll come home and find him there, he sleeps for 48 hours, we make love, and then he's gone to Bosnia, Lebanon or some other troubled spot for six weeks."

"I didn't even know I felt the things I've just told you," I said. "I feel a little foolish for laying all this on you."

I could tell by the way she looked at me that all I had to do was make the first move. But I didn't. I needed to be certain Allison wasn't a collector, that she was someone who wanted me, not the uniform, the power, the celebrity, the money.

Whatever my wife and I once had was gone. I'd known it for a couple of years, but didn't want to admit it, even subconsciously. Though we were not legally separated, when I went home to Memphis at the end of last season, we lived separately. I still saw a lot of Sandra and the kids. My phone call home, (I still call about three times a week), a call that at one time produced laughter and 'I love yous,' and, from me, a pitch by pitch recount of the plays I'd been involved in that evening, and from Sandra a recounting of her day and the cute things the kids did and said, was, as usual, only a long litany of complaints from Sandra, about the children, the weather, the house.

I listened, saying virtually nothing, wondering how things could have changed so much without either of us being conscious of it.

After I hung up, I sighed, reminding myself that I only had two or three years left as a pro. I'll muddle through, I thought. My best years are behind me, I've got to adjust to the inevitable slide, the hanging curve ball that only makes it to the warning track because my timing is off 1/1000 of a second, the step I've lost in the outfield, the lapses of concentration caused by my thinking of my deteriorating abilities. Things will improve when I'm home for good, I thought. But the thought of being *home for good* with a wife who has become a stranger, a family I barely know, left me depressed, my limbs lead weights, dragging me down.

Allison phoned about a week later.

"I've arranged for another promotion poster," she said. "One using you alone. Just got the idea last night. I pitched it to the Cardinals this morning and they love it. It will be called 'Redbird Flying High'."

"What does it involve?" I asked. A public relations person once asked several members of the Cardinals, including me, to dress in costumes identical to the team mascot, Fred Bird the Redbird. Another suggested the whole team should be photographed mud wrestling to promote Fan Appreciation Night.

"Oh, nothing to worry about, it will all be done on the tarmac. We'll rent an old biplane, the kind they used to use for stunt flying, we'll stand you out on the wing with your bat. We may put a helmet and goggles on you, I haven't decided. We'll get a big fan and the wind will be blowing the pilot's scarf and my hair, I'm going to sit behind the pilot. After the shoot we'll paint in a background of sky and cloud and ground below. It will look exactly like we're flying at a thousand feet."

I agreed to do the project. We talked on, arranging to meet for dinner after that night's game. That evening I did make the first move.

"For the rest of the night we're going to be the only two people in the world," I said. "No one else exists, family, business, baseball, whatever — all erased. Just us, we can say anything, we can . . ."

"I know," said Allison. "It's alright to be in love, just for tonight," and she placed her fingers on the back of my neck, and found her way into my arms. I lifted her hair with my left hand, kissed along her neck, nibbled her earlobe.

After long, sweet hours of lovemaking, of enjoying the terrible thrill of being close to someone after being alone for such a long time, we talked dreamily of what it would be like if we never had to open the door and go back into the real world. But the real world intruded on us soon enough, for even though I didn't want to, I began listing the many dissatisfactions of my life.

"I'm tired of baseball," I said. "It used to be my whole life, but I'm past my prime. I play for the money. I know I'm never going to hit three home runs in a game again, never going to bat in a hundred runs or hit thirty homers. I'm batting .280 but the fans boo me because I'm not the hot shot kid I was seven seasons ago."

Allison leaned over me, her hair trailing across my face; we kissed.

"I'm sorry," I said. "I was the one who was going to be sure we didn't talk this way. I've already whined about my bad marriage and my career. Sometimes I just wish I could disappear."

"What if I told you, you could," said Allison, her lips against my cheek, her musical voice a thrill.

"I'm too well known to disappear," I said matter-of-factly. "No matter where I'd go some eight-year-old would appear out of the woodwork to ask for an autograph."

"Unless you really disappeared."

"What do you mean?"

"Suppose there was a unique place," said Allison, "a very special somewhere where all the people who vanish without a trace from the face of the earth — a place where they all go to live."

"You're not serious?"

"I believed you had an imagination," said Allison. There was a hint of annoyance in her voice.

"What the heck do you mean?" I drew away from her. I sat up, swung my feet over the side of the bed, sat with my back to her.

"Take it easy," Allison said, reaching out, tentatively touching my shoulder. "There's more going on here than you're aware of."

I recall that and other conversations as I hold the telephone receiver in my hand and dial part of the number, all but the final digit, in fact — I wait and wait, then hang up. I feel like a high-school kid dialing for a date, tongue clotted, brain paralyzed with fear. I can almost hear my Cardinal teammates razzing me. I can see the freckled face and fish-like mouth of Foxy Rinehart, who fancies himself a comedian, saying, "Come on, Scotty, how scared can you get dialing long distance information?" Foxy has no idea what's at stake. Baseball and partying are his only interests. He doesn't have an imagination. He has to be constantly entertained: women, drinks, movies, TV, dancing, video games. Allison is right. I have an imagination, something that can be both a curse and a blessing, as I am finding out.

What I've decided to do is, for the first time in my life, believe in something magical. Allison has brought me the magic, or at least gifted me with the key to unlock magic.

I take a deep breath, imagine myself stepping into the batter's box against Greg Maddox or Steve Avery. I think of the way I let the tension flow out of my body, concentrating so fiercely I can hear my blood circulating as I challenge the pitcher. I'm as good as you are, I think. I've hit you before and I'll hit you again. Burn it in here, across the plate within reach of my bat.

The number I'm calling is information for a town not far from St. Louis. I dial, all the while stifling an urge to hang up at the first ring.

If Allison could see me, I think, as I often do when batting on the road, at that instant when the pitcher releases the ball, that instant when I know the pitch, from my point of view is perfect, know it will travel toward me in slow motion, almost freezing as it approaches the plate where I will make full contact driving it high and deep toward and beyond the outfield fence. I want Allison to feel the joy an instant like that brings me; I want her to share the rush that completing this seemingly innocuous phone call gives me.

"Information. For what city, please?"

"Mexico, Missouri," I reply, my voice shaky.

"Go ahead."

"A number for Fred Noonan Flying Services?" There is a long pause.

"Is that N-o-o-n-a-n?"

"Yes."

"I'm sorry, sir, but that is a silent listing."

"But, it's a business."

"I know that's unusual, but I've double checked. I'm sorry."

Relief and disappointment mix within me as I hang up. Perhaps Allison, and everything that's happened to me in the past few weeks is part of an elaborate hoax.

But who would do such a thing? If it were a scheme, it is far too elaborate to be hatched by any of my teammates; their idea of a joke is to nail someone's cleats to the floor or put Jell-o in a jock-strap.

I recall more of our first night together. Me quizzing Allison.

"Who lives in this place?"

"The truly lost. Those who need a second chance."

"Like the faces on the milk cartons? All those lost children?"

"Some of them, the ones who truly disappeared, the ones who weren't kidnapped by a parent or murdered. The ones who really ran away."

"I suppose everyone there is a descendant of Ambrose Bierce."

"Some of them might be. There are thousands of people there now."

"That's an odd idea. How did you come up with it?"

"I'm special," said Allison. "Didn't you sense I was special?"

"Where is this place and how do we get there?"

"I know a way to get there, there's a company called Fred Noonan Flying Services."

"What makes you believe this place exists?"

"Someone I know went there. Told me how to get the number of Fred Noonan Flying Services."

"Went there?"

"Took nothing with him. Caught a taxi to the airport at 1:00 a.m., gave his wristwatch to a man who was sweeping the floor, and vanished."

"Did you call the number he gave you?"

"I thought about it for a few weeks, and one night when

things were going badly, both personally and professionally, I did. But information said the listing for Fred Noonan Flying Services was silent. Isn't that strange?"

"Who is Fred Noonan?"

"Do you know the story of Amelia Earhart?"

"Of course. He was Amelia Earhart's navigator. I saw a movie about them. Susan Clark played Amelia Earhart."

"Did you know they flew into yesterday. I went and looked it all up. They flew off from New Guinea on July 3, 1937, for a 3,000-mile flight to Howland Island. But Howland was a day earlier; it was a flight into yesterday. And they were never heard from again."

"And you think they ran away?"

"There were rumors that Amelia Earhart and Fred Noonan were in love, that they found an isolated Pacific island and lived out their lives there. She was a very independent lady. He was tall and handsome, looked a little like Clark Gable, and Amelia was pretty, blond and boyish with a sensual mouth. Historians tend to think they blundered onto the Japanese doing something sneaky on a small atoll, and the Japanese executed them."

"You don't think so?"

"We're all around you, Scotty. Waiting. Anything is possible. There is a place, a town, a small city really, good climate, relatively isolated. A place where strangers are discouraged from settling, unless of course, they're running away from their past. A place where the police chief files *all* missing person reports in the waste basket."

"You have a bizarre sense of humor."

"I know."

We were silent for several minutes.

"So, Jimmy Hoffa? Was there a young woman like yourself who was turned on by dangerous men?"

"If he's with us, and I could tell you but I won't, it may be because we needed a union organizer."

"I see."

"Do you?"

"Suppose I want to go. How do I get there?"

"Fred Noonan Flying Services only flies to one destination," said Allison. "People just know. Like birds migrating."

Our eyes met, Allison's smile quizzical, challenging, full of irony. Her pink tongue peeked between scarlet lips.

"I meet some pretty odd people in my line of work," she said.

"Like ballplayers?"

"Sometimes. But there's more. I could name the town where Fred Noonan Flying Services is located. There's a song about Amelia, written and recorded literally hours after she and Fred vanished. Back in the thirties that was how disasters and major public events were dealt with." Allison began to sing, "Happy landings to you Amelia Earhart, farewell first lady of the air . . ."

Until that moment nothing truly extraordinary had ever happened to me. I'd been a successful athlete, I'd led the National League in home runs and RBIs, but I'd never experienced anything other-worldly. As Allison sang I had a vision, and I understood that she did indeed know some unusual people. I saw myself and Allison flying in a very old plane, there was a pilot in leather helmet and goggles. The pilot's scarf snapped in the wind just in front of our faces, Allison's hair flowed behind her, the wind strafed my face making my eyes water. The vision was gone in a tenth of a second.

"Name that town," I said.

Allison scratched around in the bedside table, she wrote the name of a town on the back of her business card.

"When you reach the operator, you ask for Fred Noonan Flying Services. The rest is up to you."

"I'd want you with me."

"That's the kind of beautiful lie we agreed to tell each other tonight, but just for tonight," Allison said, cuddling down into the bed, resting her head on my chest.

"It's not a lie," I said. "I mean it." Then a thought struck me. "This doesn't have anything to do with the new poster — 'Redbird Flying High'?"

"Well, it does and it doesn't. You have no idea how hard I had to think to come up with the idea. I had to see you again, and I didn't have the nerve just to call and say 'Hey, I know how you, how we can disappear forever.'"

"You wanted to tell me that, even before tonight?"

"I knew everything you told me tonight, just by looking at you. I have enough experience to recognize lonely when I see it."

"So, the poster was just an excuse."

"To get us together tonight, yes. The Fred Noonan story has nothing to do with the poster, but everything to do with what we agreed about this evening. We can say anything, do anything. Maybe Fred Noonan Flying Services is my fantasy. Scotty, I can't imagine anything as wonderful as starting all over — a completely fresh start, with you."

"Would there be baseball?" I laughed as soon as I said it. "Baseball must have a greater hold on me that I imagined."

"There would be baseball. But the kind you could enjoy; you could be a star, a big fish in a small pond, or you could coach, or just be a spectator. I can't imagine a small, quiet American city without baseball."

"Could you be happy with someone who wasn't famous? A quiet country boy from Memphis who happens to know a little about holding a bat?"

"Why did you put me off last week?" asked Allison. "We could have been together then, without my having to invent the poster."

"I know I must have puzzled you. It has nothing to do with morality. It's just that I never met a woman I thought I'd want to be alone with after we made love. With you it was different. You have no idea how much I wanted to take your hand and say, 'Would I be way out of line if I kissed you?' Of course, I knew the answer without asking the question. I may have appeared oblivious to all the signals and body language, but I wasn't. With you, Allison, I knew that if we made love, I'd never want to leave you, and I wasn't ready to carry that weight just then."

"I understand," said Allison, cuddling closer. "Are you telling me the truth?"

"What's truth?"

Before I leaned over to turn out the light, I studied the name of the town Allison had given me, committed it to memory, in case in the morning the back of the card was blank.

The next morning I made my first attempt to contact Fred Noonan Flying Services.

Allison and I spent the next four nights together. Then the Cardinal home stand ended. We left for an eight-day road trip. I had plenty of time to mull things over. Even if it was all a beautiful dream, I didn't mind. Suppose I dialed again and the operator told me the number was still silent, I thought. There would always be a lingering hope that the next time I tried I would be put through. Hope, I decided, is all anyone needs.

Lack of hope, I decided, was what was wrong with my life.

"I'll be back in St. Louis late Sunday," I said to Allison. "If I get through before then, and I've got a feeling I'm going to — like a day when I look in the mirror and can tell by my reflection that I'm going to get three hits — maybe we can take a little plane ride Monday morning?"

On the third day of the road trip, in Atlanta, I dialed information again, and as I did the same excitement filled me as when I dialed Allison's number, as when I waited to hear her throaty voice, the laugh clear as singing crystal. As the number rang, I breathed deeply, imagined myself in the on-deck circle, a game-deciding at-bat about to occur.

"What do you suppose it will be like, this town, this city, this final destination? Can you give me a clue as to where it's located?"

"It may be only a few feet away," said Allison enigmatically. "Though it may take a half day to get there. It will be peaceful, no more pressure for you to perform on the field or off, for either of us. Tree-lined streets, people working at things they love to do. Everyone will love their job. Merchants will treat their customers like human beings, and customers will act in a civilized manner. There'll be no bureaucrats, reasonable rules that everyone obeys, no alcoholics, petty criminals, no zealots of any kind."

"Did you pick me? I mean personally? I'm beginning to think chance wasn't involved."

"What do you think?"

"Are you real? Where did you come from? Did you just appear out of no where in full bloom?"

"I'm a real as you are."

"Which doesn't answer my question. What about . . . over there?"

"I'm more at home over there. There are other dimensions

chattering all about us, one or two, perhaps many. It's like when the Northern Lights envelop you, the static, the eeriness, the half-heard conversations. Have you never heard a whimper when you knew you were alone? Voices in the foliage? The phantom hand that brushes a cheek? The spooky feeling of being watched? Occasionally, one of us is able to invade dreams." Allison stared into my eyes.

"I tried. Very hard. I wanted you to dream of me. I wanted you to feel, when you first met me, like we were old friends."

"Have you done this before?"

"We're watching all the time. We always need new blood. I volunteered to find some."

"I don't care for that idea. What am I, a stud service?"

"Oh, don't be so sensitive. Of course you fill a need. Everyone does. The void you fill is my need for a life partner. I decided on you after I made certain you fit all the criteria. If we hadn't hit it off, I would have looked elsewhere. But I fell in love with you."

"Was I your first choice?"

"Of course."

"And would you tell me if I wasn't?"

"No."

"And if we hadn't hit it off?"

"Well, there's a very nice playwright in New York. A Bismarck, N.D. boy, whose first play was a massive hit, and who hasn't been able to write anything else since. He's sad, frustrated, not enjoying life."

"What will happen to him now? Will someone else save him?"

"Perhaps. That's not for you to worry about."

There is a metallic clang, like a soft door chime, as a recorded voice spells out the number for Fred Noonan Flying Services. The blood roars in my ears like the ocean as I quickly copy it down, wait for the recorded voice to repeat it so I can be certain I have it right.

I quickly dial the number.

"Fred Noonan Flying Services," says a gravelly voice.

"I'd like to book a flight," I say.

"Right. To where?"

"A special place. I'm told it's the only place you go."

"That's right. We have only one destination."

"Can you tell me where that is?"

"Sorry. It's kind of a mystery tour."

"Right."

"How many and from what city?"

"Two," I say. "St. Louis. Monday morning, if that's convenient."

"It's convenient."

"Do you mind if I ask a question?"

"Shoot?"

"Why the name?"

"Of the company, you mean? Fred Noonan? No secret. We're dealers in old aircraft, nothing newer than thirty-five years old. We supply planes and pilots to movie companies, TV shows, air shows. And we run these mystery tours; people like to fly back into the past. The early days of aviation hold a lot of mystery. You know we've got a Lockheed Electra, big silver jobby, just like the one Amelia and Fred were flying when we . . . when they disappeared.

"Fred Noonan was a lot more than Amelia's navigator. He was one of the pioneers of American aviation. Twenty-two years of flying over oceans; he helped establish Pan American Airways; he was one of the first instructors and aerial navigators. Yet he's almost completely forgotten — ask anybody and they'll tell you Amelia Earhart was alone when she disappeared."

He sounded, as I imagined Ernest Hemingway would have, rugged, ruddy, a scuffed bomber jacket, a battered pilot's cap.

"You can't take anything with you. The clothes you're wearing. Pockets empty."

"I understand."

"Good. We get people trying to sneak strange things along. Bags of money, jewelry, pets. There was this banker had ten $5,000 dollar bills in each shoe. One lady had a canary bird hid in her hairdo."

After the conversation with Fred Noonan ended, I sat quietly for a long time.

I felt the way I had almost ten years before, when I was first called up to the Cardinals from Louisville: full of anticipation, positively twitching with excitement.

I can see the plane, taxiing down the runway, Fred Noonan at the controls, crouching behind his windscreen. Allison and I behind him. Ascending. One Redbird flying high . . . flying toward yesterday.

But it isn't that simple. In fact it's ridiculous. The next time I see Allison I try to make light of the whole situation.

"This is all some kind of elaborate joke, right?"

"Do you love me?"

"That's answering a question with a question. But, yes."

"Have you ever heard of limerance."

"No."

"It's a term to do with going out on top. Quitting while you're ahead, leaving the party before the gin runs out. At it's most extreme it involves suicide. A couple like us, in the wild throes of first romance. We know things will never be so perfect. All life's problems are going to wear us down. Your career will end. Maybe we'll have children. Our priorities will change.

"If we died now . . ."

"I don't want to hear any more. Hell, anyone can have a business card made up that says Fred Noonan Flying Services, get a telephone listing . . ."

"I don't mean die, die. You know that." Allison covered my mouth with hers, her tongue electric, her taste nectar.

"Is it far?" I shout.

"A fair distance, not all in miles," Allison replies.

"Do we have enough fuel?"

"Relax. Lindy flew the Atlantic in a plane this size. Besides, Fred Noonan would never let us run out of fuel."

"Is there really a place where we can start over?"

"Of course."

"Sing to me, Allison."

Her voice is so thrilling, somewhere between sex and sunshine.

"Happy landings to you . . ."

The wind, as we whip down the runway, blows Allison's long hair and white scarf back toward me.

"Farewell . . . first lady of the air . . ."

The fringe snaps against my cheek, stinging like a willow switch.

Zanduce at Second

RON CARLSON

By his thirty-third birthday, a gray May day which found him having a warm cup of spice tea on the terrace of the Bay-side Inn in Annapolis, Maryland, with Carol Ann Menager, a nineteen-year-old woman he had hired out of the Bethesda Hilton Turntable Lounge at eleven o'clock that morning, Eddie Zanduce had killed eleven people and had that reputation, was famous for killing people, really the most famous killer of the day, his photograph in the sports section every week or so and somewhere in the article the phrase "eleven people" or "eleven fatalities." In fact, the word *eleven* now had that association first, the number of the dead — and in all the major league baseball parks his full name could be heard every game day in some comment, the gist of which would be "Popcorn and beer for ten-fifty, that's bad, but just be glad Eddie Zanduce isn't here, for he'd kill you for sure," and the vendors would slide the beer across the counter and say, "Watch out for Eddie," which had come to supplant "Here you go," or "Have a nice day," in conversations even away from the parks. Everywhere he was that famous. Even this young woman, who has been working out of the Hilton for the past eight months not reading the papers and only watching as much TV as one might watch in rented rooms in the early afternoon or late evening, not really news hours, even she knows his name, though she can't remember why she knows it and she finally asks him, her brow a furrow, "Eddie Zanduce? Are you on television? An actor?" And he smiles, raising the room-service teacup, but it's not a real smile. It is the placeholder expression he's been using for four years now since he first hit a baseball into the stands and it struck and killed a college sophomore, a young man, the papers were quick to point out, who was a straight-A student majoring in chemistry, and it is the kind of smile that makes him look nothing but old, a person who has seen it all and is now waiting for it all to be over. And in his old man's way he is patient through the next part, a talk he has had with many people all around the country, letting them know that he is simply Eddie Zanduce, the third baseman for the Orioles who has killed several people with foul balls. It has been a pernicious series of accidents really, though he won't say that.

She already knows she's not there for sex; after an hour she can tell by the manner, the face, and he has a beautiful actor's face which has been stunned with a kind of ruin by his bad luck and the weight of bearing responsibility for what he has done as an athlete. He's in the second thousand afternoons of this new life and the loneliness seems to have a physical gravity; he's hired her because it would have been impossible not to. He's hired her to survive the afternoon.

The day has been a walk through the tony shopping district in Annapolis, where he has bought her a red cotton sweater with tortiseshell buttons. It is a perfect sweater for May, and it looks wonderful as she holds it before her; she has short brunette hair, shiny as a schoolgirl's, which he realizes she may be. Then a walk along the pier, just a walk, no talking. She doesn't because he doesn't, and early on such outings, she always follows the man's lead. Later, the fresh salad lunch from room service and the tea. She explores the suite, poking her head into the bright bathroom, the nicest bathroom in any hotel she's been in during her brief career. There's a hair dryer, a robe, a fridge, and a phone. The shower is also a steamroom and the tub is a vast marble dish. There is a little city of lotions and shampoos. She smiles and he says, Please, feel free. Then he lies on the bed while she showers and dresses; he likes to watch her dress, but that too is different because he lies there imagining a family scene, the young wife busy with her grooming, not immodest in her nakedness, her undergarments on the bed like something sweet and familiar. The tea was her idea when he told her she could have anything at all; and she saw he was one of the odd ones, there were so many odd ones anymore willing to pay for something she's never fully understood, and she's taken the not understanding as just being part of it, her job, men and women, life. She's known lots of people who didn't understand what they were doing; her parents, for example. Her decision to go to work this way was based on her vision of simply fucking men for money, but the months have been more wearing than she could have foreseen with all the chatter and the posturing, some men who only want to mope or weep all through their massage, others who want to walk ahead of her into two or three nightspots and then yell at her later in some bedroom at the Embassy Suites, too many who want her to tell them about some other bastard who has abused her or broken her heart. But here this Eddie Zanduce just drinks his tea with his old man's smile as he watches the stormy summer weather as if it were a home movie. They've been through it all already and he has said simply without pretension. No, that's all right. We won't be doing that, but you can shower later. I'll have you in town by five-thirty.

The eleven people Eddie Zanduce has killed have been properly eulogized, the irony in the demise of each celebrated in the tabloid press, the potentials of their lives properly inflated, and their fame — brief though it may have been — certainly far beyond any which might have accompanied their natural passing, and so they needn't be listed here and made flesh again. They each float in the head of Eddie Zanduce in his every movement, though he has never said so, or acknowledged his burden in any public way, and it has become a kind of poor form now even in the press corps, a group not known for any form, good or bad, to bring it up. After the seventh person, a girl of nine who had gone with her four cousins to see the Orioles play New York over a year ago, and was removed from all earthly joy and worry by Eddie Zanduce's powerhouse line drive pulled foul into the seats behind third, the sportswriters dropped the whole story, letting it fall on page one of the second section: news. And even now after games, the five or six reporters who bother to come into the clubhouse — the Orioles are having a lackluster start, and have all but relinquished even a shot at the pennant — give Eddie Zanduce's locker a wide berth. Through it all, he has said one thing only, and that eleven times: "I'm sorry; this is terrible." When asked after the third fatality, a retired school principal who was unable to see and avoid the sharp shot of one of Eddie Zanduce's foul balls, if the unfortunate accidents might make him consider leaving the game, he said, "No."

And he became so stoic in the eyes of the press and they painted him that way that there was a general wonder at how he could stand it having the eleven innocent people dead by his hand, and they said things like "It would be hard on me" and "I couldn't take it." And so they marveled darkly at his ability to appear in his uniform, take the field at all, dive right when the hit required it and glove the ball, scrambling to his knees in time to make the throw either to first or to second if there was a chance for a double play. They noted that his batting slump worsened, and now he's gone weeks in the new season without a hit, but he plays because he's steady in the field and he can fill the stands. His face was the object of great scrutiny for expression, a scowl or a grin, because much could have been made of such a look. And when he was at the plate, standing in the box awaiting the pitch, his bat held rigid and ready off his right shoulder as if for business, this business and nothing else, the cameras went in on his face, his eyes, which were simply inscrutable to the nation of baseball fans.

And now, at thirty-three he lies on the queen-size bed of the Bayside Inn, his fingers twined behind his head, as he watches Carol Ann Menager come dripping into the room, her hair partially in a towel, her nineteen-year-old body a rose-and-pale pattern of the female form, five years away from any visible wear and tear from the vocation she has chosen. She warms him appearing this way, naked and ready to chat as she reaches for her lavender bra and puts it on first of all her clothing, simply as convenience, and the sight of her there bare and comfortable makes him feel the thing he has been missing: befriended.

"But you feel bad about it, right?" Carol Ann says. "It must hurt you to know what has happened."

"I do," he says, "I do. I feel as badly about it all as I should."

And now Carol Ann stops briefly, one leg in her lavender panties, and now she quickly pulls them up and says, "I don't know what you mean."

"I only mean what I said and nothing more," Eddie Zanduce says.

"What was the worst?"

He still reclines and answers: "They are all equally bad."

"The little girl?"

Eddie Zanduce draws a deep breath there on the bed and then speaks: "The little girl, whose name was Victoria Tuttle, and the tourist from Austria, whose name was Heinrich Vence, and the

Toronto Blue Jay, a man in a costume named William Dirsk, who was standing on the home dugout when my line drive broke his sternum. And the eight others all equally unlikely and horrible, all equally bad. In fact, eleven isn't really worse than one for me, because I maxed out on one. It doesn't double with two. My capacity for such feelings, I found out, is limited. And I am full."

Carol Ann Menager sits on the bed and buttons her new sweater. There is no hurry in her actions. She is thinking. "And if you killed someone tonight?"

Here Eddie Zanduce turns to her, his head rolling in the cradle of his hands, and smiles the smile he's been using all day, though it hasn't worn thin. "I wouldn't like that," he says. "Although it has been shown to me that I am fully capable of such a thing."

"Is it bad luck to talk about?"

"I don't believe in luck, bad or good." He warms his smile one more time for her and says, "I'm glad you came today. I wouldn't have ordered the tea." He swings his legs to sit up. "And the sweater, well, it looks very nice. We'll drive back when you're ready."

On the drive north, Carol Ann Menager says one thing that stays with Eddie Zanduce after he drops her at her little blue Geo in the Hilton parking lot and after he has dressed and played three innings of baseball before a crowd of twenty-four thousand, the stadium a third full under low clouds this early in the season with the Orioles going ho-hum and school not out yet, and she says it like so much she has said in the six hours he has known her — right out of the blue as they cruise north from Annapolis on Route 2 in his thick silver Mercedes, a car he thinks nothing of and can afford not to think of, under the low sullen skies that bless and begrudge the very springtime hedgerows the car speeds past. It had all come to her as she'd assembled herself an hour before; and it is so different from what she's imagined, in fact, she'd paused while drying herself with the lush towel in the Bayside Inn, her foot on the edge of the tub, and she'd looked at the ceiling where a heavy raft of clouds crossed the domed skylight, and one hand on the towel against herself, she'd seen Eddie Zanduce so differently than she had thought. For one thing he wasn't married and

playing the dark game that some men did, putting themselves closer and closer to the edge of their lives until something went over,
and he wasn't simply off, the men who tried to own her for the three
hundred dollars and then didn't touch her, and he wasn't cruel in the
other more overt ways, nor was he turned so tight that to enjoy a cup
of tea over the marina with a hooker was anything sexual, nor was
she young enough to be his daughter, just none of it, but she could see
that he had made his pact with the random killings he initiated at the
plate in baseball parks and the agreement left him nothing but the
long series of empty afternoons.

"You want to know why I became a hooker?" she asks.

"Not really," he says. He drives the way other men drive when
there are things on their minds, but his mind, she knows, has but
one thing in it — eleven times. "You have your reasons. I respect
them. I think you should be careful and do what you choose."

"You didn't even see me," she says. "You don't even know
who's in the car with you."

He doesn't answer. He says. "I'll have you back by five-thirty."

"A lot of men want to know why I would do such a thing. They
call me young and beautiful and talented and ready for the world
and many other things that any person in any walk of life would take
as a compliment. And I make it my challenge, the only one after survive, to answer them all differently. Are you listening?"

Eddie Zanduce drives.

"Some of them I tell that I hate the work but enjoy the money;
they like that because — to a man — it's true of them. Some I tell
I love the work and would do it for free; and they like that because they're all boys. Everybody else gets a complicated story
with a mother and a father and a boyfriend or two, sometimes an
ex-husband, sometimes a child who is sometimes a girl and sometimes a boy, and we end up nodding over our coffees. Or our
brandies or whatever we're talking over, and we smile at the *wis-
dom* of time, because there is nothing else to do but for them to
agree with me or simply hear and nod and then smile, I do tell
good stories, and that smile is the same smile you've been giving
yourself all day. If you had your life figured out any better than I
do, it would have been a different day back at your sailboat motel.
Sorry to go on, because it doesn't matter, but I'll tell you the truth;
what can it hurt, right? You're a killer. I'm just a whore. I'm a whore

because I don't care, and because I don't care it's a perfect job. I don't see anybody else doing any better. Show me somebody who's got a grip, just one person. Survive. That's my motto. And then tell stories. What should I do, trot out to the community college and prepare for my future as a medical doctor? I don't think so."

Eddie Zanduce looks at the young woman. Her eyes are deeper, darker, near tears. "You are beautiful," he says. "I'm sorry if the day wasn't to your liking."

She has been treated one hundred ways, but not this way, not with this delicate diffidence, and she is surprised that it stings. She's been hurt and neglected and ignored and made to feel invisible, but this is different, somehow this is personal. "The day was fine. I just wish you'd seen me."

For some reason, Eddie Zanduce responds to this: "I don't see people. It's not what I do. I can't afford it." Having said it, he immediately regrets how true it sounds to him. Why is he talking to her? "I'm tired," he adds, and he is tired — of it all. He regrets his decision to have company, purchase it, because it has turned out to be what he wanted so long, and something about this girl has crossed into his view. She is smart and pretty and he hates this — he does feel bad she's a hooker.

And then she says the haunting thing, the advice that he will carry into the game later that night. "Why don't you try to do it?" He looks at her as she finishes. "You've killed these people on accident. What if you tried? Could you kill somebody on purpose?"

At five twenty-five after driving the last forty minutes in a silence like the silence in the center of the rolling earth, Eddie Zanduce pulls into the Hilton lot and Carol Ann Menager says, "Right up there." When he stops the car, she steps out and says to him, "I'll be at the game. Thanks for the tea."

And now at two and one, a count he loves, Eddie Zanduce steps out of the box, self-conscious in a way he hasn't been for years and years and can't figure out until he ticks upon it: she's here somewhere, taking the night off to catch a baseball game or else with a trick who even now would be charmed by her unaffected love for a night in the park, the two of them laughing like teenagers over popcorn, and now she'd be pointing down at Eddie, saying, "There, that's the guy." Eddie Zanduce listens to the low murmur of twenty-four thousand people who have chosen to attend tonight's game knowing he would be here, here at bat, which was a place from which he could harm them irreparably, for he has done it eleven times before. The announcers have handled it the same after the fourth death, a young lawyer taken by a hooked line shot, the ball shattering his occipital bone, the final beat in a scene he'd watched every moment of from the tock! of the bat — when the ball was so small, a dot which grew through its unreliable one-second arc into a huge white spheroid of five ounces entering his face, and what the announcers began to say then was some version of "Please be alert, ladies and gentlemen, coming to the ballpark implies responsibility. That ball is likely to go absolutely anywhere." But everybody knows this. Every single soul, even the twenty Japanese business-men not five days out of Osaka know about Eddie Zanduce, and their boxes behind first base titter and moan, even the four babies in arms not one of them five months old spread throughout the house know about the killer at the plate, as do the people sitting behind the babies disgusted at the parents for risking such a thing, and the drunks, a dozen people swimming that abyss as Eddie taps his cleats, they know, even one in his stuporous sleep, his head collapsed on his chest as if offering it up, knows that Eddie could kill any one of them tonight. The number eleven hovers everywhere as does the number twelve waiting to be written. It is already printed on best-selling T-shirt, and there are others, "I'll be 12th," and "Take Me 12th!" and "NEXT," and many others, all on T-shirts which Eddie Zanduce could read in any crowd in any city in which the Orioles took the field. When he played baseball, when he was listed on the starting roster — where he'd been for seven years — the crowd was doubled. People came as they'd come out tonight on a chilly cloudy night in Baltimore, a night that should have seen ten thousand maybe, more likely eight, they flocked to the ballpark, crammed themselves into sold-out games or sat out — as tonight — in questionable weather as if they were asking to be twelfth, as if their lives were fully worthy of being interrupted, as if their lives — like right now with Eddie stepping back into the batter's box — they were asking, Take me next, hit me, I have come here to be killed.

Eddie Zanduce remembers Carol Ann Menager in the car. He hoists his bat and says, "I'm going to kill one of you now."

"What's that, Eddie?"

Caulkins, the Minnesota catcher, has heard his threat, but it means nothing to Eddie, and he says that: "Nothing. Just something I'm going to do." He says this stepping back into the batter's box and lifts his bat up to the ready. Things are in place. And as if enacting the foretold, he slices the first pitch, savagely shaving it short into the first-base seats, the kind of ugly truncated liner that has only damage as its intent, and adrenaline pricks the twenty-four thousand hearts sitting in that dangerous circle, but after a beat that allows the gasp to subside, a catchbreath really that is merely overture for a scream, two young men in blue Maryland sweatshirts leap above the crowd there above first base and one waves his old brown mitt in which it is clear there is a baseball. They hug and hop up and down for a moment as the crowd witnesses it all sitting silent as the members of a scared congregation and then a roar begins which is like laughter in church and it rides on the night air, filling the stadium.

"I'll be damned," Caulkins declares, standing mask off behind Eddie Zanduce. "He caught that ball, Eddie."

Those words are etched in Eddie Zanduce's mind as he steps again up to the plate. He caught the ball. He looks across at the young men but they have sat down, dissolved, leaving a girl standing behind them in a red sweater who smiles at him widely and rises once on her toes and waves a little wave that says, "I knew it. I just knew it." She is alone standing there waving. Eddie thinks that: she's come alone.

The next pitch comes in fat and high and as Eddie Zanduce swings and connects he pictures this ball streaming down the line uninterrupted, too fast to be caught, a flash off the cranium of a man draining his beer at the very second a plate of bone carves into his brain and the lights go out. The real ball though snaps on a sharp hop over the third baseman, staying in fair territory for a double. Eddie Zanduce stands on second. There is a great cheering; he may be a killer but he is on the home team and he's driven in the first run of the ballgame. His first hit in this month of May. And Eddie Zanduce has a feeling he hasn't had for four years since it all began, since the weather in his life changed for good, and what he feels is anger. He can taste the dry anger in his mouth and it tastes good. He smiles and he knows the cameras are on him but he can't help himself he is so pleased to be angry, and the view he has now of the crowd behind the plate, three tiers of them, lifts him to a new feeling that he locks on in a second: he hates them. He hates them all so much that the rich feeling floods through his brain like nectar and his smile wants to close his eyes. He is transported by hatred, exulted, drenched. He leads off second, so on edge and pissed off he feels he's going to fly with this intoxicating hatred, and he smiles that different smile, the challenge and the glee, and he feels his heart beating in his neck and arms, hot here in the center of the world. It's a feeling you'd like to explain to someone after the game. He plans to. He's got two more at bats tonight, the gall rises in his throat like life itself, and he is going to kill somebody — or let them know he was trying.

Judgment Call

JOHN KESSEL

Bottom of the first, no score, Dutch on first, Simonetti on second, two outs. In the bar afterwards, Sandy replayed it in his head.

Sandy had faced this Louisville pitcher maybe twice before. He had a decent fastball and a good curve, enough so he'd gotten Sandy out more than his share. And Sandy was in a slump (three for eighteen in the last five games), and the count was one and two; and the Louisville catcher was riding him. The ump was real quiet, but Sandy knew he was just waiting to throw his old rabbit punch to signal the big K — fist punching the air, but it might as well be Sandy's gut. It was hot. His legs felt rubbery.

Old War Memorial was quiet. There weren't more than fifteen hundred people there, tops; Louisville was leading the American Association, and the Bisons were dead last. The steel struts holding up the roof in right were ranked in the distance like the trees of the North Carolina pine forest where he grew up, lost in the haze and shadows of the top rows where nobody ever sat. The sky was overcast, and a heavy wind from the lake snapped the flag out in left center, but it was very hot for Buffalo, even for June. People were saying the climate was changing: it was the ozone layer, the Japs, the UFOs, the end of the world. Some off-duty cop or sanitation worker with a red face was ragging him from the stands. Sandy would have liked to deck him, but he had to ignore it because the pitcher was crouched over, shaking off signals. He went into his stretch.

Then something happened: suddenly Sandy knew, he just knew he could hit this guy. The pitcher figured he had Sandy plugged — curveball, curveball, outside corner and low, then high and tight with the fastball to keep him from leaning — but it hit Sandy like a line drive between the eyes that he had the *pitcher* plugged, he knew where the next pitch was going to be. And there it was, fastball inside corner, and he turned on it and *bye-bye baby!* That sweet crack of the ash. Sandy watched it sail out over the left field fence; saw the pitcher, head down, kick dirt from the mound — sorry, guy; could be you won't see the majors as soon as you thought — and jogged around the bases feeling so *good*. He was going to live forever. He was going to get laid every night.

That was just his first at bat. In the top of the sixth he made a shoestring catch in right center, and in the second and the seventh he threw out runners trying to go from first to third. At the plate he went four for five, bringing his average up to a tantalizing .299. And number five was an infield bouncer that Sandy was sure he'd beat out, but the wop ump at first called him out. A judgment call. The pud-knocker. But it was still the best game Sandy had ever played.

And Aronsen, the Sox general manager, was in town to take a look at the Bisons in the hope of finding somebody they could bring up to help them after the bad start they'd had. After the game he came by in the locker room. He glanced at Sandy's postgame blood panel. Sandy played it cool: he was at least 0.6 under the limit on DMD, not even on scale for steroids. Sandy should get ready right away, Aronsen told him, to catch the morning train to Chicago. They were sending Estivez down and bringing him up. They were going to give him a chance to fill the hole in right field. Yes, sir, Sandy said, polite, eager.

Lordy, lordy — yes, sir, he'd thought as he walked down Best with Dutch and Leon toward the Main Street tramway — good-bye, War Memorial. The hulk of the stadium, the exact color of a Down East dirt farmer's tobacco-stained teeth, loomed above them, the Art Deco globes that topped its corners covered with pigeon shit. Atop the corroded limestone wall that ran along the street was a chain-link fence, rusted brown, and atop the fence glistened new coils of barbed wire. The barbed wire was supposed to keep vagrants from living in the stadium. It made the place look like a prison.

Now it was a few hours later, and Sandy was having a drink with Dutch and Leon at the Ground Zero on Delaware. He'd already stopped by a machine and withdrawn the entire six hundred dollars in his account, had called up the rental office and told them he was leaving and they could rent the place because he wasn't coming back. Chalk up one for his side. Sandy paid for the first round. He had it figured: you paid for the first stiff one, you didn't hesitate a bit, and the others would remember that much better than how slow you were on the second or third; so if you played it right, you came out ahead on drinks when the evening was done. Even when you didn't, you got the rep with the regulars at the bar of being a generous kind of guy. Sure enough, Dutch paid for the second round and Leon for the third, and then some fans came by and got the next two. So Sandy was way ahead. His day. Only one thing was needed to make it complete.

"You lucky son-of-a-bitch," Dutch shouted over the din of the talk and the flatscreen behind the bar. "You haven't played that well in a month. The Killer decides to go crazy on the day that Aronsen's in town."

There was more than kidding in Dutch's voice. "That's when it pays to look your best," Sandy said.

Dutch stared at the screen, where a faggot VJ with a wig and ruffles and lace cuffs was counting down the Top 100 videos of the twentieth century. Most of them were from the past two years. "Wouldn't do me any good," Dutch said. "They've got two first basemen ahead of me. I could hit .350, and I wouldn't get a shot at the majors."

"Playin' the wrong position, man," said Leon. His high eyebrows gave him a perpetually innocent expression.

Dutch didn't have the glove to play anywhere else but first. Sandy felt a little sorry for Dutch, who had wrecked his chances with HGH. At eighteen he had been a pretty hot prospect, a first baseman who could hit for average and field okay. But he didn't have any power, so he'd taken the hormone in order to beef up. He'd beefed up, all right — going to six-five, 230 — but his reflexes got shot to hell in the process. Now he could hit twenty home runs in triple-A ball, but he struck out too much and his fielding was mediocre and he was slow as an ox. And the American League had abandoned the DH rule just about the time Dutch went off the drug.

It was a sad story. But Sandy got tired of his bitching, too. A real friend didn't bitch at you when you got called up. "You ought to work on the glove," he said.

A glint of hate showed in Dutch's face for a second, then he said, "I got to piss," and headed for the men's room.

"Sometimes he gets to me," Sandy said.

Leon lazily watched the women in the room, leaning his back against the bar, elbows resting on the edge, his big, gnarled catcher's hands hanging loosely from his wrists. On the screen behind him, a naked girl was bouncing up and down on a pink neon pogo stick. Sandy couldn't tell if she was real or vidsynthed.

"Got to admit, Killer, you ain't been playin' that good lately," Leon said over his shoulder. They called Sandy "The Killer" because of the number of double plays he hit into: Killer as in rally killer. "You been clutched out. Been tryin' too hard."

Now it was Leon, too. Leon had grown up in Fayetteville, not ten miles from Sandy's dad's farm, but Sandy would not have hung around with Leon back there. Leon was ten years older, his father was a noncom at Fort Bragg, and he was the wrong color. Sandy always felt like blacks were keeping secrets that he would just as soon not know.

Sandy finished his bourbon and ordered another. "You don't win without trying."

Leon just nodded. "Look at that talent there." He pointed his chin toward a table in the corner.

At the table, alone, sat a woman. He wondered how she had got there without him noticing her: she had microshort blonde hair and a pale oval face with a pointed chin. Blue lips. Her dark eyelashes were long enough so that he could see them from the bar. But what got him was her body. Even from across the room, Sandy could tell she was major league material. She wore a tight blue dress and was drinking something pale, on the rocks.

She looked over at them and calmly locked glances with Sandy. Something strange happened then. He had a feeling of vertigo, and then was overwhelmed by a vivid memory, a flashback to something that had happened to him long before.

It's the end of the summer of your junior year of high school, and you're calling Jocelyn from the parking lot of the Dairy King out near Highway 95. Brutal heat. Tapping your car keys impatiently on the dented metal shelf below the phone. Jocelyn is going to Atlantic Beach with Sid Phillips, and she hasn't even told you. Five rings, six. You had to get the news from Trudy Jackson and act like you knew all about it when it was like you'd been kneed in the groin.

An answer. "Hello?"

"Miz James, this is Sandy Ellison. Can I talk to Jocelyn?"

"Just a minute." Another wait. The sun burns the back of your neck.

"Hello." Jocelyn's voice sounds nervous.

The anger explodes in your chest. "What the fuck do you think you're doing?"

A semi blasts by on Highway 95, kicking up a cloud of dust and gravel. You turn your back to the road and hold your hand over your other ear.

"What are you talking about?"

"You better not fuck with me, Jocelyn. I won't take it."

"Slow down, Sandy. I —"

"If you go to the beach with him, it's over." You try to make it sound like a threat instead of a plea.

At first Jocelyn doesn't answer. Then she says, "You always were a jerk." She hangs up.

You stand there with the receiver in your hand. It feels hot and greasy. The dial tone mocks you. Then Jeff Baxter and Jack Stubbs drive up in Jeff's Trans Am, and the three of you cruise out to the lake and drink three six-packs. "Bitch," you call her. "Fucking bitch."

The woman was still staring at him. She didn't look at all like Jocelyn. Sandy broke eye contact. He realized that Dutch had come back, had been back for a while while Sandy was spaced-out. Fucking Jocelyn.

Sandy made a decision. "One hundred says I boost her tonight."

Leon regarded him coolly. Dutch snorted. "Gonna pull down your batting average, boy."

"Definitely a tough chance," Leon said.

"You think so? It's my day. We'll see who's trying too hard, Leon."

"You got a bet."

Sandy pulled the wad of bills out of his shirt pocket and laid two fifties on the bar. "You hold it, Dutch. I'll get it back tomorrow when I pick up my gear." Dutch stuffed the redbucks into his shirt pocket. Sandy picked up his drink and went over to the table. The woman watched him the whole way. Up close she was even more spectacular.

"Hey," he said.

"Hello. It's about time. I've been waiting for you."

He pulled out a chair and sat down. "Sure you have."

"I never lie." Her smile was a dare. "How much is riding on this?"

He couldn't tell whether she was hostile or just a tease. Well, he could go with the pitch. "One hundred," Sandy said. "That's a week's pay in triple-A."

"What is triple-A?" Her husky voice had some trace of accent to it — Hispanic?

"Baseball. My name is Sandy Ellison. I play for the Bisons."

She sipped her drink. Her ears were small and flat against her head. The shortness of her hair made her head seem large and her violet eyes enormous. He would die if he didn't have her that night.

"Are you a good player?" she asked.

"I just got called up to the majors. Monday night I'll be starting for Chicago."

"You are a lucky man."

Luck again. The way she said it made Sandy think for a moment he was being set up: Leon and Dutch and all that talk about luck. But Dutch was too dumb to pull some elaborate practical joke. Leon was smart enough, but he wasn't mean enough. Still, it would be a good idea to stay on his guard. "Not luck; skill."

"Oh, skill. I thought you were lucky."

"How come I've never seen you here before?"

"I'm from out of town."

"I figured as much. Where?"

"Lexington."

Sandy ran his finger around the rim of his glass. "Kentucky? We just played Louisville. You follow the Cards on their road trips?"

"Road trips?"

"The game we played today was against the Louisville Cardinals. They're in town on a road trip."

"What a coincidence." Again the smile. "I'm on a road trip, too. But I'm not following this baseball team. I came to Buffalo for another reason, and I'm leaving tomorrow."

"It's a good town to be leaving. You help me celebrate, and I'll help you."

"That's why I'm here."

Right. Sandy glanced over at the bar. Leon and Dutch were talking to a couple of women. On the flatscreen was a newsflash about the microwave deluge in Arizona. Shots of househubs at the supermarket wearing their aluminized suits. He turned back to the woman and smiled. "Run that by me again."

The woman gazed at him calmly over her high cheekbones. "Come on, Sandy. Read my lips. This is your lucky day, and I'm here to celebrate it with you. A skillful man like you must understand what that means."

"Did Leon put you up to this? If he did, the bet's off."

"Leon is one of those two men at the bar? I don't know him. If I were to guess, I would guess that he is the black man. I'd also guess that you proposed the bet to him, not he to you. Am I right?"

"I made the bet."

"You see. My lucky guess. Well, if you made the bet with Leon, then it's unlikely that Leon hired me to trick you. It is unlikely for other reasons, too."

This was the weirdest pickup talk Sandy had ever heard. "Why do I get the feeling there's a proposition coming?"

"Don't tell me you didn't expect a proposition to pass between us sometime during this conversation."

"For sure. But I expected to be making it."

"Go ahead."

Sandy studied her. "You northern girls are different."

"I'm not from the North."

"Then you're from a different part of the South than I grew up in."

"It takes all kinds. May I ask you a question?"

"Sure."

"Why the bet?"

"I just wanted to make it interesting."

"I'm not interesting enough unless there's money riding on me?"

Riding on her. Sandy smiled. The woman smiled back. "I just like to raise the stakes," he said. "But the bet is between me and them, to prove a point. It has nothing to do with you."

"You're not very flattering."

"That's not what I meant."

"Yes. We can make it even more interesting. You think you can please me?"

Sandy finished his bourbon. "If you can be pleased."

"Good. So let's make it very interesting." She opened her clutch purse and tilted it toward him. She reached inside and held something so that Sandy could see it. A glint of metal. It was a straight razor.

"If you don't please me, I get to hurt you. Just a little."

Sandy stared at her. "Are you kidding?"

She stared back. Her look was steady.

"Maybe you're not as good as you tell me. Maybe you'll need to have some luck."

She had to be teasing. Sandy considered the odds. Even if she wasn't, he thought he could handle her. Sandy stood up. "It's a deal."

She didn't move. "You're sure you want to try this?"

"I know what I want when I see it."

"You already know enough to make a decision?"

He came around to her side of the table. "Let's go," he said. She closed her purse and led him toward the door. Sandy winked at Leon as they passed the bar; Leon's face looked as surprised and skeptical as ever. The girl's hips, swaying as she walked ahead of him, pulled him along the way the smell of food in the dumpster by the concession stand drew the retirees living in the cardboard boxes on Jefferson Avenue.

Once in the street he slipped an arm around her waist and nudged her over to the side of the building. Her perfume was dizzying. "What's your name?" he asked her.

"Judith," she said.

"Judith." It sounded so old-fashioned. There was a Judith in the Bible, he thought. But he had never paid attention in Bible class.

He kissed her. He had to force his tongue between her lips. Then she bit it lightly. Her mouth was strong and wet. She moved her hips against him.

You are twelve. You're sitting in the Beulah Land Baptist Church with your mother. She must be thirty-five or so, a pretty woman with blonde hair, putting on a little weight. Your father doesn't go to church. Lately your mother has been going more often and reading from the Bible after supper.

Some of your classmates, including Carrie Ford and Sue Harvey, are being baptized that Sunday. The two girls ride the bus with you, and Carrie has the biggest tits in the seventh grade.

The choir sings a hymn while the Reverend Mr. Foster takes the girls into the side room; and when the song is done, the curtains in front of the baptismal font open and there stand the minister and Carrie, waist-deep in the water. Carrie is wearing a blue robe, trying nervously not to smile. Behind them is a painting of the lush green valley of the Promised Land and the shining City on the Hill. The strong light from the spot above them makes Carrie's golden hair shine, too.

The Reverend Mr. Foster puts his hand on Carrie's shoulder, lifts his other hand toward heaven, and calls on the Lord.

"Do you renounce Satan and all his ways?" he asks Carrie.

"Yes," she says, looking holy. She crosses her hands at the wrists, palms in, and folds her hands over those tits, as if to hold them in.

The minister touches the back of her neck. She jumps a bit, and you know she didn't expect that, but then lets him duck her head beneath the surface of the water. He holds her down for a long time, making sure she knows who's boss. You like that. The minister says the words of the baptism and pulls her up again.

Carrie gasps and sputters. She lifts her hands to push the hair away from her eyes. The robe clings to her chest. You can see everything. As she tries to catch her breath, you feel yourself getting an erection.

You put your hand on your lap and try to make the erection go away, but the mere contact with your pants leg makes you get even harder. You can't help it; your dick has run away with you. You turn red and shift uncomfortably in the pew, and your mother looks at you. She sees your hand on your lap.

"Sandy!" she hisses. A woman in front of you looks around.

Your mother tries to ignore you. The curtains close. You wish you were dead. At the same time you want to get up, go to the side room, and watch Carrie Ford take off her wet robe and towel herself dry.

He felt the warmth of Judith's lips on his, her arms around his neck. He pushed away from her, staring. This was no time for some drug flashback. After a moment he placed his hands on either side of her head against the wall and leaned toward her. She bit her lower lip. He had an erection after all. Whether it was because of the memory or Judith, he couldn't tell; he felt the embarrassment and guilt that had burned in him at the church. He felt mad. "Listen," he said. "Let's go to my place."

"Whatever you like." They walked down the block to the tram

station. Sandy lived in one of the luxury condos that had been built on the Erie Basin before the market crash. He had an expensive view across the lake. It was even more high-rent now that the Sunbelters were moving North to escape the drought.

They got off downtown and walked up River Street to the apartment; he inserted his ID card and punched in the security code. The lock snapped open, and Sandy ushered her in.

The place was wasted on Judith. She walked through his living room, the moon through the skylight throwing triangular shadows against the cathedral ceiling and walls, and thumbed on the bedroom light as if she had been there before. When he followed her, he found her standing just inside the door. She began to unbutton his shirt. He felt hot. He tried to undress her, but she pushed his hands away, pushed him backward until he fell awkwardly onto the water bed. She stood above him. The expression on her face was very grave.

She knelt on the undulating bed and rested her hands on his chest. He fumbled on the headboard shelf for the amyl nitrite. She pushed his hand away, took one of the caps, and broke it under his nose. His heart slammed against his ribs as if it would leap out of his chest; the air he breathed was hot and dry, and the tightness of the crotch of his jeans was agony. Eventually she helped him with that, but not before she had spent what seemed like an eternity making it worse.

The sight of her naked almost made him come right then. But she knew how to control that. She seemed to know everything in his mind before he knew it himself; she responded or didn't respond as he needed, precisely, kindly. She became everything that he wanted. She took him to the brink again and again, stopped just short, brought him back. She seemed hooked into the sources of his desire: his pain, his fear, his hope, all translated into the simple, slow motions of her sex and his. He forgot to worry about whether he was pleasing her. He forgot who he was. For an hour he forgot everything.

It was dark. Sandy lay just on the edge of sleep with his eyelids sliding closed and the distant sound of a siren in the air. The siren faded.

"You're beautiful, Sandy," Judith said. "I may not cut you after all."

Sandy felt so groggy he could hardly think. "Nobody cuts the

Killer," he mumbled, and laughed. He rolled onto his stomach. The bed undulated; he felt dizzy.

"Such a wonderful body. Such a hard dick."

She slid her hand down his backbone, and as she did, all the muscles of his back relaxed, as if it were a twisted cord that she was unwinding. It was almost a dream. In the interior of his mind was a tiny alarm, like the siren that had passed into another part of the city.

"Now," said Judith, "I want to tell you a story."

"Sure."

Lightly stroking his back, Judith said, "This is the story of Yancey Camera."

"Funny name." He felt so sleepy.

"It is. To begin with, Yancey Camera was a young man of great promise and trustful good nature. Would you believe me if I told you that he was as handsome as the leading man in a black-and-white movie? He was that handsome, and was as smart as he was handsome, and as rich as he was smart. His dick was as reliable as his credit rating. He was a lucky young man.

"But Yancey did not believe in luck. Oh, he gave lip service to luck; when people said, 'Yancey, you're a lucky boy,' he said, 'Yes, I guess I am.' But when he thought about it, he understood that when they told him how lucky he was, they were really saying that he did not deserve his good fortune; he had done nothing to earn it; and in a more rationally ordered universe he would not be handsome, smart, or rich, and his dick would be no more reliable than any other man's. Yancey came to realize that when people commented on his luck, they were really expressing their envy, and he immediately suspected those people. This lack of trust enabled him to spot more than a few phonies, for there was a large degree of truth in Yancey Camera's analysis.

"The problem was that as time went on and Yancey saw how much venality was concealed by people's talk of luck, he forgot that he had not initially done anything to earn the good looks, intellect, wealth, and hard dick that he possessed. In other words, Sandy, he came to disbelieve in luck. He thought that a man of his skills could control every situation. He forgot about the second law of thermodynamics, which tells us that we all lose, and that those times when we win are merely local statistical deviations in a universal progress from a state of lower to a state of higher entropy. Yancey's own luck was just such a local deviation. As time passed and Yancey's good fortune continued, he began ultimately to think that he was beyond the reach of the second law of thermodynamics."

Forget the alarm; forget the razor. The second law of sexual dynamics. First you screw her, then she talks. Sandy thought about the instant he had hit the home run, the feel of the bat in his hands, the contact with the ball so pure and sweet he knew it was out of the park even before he had finished following through.

"This is a sin that the Fates call hubris," Judith said, "and as soon as they realized the extent of Yancey Camera's error, they set about to rectify the situation. Now, there are several ways in which such an imbalance can be restored. It can be done in stages, or it can be done in one sudden, enormous stroke.

"And here my story divides: in one version of the story, Yancey Camera marries a beautiful young woman, fathers four sons, and opens an automobile dealership. Unfortunately, because Yancey's home is built on the site of a chemical waste dump, one of his boys is born with spina bifida and is confined to a wheelchair. The child dies at the age of twelve. One of his other boys is unable to compete in school and becomes a behavior problem. A third is brilliant but commits suicide at the age of fourteen when his girlfriend goes to the beach with another boy. Under the pressure of these disappointments, Yancey's wife becomes a shrill harridan. She gets fat and drinks and embarrasses him at parties. Yancey gets fat, too, and loses his hair. He is left with the consolation of his auto dealership, but then there is a war in the Middle East in which the oil fields are destroyed with atomic weapons. Suddenly there is no more oil. Yancey goes bankrupt. A number of other things happen that I will not tell you about. Suffice it to say that by the end of this version of the story, Yancey has lost his good looks, his money, and finally his fine mind, which becomes unhinged by the pressures of his misfortune. In the end he loses his hard dick, too, and dies cursing his bad luck. For in the end he is certain that bad luck, and not his own behavior, is responsible for his destruction. And he is right."

"That's too bad."

"That is too bad, isn't it?" Judith lifted the hair from the back of his neck with the tips of her fingers. It tickled.

"The other version of the story, Sandy, is even more interesting.

Yancey Camera grows older, and success follows success in his life. He marries a beautiful young woman who does not get fat, and fathers four completely healthy and well-adjusted sons. He becomes a successful lawyer and enters politics. He wins every election he enters. Eventually he becomes the President of the Entire Country. As president he visits every state capital. Everywhere he goes the people of the nation gather to meet him, and when Yancey departs, he leaves two groups of citizens behind. The first group goes home saying, 'What a fortunate people we are to have such a handsome, smart, and wealthy president.' Others say, 'What a smart, handsome, and wealthy people we are to have elected such a handsome, smart, and wealthy leader.' What a skilled nation, they tell themselves, they must be. Like their president, they assume that their gifts are not the result of good luck but of their inherent virtue. Therefore, all who point out this good luck must be jealous. And so the Fates or the second law of thermodynamics deal with Yancey's nation as they dealt with Yancey in the other version of this story. In their arrogance, Yancey Camera and his people, in the effort to maintain an oil supply for their automobiles, provoke a war that destroys all life on earth, including the lives, good looks, wealth, and hard dicks of all the citizens of that country, lucky and unlucky. The end.

"What do you think of that, Sandy?"

Sandy was on the verge of sleep. "I think you're hung up on dicks," he mumbled, smiling to himself. "All you women."

"Could be," Judith whispered. Her breath was warm on his ear. He fell asleep.

He woke with a start. She was no longer lying beside him. How could he have let down his guard so easily? She could have ripped him off — or worse. Where had he put the cash from the bank? He rolled over and reached for his pants on the floor beside the bed, then poked his index finger into the hip pocket. It was empty. He felt an adrenal surge, lurched out of bed, and began to haul on his pants. He was hopping toward the hallway, tugging on his zipper, when he saw her through the open bathroom door.

She turned toward him. The light behind her was on. Her face was totally in shadow, and her voice, when she spoke, was even huskier than the voice he had heard before.

"Did you find it?" she asked.

He felt afraid. "Find what?"

"Your money."

Then he remembered he had stuck the crisp bills, fresh from the machine, into the button-flap pocket of his shirt. He ran back to the bed, found the shirt on the floor, and fumbled at it. The money was there.

When he turned back to her, she was standing over him. She reached down and touched his face.

You're fifteen. You are sitting at the chipped Formica table in the kitchen of the run-down farmhouse, sweating in the ninety-degree heat, eating a peanut butter sandwich and drinking a glass of sweet tea. The air is damp and hot as a fever compress. Through the patched screen door you can see the porch, the dusty red-clay yard, and a corner of the tobacco field, vivid green, running down toward the even darker line of trees along the bend of the Cape Fear that marks the edge of the farm. The air is full of the sweet smell of the tobacco. Even the sandwich tastes of it.

You're wearing your high school baseball uniform. Your spikes and glove — a Dale Murphy autograph — rest on the broken yellow vinyl of the only other serviceable kitchen chair. You're starting in right today, at two o'clock, in the first round of the Cumberland County championships, and afterward you're going out for pizza with Jocelyn. Your heart is pulling you away from the farm, your thoughts fly through a jumble of images: Jocelyn's fine blonde hair, the green of the infield grass, the brightly painted ads on the outfield fence, the way the chalk lines glow blinding white in the summer sun, the smell of Jocelyn's shoulders when you bury your face in the nape of her neck. If you never have to suffer through another summer swamped under the sickly sweet smell of tobacco, it will be all right with you.

You finish eating and are washing out the glass and plate in the sink when you hear your father's boots on the porch and the screen door slams behind him. You ignore the old man. He comes over to the counter, opens the cupboard, and takes out the bottle of sour mash bourbon and a drinking glass. Less than an inch is left in the bottom of the bottle. He curses and pours the bourbon into the glass, then drinks it off without putting down the bottle. He sighs heavily and leans against the counter.

You dry your hands quickly and get your glove and spikes.

"Where you going?" your father asks, as if the uniform and equipment are not enough.

"We got a game today."

He looks at you. His eyes are set in a network of wrinkles that come from squinting against the sun. Mr. Witt, the high school coach, has the same wrinkles around his eyes, but his are from Playing outfield when he was with Atlanta. And Mr. Witt's eyes are not bloodshot.

Your father doesn't say anything. He takes off his billed cap and wipes his forearm across his brow. He turns and reaches into the sugar canister he keeps in the cupboard next to his bottles. You try to leave, but are stopped by his voice again. "Where's the sugar-bowl money?"

"I don't know."

His voice is heavy, slow. "There was another twelve dollars in here. What did you do with it?"

You stand in the door, helpless. "I didn't touch your money."

"Liar. What did you do with it!"

Pure hatred flares in you. "I didn't take your fucking money, you old drunk!"

You slam out the screen door and stalk over to the beat-up Maverick that you worked nights and weekends saving up to buy. You grind the gearshift into first, let the engine roar through the rotten muffler, spin the tires on the dirt in the yard. In the side mirror you see the old man standing on the porch shouting at you. But you can't hear what he's shouting, and the image shakes crazily as you bounce up the rutted drive.

Sandy flinched. He was crouched in his apartment, and the woman was standing over him. He still shook with anger at his father's accusation, still sweated from the heat; he could still smell the tobacco baking in the sun. How he hated the old man and his suspicion. For the first time in years he felt the vivid contempt he'd had then for the smallness that made his father that way.

He backed away from Judith, shaking. She reached out and touched him again.

You're in this same bedroom, leaning half out of bed where you've just gotten your ashes hauled better than you have in your entire life, in order to stick your finger into a pocket to see whether you've been robbed. On the day that you made the majors, on the day that you played better than you have in your entire life, on the day you played better than, in truth, you know you are really able to play. Sticking your finger into your pants pocket like a half-wit sticking his finger up his ass because it feels so good. A pitiful loser. Just like your father.

Sandy jerked away from her. He scrambled toward the bed, suddenly terrified. His knees were so weak he couldn't pull himself into the bed.

"What's the matter, Sandy?" She stepped toward him.

"Don't touch me!"

"You don't like my touch?"

"You're going to kill me." He said it quietly, amazed; and as he spoke, he realized it was true.

She moved closer. "That remains to be seen, Sandy."

"Don't touch me again! Please!"

"Why not?"

Cowering, he looked up at her, trying to make out her face in the darkness. It wasn't fair. But then something welled up in him, and he knew it *was* fair, and that was almost more than he could stand. "I'm sorry," he said.

She knelt beside him, wrapped her arms around him, and said nothing.

After a while he stopped crying. He wiped his eyes and nose with the corner of the bed sheet, ashamed. He sat on the edge of the bed, back to her. "I'm sorry," he said.

"Yes," she said. Then he saw that in her other hand, the one she had not touched him with, she held the straight razor. She had been holding it all the time.

"I didn't realize I might be hurting your feelings," he said.

"You can't hurt my feelings." There was no emotion in her voice. There was nothing. Looking at her face was like looking at an empty room.

"Don't worry," she said, folding the blade back into the handle. "I won't hurt you."

It was a blind voice. Sandy shuddered. She leaned toward him. Her body was excruciatingly beautiful, yet he stumbled back from the bed, grabbing for his shirt, as if the pants weren't enough, as if it were January and he was lost on the lakefront in a blizzard.

"You don't have to be afraid," she said. "Come to bed."

He stood there, indecisive. He had to get out of there. She was insane — fuck, insane; she wasn't even human. He looked into her cold face. It was not dead. It was like the real woman was in another place and this body was a receiver over which she was bringing him a message from a far distance — from another country, from across the galaxy. If he left now, he would be okay, he knew. But something that might have happened to him would not happen, and in order to find out what that was, he would have to take a big chance. He looked up at the moon through the skylight. The clouds passed steadily across it, making it seem like it was moving. The moon didn't move that fast; it moved so slowly that you couldn't tell, except Sandy knew that in five minutes the angle of the shadows on the wall and chair and bed would be all different. The room would be changed.

She was still in bed. Sandy came back, dropped the shirt, took off his pants, and got in beside her. Her skin was very smooth.

The clock read 8:45; he would have to hurry. He felt good. He got his bags out of the closet and began to pack. Halfway through, he stopped to get the shirt he had left on the floor. He picked it up and shoved it into his laundry bag, then remembered the cash and pulled it out again. She had left him fifteen dollars. One ten, five ones.

He pushed the shirt down into the bottom of the bag and finished packing. He called a cab and rode over to War Memorial.

On the Hitachi in the cab he watched the morning news, hoping to get the baseball scores. Nothing. The Reverend Mr. Gilray declares the Abomination of Desolation has begun, the Judgment is at hand. Reports the Israelis have used tactical nukes in the Djibouti civil war. Three teenagers spot another UFO at Chestnut Ridge.

When he got to the park, Sandy tipped the cabbie a redbuck and went directly to the locker room and cleaned out his locker. He was hoping to avoid Leon or Dutch, but just as he was getting ready to leave, Dutch showed up to take some hitting before the Sunday afternoon game.

"Looks like I underrated you, sport. Just like on the field." He hauled out his wallet and began to get the bills.

"Keep it," Sandy said.

"Huh?" Dutch, surprised, looked like a vanilla imitation of Leon's perpetual innocence.

"Leon won the bet."

Dutch snickered. "She got wise to you, huh?"

Sandy zipped his bag shut and picked up his glove and bats. He smiled. "You could say that. I got to go — cab's waiting. Wish me luck."

"Thought you didn't need luck."

"Goes to show you what I know. Say good-bye to Leon for me, okay?" He shook Dutch's hand and left.

In Boise

RICK WILBER

The wheel ruts are still there, aimed west toward Oregon. Drive to the south side of Boise, like I did the other day after I heard the news, and cross over the Americana Boulevard bridge and then go left into Ann Morrison Park. Pull into that parking lot with the cottonwoods all around it, then walk down that bluff and into the green grass at the north edge of the park and you'll see them for yourself: two shallow ruts, maybe six feet apart, running alongside the Boise River. A century and a half ago, Conestogas — a line of them that must have seemed to stretch all the way back to Missouri — filled those ruts all summer long, settlers heading to Oregon, looking for land and a good life in the Golden West. They knew where they were headed, and Boise wasn't anything more than a day or two's stopover on their way there. It was just a place to rest the oxen and buy some provisions before the final four-hundred-mile push along the Oregon Trail

I thought I knew where I was headed, too, back in 1941. I figured Boise for a place where I'd spend a few months before moving up to Columbus, Ohio and then to St. Louis and the big time, joining the likes of Johnny Mize and Enos Slaughter and Terry Moore and those other Cardinals of the early 1940s.

I had a fastball with a lot of movement on it, you see, and I knew that was all I needed. Rare back and let 'er rip, just blow it right by them, that was my philosophy.

I came west from Decatur, Illinois, riding the old Union Pacific through Missouri and Nebraska and Wyoming and on into Idaho. Took me two days, what with changing trains in Denver and spending one miserable night sitting upright in the Pullman coach as we rattled through the Rockies. But I didn't mind the sleepless travel, I was eighteen years old and was going to be the next Bob Feller, and some bumpy tracks weren't about to get in my way.

Boise felt cool to me for the first day of June, coming from Illinois where it'd been hot as blazes and limp-rag humid. I was met at the station by Jack McDevitt, the back-up catcher and player-manager for the Boise Pilots in the newly reformed Pioneer League. McDevitt was about five-foot-ten, wiry, with thinning brown hair under that fedora he wore. He was dressed in a suit, single-breasted with a belt in the back the way they wore them then. Under his left arm he carried, of all things, a catcher's mitt, a new Rawlings Ernie Lombardi model. He didn't say why.

He seemed a nice enough guy at first, and normal as he could be. He was on the downside of a career that saw him playing for the Phillies and then the Redlegs for a few years. A good defensive catcher and decent hitter, he was one of those guys who was up for more than a cup of coffee but never quite got a chance to be a starter. Now he was making the shift to managing and Boise was his first stop on the road back to the big leagues. We shared that, I remember thinking that first day. Both of us out in the Wild West to get started on our new careers. Both of us thinking we knew where we were headed.

McDevitt got me to my boarding house, introduced me around to Mrs. O'Connor — Mother Mary, she said she liked to be called — and the other players who lived there: Andy Harrington, Gordie Williamson, Bob King, Marvin Rickert, and Eijii Sawamura. Sawamura had been a pitcher for the old Boise Rising Suns, a popular team there for awhile in the mid 1930s. Eijii was gone a couple of weeks after I showed up, called home by his family in Nagasaki. He was the first Japanese I ever met and I liked him a lot, he had a heck of a sense of humor. A couple of years later, less pleasantly, I met a lot more of them.

We were all in the front room, going through the handshaking routine, when McDevitt stopped right in the middle of talking to a little group of us, held out his hand to tell us to be quiet, and then took that glove out from under his arm and put it up to his ear, the mitt opened wide.

I wasn't paying too much attention at first, too busy smiling and listening to Harrington warn me about Haydn Walker, the owner, who was, he said "a nice enough guy when he's sober. But that ain't often."

I laughed at that, thinking he was joking, and then I saw

McDevitt raise that hand again, listen to that mitt for a few seconds, then put the mitt in front of his mouth and start talking. "Joe," he said, "Listen, kiddo, I know what they're saying, but that's not the way it is. You're hitting the ball fine. Hell, you got a ten-game streak going, d'you know that?"

He paused, put it back to his ear to listen again, then back to his mouth, saying "There you go. Yeah, that's what I figured. You're coming around nicely, Joe, just keep swinging, OK? And don't worry about that stiff neck. You had the same thing last year, too, and it loosened up in the heat, right?" He listened, nodded. "Well, it'll be hot in St. Louis, Joey, always is. I think you'll go on a tear. Just keep those feet apart in your stance, right? And bring those wrists through first, got it?"

McDevitt listened, nodded again, "Yeah, Joe, no problem. I'm here when you need me. Yeah, sure. OK. Talk to you later, kiddo." And he closed the mitt up and shoved it back under his left arm.

I looked at Harrington, the question on my face.

Harrington just smiled, shook his head, whirled his finger around his ear and whispered "He's crazy as a loon, kid. Thinks he's talking to DiMaggio."

"Joe DiMaggio? *The* Joe DiMaggio?"

He laughed. "The very one, kid." He put his arm over my shoulder. "Look, kid, Jack McDevitt's a hell of a swell guy, but he's got some strange habits, OK? He reads all the damn time for one thing — newspapers, magazines, history books. You'd think he was a damn professor.

"And now there's this thing with DiMaggio that's been going on for the past week or so. Hell, Jack never hit better than .268 in six years in the big leagues, but he thinks DiMaggio needs his advice — not to mention they're talking to each other through a catcher's mitt." He laughed, shrugged his shoulders. "I don't think Jack even knows Joe Dee, to tell you the truth. Jack spent all his time in the National League."

Then Harrington turned away from me, smiled and walked over to McDevitt to put his arm around his shoulders and start chatting about the Pilots and how much the kid — that'd be me — could help the pitching rotation.

And I did help the rotation there at first. I was eighteen, with a rising fastball and a ton of confidence. I'd been mowing them down back home, all-star of my high-school team at Decatur Central High, and then getting great ink playing for the Central Illinois All-Stars in a tournament at St. Louis' Heinie Meinie Field after I graduated. Heck, I threw a no-hitter there in late May, and a one-hitter a couple of days later. That's when Freddie Hawn, a scout for the Cardinals, came calling, and now, here I was a professional in the Cardinal organization, on loan to the Boise Pilots.

A week later I got my first chance to pitch, in the final game of three against the first-place Twin Falls Cowboys. I was darn near perfect, throwing a two-hit shutout, with ten strike-outs and just one walk. I even had a stand-up double in the fourth to drive in one of our four runs.

Do you know what's it like to be in control of a game like that? There's no feeling like it in the world. I knew, absolutely *knew*, I could get every batter out. My fastball was hopping, with Cowboys waving at it as it went by. I even got two strikeouts with my curve. Been eating my Wheaties, you know what I mean?

The win tied us with Twin Falls for first-place and I figured I was pretty damn swell. An hour later, when we climbed into our broken-down old Ford team bus after the game and headed toward Ogden for a pair of rain-out double-headers, I was sure I was on my way to great things. The St. Louis fans would be screaming my name by August or September.

I couldn't sleep for thinking about the game. The bus rattled and groaned as McDevitt, doing the driving, ground it through what gears it had left, up toward Sawtooth Pass and then down the other side on route 83 into Ogden. There was great scenery out there somewhere, I remember thinking, but between the dirt on the inside of my window and the rain on the outside, I couldn't see any of it.

I was in the second row, behind Harrington, who had the knack for sleeping soundly even in that bus. Dizzy with my own success, and maybe a little homesick, I sat back and tried to drift off, tried not to think too much about how glorious and wonderful my future in the game was certainly going to be if only I could make a few friends and not be quite so lonely.

Eyes closed, thinking about home, I heard someone softly talking. I looked up and it was McDevitt, holding his glove to his ear with his left hand while he drove that narrow mountain road in the rain with his right. He was talking to the pocket of that old Rawlings mitt.

"Well, ain't it just like I told ya, Joe?" he was saying. "You just stay with it and it'll come. That's great, kid, just great."

He put the glove to his ear for a moment, listened, then put it back in front of his mouth to speak again. "Three hits? That's great. You got those Yanks going now, Joey. I'm telling you right now, you fellows are gonna have a great season."

He listened some more, nodded. "Yeah, that's just swell, Joe. Double-header tomorrow? Yeah, for us, too, down in Ogden. Yeah, we won tonight, the kid pitcher did a heckuva job, I think maybe he's a prospect."

He listened again, then moved the glove back and ended with, "Yeah, you, too, Joey. Knock 'em dead. Yeah, and keep that stance wide, right? Yeah, OK. Yeah, you, too."

And McDevitt set the glove down to the side of his seat and put both hands back on the wheel before leaning forward to peer through the windshield wipers as they pushed the water around on the glass. We were through the pass now and heading steeply down-hill on that slick, narrow mountain road. I wanted to ask McDevitt about what was going on. I wanted to find out if he was mad as a hatter, crazy for talking to Joe DiMaggio through his glove in the middle of the Utah rain. But I didn't ask, he was concentrating hard on keeping us on the road and I didn't want my curiosity to kill us all. And then the moment passed and Harrington woke up and started talking to me about developing a change-up and then, finally, as we drove along the edge of the Great Salt Lake and on into Ogden, I managed to catch a couple of hours sleep.

When we got to our hotel in Ogden, I bought a copy of the *Post Register* to read over breakfast and there it was, top headline on the back sports page: "DiMaggio's three hits beat Browns."

I didn't know what to make of that.

After breakfast, I got a couple more hours sleep in the Golden Spike Hotel and then it was time to get to the ballpark for our double-header. I got there early, that's the only way for a kid pitcher to get any cuts at all in batting practice. In the clubhouse — a new place, but bare, with a concrete slab floor and some wooden benches and an open wooden locker for each of us, nails tapped into the sides and backs — I sat there and pulled on my sanitaries and then my red Pilots socks with the three white stripes, rolling the socks and the bottom of my pants and the sanitaries all together up near the top of the calf. I was still at the stage of my career then when just putting on the uniform was a thrill.

McDevitt came by as I finished. He smiled at me. "C'mon kid, I want to watch you take a few swings," he said, and then he walked me through the tunnel and into the dugout and that bright Utah sunshine. It was hot, with the wind blowing in from the desert and the salt lake; the air so humid and salty you could feel the stuff on your skin and taste it in the air.

I stepped into the cage to hit a few and McDevitt talked for a minute or two about my swing, about how I needed to level it off and tighten it up some, that I wasn't ever going to be hitting home runs and I should worry about singles.

I'd hit that double off the wall the night before, but I wasn't going to say anything to him. He was the skipper and I was the rookie, and if there was anything I'd learned in just two weeks of being a professional, it was to keep my mouth shut.

And then, as I swung level and flat, slapping line-drives out over short, he said this to me: "Kid, I know you was awake last night when I was talking to Joe."

I didn't say anything.

"Joe and I was roommates back in '33, with the San Francisco Seals," he said. "Joe was having some trouble at the plate and asked me to take a look at his swing. Well, I thought he had a hitch in there, and then was trying to catch up with it, punching at the ball instead of swinging through. We worked on it some, and . . ."

"And he went on that streak," I said, stepping back from the plate. I turned to look at McDevitt. "Everyone knows about that, when he hit in 61 straight. That's the professional record."

"You got it, kid," McDevitt said, and turned to spit out a big hunk of tobacco. "He's trusted me ever since, that's all. You see me talking to him, well that's all it is, just a little free advice. I keep up with how he's doing and I give him some advice here and there."

"Sure," I said, thinking about how all that good advice was being sent through the deep pocket of a Rawlings catcher's mitt. I didn't know what else to say, so I just stepped back into the box and waited for the next pitch from Harrington to come into me, straight down the middle, perfectly understandable. See the ball. Hit the ball. It's a simple game, really.

That evening I spent the first game in the bullpen, waiting for the weather to cool down some and watching us lose the opener, 3-1, on a long home run off a sweet swing by Swish Nicholson, a guy who earned his nickname a couple of years later with the Cubs when he hit twenty-nine of them.

The nightcap I spent in the dugout, right next to McDevitt. He wanted me to watch the Ogden hitters and tell him what I saw, the strengths and weaknesses. That was harmless enough, and even got to be pretty interesting as Howie Petersen pitched a good game at them, keeping a shutout going through the first five. Then the catcher's mitt rang in McDevitt's head and it all got strange.

We were watching Petersen get behind in the count in the first two hitters he faced that inning before getting them both to fly out to left. When he went 2-0 on the third guy with a couple of breaking balls, one outside and one in the dirt, I figured it was time for serious worry; but McDevitt sat up like he'd heard something the rest of us couldn't find on any radio dial and then he picked up that mitt and gave it a listen.

He nodded. "Sure, Joe," he said, "Yeah, he's got that sloppy curve and then he'll try to run it in on you with the fastball. He never throws that curve over the plate, so wait on him and then go for the pump, OK?"

Petersen came in with a fastball and the guy drilled it, foul, to left. At least it was a strike.

"Sure, Joe," McDevitt was saying, "but you got to go down and get that fastball and knock it right out of there, OK?"

He paused, listened. Petersen, working fast, came in with another curve in the dirt. Ball three. "Joey," McDevitt was saying into his glove, "you got to trust me, he'll come in with that fastball down and in, you just be ready."

He listened again, nodding. Petersen came in one more time with the curve, in the dirt and outside for a walk.

"Joe," McDevitt said, "I got to get out there and talk to my pitcher. Stay on the line. I'll be right back." He handed me the catcher's mitt. "Here, kid. Talk to Joe while I get out there and settle Howie down, all right?"

I stared at him.

"Just say hi, kid. He won't bite," he said, and walked up the dugout steps and out onto the field.

I held the mitt to my ear. There was nothing. "Hi," I said, figuring it couldn't hurt. Still nothing.

"Mr. DiMaggio?" I tried. Silence, but then McDevitt, halfway out to the mound, turned back to look at me, put his hands out, palms up as if to ask me how the conversation was going. I shrugged, shook my head slightly.

He frowned. "Keep him on the line, kid," he yelled, and then turned back to stride out to where Petersen stood there, the ball in his hand, waiting for him.

So I tried again. "Um, Mr. DiMaggio, this is Delbert Potter. I'm a pitcher here with the Boise Pilots? Jack McDevitt — he's our manager here — he says I should say hi and keep you on the line for a couple of minutes. He's out talking to our pitcher right now and he handed me this, um, glove . . ."

The dugout was awfully quiet. I stopped talking into the mitt and looked down the bench. They were all looking at me, some of them grinning. I looked out toward the mound and McDevitt was walking back. He was giving Petersen one more hitter to get things straightened out.

"How's it going, kid?" he asked me as he reached the top of the dugout steps.

I put up my hand to shush him, listened intently to the mitt for a second, then put the pocket of the mitt close to my mouth, said "Yes, sir, Mr. DiMaggio. Absolutely. I'll tell him you said so. Yes, sir. And good luck today. That's right, fastball, low and inside, sir. Yes, sir, that's what he says." I gave it a listen again, then "And thank you, Mr. DiMaggio. OK, then. Thank you, Joe."

And I pulled the mitt away from my face, folded it together and tossed it up to McDevitt. "It's going fine, Skip," I said. "Mr. DiMaggio — Joe — says thanks for the tip. He'll be watching for that fastball."

"That's great, kid. Thanks," said McDevitt, catching the mitt as he came down the steps before plopping down on the bench. "Now let's see what old Howie can do here with the bottom of their line-up."

Howie, it turned out, couldn't do much. We lost the first game, and then the second, too, to fall out of that tie for first.

DiMaggio, in St. Louis, had three home runs and a double off the Browns.

It went on like that for the next few weeks, McDevitt talking to DiMaggio through that catcher's mitt with me acting like some sort of receptionist when McDevitt couldn't talk, chatting away with the glove like it all was for real, then listening while McDevitt gave Joe Dee plenty of advice on how to handle things as the whole nation started paying attention — a lot of attention — to The Streak.

There was a war going on in Europe, we knew, and the Japanese were marching all around China. War fever had even reached into Boise, with B-25 bombers practicing their bombing runs from Gowen Field, the big new airbase just half-a-mile past the ballpark's left-field fence.

But baseball is what mattered, from our struggles to hang onto first place in the Pioneer League to Jack McDevitt holding that big, floppy Rawlings mitt up to chat with DiMaggio about how to keep that streak going.

When Joe broke the Yankee record of twenty-nine games on a bad-hop single that ate up Luke Appling at short for the White Sox, it was McDevitt on the mitt congratulating him before handing the glove over to me so I, too, could tell Joe way-to-go.

When Bob Muncrief, a rookie right-hander for the Brownies, had Joe stymied the whole game, it was McDevitt who told Joe not to worry; he figured the kid wouldn't walk Joe in the eighth but would pitch to him out of pride, and he was right. Joe singled to save the streak. In the next day's *Boise Statesman* I read where Muncrief said, "I wasn't going to walk him. That wouldn't have been fair — to him or to me."

When the Yankees were finally in first place a couple of days later and playing at home, McDevitt was on the mitt with Joe as Tommy Henrich came up with a man on and one out. McDevitt told Joe not to worry about a double-play, Henrich would bunt the man over to help out, and sure enough that's what happened. Henrich asked Joe McCarthy if he could bunt and McCarthy said yes. The sacrifice moved the runner over and gave Joe one more at-bat. He doubled and kept the streak going.

It went on like that for weeks, the guys finding it pretty funny there for awhile. Eventually, though, the sportswriters in Boise found out about it — from Harrington, I think — and it all got pretty sour.

Most guys thought the joke had gone on way too long, and it was taking attention away from the field, where we were playing pretty good and in a race for the Pioneer League pennant.

McDevitt never let on the whole time whether he even knew we all thought it was just a prank. As far as he seemed to be concerned, it was all very simple, Joe DiMaggio needed his advice and he was happy to help. Giving advice, after all, was what he did for a living, as he told me often enough.

One afternoon, we stood out in the bullpen and he worked on teaching me how to throw a change-up while those bombers roared behind us. "It's all about keeping 'em guessing kid," he said. "If you can change speeds, it'll make that fastball of yours look a little faster and give them hitters something else to think about."

I nodded, took the ball from him and tried one, sliding the ball back from the fingertips and in toward the knuckles, like he'd taught me. It worked, but I didn't have much control with it and told him so.

"That'll come," he said, and then he smiled. "Look, kid, you got smarts, and that counts for a lot in this game, especially when you're pitching. Guy like you, you got to outsmart the hitter, know what I mean?"

I nodded again — only later did it dawn on me what he'd really been telling me about my physical tools — and then I tried a few more. I could tell the change would help me, and Lord knew I needed the help. I thanked him, after I finally got a couple of them spotted where he wanted them.

"Oh, hell, kid, don't thank me for doing my job," he said. "I'm supposed to be a coach, remember? I'm supposed to help kids like you learn to play this game a little." Then he'd grinned suspiciously. "Plus, I'm supposed to win some, too, and damned if we're not doing that, right, kid?"

He turned around and watched a bomber coming in for a landing. "You ever think about history, kid?"

"I can tell you who led the National League in hitting every year this century," I said. "Just try me."

He smiled. "I bet you can, kid. But what I was wondering about was this war we're heading into. Going to be some history made. Might not be too long before them pilots find themselves dropping the real thing instead of sacks of flour, you know what I mean?"

"You really think it'll come to that?" I asked. The way McDevitt read every newspaper he could get his hands on I figured he knew what he was talking about. Me, I hadn't read anything but the sports page in maybe my whole life.

"Yeah, kid, I do. I ain't got much of an education, but it looks like to me we're going to be in this thing one way or another, and soon. And I'll tell you what, we won't be out here playing ball if the whole country goes to war, you can count on that. There'll be more important things than baseball."

"What'll we do, then?"

"Ballplayers?" He shrugged. "Go fight, I guess. Wouldn't that be a mess?"

"Sure would," I agreed, thinking mostly of myself.

He turned his back on the bombers and looked back into the field. "Hell, we all make our own history one way or another, you know? Joe's going to get his made with this streak. Me and you, who knows? How you going to make the history books, kid?"

A month before I'd have answered with something about being in the Hall of Fame. But now I wasn't so sure. The Pilots were winning, sure, fighting it out for first all the way with Twin Falls and then, later, with Ogden, too. But my pitching had gone south as the hitters caught up with my fastball and learned to sit on my curve. After a couple more real disasters as a starter, by early July, I was in the bullpen in middle relief, trying to get my confidence back and get the ball over the plate, reduced to hoping a new change-up would cure my ills.

Somewhere along the line I realized I was in a terrible rut — like those tracks out past the left-field fence in Airway Park in Boise.

The field was new then, and a gem — I realized how lucky I was to play there once I'd seen the other parks in the league. But just beyond the fence ran those wheel ruts of the Oregon Trail. I walked in them all the time, they were on my way to the park from Mrs. O'Connor's boarding house. Walking along, knee-deep in ruts that began in Missouri and kept on going all the way to the Williamette Valley in Oregon, I could picture those wagons moving along slowly, steadily to whatever waited for them, following that trail like there were no options to go anywhere else, do it any other way. They must have been hell to get out of, those ruts. I know mine were — the fastball getting ripped, my curve not fooling anyone, my new change-up too little too late. I wanted to just pack it up, leave go of it all and head home to Decatur.

Through everything I kept helping McDevitt talk to Joe, listening in as McDevitt said Joe Dee should swing on that 3-0 count like he did to get the hit in the fourteenth game, then hearing McDevitt relay Joe's description of how he'd slapped a double off Dutch Leonard to tie Sisler's record.

And I anguished with them both when DiMaggio's favorite bat was stolen between games of that crucial double-header in Washington.

I was out on the mound, struggling to get through the fifth inning at home against Lewiston, the last-place team, when McDevitt got that call. I'd walked the first two men I faced, then dropped down a gear to get it over the plate and given up a triple off the wall, then walked the next guy. Finally, the guy after that hit a scorcher to short, but Tommy Seals at second turned it into a slick double-play that got me some outs but cost me a run. I looked into the dugout to see how McDevitt was taking it all, and he was talking to that catcher's mitt.

I was a wreck, all the craziness of that long, hot Boise summer running around in my head so fast I was dizzy with it. I stood there, looking at McDevitt, willing him to notice me out there, have some pity on me, take me out, send me home, end all this misery. Instead, when I needed him most to be my manager he was talking to that glove.

I glared at him until Harrington, sitting next to him, noticed me and elbowed him. He looked up, frowned, then stood up, climbed those dugout steps and waved at the ump for a timeout as he walked toward me, that catcher's mitt tucked away like always under his left arm.

"What's up, kid?" he asked.

"I don't have it, Skip. I think maybe, well, you know..." I said lamely, handing him the ball.

"You know what, kid," he said. "Somebody stole Joe's bat between games of that doubleheader."

"Oh, Christ Almighty." I was a religious man, even back then, and I wasn't one to use the Lord's name in vain. But I couldn't believe it. Here I was in the middle of a real mess and all McDevitt could talk about was DiMaggio and that damn streak.

He could see how mad I was at him, but it didn't faze him.

Instead, he just smiled, said, "Hey, kid, hang on a second. I got to tell Joe something." And he put the catcher's mitt up to his face to talk.

"Tell Joe something!" I yelled at him, reaching out to pull the glove away, all the worries and the anxieties and the fear boiling up out of me at last. "Why don't you tell *me* something, McDevitt? For Christ's sake, man, I'm trying to pitch to these guys and all you want to do is talk into that damn mitt!"

He just smiled. "That's good, kid. Nice to see some fire in those eyes." He tossed me back the ball. "Now let's see if that new change-up works," he said, and put the glove back up to his face, mumbling into the pocket as he turned around to walk back to the dugout.

I turned around to stare at my teammates, all of them looking at me, slapping their fists into their gloves, shouting encouragement like this was all just an ordinary part of the game.

All right, then.

I stood there for a moment, my career in a shambles before it ever got started, my manager talking to Joe DiMaggio through his mitt while I watched my dreams blow away in that hot summer breeze.

And then I started to pitch, buzzing the first one high and tight, giving the Lewiston batter a nice, clean shave for ball three. Then a curveball for strike two, and then that change-up, fat and right down the middle, but looking faster than it was so the guy swung early and hit it off the end of the bat instead of the meat, lofting a lazy flyball to left, where Mel Nelson caught it without taking a step.

From the mound, I could hear McDevitt in the dugout, saying "I'm telling you, Joe, the bat's in Newark. And I got friends in Newark. I'll call 'em and you'll have the bat back tomorrow, Joe, swear to god."

And the bat, I read in the sports page later, really was in Newark, and Joe did get it back and keep the streak going. And darned if I didn't win that game, too, 7-5, for my third — and last — professional win.

It all ended a couple of weeks later, on July 17 in Pocatello. I was on the mound in relief again. Jack Coates, our catcher, was sitting it out, so McDevitt was behind the plate, trying to teach me a few things while he could.

I was still mad as a hornet at him, and while he'd kept on with the conversations with Joe Dee, I hadn't played any of those stupid tricks with the DiMaggio mitt since that night back in Boise. But he ignored all that and treated me like everything was copacetic, smiling and grinning and telling me how great my stuff was. That just made me madder, and I reared back harder, putting about everything I had into that fastball and shaking off the sign every time he called for a curve or a change-up. Hell, I figured I'd just fire away at him. And it felt good, to tell you the truth, though the Pocatello hitters were hammering me and I was having a hard time protecting a six-run lead we'd built up in the first four innings.

In the sixth it started getting obvious. Pocatello's number-three hitter slapped a sharp liner to left that landed in front of Nelson. Then the next guy took a couple of strikes before I shook off the sign for the change and came in with my best fastball and he ripped it right back into McDevitt's glove. It would have gotten us out of the inning, but McDevitt couldn't hold onto it, and on the next pitch the guy went to the pump with a towering home run that's still up there somewhere sailing through the Idaho night sky looking for some mountain peak to plow into.

McDevitt came out to talk to me, clanking up to me in that beat-up catcher's gear, his mask up on top of his head, his glove on his left hand.

"Got that one up some," he said, and I nodded. I figured he'd be talking to DiMaggio any second now, the streak was up to fifty-six and going strong.

I was feeling mean. "You should've hung onto that third strike. We had that guy."

McDevitt smiled thinly, held up the Rawlings mitt. The web was torn from between the thumb and first finger, the leather lacing dangling there. "Didn't realize it until just now, kid. That foul tip ripped right through my mitt."

"I'm sorry."

"Yeah, me too, kid." He held the glove up to his ear. "It ain't working so I can talk to Joe, either." He shook his head. "Too bad. I got a bad feeling about Joe today."

"Sure," I said, "a bad feeling."

"And I got a bad feeling about your stuff, too, kid. I think they got you figured out. I'm gonna bring in Townie. We got to protect this lead and win this one."

I nodded. I knew I was done. Hell, I'd known I was done for the past month. If I couldn't get anybody out in the Pioneer League, I sure as hell wasn't going to be striking them out for the Cardinals any day soon.

And so I went to the bench, and then into the showers, and, just a few weeks later, back home to Decatur.

In Cleveland that night, DiMaggio was up against Al Smith, a veteran leftie. Bob Feller would face him the next night, and most people figured Feller could stop the streak if anyone could.

But Smith got the job done: a nice play at third by Ken Keltner, a walk, another nice play at third by Keltner, and then a groundball into a double-play and that was it.

In Boise, McDevitt worked on fixing that mitt between innings and got it done in five minutes, but he said it didn't work anymore. Not that it mattered. By the time our game was in the fifth, the Yankee game — and DiMaggio's streak — was over.

By September, I was back on the farm in Illinois, worrying about soybeans and corn instead of Joe Dee and Jack McDevitt's catcher's mitt. While I was out standing knee deep in corn furrows, DiMaggio went right back on another good streak and the Yankees won the pennant, seventeen games in front of the Red Sox.

Later, I heard from Andy Harrington that Jack McDevitt died at Okinawa. He was top turret gunner and flight engineer on a B-25 and they were attacking Japanese gun implacements on the beach, flying in so low that their props cut a wake through the lagoon. When they pulled up to drop their bombs some enemy sharpshooter — who knows, maybe Eijii Sawamura — got at them with anti-aircraft fire and that was that.

McDevitt and the others couldn't get out in time, and so they all made it into the history books as part of the price the country paid. I bet McDevitt wished, right there at the end, that he had that catcher's mitt with him, that it worked again and he could talk to Joe one last time before they went into the water.

I can see that in my mind, see him talking to Joe, saying goodbye as the plane's right wing caught the water, sending the plane careening in and breaking up over the reef-line.

As for me, I wound up fighting the war with a typewriter, writing about the real heroes as they waded ashore at Guadalcanal and Ie Shima. I met a lot of ballplayers along the way, guys ripping out the heart of their careers to do the right thing for themselves, for their country; guys making history. I never ran into DiMaggio in all those years or anytime after, even though he was doing his duty, too.

After the war I took advantage of the GI Bill and got my college degree and wound up teaching high-school history classes and coaching the baseball team at Decatur Central, back where I'd started.

I helped some good kids along the way, and a few of them even made the bigs. If you ever saw Del Unser roam the outfield for the Phillies, you saw one of my best. And if you watched Bobby Gamin throw his no-no against the Mets in '74, you saw Jack McDevitt's change-up in action. I taught it to Gamin eight years before and he took us to the state title with it — that and his ninety-mile-an-hour fastball.

I know — I always knew — that Jack McDevitt was crazy as a loon and none of that happened the way it seemed to be happening. Joe Dee could have cleared all that up for me just by looking at what I could show him, by putting the mitt on his left hand and chuckling a little and telling me it hadn't happened that way.

But I didn't really want to know, not like that. What I wanted, what I've kept alive, is the thought that maybe it really *did* happen that way, that my season in Boise was part of something important, something that mattered.

And that catcher's mitt? McDevitt gave it to me when I got on the train heading home, said he thought I'd earned that much, at least.

Now it sits here, looking comfortable in my bookcase, right there next to the picture of me and the kids after we won state, Bobby Gamin holding up that trophy and grinning, me standing in the background.

I've had a good, long run with this game, with this life. I married a good woman and we had fifty years together. She died a couple of years ago, so I'm lonely again the way I was in 1941; but we did fine while she was here — four kids, a pack of grandkids, even a great-grandson who looks to me like a natural hitter.

I travel some now, trying to stay busy and interested in things. I get up to St. Louis a lot for Cardinal games, and once or twice a summer I head to Chicago to see the Cubs.

I went west, to Boise, after I heard that DiMaggio had died. I made a nice little vacation out of it; saw the mountains, saw how big the city had become, walked along those wagon-wheel ruts in Ann Morrison Park, thinking about Jack McDevitt and Joe Dee and the way things were back then. And then I came on home to Decatur.

Every now and then, just for fun, I pick that catcher's mitt up, fiddle with the laces some, pound my fist into the pocket a few times. Then I start talking, chatting with McDevitt and DiMaggio, pretending that they can hear me, pretending that they care about what I have to say about teaching kids the game.

I put the glove to my ear now and then for a quick listen, but the old mitt has nothing much to say to me. Except for this one remarkable thing: 56 games, from May 15 to July 17, from a single off White Sox pitcher Edgar Smith to a double-play against the Indians, Boudreau flipping the ball to Mack to get it started. A .357 average that year, with thirty home runs, forty-three doubles, eleven triples. You can look all that up. It's in the history books, where it belongs, where it will probably be forever.

Streak

ANDREW WEINER

I

Victor Garmez was playing center field the day the aliens came. Last season, back in Double-A ball, he had mostly played left field. The Chiefs had started him there, too. But just a few weeks into the season there had been a rash of injuries on the major league team, and the regular center fielder, Mel Hewlett, had been dispatched to Toronto to join The Show.

Hewlett had been batting only .251 at the time, Garmez .305. But Hewlett was management's blue-eyed boy, a first-round pick in the college draft. Garmez was just another Dominican. Or so he imagined they thought of him, when they thought of him at all.

Garmez did not miss Hewlett. But he did envy him, all the more so as the iron gray sky over Syracuse opened up at the top of the third inning and the rain began to fall in torrents. Playing deep, he was soaked through by the time he made it back to the dugout.

They didn't get wet, up in Toronto. They just closed the roof on the dome.

In the dressing room, some of the players had resumed their endless card games. Others were watching daytime TV on the small monitor perched on top of one of the lockers. Garmez sat down to watch with them. He needed to improve his English.

The actors in the TV show were glossy and well-dressed and lived in palace-like homes. You never saw such people or such homes back in the Dominican. Garmez's mother, along with his three sisters, lived in a two-room shack. One day, though, he would make it to the big leagues, and build them a new house. If he didn't catch pneumonia and die first, this ghastly wet and chilly April.

"There's something you should know, Jill," a glossy, well-dressed man with fair wavy hair, who looked just a little like Mel Hewlett, was telling a glossy, well-dressed woman. And then, abruptly, the picture blanked.

"We interrupt this broadcast," said an authoritative sounding voice, "to bring you this special bulletin."

War, Garmez thought. These Yankees have got themselves in another war. Or someone shot their President . . .

The face of a newscaster filled the screen. At first glance, he looked like any other newscaster: dignified, sober, serious. But there was something wild about his eyes.

"Aliens," said the newscaster, "extraterrestrial visitors to our planet from another part of the galaxy, are currently meeting with world leaders in a closed session at the United Nations in New York. We take you now to Diane Kendrick at the UN Plaza. Are you there Diane?"

2

Ken Brady stared in horror at his managing editor.

"You're assigning me *where*?"

"You heard me," Hugh Vernon said. "Sports desk."

"But I'm a science writer. I don't know anything about sports."

"And they don't know shit about science. I want you on the Garmez story."

"Garmez?"

Vernon looked at Brady with a mixture of scorn and awe.

"You don't know? You really don't know?"

"I've been doing stories on the aliens," Brady said. "Who's Garmez?"

"Victor Garmez," Vernon said. "Plays left field for the Blue Jays. Got called up from Triple-A in April as a backup. Got into a game and went 3-for-4. They kept him on the team and he kept on hitting. He's now hit safely in fifty one consecutive games . . ."

"And?"

"Fifty one games," Vernon repeated. "Six more to get past Joe DiMaggio. That name ring any bells for you?"

"Sure. Wasn't there a song about him?"

"DiMaggio set the record for a hitting streak in 1941. No one else has even come close. Until this kid from the Dominican."

"And this is a big deal?"

"A big deal?" Vernon echoed. "The greatest accomplishment in the history of baseball is on the line. I think you could say that was a big deal."

"Okay," Brady said. "But what does it have to do with me?"

"I want a think piece on probability theory. What are the odds against a streak like this? Baseball fans eat up this statistical crap. I need two thousand words for Saturday. Front page of the sport section."

"What's so special about Saturday?"

"Jays finish up their home stand. And Garmez goes for number fifty seven. Assuming he gets that far."

"And if he doesn't?"

Vernon shrugged. "We'll run it on the science page."

"I was supposed to finish this piece on the aliens."

"Screw the aliens," Vernon said. "The aliens are boring. *This* is the big story."

3

Boring. While Brady did not personally agree with this assessment, he could see how interest in the aliens might have begun to wear a little thin.

Following their meeting with world leaders, and a single, carefully orchestrated press conference, the aliens had been keeping a studiously low profile. They were here, they claimed, strictly in a touristic capacity. They wished only to obtain the requisite visas to come and go as they liked, along with a supply of native currencies. In exchange for this they had offered certain philosophical constructs and technological devices. Details of their offerings had not yet been revealed, but apparently the deal had been satisfactory to all concerned.

Afterward, the aliens had flitted here, there, everywhere. They had been sighted buying jewelry at Tiffany's in New York, shopping for native art in Manila, dining on caviar in Moscow, observing the work of the Zurich sanitation department. There had even been reports, still unconfirmed, of aliens seen in Montreal, eating smoked meat, although so far none had been spotted in Toronto.

At their one press conference, the aliens had not been terribly forthcoming. They had declined to identify their planet of origin. Neither would they discuss the technology that had powered their ship. As to the nature of their own society, they offered only the barest clues. And they declined to be drawn into comment on

Earthly ideological and religious squabbles.

It was not surprising that the aliens were evasive on these issues. But it made for rather thin gruel when you had to write background pieces on them. Brady was in some ways relieved to lay down the burden of speculating endlessly on the basis of little or no data. Even to have to write about *baseball*, of all things, a game about which he knew almost nothing and cared less.

4

"Garmez, yeah," said the hitting coach. "I expected good things of him, you know. But not *this* good."

"He didn't make the team in spring training," Brady said.

"Only just came up from Double-A. We thought he needed more seasoning. Still does, to tell you the truth. But when he's hitting like that . . . I mean, when you're hot, you're hot, right?"

"Right," Brady said.

"Garmez, he's a good little hitter. Reminds me of Wade Boggs."

"Wade Boggs never hit in fifty-one consecutive games."

The coach shrugged. "Streaks," he said. "I never understood them. I mean, not to take anything away from Garmez, but he's had some real luck along the way. Back around game twelve, he hits this little looper and it just drops in because the right fielder plays it too deep. Could have been scored an error, but they give him the hit. Another time he hits a chopper back to the mound and legs it out to first base. The umpire says safe, but it looks awfully close. Take away those hits and there's no streak, just a guy having a real good season."

"DiMaggio had some luck, too," Brady said. "From what I've read, there were a couple of very close judgment calls."

"Were there? Maybe that's true. But you know, I remember seeing DiMaggio when I was a kid. He was a giant, a real giant . . . It's some strange kind of world where some green kid can come this close to topping DiMaggio. But don't print that, okay? The line around here is, we're right behind him."

5

Victor Garmez was tall and thin, with mournful eyes and a wispy moustache. According to team records, he had just turned twenty-two.

"I don't know what to tell you," he said. "Nothing like this ever happened to me before. Once I went eleven, maybe twelve games in winter ball. But fifty-one? It's crazy."

He spoke quietly, shyly. His vocabulary was quite good, but his accent was thick, and Brady had to strain to understand him.

"I guess you never expected anything like this to happen."

"Expected? I never expected to be here. It was a fluky thing, you know. One guy breaks an ankle, another guy gets the flu, another one runs into the wall trying to catch a ball and throws out his shoulder —" Garmez allowed himself a brief smile at the fate of Mel Hewlett "— no chance of catching it, he's just hot-dogging. So they got to call me."

"You must have been pleased when you got the call."

"Stunned, more like. One minute I'm watching TV and they're talking about these aliens. And then the manager comes in and tells me to pack because I'm going to The Show. Between the aliens and The Show, my head was spinning so fast I thought it was going to fall off."

Garmez was cradling a bat in his arms, waiting to take batting practice. As they watched, the man in the batting cage smashed a home run ball into the upper deck. He turned, grinning broadly, and caught sight of Garmez and the journalist. The grin turned to a scowl.

"That guy," Garmez said. "Two million dollars a year. Cleanup hitter, he's supposed to be. And you know how many RBI's he hit in April? Three."

A week ago, Brady would not have known what an RBI was. Now, after studying the sacred texts of sabremetrics, he knew all too well. At night, when he closed his eyes, all he saw were tables of names and numbers.

"They hate me," Garmez said. "All these guys. Because I'm showing them up. Me and a couple of others, we're carrying this team."

He ran his hand along his bat.

"That bat," Brady said. "Is that the one you've been using? Kind of a lucky bat?"

Garmez shook his head. "I've used five, six different bats since I came up. A lot of guys, they got lucky bats and lucky socks and lucky ninja turtles, all kinds of lucky crap. But I don't believe in that stuff. What happens to me out there, it's down to me. And God."

"You think God is helping you?"

"I don't know. Maybe so." Garmez's voice trailed down to a

whisper. "It's kind of hard to explain it any other way."

"How does it feel, taking on a legend like Joe DiMaggio?"

"I never heard too much about DiMaggio. Married Marilyn Monroe, right? They say he was a hell of a ballplayer."

"You think you're going all the way?" Brady asked.

"I know it. You see, it's like they say: when you're hot, you're hot."

"Yes," Brady said. "Like they say."

They shook hands, and Garmez headed off to the batting cage. Then he turned back. "Hey," he said. "Maybe I get to marry a movie star, too."

"Yeah," Brady said. "Maybe you do."

6

When you're hot, you're hot.

Victor Garmez believed that. So did his batting coach. So did a lot of other people. And certainly it sounded plausible: the more you succeeded, the more confident you felt, and the better you did next time up.

The only problem, Brady thought, was that it wasn't true. Not in baseball or any other sport. He had pored over the studies, and they all pointed to the same conclusion.

There was a Stanford psychologist who had studied the Philadelphia 76ers basketball team, tracking every basket for more than a season. He found that the probability of making a second basket did *not* rise after a successful shot. The number of baskets made in succession was no greater than you would predict on the basis of the laws of chance. If your chance of making each basket was one in two, for example, you would get five baskets in a row, on average, once in thirty two sequences.

Longer runs occurred, but there was no mystery to them. A more talented basketball player might shoot at, say, a 0.6 probability of success each time out. He would get five in a row about once every thirteen sequences.

The same applied to baseball. There was almost no statistic in the game, no sequence of wins or losses or hits or strikeouts, that went beyond the frequency predicted by the laws of chance.

There was no "hot" or "cold" about it: only skill intermeshing with the dance of probabilities.

Brady could have told Garmez this. But Garmez would not have believed it. No athlete would. No sports fan, either. People didn't seem able to think in probabilistic terms. They saw patterns emerging from the random flux of existence, and they rushed to impose meaning on them, to spin tales of heroism and villainy, or to look for the hand of God.

No, Garmez would not have believed it. No more than Brady's readers were going to believe it.

Besides, there *was* one exception to the rule. One gigantic, spooky exception: DiMaggio's fifty-six game hitting streak. A sequence of events, as the biologist and baseball fan Stephen Jay Gould had once observed, *"so many standard deviations above the expected distribution that it should not have occurred at all . . . the most extraordinary thing that ever happened in American sports."*

Like DiMaggio, Victor Garmez was heading off the probabilistic map. And no one could predict where he might end up.

7

Brady had Saturday off. He rose early and picked up the newspaper from his front step. His own article was on the front page of the sports section. Obviously, Garmez had come through with hit number fifty six the night before.

Brady glanced briefly at his work, then tossed it aside. It was solid stuff, but he wasn't really satisfied with it. For all his research, he had finally been unable to penetrate the mystery of Garmez's streak.

Garmez would be going for number fifty seven that afternoon. Fame and fortune — and perhaps the lifelong endorsement contract with the ketchup manufacturer than had finally eluded DiMaggio — beckoned.

Brady had liked the shy young Dominican, and wished him well. But he had no interest in seeing the game. Besides, he was supposed to meet Janice, his fiancee, at the Eaton Centre shopping mall to select a china pattern for her forthcoming bridal shower. Janice believed in doing things properly.

8

Brady was in the Eaton's china department with Janice when he spotted the alien over in housewares, examining a Eurostyle toaster.

The alien in housewares looked exactly like all the other aliens Brady had seen on TV. He looked remarkably humanoid, with only his exceptional tallness and thinness — all the aliens were more or less seven foot tall — calling attention to his alien nature.

This was, to Brady's knowledge, the first alien to be seen in Toronto. He found a store phone and called Hugh Vernon to explain the situation.

"You want me to follow him?"

"Can't hurt," Vernon said. "First person report on an alien shopping spree. What's he bought so far?"

Brady craned his head to see the alien at the cash desk.

"Looks like a non-stick frying pan."

"Jeez," Vernon said. "This is already sounding like a real thriller. But stay with it, you never know."

Abandoning Janice to select the china pattern, Brady tailed the alien out of the department store and into the mall proper. The alien led him into Chapters, a bookseller. Like all the stores in the mall, it was nearly empty this beautiful mid-June day. Half the population of the city had headed out for their cottages. The rest were probably glued to their TV sets, watching Victor Garmez go for hit number fifty-seven.

The alien browsed for some time at the magazine racks, at first flipping through the car magazines, then becoming engrossed in *Playboy*. Brady wondered whether the alien might be homesick for his own large-breasted alien wife, back home on Arcturus 3 or wherever it was that they had come from.

As far as anyone knew, there were no alien women on Earth. Or at least, all the aliens looked the same, and the general assumption was that they were male, although that assumption could have been quite unfounded. So far, none had been publicly forthcoming about their sexual natures, despite several multi-million dollar offers for syndicated rights to such disclosures. Really, very little was known about the aliens.

Finally the alien left the store and headed for the escalator, making his way down to the lowest level. Brady realized that the alien was heading for the subway station. He followed the alien to the southbound platform. A train pulled up, and the alien got on. Brady got into the next car.

The alien disembarked at Union Station. After exiting the subway, he stood for a moment, apparently confused.

Brady seized his opportunity. "Need some help?" he asked.

"Thank you, yes. Which way is the SkyDome?" The alien spoke a fluent, accentless English.

"It's this way," Brady said, pointing. "I'm going there myself, I'll show you."

"That would be appreciated," the alien said. He was still holding the Eaton's shopping bag containing his non-stick frying pan.

"You're interested in baseball?"

"Very much so," said the alien. "In fact, you might describe this as the high point of our visit."

9

Aliens. Just when everything was going so well, some *aliens* had to come along and screw everything up.

Garmez got the story from Mel Hewlett soon after arriving at the ground. Earlier that week, the Canadian government had booked off a block of tickets for the aliens, along with assorted federal, provincial and city politicians. It was supposed to be kept secret until game time, for security reasons. But Hewlett had got the word from a secretary in the front office, and he seemed delighted to pass it on to Garmez.

"Why would aliens want to see a baseball game?"

"I don't know, Vic," Hewlett said, grinning. Garmez hated being called "Vic," as Hewlett well knew. "Maybe they're here to see *you*. Maybe your fame has spread throughout the galaxy."

Garmez had been feeling excited when he arrived at the ground. It had been a pleasant excitement, full of anticipation. Now it turned into a dull agitation.

Aliens. Garmez had not had time to give much thought to the alien visitors. His own life was moving ahead much too fast. But when he thought about them at all, it was with a kind of derision. You would expect aliens to have a little more on the ball. If they were going to come all this way, you would think they would have something to tell us. Something important about God and life and the secrets of the universe. But from what he saw on the TV, they had nothing to say at all, except "that's nice" and "how much is that?"

Really, the aliens reminded Garmez as nothing so much as the North American tourists who streamed into the Dominican every winter, buying all kinds of awful crap and burning themselves up on the beach and drinking themselves into oblivion.

It must be awfully boring, he thought, back where these aliens came from. To come all this way to see us.

And now, of all the things in the world to see or buy, they had to come *here*. Shaken, he went to see the team manager.

"How come you never told me about these aliens?" he demanded.

"Only found out myself a few hours ago," the manager said, mildly. "What you got to do now is forget about it. Forget about the aliens. Forget about your streak. Just go out there and play your normal game."

"My normal game, sure," Garmez said. He gazed out through the window at the stadium. It was beginning to fill up. "These aliens. What the hell they want here, anyway?"

"Someone invited them, I guess."

"You think they know about my streak?"

"I'm sure someone told them. Although it probably doesn't mean a hell of a lot to them. I mean, how could it?"

"Yeah," Garmez echoed. "How could it?"

10

Brady used his press credentials to gain entry into the ground. But instead of heading for the press box, he followed the alien to a special roped-off section. Within this section were dozens of aliens, along with various local dignitaries.

A security officer rose to bar his progress.

"It's alright," the alien said. "He's with me."

Gratefully, Brady sank down into an unoccupied seat next to his unexpected sponsor. He realized that he was staring at the thick, reddish neck of the Prime Minister of Canada in the seat ahead of him.

"Very kind of you," he told the alien.

"Think nothing of it, Mr. Brady."

"How do you know my name?"

"I saw it on your press pass."

Brady distinctly remembered that the alien had been ahead of him at the time. But perhaps he was wrong. Or perhaps the aliens were somehow possessed of 360° vision.

He could not help but wonder why the alien would knowingly invite a journalist to sit beside him. Since their initial press conference, the aliens had granted no further interviews to the media.

"I most enjoyed your article in this morning's *Tribune*," the alien said, as if in answer to this unspoken question. "Highly insightful."

"You're interested in probability theory?"

"Fascinated by it."

The alien leaned forward in his seat to watch the proceedings on the field. The Red Sox were batting at the top of the second inning. There was no score as yet, but the Sox, with only one out in the inning, had runners at first and second.

"If there's anything you don't understand," Brady told the alien, "go ahead and ask."

This was rather a bold offer from a man who, for all his recent research, still had at best a dim understanding of the intricacies of the game.

"Thank you," said the alien, "but I am quite well acquainted with the game, having made a certain study of it. In some ways, it is much like our own . . ." Here he said something untranslatable into Earthly phonetics.

Mumblypobble, Brady scribbled into his notebook, this being the best approximation he could manage.

"Ah," said the alien. "I believe the Sox will certainly sacrifice in this situation, in all likelihood a bunt down the third base line."

Brady scribbled down this alien prognosis.

"Games," said the alien, "are in a way the essence of a culture. The externalization of its most deeply held values about life, time and existential meaning."

Polite applause rippled through the ground as the Red Sox hitter fulfilled the alien's prediction and gave himself up, laying down a bunt that moved the runners to second and third.

A new hitter took his place. He walked stiffly, and his hair was peppered with gray. "Batting .425 lifetime with runners in scoring position," murmured the alien. "But this will certainly be his last season. It's all so wildly nostalgic, is it not?"

"Nostalgic?"

The alien waved his hand in a disconcertingly human gesture. "The knowledge that each moment is precious precisely because it is ephemeral, and will never recur in quite the same way. The awareness of the fleetingness of life, the immediateness of death. The infinite poignancy of history in the making. Consider Victor Garmez." He gestured toward the Blue Jays left fielder. "Will he ever have a finer moment than today?"

The alien smiled. It was a perfectly pleasant smile, yet it was also oddly chilling. Because somehow Brady knew that Victor Garmez would never have a finer moment. Ever, ever again.

II

A roar went up around the ground as Victor Garmez stepped into the batter's box in the bottom of the second.

Sure, he thought. Today I'm their hero. But if I don't get a hit, it's back to being a bum. I'll be the guy who couldn't quite get past DiMaggio.

He stared sightlessly into the crowd to where the aliens were supposed to be sitting. He couldn't pick them out. Maybe they hadn't come. But of course, the aliens looked pretty much like humans.

The roar of applause continued. Some idiot was trying to get a wave going. Garmez called time-out and stepped back for a moment to review the situation. One out, a man on second, Red Sox leading five to nothing. A sacrifice fly would bring home the run, but one run would not make enough difference.

What he needed to do was get on base. He would look for the hit, but accept the walk.

"They're not going to give you anything to hit," the manager had told him. "They'd rather walk you than let you get number fifty-seven against them. If they offer the walk, take it."

"What if they walk me every time?"

"The way they count it now, the streak stays alive. You get another shot tomorrow."

"But what about then? How did they count it *then*?"

"For DiMaggio, you mean? Back then, it had to be consecutive games."

"Then that's how I got to do it, too."

Bold words. A lot bolder than he felt, right now, facing the ace of the Red Sox staff, a big tough right-hander with a fastball averaging 95 miles per hour.

He watched, mesmerized, as the Boston pitcher went into his wind-up. And stood, transfixed, as the ball hurtled into his face.

12

"A close one," remarked the alien, as the hitter seemed to wait until the very last moment to weave out of the way from a high, tight fastball. "Very close. This is a game of surprising violence. And all so very much more vivid in its actuality."

"Actuality?" echoed Brady. "You mean, you used to watch it on TV?"

"Hush," said the alien. "Let us savor the opening round of this most fascinating duel."

Brady watched as, to applause and scattered boos, Garmez walked on four deliveries, without once having attempted contact with the ball.

13

The afternoon wore on. The Blue Jays picked up a couple of runs, cashing in Garmez's walk. Boston replied with another in the third. Garmez came out to bat again in the fourth with the bases empty, but grounded out to the short stop. The next player up hit a solo home run.

The heat of the fierce afternoon sun was making Brady sleepy. He had difficulty keeping his eyes open during the scoreless fifth inning.

"Ah, baseball," the alien said. "Its hypnotic tedium, its mystic transformation of the immediate."

Brady stared at him blankly.

"Philip Roth," the alien said, apparently surprised. "*My Baseball Years*. Surely you've read it?"

"Actually, no."

"It breaks your heart," the alien said. "It is designed to break your heart. Bart Giamatti."

"Who?"

The alien shook his head in apparent disappointment, and returned his attention to the game.

14

In the sixth, Garmez walked again but was left stranded. The Red Sox continued to lead, six to three.

The Blue Jays scored another run in the seventh and threatened to score more, as the starting pitcher began to tire, but a relief pitcher came on and shut them down.

"You think Garmez is going to do it?" Brady asked, during the seventh inning stretch.

"Surely," the alien said, "you wouldn't want me to spoil it for you?"

15

Neither side scored in the eighth.

There was an almost palpable air of expectation in the alien section now, as the Red Sox went quietly in the top of the ninth.

The first Blue Jay hitter of the ninth grounded out to first base. Waiting in the on-deck circle was Victor Garmez.

"Why are there so many of you here?" Brady asked.

The alien seemed surprised at this question.

"To see Victor Garmez, of course. As your article points out, this man defies probability. Against astounding odds, he achieves continuity in a universe of flux. In a sense, he defies death. For all of us."

The alien leaned forward in his seat as Garmez took his stance in the batter's box. "Besides," the alien said, "you wouldn't expect us to miss this? To miss the wonderful aching poignancy of it all?"

The crowd gasped as Garmez played and missed at a breaking ball in the dirt. But Brady was not watching. He was consumed, suddenly, by a terrible intuition.

"Wait a minute," he said. "You're not aliens at all. You're *time travellers*, isn't that right? On some kind of baseball junket."

"We are indeed aliens," the alien said, "by any possible yardstick you could imagine. There is a certain quality of brilliance to your deduction, but I am really not at liberty to discuss it with you. At any rate, I now wish to turn my fullest attention to this most diverting spectacle."

16

Behind 0 and 2. One more strike and it would be over, the whole crazy circus.

Maybe it was better that way, Garmez thought. Better to be a footnote in baseball history than the man who beat DiMaggio. There would be less to live up to afterward.

He wiped the sweat from his brow, took his stance, waggled the bat. Easy, he told himself. Nice and easy.

Curveball, floating way outside. 1 and 2.

Breaking ball, in the dirt.

Fastball, high and inside, jack-knifing him off the plate.

A full count. Another walk? If it came, it came. He watched the pitcher go into his wind-up.

He's got to throw me a strike, Garmez thought. Streak or not, he doesn't want to bring up the tying run. Got to be a fastball straight up the middle.

He watched it coming all the way, as though it were traveling in slow motion. He felt as if he had all the time in the world. The cheers of the crowd damped down to a dull roar, as he brought his bat around. There was a satisfying crack, and he watched the ball streaking into the right field corner. Then he was rounding second base and being waved on to third.

17

As the crowd sank back into their seats to watch the next batter, the aliens remained standing. Then they began to file out of the ground.

"Don't you want to see who wins?" Brady asked his alien seat-mate.

The alien shrugged. "It doesn't really matter who wins. Either way, the outcome is well within the normal distribution. We've seen quite enough, thank you."

Brady realized that the Prime Minister had turned around in his seat and was watching this exchange.

"Surely you're staying for the reception?" the Prime Minister asked, a little petulantly.

"Oh no," the alien said. "This has been extremely entertaining, but it really is time to be moving on."

18

The departure of the aliens caused considerable discussion among the crowd. The umpires called time-out as they waited for the noise to subside. Garmez stood patiently at third base.

"Aliens," the third base coach said. "Go figure them."

19

With the help of Garmez's triple, the Blue Jays tied up the game in the ninth, sending it into extra innings. The Red Sox, however, finally prevailed in the twelfth. Brady, slumped low in his seat, stayed until the end. It was the first and last major league baseball game he would ever attend.

Garmez's streak was broken off the following night, at the County Stadium in Milwaukee. But he continued to hit well, and was named Rookie of the Year. Endorsement contracts, including offers from rival ketchup manufacturers, poured in. He was able to build a house for his family in the Dominican, and another for himself in Florida. He did not, however, marry a movie star.

Brady married Janice, but they separated a year later. She took the china, which he had never liked.

The aliens, after their visit to the SkyDome, were not seen again.

Life, within the normal distribution, continued.

Author's Note: I am indebted to Stephen Jay Gould's lucid and poetic article "The Streak of Streaks" (*New York Review of Books* 16.8.88) for the information on sports probabilities used in this story.

Lost October

DAVID SANDNER AND JACOB WEISMAN

DeRosa watched the boys play baseball in the street below. They played with a tennis ball. First base was a rear tire of a car. Second base was a dark patch of asphalt in the middle of the road, the pitcher's mound another. Third base was the tire of the car across from first. Home plate was a crushed tin can.

DeRosa rested in a large deck chair on the balcony of his third floor apartment, his right knee turned inward and his ankle twisted around the front chairleg. Only his eyes moved, following the high, bounding hops of the tennis ball.

One of the boys drove a deep fly ball that sailed the length of the street and bounced several times before coming to rest beneath the wheel of a parked car. An outfielder closed on the ball, chased it down and threw a two-hopper to the plate. The catcher caught the ball to his right, pivoted violently to his left, throwing himself to the ground to make the tag. An argument ensued.

The arguments always bored DeRosa. The balcony swirled in sunlight. DeRosa lay back, content in the brightness, sitting as still as empty bleachers. He dozed, listening to shrill voices punctuated by the womp of a flattened tennis ball.

DeRosa awoke uncomfortably, the tough fabric of the chair biting into his arm, etching deep, criss-crossing patterns into the flesh. He had on only a short-sleeved shirt, faded green, unbuttoned to his white undershirt. DeRosa rubbed his arm tenderly. His head swam. Gingerly, he turned his neck from side to side. He slipped his black-socked feet into a pair of white leather shoes and stood slowly, keeping his hands firmly on his knees for support. He opened the sliding glass door and crossed the living room to the kitchen to splash some water on his face.

Standing at the sink, water dripping from his chin, DeRosa looked out his open kitchen window over the backyard. The trees were

deathly still, yet he heard the branches creaking. It seemed unnatural
to him, put him on edge. A German Shepherd crossed into the shade
of a eucalyptus and sniffed at the trunk. It had been too close to the
house to be seen before. The dog was old, gray mixed in his soft colored tan and brown coat. He was big shouldered.

DeRosa leaned out the window, holding tight at the sill.

"Hey," DeRosa called. "Hey. Get out of there. Shoo."

The dog turned, eyeing DeRosa evenly before moving across
the yard to a hole in the fence. He looked back again and the sun
glowed in his eyes, then he ducked through the hole and was gone.

DeRosa drank a glass of water and sighed. He felt tiredness
heavy in his eyes and shoulders. Maybe the heat had gotten to him,
or maybe he was still sluggish from sleeping on the balcony. He shuffled to the couch, sat, lay back and slept. He dreamed of the trees, full
with thin, earth-tone eucalyptus leaves and overfull with the moist,
drunken smell of spring.

DeRosa awoke to footsteps and then the doorbell chimed.
Eugene Kelly opened the door and walked in carrying an over-
stuffed bag of groceries. He dropped it on the counter.

"You looked good playing ball out there, Eu," said DeRosa, sitting up. "You're really starting to give the ball a whack. How much
do I owe you?"

The bill came to twenty four dollars. DeRosa came up to the
counter and counted out the money.

"Thanks, Eu."

DeRosa stuffed the crumpled bills into Eugene's hand, grasping
the boy's hand in his own. Eugene's hand was smooth and small.

"That was a great play you made behind the plate today."

"Yea." Eugene shrugged. "Thanks."

DeRosa walked over to a closet by the door, reached in and
grabbed his jacket, holding it by the collar until he had extracted
another five. DeRosa saw his own shadowed face reflected in the
mirror hanging inside the closet door. He thought he looked worried. Deep lines cut down his cheeks, bruises weighted under his
eyes and wisps of white hair stuck out from atop his head at odd
angles. He wondered what Eugene must think of him, looking the
way he did. DeRosa hung the jacket back in the closet.

"Something for you," he said, dropping the wadded bill on the
counter between them.

"It's too much." Eugene turned his head.

DeRosa backed away.

"Take it." He smiled and nodded his head too much.

Eugene rubbed his nose. His face was blank, unreadable. He took the five and wiped it flat. He folded all the bills together and tucked them in his front pocket.

"I've got to go," Eugene said, turning his shoulder away from DeRosa toward the door.

"I was hoping you'd catch a few with me." DeRosa came forward, leaned his bare forearms against the edge of the counter to support himself. He grinned at Eugene. "Still plenty of time before the game. You are coming back up for the game?"

Eugene shrugged, nodded without turning. "I'll be back around five. I've got some homework to do."

"Homework? You can forget about that right now." DeRosa moved back into the closet. He took down a ball and glove from a shelf. The mitt was old, dark from many oilings, with short, squat fingers that barely covered DeRosa's hand. "These are the Giants in the World Series. Doesn't happen very often. We almost won it, you know, back in '62."

"Yes," Eugene said with a trace of boredom. "If the Yankees' second baseman doesn't catch McCovey's line drive in the seventh game. I know."

"That was Bobby Richardson, an excellent second baseman. Think about it, will you? That was twenty seven years ago. Haven't been back since. Besides if Whitey Lockman had just sent Matty Alou home from third on Mays' double, McCovey wouldn't even have gotten up to the plate."

"I don't know," Eugene said.

"Come on." DeRosa put his jacket on, turning the collar down. The nylon rustled as he strapped the velcro straps around his wrists. The jacket had Giants scripted in black across the back. The orange had worn to white at the forearms. The gold lining had dirtied.

They walked down the front stairs and set up in front of the garage. DeRosa warmed his arm up slowly, his pitches barely reaching Eugene who squatted on the balls of his feet fifteen feet away. Eugene looked bored, but then the ball started to break. It would cross the plate, flutter, and shift suddenly, all at once, exploding in all sorts of directions.

"Could you show me that?"

DeRosa moved forward and took the ball.

"Hold the ball by your fingertips. Don't use your knuckles."

Eugene walked out and threw the ball a couple times, nothing.

"The ball should barely have any rotation at all," DeRosa said. "Too much rotation or no rotation at all and nothing happens. If you throw it right, you should be able to see the ball tumble." DeRosa demonstrated, turning the ball an inch on its axis. "Try it again."

The sky was clear, without a trace of clouds or wind.

"It's a great day," said Eugene, wiping the perspiration from his cheek.

"Not really," DeRosa said. "Not really."

"What do you mean?" Eugene licked his lips.

"Nothing. Its just bad luck to have weather like this in San Francisco, that's all. It's no big deal. Throw the ball."

DeRosa's dream was sharp as morning light. He was sitting on the warm grass outside the stable where the milk men parked the horses after the morning run, watching Joe DiMaggio. Not the Yankee Clipper. Not yet. Not even the pride of the Seals or Galileo High School.

DeRosa's older brother, Monty, was hitting batting practice to a bunch of his friends, while the younger DeRosa sat in foul territory watching the players and guarding the extra equipment.

DiMaggio played third, his usual position back then. He was tall and gawky, thin with a strong but erratic throwing arm. It was only when he batted that one could see the savage, slashing swing that would one day lead him to stardom.

On this day, DiMaggio played more fluidly than usual, handling even the toughest short hops effortlessly with soft hands, gunning the ball over to first with perfect crisp throws. DiMaggio's delight was obvious. Unlike his later days with the Yankees, when cameras hounded him everywhere, DiMaggio was relaxed without even a hint of self-consciousness. Baseball was his escape from the world, from his family's fishing business, from his father.

The morning light swirled warmly about DeRosa's cheeks as he laid back in the shallow grass. Dom DiMaggio sat next to DeRosa pounding his fist into his tiny child's glove, longing for his chance to play. DeRosa picked up an extra ball, stained green from overuse, and tossed it to Dom. Dom smiled and threw the ball back, lobbing it gently, allowing his arm to loosen up slowly.

They continued throwing the ball back and forth, looping high arcing tosses and sharp ground balls, forcing one another to move left or right into the hole or back for a high fly ball. Even as they threw, DeRosa knew Dom would be great, eventually following his older brothers, Vince and Joe, into the major leagues, leaving DeRosa behind to scan the box scores over his morning cereal before making his way to work.

DeRosa awoke with a start. The kitchen door was rattling loudly. He stood up and a force bigger than himself knocked him back. Spider web cracks burst suddenly through the plaster board walls with a crack like the snap of a whip. A green glass ashtray fell from a kitchen counter, ringing off the linoleum. Stacks of magazines slid from a shelf and spread across the floor. A glass on the table beside DeRosa rocked, waves of brown ice tea sloshing over the rim, tipped and spilled, clanging on the table. Plates and glasses clinked in the kitchen cupboards and the whole house, the walls and floors, and below the floors, rumbled like heavy machinery.

Before DeRosa struggled to his feet again, it was over. He was breathing heavy.

"That was a big one," he said.

Books leaned askew on their shelves; ice tea drained noisily from the table to the hardwood floor; a photograph finally tipped off the edge of a mantel and fluttered down to where the baseball rocked, slowed, stopped.

"The game was just starting," Eugene said.

Eugene surveyed the room from where he sat in front of the blank television set. Eugene knelt in front of the television and clicked the on/off button several times. DeRosa turned a switch on a lamp beside the couch. Stepping over the puddle of ice tea, he walked over to the open counter between living room and kitchen and picked up the phone receiver.

"Dial tone," he said. "But no power."

Eugene stood and walked, steadying himself along the wall and doorframe, into the bathroom.

"Let's go outside," DeRosa called, retrieving his Giants jacket from the couch and shuffled over to the door. Eugene emerged from the bathroom.

"What about the mess?"

"Leave it, come on."

They walked downstairs and out into the street. Neighbors were emerging, or standing staring at their houses; a group had gathered down the street around a portable radio to listen to reports and exchange stories about the quake.

"You O.K.?" someone asked without bothering to stop, moving toward the throng. A man with a wrench offered to turn off DeRosa's gas line. DeRosa conferred with him, then stared up at his house. No cracks along the foundation. Eugene returned from talking with his mother.

"Look," Eugene said. "What's that?"

DeRosa turned and looked out from Telegraph Hill. Off to the left, towering over the row of houses and trees, he saw something dark and menacing. He had to walk further down the street before the image took shape. Thick smoke mushroomed over the Marina.

DeRosa headed for an old white fifty-eight Cadillac and unlocked the driver's seat.

"Get in. I'll turn on the radio."

They sat in DeRosa's car and listened to the radio until the main news stories, the fire in the Marina, the cancellation of the Series, the collapse of the Bay Bridge and the I-80 expressway, began to repeat. Out in the Pacific, the sun set — canary yellow spreading over the sea.

"Come on," DeRosa said. "Let's drive."

"They said not to," Eugene said. "There's no street lights or signal lights."

"It's all right. We won't go far."

DeRosa started the car and pulled out into the street. Tipping over the edge, they rolled downhill.

They drove in silence, slowing down only when something caught their attention: the fallen brick of a house front, long cracks in the sidewalk, or the long drifts of smoke rising over whatever remained of the Marina. The city was quiet as the sun melted away like margarine, sickly yellow burning to black.

As the sky darkened, no lights came on anywhere. The city felt strange and empty, somehow different.

"I've never seen anything like it," DeRosa said. "A night like this could promise anything. You could remake the world on a night like this. Just fold it up and start over. Look at it. No lights to anchor it down and make you believe in it."

Eugene rubbed his leg and looked out the window, away from DeRosa.

DeRosa smiled. "This is history you're seeing. Living history."

Eugene didn't respond.

"O.K., I guess it's time to head back."

"What's that?" Eugene asked.

"What?"

"That."

A bright light lit up the sky, obvious and out of place in the dark city.

DeRosa drove towards the light, sometimes losing it altogether behind houses and hills, sometimes just following the glare in the sky. DeRosa rolled down the dark streets, winding his way to the light, finally turning a corner and heading straight into the glare. For a moment, he couldn't see a thing.

"Hey," DeRosa said.

"What is it?"

DeRosa leaned forward over the dash and looked up, as if getting closer would clear his vision and make the stadium and the lights resolve and disappear.

"That's Seal stadium."

"How come the lights are on?"

"They tore it down years ago. There's supposed to be a Safeway here now."

Eugene turned and looked at DeRosa.

"I don't understand."

DeRosa stared up at the lights.

"Neither do I, but it's really here."

DeRosa turned off the engine of the car, flipped off the car lights.

"Let's take a look," DeRosa said, stepping out, leaving the door hanging open. He walked in front of the car and stared upward. A cheer sounded from inside.

Eugene sat and watched DeRosa, who was smiling, bathed in

an even white sheet of electric glare.

"Let's go in," DeRosa said. "Sounds like there's a game going on."

Eugene got out slowly, pushed his door closed with both hands. DeRosa had already swept off into the deep shadows around the edges of the stadium.

"Wait up," Eugene said, then hurried after him.

They entered the ballpark along the first baseline. The thick, richly colored grass, lit up by the lights, glowed like an emerald. A series of goose eggs on a narrow hand-held scoreboard in dead away centerfield showed the score tied at zero midway through the sixth inning. Seals and Oaks. Pacific Coast League.

They found a pair of empty seats farther down the left field line among a swirl of orange pennants.

The Seals wore white uniforms with navy pinstripes and the letters "ea" and "ls" written inside the upper and lower halves of a large letter "S" to form the word "Seals." The Oaks wore more conventional navy blue uniforms with Oaks inscribed across the chest.

"Pretty nice," said DeRosa, looking around. "That's Joe Marty, the Seals right fielder at the plate. He played a couple of years in the Major Leagues. A friend of mine once went to his bar in Sacramento, said he was the most foul-mouthed person he'd ever met. That's what can happen, I guess, when you get to be around my age."

"Who's pitching?" asked Eugene.

"I don't know," DeRosa admitted. The Oakland pitcher looked young, baby fat still resting heavy in his cheeks. "Might be Ed Walsh, Jr."

Marty lined a two-two pitch down the line at third. The third baseman dove to his right, picked the ball off the short hop and gunned a throw to the bag at first, beating Marty easy.

"Nice play," said Eugene. "These guys are good."

"Yes." DeRosa smiled, not the shy smile that Eugene was used to, but rather a big grin.

A Seals left-hander lined out to deep right for the third out of the inning. The Oakland outfielder caught the ball on the dead run, took off his glove and threw it behind him as he walked off the field into the dugout.

"What's all this doing here?" Eugene asked.

"What? This game? I don't know."

"Are you here. I mean, do you think you might have you been to this game before?"

"You mean as a kid? Maybe. I hadn't thought of that."

DeRosa scanned the people in the seats around them.

"What did you look like then?" Eugene asked.

"A lot like I do now, only younger."

"That's a big help. What color was your hair?"

An Oaks batter lashed a line drive into the gap between right and center. DiMaggio seemed miles away as he charged the ball, closing the gap slowly with long, loping strides. DiMaggio caught up with the ball suddenly on the third hop, extended his glove effortlessly across the width of his body, changed directions in mid-stride, and threw a strike to second base, holding the batter to a long single. The crowd stood to cheer.

"I thought he didn't have a chance," said Eugene.

"He made plays greater than that when he played for the Yankees. The fans in New York took it for granted after awhile."

DeRosa's palms began to sweat and his body felt light and a little strange. He rubbed his hands against his legs, his nerves starting to feel the heightened tension of a scoreless game.

Marty doubled off the right-centerfield wall to start the eighth, but was thrown out at third on a perfect relay throw from the Oaks second baseman who went out onto the outfield grass in rightfield to take the throw.

Still tied, 0-0 with one out in the ninth, the Seals' shortstop, Hal Rhyne, beat out a bunt down the first baseline, bringing up DiMaggio. DiMaggio knocked the heel of his bat against the ground, dislodging the circular weight around the barrel and walked intently toward the plate, head down, but with his eyes up, tracking the pitcher.

"Watch this," said DeRosa, pointing.

DiMaggio dug in, redistributing the dirt around the back of the batter's box. He fouled the first pitch straight back, missing the ball by less than an inch. His swing was pure and savage — his weight shifting forward, his face contorting in expectation.

The second pitch, just off the outside corner, was called a ball. DiMaggio stepped out of the box, looked over at the third base coach who flashed a long series of signals.

DiMaggio took a sharp curve ball, just catching the inside

corner above the knees, for another strike.

DeRosa shifted nervously in his seat. Eugene rubbed his hands together.

DiMaggio ripped a line drive down the third base line that just hooked foul. He fouled off the next couple of pitches before laying off a ball in the dirt — evening the count at 2-2.

"I don't know," muttered Eugene.

DiMaggio stepped back out of the box, turned to face the fans behind homeplate. His face was young; his hair was dark. He looked more uncertain than DeRosa ever remembered seeing him before. He couldn't be much more than nineteen or twenty years old, his whole life ahead of him.

"Get him, Joe," yelled DeRosa.

DiMaggio stepped back in, took a fastball, high, 3-2. The fans rose to their feet.

The catcher threw the ball back to the pitcher, walked slowly out to join him on the mound. The manager popped his head out of the dugout, walked out toward the mound, pausing for a second as he passed over the foul line. He said a few words to his catcher, looked over to the bullpen where a pair of righthanders warmed up, before focusing his attention back to his pitcher, gesturing with sharp movements of his hands how he wanted DiMaggio pitched. At last, the home plate umpire broke up the meeting, starting in toward them, waving his arms.

The manager jogged slowly back to the dugout. The pitcher milled about behind the plate, picked up the rosin bag while the catcher settled back behind the plate. The fans stood up. DiMaggio stepped in.

The catcher stuck his bare right hand out to his side. The crowd booed loudly.

DeRosa snorted. "They're going to walk him." The pitcher delivered the ball two feet outside and the catcher stepped outside to take the throw — ball four. DiMaggio tossed his bat and jogged to first.

"Damn," DeRosa muttered. "Looks like extra innings."

The Seals' next batter, Ernie Sulik, received a smattering of applause when his name was announced, but it was clear that the fans' hearts weren't in it, thinking instead to the top of the tenth when the Oaks would send the heart of their order to the plate against the Seals' ace Walter Mails.

Sulik swung at the first pitch, in at the hands, pulling it down the line at third. The Oaks third baseman dove to his right, fielded the ball, dropped it, picked it up again, spun on his knees, throwing over to second for the force out on a sliding DiMaggio — wide! The ball kicked off the fielder's glove and out into center field. The runner at second, running all the way with two outs, scored easily and just like that the game was over and the Seals had won.

DeRosa and Eugene sat in silence while the crowd filtered past them out of the stadium, neither of them looking at the other. At last power was cut to half of the lights, and the playing field dulled, lost its luster.

"We better go now," said Eugene.

"Sure, Eu." DeRosa's voice was tired, defeated. He made no attempt to rise out of his seat.

"Here," Eugene said. "Lean on my shoulder."

"I'll be all right, Eu. Just give me a second."

"No hurry." Eugene stood, stretched, waiting for DeRosa.

"All right." DeRosa stuck out his hand and Eugene helped him to his feet. A soft wind greeted them as they exited the stadium. DeRosa led Eugene across the street to a large tree-filled park where he sat down on a short concrete embankment. The lights, still at half power, cast sharp, elongated shadows across the illuminated landscape of the park. They watched the silent empty ballpark as the lights winked out entirely. The power in the city was still out except for the soft emergency lights of a hospital in the distance.

"I can't believe they walked him," said DeRosa, his voice muffled in darkness.

"It doesn't seem fair, does it?"

"No, it doesn't."

"What would you have done?"

"You mean if I was the manager? I don't know. I might have walked him, I suppose."

"Their manager lost the game because of the walk. He put the go ahead run at second base where the runner could score on the error."

"I just don't understand, Eu. I get a chance to go back fifty years and ..."

"And it doesn't come out the way you wanted it to, does it. That's all right. We saw a good game, a great game. When's the last time you saw anything from the thirties that didn't look ancient?

Everything always looks so scratched and grainy, without color, from another era. Tonight was real. Isn't that enough?"

"Yes, I guess so." DeRosa took a deep, heaving breath. Footsteps echoed down the long, dark street. Eugene helped DeRosa back to his feet.

A tall, angular figure approached, obscured in darkness.

"Is everything O.K.?" the figure asked. "Do you need any help?"

"Joe?" asked DeRosa.

"Do I know you?" The figure's hands were tucked casually inside the pockets of a heavy, wool jacket with alternating vertical stripes of navy and orange.

"You did, once."

"You do look a little familiar. Must have been a long time ago, though."

"Ages. I knew your parents," DeRosa lied.

Together Eugene and DiMaggio led DeRosa across the street, around the corner, to the car. Someone had closed and locked the door DeRosa had left open. DeRosa searched in his pockets for the keys, found them, fumbled with the lock.

"You're a young man, Joe," said DeRosa. "You should be out celebrating."

"The rest of the players went over to the Double Play for drinks. I won't turn 21 for another year." DiMaggio shrugged, averted his eyes down to his feet.

"Don't worry, Joe. Next year you'll be able to drink anywhere you want. Just don't forget where you come from." DeRosa finally got the key in the lock. He got in and opened the passenger door from the inside.

They pulled up in front of DeRosa's blacked-out building just past midnight. A neighbor must have watched them approach and now appeared to greet them.

"Is he O.K.?" the neighbor asked.

"He's fine," Eugene answered, "just a little tired. It's been quite a night."

Eugene helped DeRosa up the stairs and into his apartment, fumbling in the darkness. DeRosa smiled at Eugene, placed a hand heavy across his shoulder. "Don't forget where you come from, either, Eugene. Don't forget."

Eugene shook his head.

DeRosa lay back on the couch, too tired to undress and get into bed. He closed his eyes and listened to Eugene move through the apartment, shut the door softly and retreat into darkness. That night DeRosa's sleep was dreamless.

Naked to the Invisible Eye

GEORGE ALEC EFFINGER

There were fewer than a thousand spectators in the little ballpark, their chatter nearly inaudible compared to the heartening roar of the major league crowds. The fans sat uneasily, as if they had wandered into the wake of a legendary hero. No longer was baseball the national pastime. Even the big league teams, roving from franchise to franchise in search of yesterday's loyal bleacher fanatics, resorted to promotional gimmicks to stave off bankruptcy. Here the Bears were in third place, with an unlikely shot at second. The Tigers had clinched the pennant early, now leading the second-place Kings by nine games and the Bears by an even more discouraging number. There was no real tension in this game — oh, with a bad slump the Bears might fall down among the cellar teams, but so what? For all intents and purposes, the season had ended a month ago.

There was no real tension, no pennant race any longer, just an inexpensive evening out for the South Carolina fans. The sweat on the batter's hands was the fault of his own nervous reaction; the knots in his stomach were shared by no one. He went to the on-deck circle for the pine-tar rag while he waited for the new pitcher to toss his warm-ups.

The Bear shortstop was batting eighth, reflecting his lame .219 average. Like a great smoothed rock this fact sat in the torrent of his thinking, submerged at times but often breaking through the racing surface. With his unsteady fielding it looked as if he would be out of a job the next spring. To the players and to the spectators the game was insignificant; to him it was the first of his last few chances. With two runs in already in the eighth, one out and a man on first, he went to the plate.

He looked out toward the kid on the mound before settling himself in the batter's box. The pitcher's name was Rudy Ramirez, he was only nineteen and from somewhere in Venezuela. That was all anyone knew about him; this was his first appearance in a professional ball game. The Bear shortstop took a deep breath and stepped in.

This kid Ramirez looked pretty fast during his warm-ups, he thought. The shortstop damned the fate that made him the focus of attention against a complete unknown. The waters surged; his thoughts shuffled and died.

The Venezuelan kid looked in for his sign. The shortstop looked down to the third base coach who flashed the *take* signal; that was all right with him. *"I'm only batting two-nineteen, I want to see this kid throw one before . . ."*

Ramirez went into his stretch, glanced at the runner on first . . .

With that kid Barger coming off the disabled list, I might not be able to . . . Ramirez' right leg kicked, his left arm flung back . . .

The shortstop's shrieking flood of thought stilled, his mind was as quiet as the surface of a pond stagnating. The umpire called the pitch a ball.

Along the coaching lines at third Sorenson was relaying the *hit-and-run* sign from the dugout. *All right,* thought the shortstop, *just make contact, get a good ground ball, maybe a hit, move the man into scoring position . . .*

Ramirez nodded to his catcher, stretched, checked the runner . . .

My luck, I'll hit an easy double-play ball to the right side . . .

. . . kicked, snapped, pitched . . .

The shortstop's mind was silent, ice-cold, dead, watching the runner vainly flying toward second, the catcher's throw beating him there by fifteen feet. Two out. One ball and one strike.

Sorenson called time. He met the shortstop halfway down the line.

"You damn brainless idiot!" said the coach. "You saw the sign, you *acknowledged* the sign, you stood there with your thumb in your ear looking at a perfect strike! You got an awful short memory?"

"Look, I don't know —"

"I'll tell you what I *do* know," said Sorenson. "I'll bet that'll cost you twenty dollars. Maybe your spot in the lineup."

The shortstop walked to the on-deck circle, wiped his bat again with the pine-tar. His head was filled with anger and frustration. Back in the batter's box he stared toward the pitcher in desperation.

On the rubber Ramirez worked out of a full windup with the

bases empty. His high kick hid his delivery until the last moment. The ball floated toward the plate, a fat balloon belt-high, a curve that didn't break . . .

The hitter's mind was like a desert, his mind was like an empty glass, a blank sheet of paper. His mind was totally at rest . . .

The ball nicked the outside corner for a called strike two. The Tiger catcher chuckled. "Them people in the seats have to pay to get in," he said. "They're doin' more'n you!"

"Shut up." The Bear shortstop choked up another couple of inches on the handle. *He'll feed me another curve, and then the fast ball* . . .

Ramirez took the sign and went into his motion.

Lousy kid. I'm gonna rap it one down his lousy Cuban throat . . .

The wrist flicked, the ball spun, broke . . .

The shortstop watched, unawed, very still, like a hollow thing, as the curve broke sharply, down the heart of the plate, strike three, side retired.

The Tigers managed to score an insurance run in the top half of the ninth, and Rudy Ramirez went back to the mound with a 5-3 lead to protect. The first batter that he was scheduled to face was the Bear pitcher, who was replaced in the order by pinch hitter Frank Asterino.

A sense of determination, confidence made Asterino's mind orderly. It was a brightly lit mind, with none of the shifting doubt of the other. Rudy felt the will, he weighed the desire, he discovered the man's dedication and respected it. He stood off the rubber, rubbing the shine from the new ball. He reached for the rosin bag, then dropped it. He peered in at Johnston his catcher. The sign: the fast ball.

Asterino guarded the plate closely. Johnston's mitt was targeted on the inside — start off with the high hard one, loosen the batter up. Rudy rocked back, kicked that leg high, and threw. The ball did not go for the catcher's mark, sailing out just a little. A not over-powering pitch right down the pipe — a perfect gopher ball.

Rudy thought as the ball left his hand, he found Asterino's will, and he held it gently back. *Be still. Do not move; yes, be still,* and Asterino watched the strike intently as it passed.

Asterino watched two more, both curves that hung tantalizing but untouched. Ramirez grasped the batter's desire with his own, and blotted up all the fierce resolution there was in him. Asterino returned to the bench, disappointed but unbewildered, amid the boos of the fans. He had struck out but, after all, that was not so unusual.

The top of the batting order was up, and Rudy touched the minds of the first and second hitters. He hid their judgment behind the glare of his own will, and they struck out; the first batter needed five pitches and the second four. They observed balls with as much passive interest as strikes, and their bats never left their shoulders. No runs, no hits, no errors, nothing across for the Bears in the ninth. The ball game was over; Rudy earned a save for striking out the four batters he faced in his first pro assignment.

Afterward, local reporters were met by the angry manager of the Bears. When asked for his impression of the young Tiger relief pitcher, he said, "I didn't think he looked that sharp. I mean, Queen Elizabeth would look good pitching to the bunch of zombies I've got on this team. How you supposed to win?" In the visitors' clubhouse, the Tiger manager was in a more expansive mood.

"Where did Ramirez come from?" asked one reporter.

"I don't really know," he said. "Charlie Cardona checks out Detroit's prospects down there. All I know is the telegram said that he was signed, and then here he is. Charlie's dug up some good kids for us."

"Did he impress you tonight?"

Marenholtz settled his wire-rim glasses on his long nose and nodded. "He looked real cool for his first game. I'm going to start him in the series with the Reds this weekend. We'll have a better idea then, of course, but I have a feeling he won't be playing Class B baseball very long."

After the game with the Bears, the Tigers showered quickly and boarded their bus. They had a game the next night against the Selene Comets. It was a home game for the Tigers, and they were all glad to be returning to Cordele, but the bus ride from the Bears' stadium would be four or five hours. They would get in just before dawn, sleep until noon, have time for a couple of unpleasant hamburgers, and get out to the park in time for practice.

The Tigers won that game, and the game the next night also. The Comets left town and were replaced by the Rockhill Reds, in for a Saturday afternoon game and a Sunday doubleheader. This late in the summer the pitching staffs were nearly exhausted. Manager Marenholtz of the Tigers kept his promise to the newspapermen; after the Saturday loss to the Reds, he went to Chico Guerra, his first-string catcher, and told him to get Rudy Ramirez ready for the second game the next day.

Ramirez was eager, of course, and confident. Marenholtz was sitting in his office when Rudy came into the locker room before the Sunday doubleheader, a full half hour before practice began. Marenholtz smiled, remembering his own first game. He had been an outfielder; in the seventh inning he had run into the left field wall chasing a long fly. He dropped the ball, cracked his head, and spent the next three weeks listening to the games on the radio. Marenholtz wished Ramirez better luck.

The Tigers' second-string catcher, Maurie Johnston, played the first game, and Guerra sat next to Ramirez in the dugout, pointing out the strengths and weaknesses of the opposing batters. Ramirez said little, just nodding and smiling. Marenholtz walked by them near the end of the first game. "Chico," he said, "ask him if he's nervous."

The catcher translated the question into Spanish. Ramirez grinned and answered. "He say no," said Guerra. "He jus' wan' show you what he can do."

The manager grunted a reply and went back to his seat, thinking about cocky rookies. The Tigers lost the first game, making two in a row dropped to the last-placed Reds. The fans didn't seem to mind; there were only twenty games left until the end of the season, and there was no way possible for the Tigers to fall from first place short of losing all of them. It was obvious that Marenholtz was trying out new kids, resting his regulars for the Hanson Cup playoffs. The fans would let him get away with a lot, as long as he won the cup.

Between games there was a local high school band marching in the outfield, and the local Kiwanis club presented a plaque to the Tigers' center fielder, who was leading the league with forty-two home runs. Ramirez loosened up his arm during all this; he stood along the right field foul line and tossed some easy pitches to Guerra. After a while the managers brought out their lineup cards to the umpires and the grounds crew finished grooming the infield.

Ramirez and Guerra took their positions on the field, and the rest of the team joined them, to the cheers of the Tigers' fans.

Kip Stackpole, the Reds' shortstop and leadoff better, was settling himself in the batter's box. Rudy bent over and stared toward Guerra for the sign. An inside curve. Rudy nodded.

As he started into his windup he explored Stackpole's mind. It was a relaxed mind, concentrating only because Stackpole enjoyed playing baseball; for him, and for the last-placed Reds, the game was without urgency. Rudy would have little difficulty.

Wait, thought Rudy, forcing his will directly into Stackpole's intellect. *Not this one. Wait.* And Stackpole waited. The ball broke sharply, over the heart of the plate, for the first strike. There was a ripple of applause from the Tiger fans.

Guerra wanted a fast ball. Rudy nodded, kicked high, and threw. *Quiet*, he thought, *do not move.* Right down the pipe, strike two.

This much ahead of the hitter, Guerra should have called for a couple of pitches on the outside, to tease the batter into swinging at a bad pitch. But the catcher thought that Stackpole was off balance. The Reds had never seen Ramirez pitch before. Guerra called for another fast ball. Rudy nodded and went into his windup. He kept Stackpole from swinging. The Reds' first hitter was called out on strikes; the Tiger fans cheered loudly as Guerra stood and threw the ball down to third base. Ramirez could hear his infielders chattering and encouraging him in a language that he didn't understand. He got the ball back and looked at the Reds' second man.

The new batter would be more of a challenge. He was hitting .312, battling with two others for the last place in the league's top ten. He was more determined than anyone Ramirez had yet faced. When Rudy pitched the ball, he needed more mental effort to keep the man from swinging at it. The pitch was too high. Ramirez leaned forward; Guerra wanted a low curve. The pitch broke just above the hitter's knees, over the outside corner of the plate. One ball, one strike. The next pitch was a fast ball, high and inside. Ball two. Another fast ball, over the plate. *Wait*, thought Rudy, *wait.* The batter waited, and the count was two and two. Rudy tried another curve and forced the batter to watch it helplessly. Strike three, two out.

Ramirez felt good now. The stadium full of noisy people didn't make him nervous. The experienced athletes on the other team posed no threat at all. Rudy knew that he could win today; he knew that there wasn't a batter in the world that could beat him. The third hitter was no problem for Rudy's unusual talent. He struck out on four pitches. Rudy received a loud cheer from the fans as he walked back to the dugout. He smiled and waved, and took a seat next to the water cooler with Guerra.

The Tigers scored no runs in their part of the first inning, and Rudy went back to the mound and threw his allotment of warm-ups. He stood rubbing up the ball while the Reds' cleanup hitter settled himself at the plate. Rudy disposed of the Reds' best power hitter with three pitches, insolently tossing three fast balls straight down the heart of the plate. Rudy got the other two outs just as quickly. The fans gave him another cheer as he walked from the mound.

The Tigers got a hit but no runs in the second, and Ramirez struck out the side again in the top of the third. In the bottom of the third Doug Davies, the Tiger second baseman, led off with a sharp single down the left field line. Rudy was scheduled to bat next; he took off his jacket and chose a light bat. He had never faced an opposing pitcher under game conditions before. He had never even taken batting practice in the time he had been with the Tigers. He walked to the plate and took his place awkwardly.

He swung at two and watched two before he connected. He hit the ball weakly, on the handle of the bat, and it dribbled slowly down the first base line. He passed it on his way to first base, and he saw the Reds' pitcher running over to field it. Rudy knew that he'd be an easy out. *Wait*, he thought at the pitcher, *stop. Don't throw it.* The pitcher held the ball, staring ahead dazedly. It looked to the fans as if the pitcher couldn't decide whether to throw to first or try for the lead runner going into second. Both runners were safe before Rudy released him.

Rudy took a short lead toward second base. He watched the coaches for signs. On the next pitch Davies broke for third. Rudy ran for second base. The Reds' catcher got the pitch and jumped up. *Quiet*, thought Rudy. *Be still.* The catcher watched both Davies and Rudy slide in safely. Eventually the Tigers' leadoff man struck out. The next batter popped up in the infield. The third batter in the line-up, Chico Guerra, hit a long fly to right field, an easy enough chance for the fielder. But Rudy found the man's judgment and blocked it with his will. *Not yet,* he thought, *wait.* The outfielder hesitated, seeming as if he had lost the ball in the setting sun. By the time he ran after it, it was too late. The ball fell in and rolled to the wall. Two runs scored and Guerra huffed into third base. "Now we win!" yelled Rudy in Spanish. Guerra grinned and yelled back.

The inning ended with the Tigers ahead, three to nothing. Rudy was joking with Guerra as he walked back on the field. His manner was easy and supremely confident. He directed loud comments to the umpire and the opposing batters, but his Spanish went uninterpreted by his catcher. The top of the Reds' batting order was up again in the fourth inning, and Rudy treated them with total disregard, shaking off all of Guerra's signs except for the fast ball, straight down the middle. Stackpole, the leadoff batter, struck out again on four pitches. The second batter needed only three, and the third hitter used four. No one yet had swung at a pitch. Perhaps the fans were beginning to notice, because the cheering was more subdued as the Tigers came back to the bench. The Reds' manager was standing up in the dugout, angrily condemning his players, who went out to their positions with perplexed expressions.

The game proceeded, with the fans growing quieter and quieter in the stands, the Reds' manager getting louder in his damnations, the Tiger players becoming increasingly uneasy about the Reds' lack of interest. Rudy didn't care; he kept pitching them in to Guerra, and the Rockhill batters kept walking back to their dugout, shrugging their shoulders and saying nothing. Not a single Rockhill Red had reached first base. The ninth inning began in total silence. Rudy faced three pinch hitters and, of course, struck them out in order. He had not only pitched a no-hit game, not only pitched a *perfect* game, but he had struck out twenty-seven consecutive batters. Not once during the entire game did a Rockhill player even swing at one of his pitches.

A perfect game is one of the rarest of baseball phenomena. Perhaps only the unassisted triple play occurs less frequently. There should have been a massive crowd pouring out to congratulate Rudy. Players and fans should have mobbed him, carried him off the field, into the clubhouse. Beer should have been spilled over his head. Pictures should have been taken with Fred Marenholtz' arm around Rudy's neck. Instead, the infielders ran off the field as quickly as they could. They patted Rudy's back as they passed him on the way to the dugout. The fans got up and went home, not even applauding the Tiger victory. Marenholtz was waiting in the dugout. "Take a shower and see me in my office," he said, indicating both Guerra and Ramirez. Then the manager shook his head and went down the tunnel to the dressing room.

Marenholtz was a tall, thin man with sharp, birdlike features. He was sitting at his desk, smoking a cigar. He smoked cigars only when he was very angry, very worried, or very happy. Tonight, while he waited for Guerra and the new kid, he was very worried. Baseball, aged and crippled, didn't need this kind of notoriety.

There were half a dozen local newsmen trying to force their way into the dressing room. He had given orders that there would be no interviews until he had a chance to talk to Ramirez himself. He had phone calls from sportswriters, scouts, fans, gamblers, politicians, and relatives. There was a stack of congratulatory telegrams. There was a very worried telegram from the team's general manager, and a very worried telegram from the front office of the Tigers' major league affiliate.

There was a soft knock on the door. "Guerra?" Marenholtz called out.

"*Si.*"

"Come on in, but don't let anybody else in with you except Ramirez."

Guerra opened the door and the two men entered. Behind them was a noisy, confused crowd of Tiger players. Marenholtz sighed; he would have to find out what happened, and then deal with his team. Then he had to come up with an explanation for the public.

Ramirez was grinning, evidently not sharing Mareholtz' and Guerra's apprehension. He said something to Guerra. The catcher frowned and translated for Marenholtz. "He say, don' he do a good job?"

"That's what *I* want to know!" said Marenholtz. "What *did* he do? You know, it looks a little strange that not a single guy on that team took swing number one."

Guerra looked very uncomfortable. "*Si*, maybe he just *good.*"

Marenholtz grunted. "Chico, did he look *that* good?"

Guerra shook his head. Ramirez was still smiling. Marenholtz stood up and paced behind his desk. "I don't *mind* him pitching a perfect game," he said. "It's a memorable achievement. But I think his effort would be better appreciated if one of those batters had tried *hitting*. At least *one*. I want you to tell me why they didn't. If you can't, I want you to ask *him*."

Guerra shrugged and turned to Ramirez. They conversed for a few seconds, and then the catcher spoke to Marenholtz. "He say he don' wan' them to."

Marenholtz slammed his fist on this desk. "That's going to make a great headline in *The Sporting News*. Look, if somehow he paid off the Reds to throw the game, even *they* wouldn't be so stupid as to do it that way." He paused, catching his breath, trying to control his exasperation. "All right, I'll give him a chance. Maybe he *is* the greatest pitcher the world has ever known. Though I doubt it." He reached for his phone and dialed a number. "Hello, Thompson? Look, I need a favor from you. Have you turned off the field lights yet? Okay, leave 'em on for a while, all right? I don't care. I'll talk to Mr. Kaemmer in the morning. And hang around for another half hour, okay? Well, screw the union. We're having a little crisis here. Yeah, Ramirez. Understand? Thanks, Jack." Marenholtz hung up and nodded to Guerra. "You and your battery mate here are going to get some extra practice. Tell him I want to hit some off him, right now. Don't bother getting dressed again. Just put on your mask and get out on the field." Guerra nodded unhappily and led Rudy away.

The stadium was deserted. Marenholtz walked though the dugout and onto the field. He felt strangely alone, cold and worried; the lights made odd, vague shadows that had never bothered him before. He went to the batter's box. The white lines had been all but erased during the course of the game. He leaned on the bat that he had brought with him and waited for the two men.

Guerra came out first, wearing his chest protector and carrying his mask and mitt. Behind him walked Ramirez silently, without his usual grin. He was dressed in street clothes, with his baseball spikes instead of dress shoes. Rudy took his place on the mound. He tossed a ball from his hand to his glove. Guerra positioned himself and Marenholtz waved to Rudy. No one had said a word.

Rudy wound up and pitched, a medium fast ball down the middle. Marenholtz swung and hit a low line drive down the right field line that bounced once and went into the stands. Rudy threw another and Marenhotz hit it far into right center field. The next three pitches he sent to distant, shadowed parts of the ball park. Marenholtz stepped back for a moment. "He was throwing harder during the game, wasn't he?" he asked.

"I think so," said Guerra.

"Tell him to pitch me as hard as he did then. And throw some good curves, too." Guerra translated, and Ramirez nodded. He leaned back and pitched. Marenholtz swung, connected, and watched the ball sail in a huge arc, to land in the seats three hundred and fifty feet away in right field.

Rudy turned to watch the ball. He said nothing. Mareholtz tossed him another from a box on the ground. "I want a curve now," he said.

The pitch came, breaking lazily on the outside part of the plate. Marenholtz timed it well and sent it on a clothesline into center field, not two feet over Ramirez' head. "All right," said the manager, "tell him to come here." Guerra waved, and Rudy trotted to join them. "One thing," said Marenholtz sourly. "I want him to explain why the Reds didn't hit him like that."

"I wanna know, too," said Guerra. He spoke with Ramirez, at last turning back to Mareholtz with a bewildered expression. "He say he don' wan' *them* to hit. He say you wan' hit, he *let* you hit."

"Oh, hell," said Marenholtz. "I'm not stupid."

Rudy looked confused. He said something to Guerra. "He say he don' know why you wan' hit *now,* but he do what you say."

The manager turned away in anger. He spat toward the dugout, thinking. He turned back to Guerra. "We got a couple of balls left," he said. "I want him to pitch me just like he did to the Reds, understand? I don't want him to let me hit. Have him try to weave his magic spell on me, too."

Rudy took a ball and went back to the mound. Marenholtz stood up to the plate, waving the bat over his shoulder in a slow circle. Ramirez wound up, kicked, and threw. His fastest pitch, cutting the heart of the plate.

Quiet, thought Rudy, working to restrain his manager's furious mind. *Easy,now. Don't swing. Quiet.*

Marenholtz' mind was suddenly peaceful, composed, thoughtless. The pitch cracked into Guerra's mitt. The manager hadn't swung at it.

Rudy threw ten more pitches, and Marenholtz didn't offer at

any of them. Finally he raised his hand. Rudy left the mound again. Marenholtz stood waiting, shaking his head. "Why didn't I swing? Those pitches weren't any harder than the others." Guerra asked Rudy.

"He jus' say he don' wan' you to swing. In his head he tell you. Then you don' swing. He say it's easy."

"I don't believe it," said the manager nervously. "Yeah, okay, he can do it. He *did* do it. I don't like it." Guerra shook his head. The three stood on the empty field for several seconds in uneasy silence. "Can he do that with anybody?" asked Marenholtz.

"He say, *si*."

"Can he do it any time? *Every* time?"

"He say, *si*."

"We're in trouble, Chico." Guerra looked into Mareholtz' frightened face and nodded slowly. "I don't mean just us. I mean *baseball*. This kid can throw a perfect game, every time. What do you think'll happen if he makes it to the majors? The game'll be dead. Poor kid. He scares me. Those people in the stands aren't going to like it any better."

"What you gonna do, Mr. Marehol'?" asked Guerra.

"I don't know, Chico. It's going to be hard keeping a bunch of perfect games secret. Especially when none of the hitters ever takes the bat off his shoulder."

The following Thursday, the Tigers had a night game at home against the Kings, and Rudy came prepared to be the starting pitcher, after three days rest. But when Marenholtz announced the starting lineup, he had the Tigers' long relief man on the mound. Rudy was disappointed, and complained to Guerra. The catcher told him that Marenholtz was probably saving him for the next night, when the Kings' ace left-hander was scheduled to pitch.

On Friday, Ramirez was passed over again. He stayed in the dugout, sweating in his warm-up jacket, irritated at the manager. Guerra told him to have patience. Rudy couldn't understand why Marenholtz wouldn't pitch him after the great game Ramirez had thrown in his first start. Guerra just shrugged and told Rudy to study the hitters.

Rudy didn't play Saturday, or in either of the Sunday doubleheader's games. He didn't know that the newspapermen were as mystified as he. Marenholtz made up excuses, saying that Rudy had pulled a back muscle in practice. The manager refused to make any comments about Ramirez' strange perfect game, and as the days passed the clamor died down.

The next week Rudy spent on the bench, becoming angrier and more frustrated. He confronted Marenholtz several times, with Guerra as unwilling interpreter, and each time the manager just said that he didn't feel that Ramirez was "ready." The season was coming to its close, with only six games left, and Rudy was determined to play. As the games came and went, however, it became obvious that he wasn't going to get the chance.

On the day of the last game, Marenholtz announced that Irv Tappen, his number two right-hander, would start. Rudy stormed into the clubhouse in a rage. He went to his locker and started to change clothes. Marenholtz signaled to Guerra, and they followed Ramirez.

"All right, Ramirez, what're you doing?" asked the manager.

"He say he goin' home," said Guerra, translating Rudy's shouted reply.

"If he leaves before the games is over, he's liable to be fined. Does he know that?"

"He say he don' care."

"Tell him he's acting like a kid," said Marenholtz, feeling relieved inside.

"He say go to hell."

Marenholtz took a deep breath. "Okay, Chico. Tell him we've enjoyed knowing him, and respect his talent, and would like to invite him to try out for the team again next spring."

"He say go to hell."

"He's going home?" asked Marenholtz.

"He say you 'mericanos jealous, and waste his time. He say he can do other things."

"Well, tell him we're sorry, and wish him luck."

"He say go to hell. He say you don' know you *ano* from a hole in the groun'."

Marenholtz smiled coldly. "Chico, I want you to do me a favor. Do yourself a favor, too; there's enough here for the two of us. You let him finish clearing out of here, and you go with him. I don't know where he's going this time of day. Probably back to the hotel where he stays. Keep with him. Talk to him. Don't let him get away, don't let him get drunk, don't let him talk to anybody else, okay?"

Guerra looked puzzled, but nodded. Ramirez was turning to leave the clubhouse. Marenholtz grabbed Guerra's arm and pushed him toward the furious boy. "Go on," said the manager, "keep him in sight. I'll call the hotel in about three or four hours. We got a good thing here, Chico, my boy." The catcher frowned and hurried after Rudy. Marenholtz sighed; he walked across the dressing room, stopping by his office. He opened the door and stared into the darkened room for a few seconds. He wanted desperately to sit at his desk and write the letters and make the phone calls, but he still had a game to play. The job seemed so empty to him now. He *knew* this would be the last regular game he'd see in the minor leagues. Next spring he and Ramirez would be shocking them all at the Florida training camps. Next summer he and Ramirez would own the world of major league baseball.

First, though, there was still the game with the Bears. Marenholtz closed the door to the office and locked it. Then he went up the tunnel to the field. All that he could think of was going back to the Big Time.

After the game, Fred Marenholtz hurried to his office. The other players grabbed at him, swatting at his back to congratulate him on the end of the season. The Tigers were celebrating in the clubhouse. Cans of beer were popping open, and sandwiches had been supplied by the front office. The manager ignored them all. He locked the door to the office behind him. He called Ramirez' hotel and asked for his room.

Guerra answered, and reported that Ramirez was there, taking a nap. The catcher was instructed to tell Rudy that together they were all going to win their way to the major leagues. Guerra was doubtful, but Marenholtz wouldn't listen to the catcher's puzzled questions. The manager hung up. He pulled out a battered address book from his desk drawer, and found the telephone number of an old friend, a contract lawyer in St. Louis. He called the number, tapping a pencil nervously on the desk top while the phone rang.

"Hello, Marty?" he said when the call was finally answered.

"Yes. Who's this calling, please?"

"Hi. You won't remember me, but this is Fred Marenholtz."

"Freddie! How are you? Lord, it's been fifteen years. Are you in town?"

Marenholtz smiled. Things were going to be all right. They chatted for a few minutes, and then Marenholtz told his old friend that he was calling on business.

"Sure, Freddie," said the lawyer. "For Frantic Fred Marenholtz, anything. Is it legal?" Marenholtz laughed.

The photographs on the office wall looked painfully old to Marenholtz. They were of an era too long dead, filled with people who themselves had long since passed away. Baseball itself had withered, had lost the lifeblood of interest that had infused the millions of fans each spring. It had been too many years since Fred Marenholtz had claimed his share of glory. He had never been treated to his part of the financial rewards of baseball, and after his brief major league career he felt it was time to make his bid.

Marenholtz instructed the lawyer in detail. Old contracts were to be broken, new ones drawn up. The lawyer wrote himself in for five percent as payment. The manager hung up the phone again. He slammed his desk drawer closed in sheer exuberance. Then he got up and left his office. He had to thank his players for the cooperation during the past season.

"Tell him he's not going to get anything but investigated if he doesn't put in with us." It was late now, past midnight. Ramirez' tiny hotel room was stifling. Rudy rested on the bed. Guerra sat in a chair by the single window. Marenholtz paced around, his coat thrown on the bed, his shirt soaked with perspiration.

"He say he don' like the way you run the club. He don' think you run him better," said Guerra wearily.

"All right. Explain to him that we're not going to cost him anything. The only way *we* can make money is by making sure *he* does okay. We'll take a percentage of what he makes. That's his insurance."

"He wan' know why you wan' him now, you wouldn't play him before."

"Because he's a damn fool, is why! Doesn't he know what

would happen if he pitched his kind of game, week after week?"

"He think he make a lot of money."

Marenholtz stopped pacing and stared. "Stupid Spanish bastard!" he said. Guerra, from a farming village in Panama, glared resentfully. "I'm sorry, Chico. Explain it to him." The catcher went to the edge of the bed and sat down. He talked with Rudy for a long while, then turned back to the manager.

"Okay, Mr. Marenhol'. He didn't think anybody noticed that."

"Fine," said Marenholtz, taking Guerra's vacated chair. "Now let's talk. Chico, what were you planning to do this winter?"

Guerra looked puzzled again. "I don' know. Go home."

Marenholtz smiled briefly and shook his head. "No. You're coming with me. We're taking young Mr. Ramirez here and turning him into a pitcher. If not that, at least into an educated thrower. We got a job, my friend."

They had six months, and they could have used more. They worked hard, giving Rudy little time to relax. He spent weeks just throwing baseballs through a circle of wire on a stand. Guerra and Marenholtz helped him learn the most efficient way to pitch, so that he wouldn't tire after half a game; he studied tapes of his motions, to see where they might be improved, to fool the hitters and conserve his own energy. Guerra coached him on all the fundamentals: fielding his position, developing a deceptive throw to first base, making certain that his windup was the same for every different pitch.

After a couple of months, Ramirez' control was sharp enough to put a ball into Guerra's mitt wherever the catcher might ask. Marenholtz watched with growing excitement — they were going to bring it off. Rudy was as good as any mediocre pitcher in the majors. Marenholtz was teaching him to save his special talent for the tight situations, the emergencies where less attention would be focused on the pitcher. Rudy was made to realize that he had eight skilled teammates behind him; if he threw the ball where the catcher wanted it, the danger of long hits was minimized. A succession of pop-ups and weak grounders would look infinitely better than twenty-seven passive strikeouts.

Before the spring training session began, Rudy had developed a much better curve that he could throw with reasonable control, a passable change-up, a poor slider, and a slightly offspeed fast ball. He relied on Guerra and Marenholtz for instructions, and they schooled him in all the possible situations until he was sick of the whole scheme.

"Freddie Marenholtz! Damn, you look like you could still get out there and play nine hard ones yourself. Got that phenom of yours?"

"Yeah, you want him to get dressed?" Marenholtz stood by a batting cage in the training camp of the Nashville Cats, a team welcomed into the American League during the expansion draft three years previously. The Florida sun was already fierce enough in March to make Marenholtz uncomfortable, and he shielded his eyes with one hand as he talked to Jim Billy Westfahl, the Cats' manager.

"All right," said Westfahl. "You said you brought this kid Ramirez and a catcher, right? What's his name?"

"Guerra. Only guy Ramirez ever pitched to."

"Yeah, well, you know we got two catchers in Portobenez and Staefler. If Guerra's going to stick, he's going to have to beat them out."

Marenholtz frowned. Guerra was *not* going to beat them out of their jobs. But he had to keep the man around, both because he could soothe Ramirez' irrational temper and because Guerra presented a danger to the plan. But the aging catcher might have to get used to watching the games from the boxes. He collected three and a half percent of Rudy's income, and Marenholtz couldn't see that Guerra had reason to complain.

Rudy came out of the locker room and walked to the batting cage. Guerra followed, looking uneasy among the major league talents on the field. Ramirez turned to Westfahl and said something in Spanish. Guerra translated. "He say he wan' show you what he can do."

"Okay. I'm game. *Somebody's* going to have to replace McAnion. It may as well be your kid. Let's see what he looks like."

Rudy pitched to Guerra, and Westfahl made a few noncommittal remarks. Later in the day Rudy faced some of the Cats' regulars, and the B squad of rookies. He held some of them back, pitched to some of them, and looked no less sharp than any of the other regular pitchers after a winter's inactivity. In the next two weeks Marenholtz and Guerra guided Rudy carefully, letting him use his invisible talent sparingly, without attracting undue notice, and Ramirez seemed sure to go north with the team when the season began. Guerra didn't have the same luck. A week before spring training came to an end, he was optioned to the Cats' AA farm club. Guerra pretended to be upset, and refused to report.

By this time Marenholtz had promoted a large amount of money. The newly appointed president of *RR Star Enterprises* had spent the spring signing contracts while his protégé worked to impress the public. Permissions and royalty fees were deposited from trading card companies, clothing manufacturers, fruit juice advertisements, sporting goods dealers, and grooming product endorsements — Rudy was hired to look into a camera and say, "I like it. It makes my hair neat without looking greasy." He was finally coached to say, "I like it," and the rest of the line was given to a sexy female model.

The regular season began at home for the Cats. Rudy Ramirez was scheduled to pitch the third game. Rudy felt little excitement before his game; what he did was in no way different in kind or quantity from his nervousness before his first appearance with the Cordele Tigers. The slightly hostile major league crowd didn't awe him: he was prepared to awe the four thousand spectators who had come to watch the unknown rookie.

Fred Marenholtz had briefed Rudy thoroughly; before the game they had decided that an impressive but nonetheless credible effort would be a four- or five-hit shutout. For an added touch of realism, Rudy might get tired in the eighth inning, and leave for a relief pitcher. Marenholtz and Guerra sat in field boxes along the first base side, near the dugout. Ramirez could hear their shouts from the mound. He waved to them as he took his place before the "National Anthem" was sung.

Rudy's pitches were not particularly overpowering. His fast ball was eminently hitable; only the experience of the Cats' catcher prevented pitches from sailing time after time over the short left field fence. Ramirez' weeks of practice saved him: his pitches crossed the plate just above the batters' knees, or handcuffed them close around the fists, or nicked the outside edge of the plate. Rudy's curve was just good enough to keep the hitters guessing. The first batter hit a sharp ground ball to short, fielded easily for the first out. The second batter lofted a fly to right field for the second out. Rudy threw three pitches to the third batter, and then threw his first mistake, a fast ball belt high, down the middle. Rudy knew what would happen — a healthy swing, and the a quick one-run lead for the White Sox. Urgently, desperately he sought the batter's will and grasped it in time. The man stood stupidly, staring at the most perfect pitch he would see in a long while. It went by for a called strike three, and Rudy had his first official major league strikeout.

Marenholtz stood and applauded when Rudy trotted back to the dugout. Guerra shouted something in Spanish. Ramirez' teammates slapped his back, and he smiled and nodded and took his place on the bench. He allowed a double down the line in the second inning, sent the White Sox down in order in the third and fourth, gave up a single and a walk in the fifth, a single in the sixth, no hits in the seventh and eighth, and two singles to the first two batters in the ninth. Rudy had pitched wisely, combining his inferior skill with judicious use of his mental talent. Sometimes he held back a batter for just a fraction of a second, so that the hitter would swing late. Other times he would prevent a batter from running for an instant, to insure his being thrown out at first. He caused the opposition's defense to commit errors so that the Cats could score the runs to guarantee victory.

The manager of the Cats came out to the mound to talk with Ramirez in the ninth. Carmen Velillo, the Cats' third baseman, joined the conference to translate for Rudy. Ramirez insisted that he was strong enough to finish, but the manager brought in a relief pitcher. Rudy received a loud cheer from the fans as he went off the field. He didn't watch the rest of the game, but went straight to the showers. The Cats' new man put down the rally, and Ramirez had a shutout victory. After Rudy and Velillo had answered the endless questions of the newsmen, Marenholtz and Guerra met him for a celebration.

Marenholtz held interviews with reporters from national magazines or local weeklies. Coverage of Ramirez' remarkable successes grew more detailed: as the season progressed Rudy saw his picture on the front of such varied periodicals as *Sports Illustrated* and *People Magazine*. By June, Rudy had won eleven games and lost none. His picture appeared on the cover of *Time* after he won his fifteenth in a row. An article in the *New York Post* announced that he was the greatest natural talent since Grover Cleveland Alexander. He appeared briefly on late-night television programs. He was hired to attend shopping center openings in the Nashville area. He loved winning ball games, and Marenholtz, too, gloried in returning a success to the major leagues that had treated him so shabbily in his youth.

The evening before Ramirez was to start his sixteenth ball game, he was having dinner with Marenholtz and Guerra. The older man was talking about his own short playing career, and how baseball had deteriorated since then. Guerra nodded and said little. Ramirez stared quietly at his plate, toying with his food and not eating. Suddenly he spoke up, interrupting Marenholtz' flow of memories. He spoke in rapid Spanish; Marenholtz gaped in surprise. "What's he saying?" he asked.

Guerra coughed nervously. "He wan' know why he need us," he said. "He say he do pretty good by himself."

Marenholtz put his cigar down and stared angrily at Ramirez. "I was wondering how long it would take him to think he could cut us out. You can tell him that if it hadn't been for us he'd either be in trouble or in Venezuela. You can tell him that if it hadn't been for us he wouldn't have that solid bank account and his poor gray mama wouldn't have the only color television in her banana wonderland. And if that doesn't work, tell him maybe he *doesn't* need us, but he signed the contract."

Guerra said a few words, and Rudy answered. "What's he say now?" asked Marenholtz.

"Nothing," said Guerra, staring down at his own plate. "He jus' say he thank you, but he wan' do it himself."

"Oh, hell. Tell him to forget that and pitch a good game tomorrow. I'll do the worrying. That's what I'm for."

"He say he do that. He say he pitch you a good game."

"Well, thank you, Tom, and good afternoon, baseball fans everywhere. In just a few moments we'll bring you live coverage of the third contest of this weekend series, a game between the Nashville Cats, leaders in the American League Midlands Division, and the Denver Athletics. It looks to be a pitchers' duel today, with young Rudy Ramirez, Nashville's astonishing rookie, going against the A's veteran right-hander, Morgan Stepitz."

"Right, Chuck, and I think a lot of the spectators in the park today have come to see if Ramirez can keep his amazing streak alive. He's won fifteen now and he hasn't been beaten so far in his entire professional career. Each game must be more of an ordeal than the last for the youngster. The strain will be starting to take its toll."

"Nevertheless, Tom, I have to admit that it's been a very long time since I've seen anyone with the poise of that young man. The interesting thing is that he hasn't let his success make him over-confident, which is possibly the greatest danger to him now. I'm sure that defeat, when it comes, will be a hard blow, but I'm just certain that Rudy Ramirez will recover and go on to have a truly remarkable season."

"A lot of fans have written in to ask what the record is for most consecutive games won. Well Ramirez has quite a start on that, but he has a little way to go. The major league record is nineteen, set in 1912 by Rube Marquard. But even if Ramirez doesn't go on to break that one, he's still got the makings of a spectacular year. He's leading both leagues with an earned run average of 1.54, and it looks like he has an excellent shot at thirty wins —"

"All right, lets' go down to the field, where it's time for the singing of 'The Star-Spangled Banner'."

After the spectators cheered and settled back into their seats, after the Cats' catcher whipped the ball down to second base, and after the infielders tossed it around and, finally, back to the pitcher, Rudy looked around the stadium. The Nashville park was new, built five years ago in hopes of attracting a major league franchise. It was huge, well-designed, and generally filled with noisy fans. The sudden success of the usually hapless Cats was easily traced: Rudy Ramirez. He was to pitch again today, and his enthusiastic rooters crowded the spacious park. Bedsheet banners hung over railings, wishing him luck and proclaiming Ramirez to be the best-loved individual on the continent. Rudy, still innocent of English, did not know what they said.

He could see Marenholtz and Guerra sitting behind the dugout. They saw him glance in their direction and stood, waving their arms. Rudy touched the visor of his cap in salute. Then he turned to face the first of the Athletics' hitters.

"Okay, the first batter for the A's is the second baseman, number twelve, Jerry Kleiner. Kleiner's batting .262 this season. He's a switch-hitter, and he's batting right-handed against the southpaw, Ramirez.

"Ramirez takes his sign from Staefler, winds, and delivers. Kleiner takes the pitch for a called strike one. Ramirez has faced the A's only once before this season, shutting them out on four hits.

"Kleiner steps out to glance down at the third base coach for the signal. He steps back in. Ramirez goes into his motion. Kleiner lets it go by again. No balls and two strikes."

"Ramirez is really piping them in today, Tom."

"That's right, Chuck. I noticed during his warm-ups that his fast ball seemed to be moving exceptionally well. Today it will tend to tail in toward the a right-handed hitter. Here comes the pitch — strike three! Kleiner goes down looking."

"Before the game we talked with Cats' catcher Bo Staefler, who told us that Ramirez's slider is improving as the season gets older. You know that can only be bad news for the hitters in the American League. It may be a while before they can solve his style."

"Stepping in now is the A's right fielder, number twenty-four, Ricky Gonzalvo. Gonzalvo's having trouble with his old knee injury this year, and his average is down to .244. He crowds the plate a little on Ramirez. The first pitch is inside, knocking Gonzalvo down. Ball one.

"Ramirez gets the ball back, leans forward for his sign. And the pitch — in there for a called strike. The count is even at one and one."

"He seems to have excellent control today, wouldn't you say, Tom?"

"Exactly. Manager Jim Westfahl of the Cats suggested last week that the pinpoint accuracy of his control is sometimes enough to intimidate a batter into becoming an easy out."

"There must be *some* explanation, even if it's magic."

"Ramirez deals another breaking pitch, in there for a called strike two. I wouldn't say it's all magic, Chuck. It looked to me as though Gonzalvo was crossed up on that one, probably expecting the fast ball again."

"Staefler gives him the sign. Ramirez nods, and throws. Fast ball caught Gonzalvo napping. Called strike three. Two away now in the top of the first.

"Batting in the number three position is the big first baseman, Howie Bass. Bass' brother, Eddie, who plays for the Orioles, has the only home run hit off Ramirez this season. Here comes Ramirez' pitch — Bass takes it for strike one."

"It seems to me that the batters are starting out behind Ramirez, a little overcautious. That's the effect that a winning streak like his can have. Ramirez has the benefit of a psychological edge working for him, as well as his great pitching."

"Right, Tom. That pitch while you were talking was a call strike two, a good slider that seemed to have Bass completely baffled."

"Staefler gives the sign, but Ramirez shakes his head. Ramirez shakes off another sign. Now he nods, goes into his windup, and throws. A fast ball, straight down the middle, strike three. Bass turns to argue with the umpire, but that'll do him no good. Three up and three down for the A's, no runs, no hits, nothing across."

The Cats' fans jumped to their feet, but Fred Marenholtz listened angrily to their applause. He caught Rudy's eye just as the pitcher was about to enter the dugout. Before Marenholtz could say anything, Rudy grinned and disappeared inside. Marenholtz was worried that the sophisticated major league audience would be even less likely to accept the spectacle of batter after batter going down without swinging at Ramirez' pitches. The older man turned to Guerra. "What's he trying to do?" he asked.

Guerra shook his head. "I don' know. Maybe he wan' strike out some."

"Maybe," said Marenholtz dubiously, "but I didn't think he'd be that dumb."

The Cats got a runner to second base in their part of the first inning, but he died there when the cleanup hitter sent a line drive over the head of the A's first baseman, who leaped high to save the run. Rudy walked out to the mound confidently, and threw his warm-ups.

"All right," said Marenholtz, "let's see him stop that nonsense now. This game's being televised all over the country." He watched Ramirez go into his motion. The first pitch was a curve that apparently didn't break, a slow pitch coming toward the plate as fat as a basketball. The A's batter watched it for a called strike. Marenholtz swore softly.

Rudy threw two more pitches, each of them over the plate for strikes. The hitter never moved his bat. Marenholtz' face was turning red with controlled fury. Rudy struck out the next batter on three pitches. Guerra coughed nervously and said something in Spanish. Already the fans around them were remarking on how strange it was to see the A's being called out on strikes without making an effort to guard the plate. The A's sixth batter took his place in the batters box, and the three pitches later he, too, walked back to the bench, a bewildered expression on his face.

Marenholtz stood and hollered to Ramirez. "What the hell you doing?" he said, forgetting that the pitcher couldn't understand him. Rudy walked nonchalantly to the dugout, taking no notice of Marenholtz.

Guerra rose and edged past Marenholtz to the aisle. "You going for a couple of beers?" asked Marenholtz.

"No," said Guerra. "I think I jus' *goin'*."

"Well, Tom, it's the top of the third, score tied at nothing to nothing. I want to say that we're getting that pitcher's battle we promised. We're witnessing one heck of a good ballgame so far. The Cats have had only one hit, and rookie Rudy Ramirez hasn't let an Athletic reach first base."

"There's an old baseball superstition about jinxing a pitcher in a situation like this, but I might mention that Ramirez has struck out the first six men to face him. The record for consecutive strikeouts is eleven, held by Cannon Shen of the old Cleveland Indians. If I remember correctly, that mark was set the last year the Indians played in Cleveland, before their move to New Orleans."

"This sort of game isn't a new thing for Ramirez, either, Tom. His bio in the Cats' pressbook mentions that in his one start in the minor leagues, he threw a perfect game and set a Triangle League record for most strikeouts in a nine-inning game."

"Okay, Chuck. Ramirez has finished his warm-ups here in the top of the third. He'll face the bottom of the A's order. Batting in the seventh position is the catcher, number sixteen, Tolly Knecht. Knecht's been in a long slump, but he's always been something of a spoiler. He'd love to break out of it with a hit against Ramirez here. Here's the pitch — Knecht was taking all the way, a called strike one."

"Maybe the folks at home would like to see Ramirez' form here on the slow-motion replay. You can see how the extra-high kick tends to hide the ball from the batter until the very last moment. He's getting the gull force of his body behind the pitch, throwing from the shoulder with a last powerful snap of the wrist. He ends up here perfectly balanced, ready for any kind of defensive move. From the plate, the white ball must be disguised by the uniform, appearing suddenly out of nowhere. A marvelous athlete and a terrific competitor."

"Thanks, Chuck. That last pitch was a good breaking ball; Knecht watched it for strike two. I think one of the reasons the hitters seem to be so confused is the excellent arsenal of pitches that Ramirez has. He throws his fast ball intelligently, saving it for the tight spots. He throws an overhand curve and a sidearm curve, each at two different speeds. His slider is showing up more and more as his confidence increases."

"Ramirez nods to Staefler, the catcher. He winds up and throws. Strike three! That's seven now. Knecht throws his bat away in frustration. The fans aren't too happy either. Even the Cats' loyal crowd is beginning to boo. I don't think I've ever seen a team as completely stymied as the A's are today."

"I tell you, I almost wish I could go down there myself. Some of Ramirez' pitches look just too good. It makes me want to grab a bat and take a poke at one. His slow curves seem to hang there, inviting a good healthy cut. But, of course, from our vantage point we can't see what the batters are seeing. Ramirez must have tremendous stuff today. Not one Athletic hitter has taken a swing at his pitches."

When the eighth Athletic batter struck out, the fans stood and jeered. Marenholtz felt his stomach tightening. His mouth was dry and his ears buzzed. After the ninth batter fanned, staring uninterestedly at a mild pitch belt high, the stadium was filled with shouts and catcalls. Marenholtz couldn't be sure that they were all directed at the unlucky hitters.

Maybe I ought to hurry after Guerra, thought Marenholtz. *Maybe it's time to talk about that bowling alley deal again. This game is rotten at its roots already. It's not like when I was out there.*

We cared. The fans cared. Now they got guys like Grobert playing, they're nearly gangsters. Sometimes the games look like they're produced from a script. And Ramirez is going to topple it all. The kid's special, but that won't save us. Good God, I feel sorry for him. He can't see it coming. He won't see it coming. He's out there having a ball. And he's going to make the loudest boom when it all falls down. Then what's he going to do? What's he going to do?

Rudy walked jauntily off the field. The spectators around Marenholtz screamed at the pitcher. Rudy only smiled. He waved to Marenholtz and pointed to Guerra's empty seat. Marenholtz shrugged. Ramirez ducked into the dugout, leaving Marenholtz to fret in the stands.

After the Cats were retired in the third, Rudy went out to pitch his half of the fourth. A policeman called his name, and Rudy turned. The officer stood in the boxes, at the edge of the dugout, stationed to prevent overeager fans from storming the playing field. He held his hand out to Rudy and spoke to him in English. Rudy shook his head, not understanding. He took the papers from the policeman and studied them for a moment. They were the contracts that he had signed with Marenholtz. They were torn in half. Ramirez grinned; he looked up toward Marenholtz' seat behind the dugout. The man had followed Guerra, had left the stadium before he could be implicated in the tarnished proceedings.

For the first time since he had come to the United States, Rudy Ramirez felt free. He handed the contracts back to the mystified police officer and walked to the mound. He took a few warm-ups and waited for Kleiner, the A's lead-off batter. Ramirez took his sign and pitched. Kleiner swung and hit a shot past the mound. Rudy entered Kleiner's mind and kept him motionless beside the plate for a part of a second. The Cats' shortstop went far to his left, grabbed the ball and threw on the dead run; Kleiner was out by a full step. There were mixed groans and cheers from the spectators, but Rudy didn't hear. He was watching Gonzalvo take his place in the batter's box. Maybe Rudy would let him get a hit.

The Vampire Shortstop

SCOTT NICHOLSON

Jerry Shepherd showed up at first practice alone.

I mean, *showed up*, as if he'd just popped into thin air at the edge of the woods that bordered Sawyer Field. Most kids, they come to first practice book-ended by their parents, who glower like Mafia heavies willing to break your kneecaps if their kid rides the pine for so much as an inning. So in a way, it was a relief to see Jerry materialize like that, with no threat implied.

But in another way, he made me nervous. Every year us Little League coaches get handed two or three players who either recently moved to the area or were given their release (yeah, we're that serious here) by their former teams. And if there's one thing that's just about universal, it's the fact that these Johnny-come-latelys couldn't hit their way out of a paper bag. So I figured, here's this spooky kid standing there at the fence, just chewing on his glove, real scared-like, so at least there's one brat who's not going to be squealing for playing time.

I figured him for a vampire right off. He had that pale complexion, the color of a brand new baseball before the outfield grass scuffs up the horsehide. But, hey, these are enlightened times, everybody's cool with everybody, especially since "Transylvania" Wayne Kazloski broke the major league undead barrier back in '29. And that old myth about vampires melting in the sun is just that, an old myth.

The league powers figured I wouldn't raise a fuss if they dumped an undesirable on me. I had eleven kids on the roster, only five of them holdovers from the year before, so I was starting from scratch anyway. I didn't mind a new face, even if I was pretty much guaranteed that the vampire kid had two left feet. Coming off a three-and-thirteen season, the Maynard Solar Red Sox didn't have any great expectations to live up to.

All the other players had clustered around me as if I were giving out tickets to see a rock band, but Jerry just hung out around first base like a slow-thawing cryogenic.

"I'm Coach Ruttlemyer," I said, loudly enough to reach Jerry's pointy ears. "Some of you guys know each other and some of you don't. But on my team, it's not who you know that counts, it's how hard you play."

At this point in the first preseason speech, you always catch some kid with a finger in his or her nose. That year, it was a sweet-faced, red-headed girl. She had, at that moment, banished herself to right field.

"Now, everybody's going to play in every game," I said. "We're here to have fun, not just to win."

The kids looked at me like they didn't buy that line of bull. I barely believed it myself. But I always said it extra-loud so that the parents could hear. It gave me something to fall back on at the end of a lousy season.

"We're going to be practicing hard because we only have two weeks before the first game," I said, pulling the bill of my cap down low over my eyes so they could see what a serious guy I was. "Now, let's see who's who."

I went down the roster alphabetically, calling out each player's name. When the kid answered "Here," I glanced first at the kid, then up into the bleachers to see which parents were grinning and straining their necks. That's a good way to tell right off who's going to want their kid to pitch: the beefy, red-faced dad wearing sunglasses and too-tight polyester shorts, and the mom who's busy organizing which parent is bringing what snack for which game.

When I called out Jerry's name, he croaked out a weak syllable and grimaced, showing the tips of his fangs. I waved him over to join the rest of the team. He tucked his glove in his armpit and jogged to the end of the line. I watched him out of the corner of my eye, waiting for him to trip over the baseline chalk. But he didn't stumble once, and that's when I got my first glimmer of hope that maybe he'd be able to swipe a couple of bases for me. He was gaunt, which means that if he's clumsy you call him "gangly," but if he's well-coordinated you call him "sleek." So maybe we're not as enlightened as we claim to be, but hey, we're making progress.

I liked to start first practice by having the kids get on the infield dirt and snag some grounders. You can tell just about everything you need to know about a player that way. And I don't mean just gloving the ball and pegging it over to first. I mean footwork, hand-eye, hustle, aggressiveness, vision, all those little extras that separate the cellar-dwellers from the also-rans from the team that takes home the Sawyer Cup at the end of the season. And it's not just the way they act when it's their turn; you get a lot of clues by how they back each other up, whether they sit down between turns, whether they punch each other on the arm or hunt for four-leaf clovers.

By the first run through, ten ground balls had skittered through to the deep grass in centerfield. But one, *one*, made up for all those errors. Jerry Shepherd's grounder. He skimmed the ball off the dirt and whizzed it over to first as if the ball were a yo-yo and he held the string. My assistant coach and darling wife Dana grinned at me when the ball thwacked into her mitt. I winked at her, hoping the play wasn't a fluke.

But it was no fluke. Six turns through, and six perfect scoops and tosses by Jerry Shepherd. Some of the other kids were fifty-fifty risks, and one, you'd have guessed the poor little kid had the glove on the wrong hand. You know the kind, parents probably raised him on computer chess and wheat bran. Oops, there I go again, acting all unenlightened.

Another bright spot was Elise Stewart, my best returning player. She only made the one error on her first turn, and I could chalk that up to a long winter's layoff. She was not only sure-handed, she was also the kind of girl you'd want your son to date in high school. She had a happy heart and you just knew she'd be good at algebra.

All in all, I was pleased with the personnel. In fifteen years of coaching Little League, this was probably the best crop of raw talent that I'd ever had. Now, I wasn't quite having delusions of being hauled out of the dugout on these guys' shoulders (me crushing their bones and hoisting the Sawyer Cup over my head), but with a little work, we had a chance at a winning season.

I made a boy named Biff put on the catcher's gear and get behind the plate. In baseball films, the chunky kid always plays catcher, but if you've ever watched even one inning of a real Little League game, you know the catcher needs to be quick. He spends all his time against the backstop, stumbling over his mask and jerking his head around looking for the baseball. Besides, Biff had a great name for a catcher, and what more could you ask for?

I threw batting practice, and again each kid had a turn while the others fanned out across the diamond. I didn't worry as much about hitting as I did fielding, because I knew hitting was mostly a matter of practice and concentration. It was a skill that could be taught. So I kind of expected the team to be a little slow with the bat, and they didn't disappoint me.

Except when Jerry dug into the batter's box. He stared at me with his pupils glinting red under the brim of his batting helmet, just daring me to bring the heat. I chuckled to myself. I liked this kid's cockiness at the plate. But I used to be a decent scholarship prospect, and I still had a little of the old vanity myself. So instead of lobbing a cream puff, I kicked up my leg and brought the Ruttlemyer Express.

His line drive would have parted my hair, except for two things: I was wearing a cap and my hairline barely reached above my ears. But I felt the heat off his scorcher all the same, and it whistled like a bullet from a gun. I picked up the rosin bag and tossed it in the air a few times. Some of the parents had stopped talking among themselves and watched the confrontation.

Jerry dug in and Biff gave me a target painting the black on the inside corner. I snapped off a two-seamer curveball, hoping the poor batter didn't break his spine when he lunged at the dipping pitch. But Jerry kept his hips square, then twisted his wrists and roped the ball to right field for what would have been a stand-up double. I'd never seen a Little Leaguer who could go with a pitch like that. I tossed him a knuckleball, and most grown-ups couldn't have hit it with a tennis racket, but Jerry drilled it over the fence in left-center.

Okay. *Okay.*

He did miss one pitch and hit a couple of fouls during his turn. I guess even vampires are only human.

After practice, I passed out uniforms and schedules and talked to the parents. I was hoping to tell Jerry what a good job he'd done and how I'd be counting on him to be a team leader, but he snatched up his goods and left before I had the chance. He got to the edge of the woods, then turned into a bat (the flying kind, not the kind you hit with) and flitted into the trees, his red jersey dangling from one of his little claws. His glove weighed him down a little and he was blind, of course, so he bumped into a couple of tree limbs before he got out of sight.

And so went the two weeks. Jerry was a natural shortstop, even the other kids saw that. Usually, everybody wanted to pitch and play shortstop (both positions at the same time, you know), but nobody grumbled when I said Jerry would be our starting shortstop. Elise was starting pitcher, and Wheat Bran and the redhead were "designated pinch hitters." I told everybody to get a good night's sleep, because we would be taking on the Piedmont Electric Half-Watts, which was always one of the better teams.

I could hardly sleep that night, I was so excited. Dana rolled over at about 1:00 a.m. and stole her pillow back.

"What's wrong?" she grunted.

"The game," I said. I was running through lineups in my mind, planning strategies for situations that might arise in the sixth inning.

"Go to sleep. Deadline's tomorrow."

"Yeah, yeah, yeah." I was editor of the *Sawyer Creek E-Weekly*, and Thursday noon was press time. I still had some unfinished articles. "That's just my job, but baseball is my lifeblood."

Thinking of lifeblood made me think of Jerry. The poor kid must have lost his parents. Back a few centuries ago, there had been a lot of purging and staking and garlic-baiting. Yeah, like I said, we're making progress, but sometimes I wonder if you can ever really change the human animal. I hoped nothing would come up about his being a vampire.

I knew how cruel Little League could be. Not the kids. They could play and play and play, making up rules as they went along, working things out. No, it was the parents who sometimes made things ugly, who threw tantrums and called names and threatened coaches. I'd heard parents boo their own kids.

In one respect, I was glad Jerry was an orphan. At least I didn't have to worry about his parents changing into wolves, leaping over the chain-link fence, and ripping my throat out over a bad managerial decision. Not that vampires perpetrated that sort of violence. Still, all myths contain a kernel of truth, and even a myth can make you shiver.

I finally went to sleep, woke up and got the paper online. I drove out to the ballfield and there were four dozens vehicles in the parking lot. There's not much entertainment in Sawyer Creek. Like I said, Little League's a big deal in these parts, plus it was a beautiful April day, with the clouds all puffy and soft in the blue sky. Dana was already there, passing out baseballs so the kids could warm up.

I looked around and noticed Jerry hadn't arrived.

"He'll be here," Dana said, reading my nervousness.

We took infield and I was filling out the lineup card when Elise pointed to centerfield. "Hey, looky there, Coach," she said.

Over the fence loped a big black dog, with red socks and white pin-striped pants. Propped between the two stiff ears was a cockeyed cap. The upraised tail whipped back and forth in the breeze, a worn glove hooked over its tip. The dog transformed into Jerry when it got to second base.

A murmur rippled through the crowd. I felt sorry for Jerry then. The world may be enlightened, but the light's a little slower in reaching Sawyer Creek than it is most places. There are always a few bigots around. Red, yellow, black, and white, we had all gotten along and interbred and become one race. But when you get down to the equality of the living and the living dead, some people just don't take to that notion of unity as easily.

And there was something else that set the crowd on edge, and even bothered *me* for a second. Hanging by a strap around his neck was one of those sports bottles all the kids have these days. Most of the kids put in juice or Super-Ade or something advertised by their favorite big leaguers. But Jerry's drink was thick and blood-red. Perfectly blood-red.

"Sorry I'm late," he said, sitting down on the end of the bench. I winced as he squirted some of the contents of the sports bottle into his throat.

"Play ball," the umpire yelled, and Elise went up to the plate and led off with a clean single to right. The next kid bunted her over, then Jerry got up. The first pitch bounced halfway to home plate and Elise stole third. Dana, who was coaching third base, gave her the "hold" sign. I wanted to give Jerry a chance to drive her in.

The next pitch was a little high, but Jerry reached out easily with the bat. The ball dinged off the titanium into center and we were up, one to nothing. And that was the final score, with Elise pitching a three-hitter and Jerry taking away a handful of hits from deep in the hole. Jerry walked once and hit another double, but Wheat Bran struck out to leave him stranded in the fifth.

Still, I was pleased with the team effort, and a "W" is a "W," no matter how you get it. The kids gathered around the snack cooler after the game, all happy and noisy and ready to play soccer or something. But not Jerry. He had slipped away before I could pat him on the back.

"Ain't no fair, you playing a slanty-eyed vampire," came a gruff voice behind me. "Next thing you know, they'll allow droids and other such trash to mix in. Baseball's supposed to be for normal folks."

I turned to find myself face-to-face with Roscoe Turnbull. Sawyer Creek's Mister Baseball. Coach of the reigning champs for the past seven years. He'd been watching from the stands, scouting the opposition the way he always did.

"Hey, he's got just as much right to play as anybody," I said. "I know you're not big on reading, but someday you ought to pick up the U.S. Constitution and check out the 43rd Amendment."

The Red Sox had never beaten one of Turnbull's teams, but at least I could be smug in my intellectual superiority.

"Big words don't mean nothing when they're giving out the Sawyer Cup," Turnbull hissed through his Yogi Berra teeth. He had a point. He'd had to build an addition onto his house just so he could store all the hardware his teams had won.

"We'll see," I said, something I never would have dared to say in previous years. Turnbull grunted and got in his panel truck. His son Ted was in the passenger seat, wearing the family scowl. I waved to him and went back to my team.

We won the next five games. Jerry was batting something like .900 and had made only one error, which occurred when a stray moth bobbed around his head in the infield. He'd snatched it out of the air with his mouth at the same moment the batter sent a three-hopper his way. I didn't say anything. I mean, instincts are instincts. Plus, we were winning, and that was all that mattered.

The seventh game was trouble. I'd been dreading that line on the schedule ever since I realized that my best player was a vampire. Maynard Solar Red Sox versus The Dead Reckoning Funeral Parlor Pall Bearers. Now, no self-respecting parlors were *selling* the blood that they drained. But there had been rumors of underground activity, a black market for blood supplies.

And Jerry had slowly been catching the heat, anyway. The grumbles from the stands had gotten louder, and whenever Jerry got up to bat or made a play in the field, some remark would come from the opposing bleachers. Oh, they were the usual unimaginative kind, like the old "Kill the vampire," the play on the resemblance between the words "vampire" and "umpire." The other common one was "Vampires suck." And these were the parents, mind you. They wonder where kids get it from.

The cruelest one, and the one that caught on the fastest, came from the unlikely mouth of Roscoe Turnbull, who'd made a habit of bringing his son Ted to our games just so they could ride Jerry's case. Jerry had launched a three-run homer to win in the last inning of one of our games. As he crossed the plate, Turnbull yelled out, "Hey, look, everybody. It's the Unnatural." You know, a play on the old Robert Redford film. Even *I* had to grudgingly admit that was a good one.

Now we were playing a funeral parlor and I didn't know where Jerry got his blood. I usually didn't make it my business to keep up with how the kids lived their lives off the diamond. But Jerry didn't have any parents, any guidance. Maybe he could be bribed to throw a game if the enticements were right.

So I was worried when Jerry came to bat in the sixth with two outs. We were down, four-three. Biff was on second. It was a situation where there was really no coaching strategy. Jerry either got a hit or made an out.

He had made hits in his three previous trips, but those were all in meaningless situations. I couldn't tell if he was setting us up to lose. Until that moment.

"Come on, Jerry," I yelled, clapping my hands. "I know you can do it."

If you *want* to, I silently added.

Jerry took two strikes over the heart of the plate. The bat never left his shoulder. All my secret little fantasies of an undefeated season were about to go up in smoke. I started mentally rehearsing my after-game speech, about how we gave it all we had, we'll get 'em next time, blah blah blah.

The beanpole on the mound kicked up his leg and brought the cheese. Jerry laced it off the fence in right-center. Dana waved Biff around to score, and Jerry was rounding second. I didn't know whether I hoped Dana would motion him to try for third, because Wheat Bran was due up next, and he'd yet to hit even a foul tip all season. But the issue was decided when their shortstop, the undertaker's kid, rifled the relay throw over the third baseman's head as Jerry pounded down the basepath. We won, five-four.

"I never doubted you guys for a second," I told the team

afterward, but of course Jerry had already pulled his disappearing act.

Dana was blunt at dinner as I served up some tastiwhiz and fauxburger. I'd popped a cork on some decent wine to celebrate.

"Steve, I think you're beginning to like winning just a little too much," she said, ever the concerned wife.

I grinned around a mouthful of food. "It gets in your blood," I said. "Can't help it."

"What about all those seasons you told the kids to just give it their best, back when you were plenty satisfied if everyone only showed a little improvement over the course of the season?"

"Back when I was just trying to build their self-esteem? Well, nothing builds character like winning. The little guys are practically *exploding* with character."

"I wish you were doing more for Jerry," she said. "He still doesn't act like part of the team. And the way he looks at you, like he wants you for a father figure. I think he's down on himself."

"Down on himself? *Down* on himself?" I almost sprayed my mouthful of wine across the table, and that stuff was ten bucks a bottle. I gulped and continued. "I could trade him for an entire *team* if I wanted. He's the best player to come out of Sawyer Creek since —"

"— since Roscoe Turnbull. And you see how *he* ended up."

I didn't like where this discussion was headed. "I'm sure Jerry's proud of his play. And the team likes him."

"Only because the team's winning. But I wonder how they would have reacted, how their *parents* would have reacted, if Jerry had struck out that last time today? I mean, nobody's exactly inviting him for sleep-overs as it is."

"He's just quiet. A lone wolf. Nothing wrong with that," I said, a little unsure of myself.

"Nothing wrong with vampires as long as they hit .921, is that what you mean?"

"Hey, we're winning, and that's what counts."

"I don't know," Dana said, shaking her pretty and sad head. "You're even starting to *sound* like Roscoe Turnbull."

That killed *my* mood, all right. That killed my mood for a lot of things around the house for a while. Lying in bed that night with a frigid three feet between us, I stared out the window at the full moon. A shape fluttered across it, a small lonely speck lost in that great circle of white. It most likely wasn't Jerry, but I felt an ache in my heart for him all the same.

At practice, I sometimes noticed the players whispering to each other while Jerry was at bat. I don't think for a minute that children are born evil. But they have parents who teach and guide them. Parents who were brought up on the same whispered myths.

I tried to be friendly toward Jerry, and kept turning my head so I could catch the look from him that Dana had described. But all I saw were a pair of bright eyes that could pierce the back of a person's skull if they wanted. Truth be told, he *did* give me the creeps, a little. And I could always pretend my philosophy was to show no favoritism, despite Dana's urging me to reach out to him.

Dana was a loyal assistant regardless of our difference of opinion. She helped co-pilot the Red Sox through the next eight victories. Jerry continued to tear up the league's pitching and played shortstop like a strip of flypaper, even though he was booed constantly. Elise pitched well and the rest of the kids were coming along, improving every game. I was almost sad when we got to the last game. I didn't want the season to end.

Naturally, we had to play the Turnbull Construction Claw Hammers for the championship. They'd gone undefeated in their division again. Ted had a fastball that could shatter a brick. And Roscoe Turnbull started scouting his draft picks while they were still in kindergarten, so he had the market cornered on talent.

I was so nervous I couldn't eat the day of the game. I got to the field early, while the caretaker was still trimming the outfield. Turnbull was there, too. He was in the home team's dugout shaving down a wooden bat. Wooden bats weren't even used in the majors anymore. Turnbull could afford lithium compound bats. That's when I first started getting suspicious.

"I'm looking forward to the big game," Turnbull said, showing the gaps between his front teeth.

"Me, too," I said, determined not to show that I cared. "And may the best team win."

"What do you mean? The best team always wins."

I didn't like the way he was running that woodshaver down the bat handle.

"You getting all nostalgic?" I asked, tremblingly nonchalant. "Going back to wood?"

"Good enough for my daddy. And my great-great-grandpaw on my mother's side. Maybe you heard of him. Ty Cobb."

Tyrus Raymond Cobb. The Hall-of-Famer. The Georgia Peach. The greatest hitter in any league, ever. Or the dirtiest player ever to set foot on a diamond, depending on whom you asked.

"Yeah, I've heard of him," I said. "That's quite a bloodline."

"Well, *we've* always managed to win without no low-down, stinking vampires on our team."

"Jerry Shepherd deserves to play as much as any other boy or girl."

"It ain't right. Here this —" he made a spitting face "— *creature* has all these advantages like being able to change into an animal or throw the hocus-pocus on other players."

"You know that's against the rules. We'd be disqualified if he tried something like that. There's no advantage."

"It's only against the rules if you get caught." Turnbull held the tip of the bat up in the air. It was whittled to a fine, menacing point. "And sometimes, you got to *make* your advantages."

"Even you wouldn't stoop that low," I said. "Not just to win a game."

A thin stream of saliva shot from his mouth and landed on the infield dirt. He smiled again, the ugliest smile imaginable. "Gotta keep a little something on deck, just in case."

I shuddered and walked back to my dugout. Turnbull wasn't that bloodthirsty. He was just trying to gain a psychological edge. Sure, that was all.

Psychological edges work if you let them, so I spent the next fifteen minutes picking rocks from the infield. The kids were starting to arrive by then, so I watched them warm up. Jerry was late, as usual, but he walked out of the woods just as I was writing his name into the lineup. I nodded at him without speaking.

We batted first. Ted was starting for the Claw Hammers, of course. He was the kind of pitcher who would throw a brushback pitch at his own grandmother, if he thought she were digging in on him. He stood on the mound and practiced his battle glare, then whipped the ball into the catcher's mitt. I had to admit, the goon sure knew how to bring it to the plate.

Half the town had turned out. The championship game always drew better than the town elections. Dana patted me on the back.

She wasn't one to hold a grudge when times were tough.

"Play ball," the umpire shouted, and we did.

Elise strode confidently to the plate.

"Go after her, Tedder," Turnbull shouted through his cupped hands from the other dugout. "You can do it, big guy."

The first pitch missed her helmet by three inches. She dusted herself off and stood deeper in the batter's box. The next pitch made her dance. Ball two. But she was getting a little shaky. No one likes being used for target practice. The next pitch hit her bat as she ducked away. Foul, strike one.

Elise was trembling now. I hated the strategy they were using, but unfortunately it was working. The umpire didn't say a word.

"Attaboy," Turnbull yelled. "Now go in for the kill."

Ted whizzed two more strikes past her while she was still off-balance. Biff grounded out weakly to second. Jerry went up to the plate and dug in. Ted's next offering hit Jerry flush in the face.

Jerry went down like a shot. I ran up to him and knelt in the dirt, expecting to see broken teeth and blood and worse. But Jerry's eyes snapped open. Another myth about vampires is that they don't feel pain. There are other kinds of pain besides the physical, though, and I saw them in Jerry's red irises. He could hear the crowd cheering as clearly as I could.

"Kill the vampire," one parent said.

"Stick a stake in him," another shouted.

"The Unnatural strikes again," a woman yelled.

I looked into the home team's dugout and saw Turnbull beaming as if he'd just won a trip to Alpha Centauri.

I helped Jerry up and he jogged to first base. I could see a flush of pink on the back of the usually-pale neck. I wondered whether the color was due to rage or embarrassment. I had Dana give him the "steal" sign, but the redhead popped up to the catcher on the next pitch.

We held them scoreless in their half, despite Ted's getting a triple. My heart was pounding like a kid's toy drum on Christmas Day, but I couldn't let the players know I cared one way or the other. When we got that third out, I calmly gave the kids high fives as they came off the field. Sure, this was just another game like the Mona Lisa was just another painting.

So it went for another couple of innings, with no runners getting past second. Jerry got beaned on the helmet his next trip up. The crowd was cheering like mad as he fell. I looked out at the mob sitting in the bleachers, and the scariest thing was that it wasn't just our opponent's fans who were applauding.

There was the sheriff, pumping her fist in the air. The mayor looked around secretively, checked the majority opinion, then added his jeers to the din. Biff's mother almost wriggled out of her tanktop, she was screaming so enthusiastically. A little old lady in the front row was bellowing death threats through her megaphone.

I protested the beaning to the umpire. He was a plump guy, his face melted by gravity. He looked like he'd umpired back before the days of protective masks and had taken a few foul tips to the nose.

"You've got to warn the pitcher against throwing at my players," I said.

"Can't hurt a vampire, so what's the point?" the umpire snarled, spitting brown juice towards my shoes. So that was how it was going to be.

"Then you should throw the pitcher out of the game because of poor sportsmanship."

"And I ought to throw *you* out for delay of game." He yanked the mask back over his face, which was a great improvement on his looks.

I squeezed Jerry's shoulder and looked him fully in the eyes for the first time since I'd known him. Maybe I'd been afraid he would mesmerize me.

"Jerry, I'm going to put in a pinch-runner for you," I said. "It's not fair for you to put up with this kind of treatment."

I'd said the words that practically guaranteed losing the game, but I wasn't thinking about that then. The decision was made on instinct, and instinct is always truer and more revealing than a rationalizing mind. Later on, that thought gave me my only comfort.

I signaled Dana to send in a replacement. But Jerry's eyes blazed like hot embers and his face contorted into various animal faces: wolf, bat, tiger, wolverine, then settled back into its usual wan constitution.

"No," he said. "I'm staying in."

He jogged to first before I could stop him.

"Batter up," the umpire yelled.

I went into the dugout. Dana gave me a hug. There were tears in her eyes. Mine, too, though I made sure no one noticed.

Jerry stole second and then third. Wheat Bran was at the plate, waving his bat back and forth. I knew his eyes were closed. Two strikes, two outs. I was preparing to send the troops back out onto the field when Wheat Bran blooped a single down the line in right. Jerry scored standing up.

Elise shut out the Claw Hammers until the bottom of the sixth. She was getting tired. This was ulcer time, and I'd quit pretending not to care about winning. Sweat pooled under my arms and the band of my cap was soaked. I kept clapping my hands, but my throat was too tight to yell much encouragement.

Their first batter struck out. The second batter sent a hard grounder to Jerry. I was mentally ringing up the second out when someone in the stands shouted, "Bite me, blood-breath!"

The ball bounced off Jerry's glove and went into the outfield. The runner made it to second. Jerry stared at the dirt.

"Shake it off, Jerry," I said, but my voice was lost in the chorus of spectators, who were calling my shortstop every ugly name you could think of. The next batter grounded out to first, advancing the runner to third.

Two outs, and you know the way these things always work. Big Ted Turnbull dug into the batter's box, gripping the sharpened wooden bat. But I wasn't going to let him hurt us. I did what you always do to a dangerous hitter with first base open: I took the bat out of his hands. I told Elise to walk him intentionally.

Roscoe Turnbull glared at me with death in his eyes, but I had to protect my shortstop and give us the best chance to win. Ted reached first base and called time out, then jogged over to his team's bench. Roscoe gave me a smile. That smile made my stomach squirm as if I'd swallowed a dozen large snakes.

Ted sat down and changed his shoes. I didn't understand until he walked back onto the infield. The bottom of his cleats were so thick that they resembled those shoes the disco dancers wore after disco made its fourth comeback. The shoes made Ted six inches taller. The worst part was that the spikes were made of wood.

I thought of Ted's ancestor, Ty Cobb, how Cobb was legendary for sliding into second with his spikes high. I rocketed off the bench.

"Time!" I screamed. "Time out!"

The umpire lifted his mask.

"What now?" he asked.

I pointed to the cleats. "Those are illegal."

"The rule book only bans *metal* cleats," he said. "Now, batter up."

"Second baseman takes the throw on a steal," I shouted as instruction to my fielders.

"No," Jerry shouted back. He pointed to the plate. "Left-handed batter."

Shortstop takes the throw when a lefty's up. The tradition of playing the percentages was as old as baseball itself. Even with the danger, I couldn't buck the lords of the game. Unwritten rules are sometimes the strongest.

I sat on the bench with my heart against my tonsils. The crowd was chanting, "Spike him, spike him, spike him," over and over. Dana sat beside me and held my hand, a strange mixture of accusation and empathy in her eyes.

"Maybe the next batter will pop up," she said. "There probably won't even *be* a play at second."

"Probably not."

She didn't say anything about testosterone or my stubborn devotion to the percentages. Or that Elise was getting weaker and we had no relief pitcher. Or that we had to nail the lid on this victory quick or it would slip away. I knew what Dana was thinking, though.

"I'd do it even if it was my own son out there," I muttered to her. I almost even believed it.

They tried a double-steal on the next pitch. It was a delayed steal, where the runner on third waits for the catcher to throw down to second, then tries for home. Not a great strategy for the game situation, but I had a feeling Turnbull had a lower purpose in mind.

Biff gunned a perfect strike to Jerry at second. The play unfolded as if in slow motion. Ted was already leaning back, launching into his slide.

Please step away, Jerry, I was praying. The runner on third was halfway home. If Jerry didn't make the tag, we'd be tied and the Claw Hammers would have the momentum. But I didn't care. I'd gladly trade safe for safe.

Jerry didn't step away. His instincts were probably screaming at him to change into a bat and flutter above the danger, or to paralyze Ted in his tracks with a deep stare. Maybe he knew that would have caused us to forfeit the game and the championship. Or maybe he was just stubborn like me.

He gritted his teeth, his two sharp incisors hanging over his lip in concentration. Ted slid into the bag, wooden spikes high in the air. Jerry stooped into the cloud of dust. He applied the tag just before the spikes caught him flush in the chest.

The field umpire reflexively threw his thumb back over his shoulder to signal the third out. But all I could see through my blurry eyes was Jerry writhing in the dirt, his teammates hustling to gather around him. I ran out to my vampire shortstop, kneeling beside his body just as the smoke started to rise from his flesh.

He gazed up at me, the pain dousing the fire in his eyes. The crowd was silent, hushed by the horror of a wish come true. The Red Sox solemnly removed their hats. I'd never heard such a joyless championship celebration. Jerry looked at me and smiled, even as his features dissolved around his lips.

"We won, Coach," he whispered, and that word "we" was like a stake in my own heart. Then Jerry was dust, forever part of the infield.

Dana took the pitcher's mound, weeping without shame. She stared into the crowd, at the umpires, into Turnbull's dugout, and I knew she was meeting the eye of every single person at Sawyer Field that day.

"Look at yourselves," she said, her voice strong despite the knots I knew were tied in her chest. "Just take a good long look."

Everybody did. I could hear a hot dog wrapper blowing against the backstop.

"All he wanted was to play," she said. "All he wanted was to be just like you."

Sure, her words were for everybody. But she had twenty-two years of experience as Mrs. Ruttlemyer. We both knew whom she was really talking to.

"Just like you," she whispered, her words barely squeezing out yet somehow filling the outfield, the sky, the little place in your heart where you like to hide bad things. She walked off the mound with her head down, like a pitcher that had just given up the game-winning hit.

So many tears were shed that the field would have been unplayable. People had tasted the wormwood of their prejudice.

They had seen how vicious the human animal could be. Even vampires didn't kill their young, even when the young were decades old.

There was no memorial service. I wrote the eulogy, but nobody ever got to read it, not even Dana. There was talk of filing criminal charges against the Turnbulls, but nobody had the stomach to carry it through. What happened that day was something that people spent a lot of time trying to forget.

But that victory rang out across the ensuing years, a Liberty Bell for the living dead in Sawyer Creek. Vampires were embraced by the community, welcomed into the Chamber of Commerce, one was even elected mayor. Roscoe Turnbull has three vampires on his team this season.

That Sawyer Cup still sits on my mantel, even though I never set foot on a diamond after that day. Sometimes when I look at the trophy, I imagine it is full of blood. They say that winning takes sacrifice. But that's just a myth.

Still, all myths contain a kernel of truth, and even a myth can make you shiver.

Ted Williams Storms the Gates of Heaven

LOUIS PHILLIPS

So much of life is waste. Pure waste. You send out stories, and the editors send them back. You send out poems, and the editors send them back. You send out essays, and the editors send them back. Where does all that wasted energy lead? Merely to an expanded and slothful postal service.

Libraries, of course, are mines of wasted energies, of men and women who have labored long and hard to produce materials nobody reads. Thus, whenever I go to a library I feel overwhelmed by loss. I track down and check out, if possible, those books and pamphlets that nobody has read. Salvage operations. Yes, call them salvage operations.

For example: in 1879 some nobody, because in America if you are not world famous, you are nobody, some nobody bearing toward oblivion the name T.S. Arthur, and not, alas!, T.S. Eliot (just the other day I noticed that the *Village Voice* spelled it T.S. Elliot — let that be a lesson to all students of immortality) wrote a book, yes for want of a better term let's call it a book, not relegate his unadorned prose to the lower level of pamphlets and ephemera, entitled *The Strike at Tivoli and What Came of It*. Published in Philadelphia by some long gone company named Garrigue, Mr. Arthur's book starts out to be about labor/management, for want of a better term let's call it relationship, but ends up to be just another sordid tract against the evils of drunkenness.

"They couldn't beat the spread," the black man at the bar had told me before I came to the park. "I told you they couldn't beat the spread. And none of you cowards wanted to bet with me."

You start in one direction and you end up in the other. You start a project and the project never gets finished. It gets lost or abandoned. There may be a planet where all the false starts, all the wasted efforts pile up like a mountain without name.

"Why are you telling me this?" Ted Williams asks.

Hiroshima Mon Amour. Approximately twenty years ago, I started an essay upon the great movie. I was a true film scholar at the time.

"Why are you telling me this?" Ted Williams asks.

SUPERINTENDENT (MR. THORNE)

If you men do not go back to work within the week, the owners of the mill are going to bring in hands from a distance and throw out all the strikers.

I even tracked down the film script. Read everything I could about the film. Studied it as best I could in a time long before video recorders made film analysis so accessible, so possible, so triumphantly minute.

"Why are you telling me all this??????????????????" Ted Williams asks, getting more impatient with me all the time. And who can blame him? He's almost eighty years old and he's come out of retirement to lead another left-handed assault against the record books. Of course, anything an eighty-year-old man does on the baseball field is going to be a record.

He's eighty years old but he's still everything he was. The rage inside him is pure. The Splendid Splinter. The Kid. The man who once spat at sports reporters, criticized draft boards, gave up five of the most splendid seasons of his career to serve his country in the marines. And today his sympathies go out not to the belly-achers and academic air-heads, blow-hards who retreat behind columns of rhetoric to defend their exploitation of fellow creatures less fortunate than themselves, treating their part-time colleagues with absolute contempt, or, even worse, complete indifference, part-time instructors exploited through the teeth, while the tenured and sinecured great minds roam the corridors humming the tunes of sabbatical. But Ted is right. Why am I telling him all this? Today his sympathies are with the poor down-and-out Irish fighting for their jobs. Real people with real problems.

SUPERINTENDENT

Take my advice and keep yourself and your friends out of the clutches of the law. No one questions your right to lay down our work, if you are not satisfied with the wages paid. But if other men can be found who are ready and willing to take up your work as you are laying it down, they must be left free to come into the places you have been foolish enough to abandon. So I give you fair warning. The Corporation doesn't intend to wait much longer, and it doesn't mean to advance the rate of wages.

"Did you decide to return to baseball because of the money, Ted?"

Williams shakes his head. The way he talks, the way he stands, the absolute authority that he emanates — it makes you think of John Wayne, how John Wayne should have played the lead in *The Ted Williams Story*. And probably now it never will be made because the time has passed for those kinds of films. The age of heroism is dead. Long gone. And I wonder if that perhaps is not the real reason why the Kid, even at eighty we dare not call him anything else, bears with him, in his legends and towering home runs, something that is ageless and priceless.

"Couldn't beat the spread. All they did in the fourth quarter," the man at the bar told me, "was blitz, blitz, blitz."

Of course, coming out of retirement at age eighty has thrown the Hall Of Fame people into a tizzie. You have to be inactive to be in Baseball's Hall Of Fame. Your career has to be all over. Finuto. Caput. Ted's return to Boston has caused the rules committee to rupture a duck.

ANDY
    Two sides will have to say to that, Mr. Thorne. And I give you fair warning, Mr. Superintendent, that we're none of us going to submit to any interference in this business. It's our strike; and it'll be a sorry day for him as dares come in between us and our rights — it will!

"Was it the money?"

Ted shakes his head, pulls a cap from his back pocket, picks up one of his customized Louisville Sluggers. "It's not the money. The owners can give their players $50,000,000 a year and it wouldn't make a difference to me. If Musial and myself and DiMaggio had played in the hey-day of the super-contract, they could never pay us what we would be worth. There's got to be satisfaction in that, in knowing that nobody can ever pay you what you're worth."

I guess he's right about that, but I have never been in that position.

"What's Bertrand Russell getting?"

"What's he batting?" Ted asks. With him that's the essential question. Not the religion. Not the philosophic stance. Not the color of skin. Not the status in society. Not the weekly payroll check. Just simply and forever: "What's his average? How many home runs? How many runs batted in?"

"Nothing. He can't hit."

"Couldn't beat the spread, and nobody had the guts to bet with me," the black man had said.

Ted shakes his head. "What's money to me? Didn't I always have enough? Didn't my family? My family never wanted for things."

"After the '46 World Series, didn't you give your whole share away to Johnny Orlando, the clubhouse boy? Didn't you?"

"That's me. Saint Francis Assisi of Fenway Park." He runs, jogs rather, to take his place in left field. An eighty-year-old man with the sun falling on his shoulders, his white hair gleaming in the sun. The pigeons and the larks and the nightingales and the vultures — everything with feathers and fur — gather about him while he tosses them bread and cracker crumbs. Fox and possum and bear run from beneath the bleachers. Ted pulls his cap to his head as if to say to the empty stands, to the world at large, "Take that, you bastards! The Kid is back and what are you going to do about it?"

The committee has already done something about it. The plaque honoring the Kid has been temporarily removed from the wall. A gray canvas covers the larger than life statue of Number 9 swinging from his heels.

The Kid's alive but the statues and trinkets are dead.

SUPERINTENDENT (MR. THORNE)

There's no reason in arguing the matter, Andy, nor in losing your temper over it. So far as the corporation is concerned, the question is settled. In three weeks from today, the engines will be fired up, the machinery set into motion. The mills will have their full complement of hands. Whether you or your friends in this useless strike shall be found among them or not will depend on yourselves. And now, gentlemen, I want to say a word to you about this striking business. There is no denying the fact that, somehow, things have gone wrong with you, and that you are getting worse and worse off every year, instead of better. How are you going to keep bodies and souls together much longer, unless some change takes place, is more than I can tell.

COMMITTEE MEMBER

We can't, sir, on the present wages, Mr. Thorne, and that's just why we're on strike. It's the wages, sir. That's what's the matter.

It's as if the men of Tivoli are speaking directly to Ted. It's not only his eyesight that is so extraordinary, even at his advanced age (it was said he could count the stitches on a ball in flight or number the angels on the head of a pin, the scales on a salmon from one of his Canadian rivers, the miles of the rivers themselves, and the droplets, dig, tug, and thickness of moonlight upon a forest carpet, the wattage of floodlights balanced precariously beyond the green monster), but also his hearing that allows him to hear the most minute throbbings of the heart.

"Why are you saying all these things about me?" Ted asks, suddenly overwhelmed and ashamed, like a man who has had just so much good luck thrust into his hands and then becomes forever afraid to open them for fear the luck will fall through, drain away, leach toward the lines that demark foul from fair. What you do in that case is form a fist and batter the gods into submission or take up a bat and swing with so much grace that it becomes not a matter of mechanical motion, but something far beyond anatomy, something of the natural, like the fall of rain or a slight turning of wind or a shadow.

"What about the changes in the strike zone?" I ask him.

"There's only one strike zone in baseball now," he says, now laughing, because there is no one in the stands to boo him, no die-hard blow-hard to rub the magic from the game because of envy or fear. "It's from early April to the middle of June. Usually by then the strike is settled." He roars. His own jokes please him, just as his own singles, doubles, triples, and home runs soothe him.

But the strike at the Tivoli Mills is not so easily settled. Nor anything of the past. We think of History as events that have been settled, but of course they never are. Someone is always coming out of retirement to knock over the apple cart.

SUPERINTENDENT THORNE

Gentlemen, I understand you. I don't blame you for striking. I don't see how you can help it, or how anything else can save you from ruin and starvation. The only wonder to me is that you didn't strike long ago.

ANDY

What do you mean by this, Mr. Thorne ... is it trifling with us, you are?

"You talk about waste," Ted says, "but think of the year I hit .400, the last major leaguer ever to do it. What does it mean? It means for every ten times I went to bat, there were six times I came up with nothing, came up empty. Does that mean those six times at bat were useless? I should say not," Ted says, turning his head to look out at the landscape, the broken glass, the homeless, the vultures feeding on carcasses of dead lions. We are on the way to Tivoli. Not the Garden of Tivoli, that old pleasure garden, but to the mills where the men and women and children are starving. Starving because all they want is a living wage, fair wages for fair work. Because all they want is not to be exploited, not to be trampled upon, not to be turned inside out by a system whose philosophy centers around one simple but intricate proposition: How did that money or property get into the other person's pocket in the first place? Implying, of course: Is that other person with property more deserving than I who have none?

"No," Ted continues. "Maybe when I struck out, I was learning something about the pitcher, what he threw in that particular situation. Maybe I was learning something about myself. How to wait and swing from, not the heels, but the hips. The secrets of hitting are in the hips and wrist. Hitting a baseball is one of the most difficult things a human being can do, and six out of ten, or seven out of ten, the attempt leads to failure. But wasted effort? One might as well claim that all the past is failure."

SUPERINTENDENT THORNE

This affair is altogether too serious for trifling. Striking is well enough in its way, and men ought to strike against wrong, oppression, and plunder. As I have said, I don't blame you for striking;

but I do blame you for striking against your friends instead of your enemies; against those who are helping you to feed and clothe yourselves and your children, instead of against those who are wasting your substance, and sucking out your very life's blood.

"The truth is," I tell Ted, "that the aim of society is to make you hate yourself. Once you have learned to blame yourself for every failure, once you have become riddled with self-loathing, then society takes you by the hand and says, 'Welcome, friend, now you are one of us.'"

"I never listen to sentences that begin 'the truth is,'" Ted says, as we scramble aboard the trolley car that will take us from Fenway Park, that beautiful bandbox, that icon of summer, that core of whatever is pastoral within us. I, with my arms laden with Louisville sluggers and boxes of baseballs, follow him up the narrow steps. Clang, clang, clang, go the bells of my heart.

All my youth I was Williams's greatest fan. I followed his every action, his every batting title, his every fall from grace, as if he were, as all childhood heroes must be, some extension of my secret wish. Go against the shift. If they put ten people between first and second, still knock the ball there with all your might, all your fury. Don't go the other way. God has constructed a Boudreau Shift as a test against all inferior souls. Self-destructive behavior? Perhaps. But there is no need to destroy one's self when there are so many strangers and friends out there ready, willing, and able to do it for you.

SUPERINTENDENT THORNE

Strike against the whiskey mills and you'll have no need to go any farther! The trouble lies there and not in your wages. If you were getting double what you receive, and didn't strike against the whiskey mills, you'd be no better off than you are today. Tom Maguire and Bill Maloney would only go dressing up their wives and daughters at your expense, while your own children go about in dirt and rags.

ANDY

You are insulting me and my friends and we won't stand to hear any more of your lies.

When the men at the Tivoli Mills see Ted Williams climb down from the trolley, a great cheer goes up from the crowd.

"You with us, Ted? You with us?"

The question is an insult, because the answer is obvious. Ted merely nods. The owners of the Mills peer through their top-floor windows and turn white.

"What's an eighty-year-old baseball player doing here?" one of the owners asks, taking out his pocket watch and playing loosely with the winding knob.

"What's he going to do? Spit at us?" The owners, all four of them overweight and paunch-bellied, and dressed in black suits, break out with fits of laughter. But their hands tremble as they reach for the water pitcher that stands like an island of ice atop the long mahogany table.

The wives of the striking men are not that impressed with the Splendid Splinter. After all, he is eighty years old. And he is alone. He has not brought anyone else along. Only me, the perfect factotum, the chronicler of his exploits and supplier of equipment. Perhaps I should have done more with my life, but the strikers at Tivoli and I share a terrible burden, knowing as we do that America is not exactly the land of opportunity for everyone. It is the land of illusion, the illusion of opportunity, a network of secret societies and Good Old Boy Clubs. Insider trading and all that. Good Old American Pie.

One of the women calls out to my brother-in-law Andy who is leading the strike. "I say, Andy Sullivan, we're starving, we are, and the babies are crying. You must give in."

Give in. Give in. The very words make my blood go cold. They are the words I have heard all my life. Play by the rules of the game, and don't waste time trying to fight city hall. Just what Oceanos, father of all those daughters just as fear is the father of story telling, told to Abner Doubleday when he stole fire from the gods.

"It's just a myth," Ted says, picking up his bat, feeling the exact weight of his life in his arms and wrists and hands.

"Prometheus," I say, wiping the sweat from my forehead and eyes. The August heat is stifling. The women in their rags and the children in their nakedness walk around and around the red-brick buildings, the dust rising behind them in the sunlight. A swirl of fire inside and out.

"Prometheus," Ted repeats, plucking a brand new, tightly

wound cork-cored baseball from the dozens or so I have carried, have lifted down from the fire-red clanging trolley car as if they were jewels of great price. This is the far edge of the world we have come to, where Might speaks first, and Violence is a *muta persona*. "What did he hit?"

WOMAN #2

If we keep on much longer, there'll not be half a dozen men in the room worth the powder it would take to shoot 'em. That's what we're getting from this strike! It's only an excuse for our men to loaf and to laze about and to drink, with our children crying until my heart almost breaks to hear them.

One of the strikers reaches out and grabs the woman by her bird-like wrists, shoving her with unpremeditated fury backwards. "Shut up," he shouts red-faced into the woman's red face. "Take yourself home, or I'll break every bone in your body."

ANDY

You don't know what you're talking about, woman. We can't give in! We'll just be trod under foot as if we were dogs. It's starving we've been, with the old wages: and it's for life that we're a-struggling. Just see how it is with ye all; and they living like kings with their broadcloth and silks and their satins, and their feastings and carousings. I tell you we pay for it. We pay for it all with our sweat and our very life's blood, and they grudging us every bit of crust, and turning their noses up at us if we were scum and filth instead of men and women like themselves, and just as good as they are. Give in! I'm ashamed of yez.

The Kid points to one of the third floor windows and all eyes follow. The men stop arguing. Children stop weeping. The sun sizzles in the wind like a firestorm. With his right hand he tosses the ball into the air. The bat is resting slightly off his shoulder.

WOMAN IN THE CROWD (KATE BARKER)

And I'm ashamed of you, Andy Sullivan, talkin' that sort of stuff among starving women and children instead of going to work as ye might, to feed 'em. The Corporation says, here's a dollar for you, and dollar and a half, or two dollars, according to the work;

and ye say here's nothing, according to the loafing, idling, and drinking.

TOM BARKER
    Shut up, Kate.

MRS. BARKER
    Go to work and feed your children, Tom Barker, but don't talk to me about shuttin' up! I won't go down. I never will believe in your striking.

And the Kid's bat whips through the air and everybody stops. The mouths of children hang open, eating more dust than they have eaten in their lifetimes. And the sound of the bat hitting the ball becomes a kind of timeless music, a clash of galaxies, and the ball leaves the bat with black dirt smeared over their faces as if they had crawled out of a mine somewhere, confronting the sunlight for the first time, lean ever so slightly backwards, their mouths too gaping, as the ball smashes through its target, one of the pristine panes of a third-floor window.

    "Another one, kid," he says to me. And I fetch it as fast as I can, as if my entire life had been building up to this rage, rage for the poor, the hurt the maimed, the exploited, the neglected, the hungry, the homeless, the blind, the toothless, the ulcerated, the psychotic, the neurotic, the drunk, the sober. And another perfect arc and the bat meeting the ball, freeing one sphere from gravity, and the sound of glass splintering and the owners running for cover.

    Even the women, tugging and pulling at their aprons, stop bickering and sense in the defeat of their men a slight moment of what everything could have been like if there had been only one slight splinter of justice in the universe.

    Up, up, through the third windows, and the glass splintering. The Splendid Splinter. And the children, bare-legged, bare-footed, bellies rumbling, jumping up and down, applauding. No boos here. And the thunderclouds are gathering.

    The Kid has worked himself into a fury. Every pitcher who ever struck him out, who ever tried to take a morsel of food from his mouth, every seen and unseen enemy. Karooooooooooom! Barooooooo-ooooooom! Crash! Ball after ball. And then running out of baseballs, the children start fetching him stones and pebbles and boulders, until his Louisville slugger becomes pockmarked and dented. And his hands are blistering and bleeding. He's eighty years old for god's sake.

And now the thunderstorm is letting loose. But nobody breaks rank. Nobody runs for cover. Children still fetch stones. Women still wipe tears from their eyes. Men stand as if they had been stripped to nakedness, their eyes searching every broken window for salvation.

He turns to me. All the windows on the second and third floors have been smashed. Not one pane of glass intact. Now there are only the first floor windows to take care of. Simple line drives.

The police have arrived with their Paddy Wagons, but they too, handcuffs and billy clubs at belt, are frozen in their tracks. They feel helpless against the onslaught of History. Of Myth. Hollywood and Baseball. The only true myths America has ever had.

"You can't do that, Ted, I'm telling you," the police sergeant says apologetically.

"Who says?" Karooooooooooom. A clean white stone leaves the bat and smashes yet another pane of glass. The men, women, and children have formed a circle around the batter, a living batter's circle, to protect their leader from further outrage. Would police interrupt Beethoven at his symphonies, Rembrandt at his portraits, Einstein at his equations? Something perfect needs perfect concentration.

"A hot dog," The Kid says. "I could use some hot dogs."

"How many?" I ask.

"I don't know. Two dozen. Three dozen. And some milkshakes. I'm hungry and I'm thirsty."

"Tired?"

"How can I be tired when I'm doing what I was meant to do with my life?"

"There's a lunch wagon two blocks down," Andy says. They're all ready to take my place, ready to go forth for stones or hot dogs or milkshakes or the gods and goddesses themselves.

But I assert myself and hot-foot it off in the general direction of the hot dog wagon, standing pure and white with a striped awning on a side street. The police still have made no move to destroy the magic circle.

I guess they're waiting for reinforcements.

"Blitz, Blitz, Blitz. All afternoon," the man at the bar had said.

And the old Greek couple husbanding and wiving the hot dog wagon tear, burn, sizzle, mustard, and relish. Hurry, please, hurry.

I hear shooting and yelling at the factory grounds, but I decide to stay put. It's like most things in life: it is my affair and it isn't.

"You know the largest hot dog ever made in the United States," the Greek says, turning the dogs over on the grill, "was seventeen feet long, and five inches in diameter?"

"I'd like to get my hands on that," says a woman who stands next to me. She has red hair and a tight blue skirt, a white blouse. I recognize her as one of the Tivoli women, one of them working the crowd.

"Take your foul mouth somewhere else, Hillary," the Hot Dog man says. "Can't you see we're busy?"

"I really don't have time for a lecture on the history of hot dogs," I tell him.

"We're doing the best we can, son."

"Want a good time?" Hillary asks me. She reaches for a napkin to wipe a spot from her blouse, over her left nipple.

"I had a good time once," I tell her. "Once. A long time ago."

"Once is not enough." Sounds like someone is tossing bombs by the mills.

So much waste. Oh, hurry. Hurry.

My arms are loaded with hot dogs and milkshakes. I pay with money, old and crumbled and dull. The change falls to the sidewalk, but I am too impatient to pick it up.

"Now there's a man in a hurry," Hillary says. She goes for the silver. The pennies she leaves in place.

Blitz. Blitz. Blitz.

"Harry M. Stevens discovered the hot dog, and Tad Dugan named them."

"Big deal."

The rain is coming down harder, making the hot dog buns soggy. And I'm only a block or two away from the white and awninged hot dog wagon when the rolls burst open and four or five of the hot-dogs fall to the street. I bend over to pick them up but, in doing so, I spill the chocolate milkshakes over my pants and shirt and tie and coat and shoes. This is not my day, I think, remembering the time the bat boy for the New York Yankees brought his idol Babe Ruth enough hot dogs to give the Great Bambino a stomachache heard around the world. The bat boy's name was William Bendix.

The Babe and The Kid. Is that a meeting of onomastic destiny? I step on a couple more hot dogs, then into a puddle. My shoes fill with water as do the cuffs of my pants. The napkins are so wet that they fall apart.

Frankfurters. Franks. Red Hots. Pups. Viennas. Wienies. Wieners. Here they are. In all their glory. Broken. Bruised. Dirty. Wet. Soggy. When I reach the mill, no one is there. The thunderstorm has driven everyone away.

Or the militia has.

The ground is littered with dead bodies. Andy Sullivan is face down in the mud. There's a hole through the back of his neck. His shirt is pressed to his body by the rain and blood. I put the remains of the hot dogs and chocolate shakes on the ground, and turn the body over. Poor Andy Sullivan. All he wanted was a fair shake in life. Frankfurters. Franks. Red Hots. Pups. Viennas. Wienies. Wieners. What is a baseball game without them? But Andy Sullivan has no use for them now.

I feel a hand tighten upon my shoulder. It's The Kid. I know it is. But I don't turn to look at him. I don't want him to see me crying.

"I've ruined the hot dogs," I tell him.

"It doesn't matter," he says. "They were ruined a long time ago."

"What happened?"

"The owners were pissed that I destroyed all their windows, and so they called out the National Guard to bring a halt to the strike."

"They can't do that."

"They've got the money. People with money can do anything they want."

"How come you didn't get hurt?" I turn to face him. He stands without a wound, a scratch. An eighty-year-old living wonder on the comeback trail. He has won the comeback of the year so many times.

"I kept hitting the bullets back as fast as they could shoot them. Besides they knew what would happen if they harmed me. It would spark a whole goddamn rebellion, a full-scale revolution. Besides I have a game to play tonight."

Together we walk back to the trolley.

"Why would you play tonight?"

He shakes his head.

All the while, I imagine him in another eternity, imagine him in heaven, standing in front of St. Peter's Gate. He holds a ball and a bat, and he tosses the ball into the air, and then he hammers it as hard as he can against the pearly gates. Smash. Smash. Smash. And the angels are singing "Hallelujah!" For the first time in the history of salvation, a mortal, though not a mere one, using spit and determination and all the skills at his command, fantastic hand-to-eye, eye-to-muscle coordination, is going to crash through the gates of heaven. Not even Christ is going to keep him out. Smash. And the ball sizzles into the golden lock. He's worked himself up into a fury and is smashing ball after ball into the giant gate. Gabriel and Michael and St. Peter try to interpose their nonsubstantial bodies between the line drives and the gate. Smash. Kaboooooooooooom! Hallelujah.

The milkshakes and hot dogs remain on the field of battle. "Such a waste," Ted says. "Everything is such a goddamn waste." It's a good thing he hadn't eaten them because he would have only gotten a fantastic stomachache.

"How can you play after all you've seen?" I ask him, but he doesn't answer. He senses the terrible waste inherent in words, in story-telling, in reaching toward the hearts of others. He stares straight ahead, perhaps imagining the wide assortment of pitches that are going to be tossed him in the game that lies ahead.

The trolley car rumbles and the bells ring. Terrible Teddy. Teddy Ballgame.

I tell him my fantasy about him knocking down the gates of heaven with his line drives, but even as I speak, a pained expression clouds his face.

"Why are you telling me all this?" he asks.

And the trolley car, newly painted, oblivious to the burdens it carries, turns toward Fenway Park with its thousands upon thousands of screaming and adoring fans.

"Why are you telling me all this?" he asks. "Why are you telling me all this?"

"You can't beat the spread," the man at the bar had said.

Two Men On, Bases Empty

STEFANO DONATI

I got to get this down fast, 'cause pretty soon I won't be me anymore. Not the way I look at it.

Zeke would be the first to tell you: he didn't think it'd help much when they brought in Skip Dixon to manage. A bad team's a bad team, and it sure can't be fixed by some squat little redneck no one's hardly heard of. But we took two of three in Detroit, three of four in New York, and pretty soon it was twenty-five of thirty-two overall. By mid-July we were two games in front.

And I was pitching better than I had in years. At least the stats said so, and I wasn't going to fight with them. I was still hanging sliders, and couldn't get my fastball past ninety much anymore; but in the weeks since Skip had took over, I'd brung my ERA down to 3.74.

Zeke, too: my roomie was just a platoon guy, thirty-two the same as me, and you could have a sandwich and Coke in the time he'd need to get from first base to third. But he was up near .300. Best year of his life.

Till he was traded.

"Baltimore," he said, coming back to our hotel room from the lobby and his meeting with Skip. He walked straight to the window and I was afraid he might jump. "*Baltimore. For Mellora, no less.*"

I blinked. Phil Mellora: there was even a song about him that ran through the league. Set to the tune of "That's Amore":

When the ball hits the fat
Juicy end of the bat
That's Mellora.

For Phil Mellora you give up maybe one broken-in glove; you don't give up Zeke. This was Skip Dixon's first trade as manager, and it told me he was no goddamn genius after all.

"Skip made the right move," Zeke said.

"I don't see how."

"Neither do I. But all the success this club's been having since he took over . . . it's a lot more than random variation." He winked, all ready to learn me what he meant.

So I asked. "Random variation?"

"Sure." He sat on his bed, facing me, and flipped through the book he'd been reading since Boston: *Quantum Mechanics & Probability Something or Other*. "When I go eight for sixteen with a couple of homers, I'm not really swinging the bat any better than when I go, oh, for twelve. It's just like when a coin comes up tails five times in a row. With enough flips, a streak like that is inevitable."

"You really should go back to school, Zeke, and get that degree. You're smarter than a lot of them college boys."

"School is for morons."

"But this random thing, this random . . ."

"Variation."

"Yeah. Roomie, the whole club's playing well; we ain't just some coin."

"Exactly. We're puppets." Zeke was near tears. *Baltimore*.

So I said, comforting like, "What do you mean, 'puppets'?"

He looked at me the way Dorothy used to look, sorry for me, back when I was pitching bad. "I didn't mean anything, Vernon. You're going to keep having a great year."

Not without you, I thought. But you can't say stuff like that. Not even to a guy like Zeke. In eleven years in the bigs I'd seen maybe a hundred teammates get traded or cut or sent down, and so what if losing Zeke hurt the worst. In Baltimore, he'd at least be in the lineup every day. And Phil Mellora, well, lucky him; he was gonna get to come play for a champion.

That's how you got to think in this game.

But puppets, Zeke had said. My next start I went six and a third against Oakland, five hits and three walks but only two runs, even though my slider still wasn't working too good, my curve wouldn't curve, and my fastball kept getting lined hard. But with every jam, Skip came out of the dugout and calmed me, even overruled Birdsall on what pitch I should throw, and I watched him waddle back to the dugout, soaking his spikes with tobacco juice all the way, and I thought there was just no way a guy like that could know what the hell he was talking about.

But he did; seemed to. 'Cause each time, I got the next batter to strike out. Even if I hadn't been missing ol' Zeke, I still would have thought of him. Him and his theories. Skip had something going for him, all right.

And he'd made a good trade after all. Every time I looked at a Baltimore box score, I saw Zeke's average was falling faster than a bike off a roof. Pretty soon he was back to only platooning. And my new roomie Mellora was doing okay for us. More than okay. Even if I did keep stealing his room key and short-sheeting his bed.

Baltimore's in town now for three games. Last night, after getting in, Zeke called me and Dorothy let me meet him at his hotel bar. The juke was shrieking out heavy metal, and Zeke was flinching, twitching, the way you do when the mix of a slump and bad music gets to be too much. "Too bad about your sorry-ass season," I said, as the waitress brought over two beers.

"Don't be," he said. "I've figured it out."

"What?"

"Why you're winning so much."

I preened like a rooster. "'Cause we're good. I'm good."

"You don't suddenly turn into one of the best lefties in the league, not at your age."

Fuck you, I thought. "It's happened to other guys."

"Vernon," he said, "is your arm really any livelier than it was last year? You really think Hubbin's eye is so improved he could naturally, just on his own, be up to .320-whatever? You think Falooza could really only have five errors at short?"

"My arm ain't livelier, no. But stats is stats."

"Because of Skip."

"Managers don't play the game." You're just mad, I thought. Stuck on a loser while your old buddy's going good. You're mad, okay, but don't let it make you go nuts.

"Managers don't play the game, Vernon, but they can help win it."

I shrugged in mid-swig. "Skip couldn't tell the left side of his asshole if you gave him three guesses."

"Okay, then. It's Skip and his machine."

"What kind of machine?"

Vernon gave me one of them ain't-I-Einstein looks. "Time machine."

And I gave him back one of them no-you-ain't glares.

"Think about it, Vernon," he said. "Bringing the infield in, calling for pitchouts, playing some pull hitter straightaway; deciding to bunt or steal or hit and run. How often does Skip make the right move?"

"Not all the time," I said.

"No. And that's why nobody suspects him. If he keeps it to eight smart moves out of ten, nine out of ten even, he's just some managerial genius. Say every now and then he brings Perkins in from the pen and Perkins gets hammered, or he pinch-hits Seguno and Seguno strikes out . . . if Skip just remembers to preserve a bad move like that now and then, you'll lose just enough games that nobody would ever think he's time-traveled the other losses away. But he has."

"No."

"Yes. I wish very much, Vernon, that your low ERA were honestly won. But why do you think sometimes Skip tells Birdsall to tell you what to throw? It's because he's already lived through the game, and he doesn't want to see the same big hit twice. So he calls the right pitch this time, and you get the guy out."

"That'd be cheating."

"Of course it would, Vernon." Zeke clutched his beer with both hands. This was still just his first drink of the night, and he'd never talked crazy before, but what could I say? It was playing for Baltimore, that was it. All those blowout losses had messed up his head.

"Another reason, Vernon, why you guys don't win all the time: Skip gets bored if he takes too many trips back. Imagine him trying to live through four or six ballgames every day. Plus, maybe your bodies would get tired from too much travel through time and from the gobs of innings you'd play. So he replays the game once or twice, maybe three times, and if you guys still haven't won he just shrugs and gets ready for tomorrow."

Zeke had thrown me some horseshit theories before, everything from Jesus Christ being hooked on pain to why turkeys open their mouths in a rainstorm. But this time his voice had a little panic in it, like he meant what he said.

"Okay. But tell me this, Zeke: where the hell would Skip get his hands on a time machine?"

"Must be from Feinbrusser."

"The owner? Feinbrusser knows less about baseball than you do about hunting."

"Doesn't need to know baseball. He's got the capital and the contacts; could probably buy MIT if he wanted. He pays some schmuck to build him a machine, and pays him even more to keep quiet, and all Skip has to do is learn how to use the damn thing."

This sweet season, I thought, ain't due to no MIT. It's due to my sweat and good pitches and pluck at working my way out of jams. My own way. I'm in the top twenty in ERA, first time since my rookie year, and all that crud about me being washed up, I don't hear none of it anymore.

Screw the machine.

I said, "Why was you traded, then? Tell me that."

Zeke sighed like somebody who wished he wasn't so smart. "Maybe to keep me at .300, Skip had to use his machine more times than he liked. Maybe it's only good for so many trips, and he has to budget them."

"You can still hit, Zeke. You're just in a slump now. Playing for the Orioles can do that to a guy."

"But even before . . . remember in Chicago, my pinch dinger in the twelfth? I wonder how many times poor Skip sent me up till I managed it."

"Poor Skip? He traded you."

"Because I was a strain on his machine — striking out in the clutch too damn much, the way I am now. And maybe he thought I suspected."

"You want me to tell on him?"

Zeke smiled. "No, Vernon. I like to see you doing well."

"But it ain't me; it's the machine."

"It's also you. Partly. The first run-through's no more valid than the third; there's so much luck in this game anyway. If you got to live a thousand years, and got thirty thousand starts, you'd pitch four or five no-hitters. Guaranteed. Maybe even a perfect game. Just like if we all lived a thousand times, we'd find our perfect woman — just by chance. Why should you lose out on happiness, just because the best luck you could get didn't come to you first time out?"

I remembered my beer. The look of it, the smell of it, seemed like something from some other world now. Everything did. I took a long gulp, and when I finished Zeke was still across from me. What he'd said was still burning inside my brain.

Even if it was only horseshit.

I could picture Dorothy giggling if I ever told her his theory. I'd sure leave out the part about the perfect woman. "If you ain't telling no one else," I said, "then why tell me?"

He leaned forward to say, but then the waitress came by to ask if everything was okay with our orders. What could be wrong with two beers? What could be right with all he'd said? We both nodded and she went away.

"Zeke?" I said. "Why tell me?"

"I want somebody out there to know why my season's gone so far south since the trade."

Fine way to treat an old friend, I thought, driving home — making him feel he ain't earned his success. I tugged open the sack of fan mail Totter had left on my doorstep. Autograph pleas written in little-kid scrawls; people I dropped out of high school with, asking for free tickets; photos from women, not all of them clothed.

You never get photos like this if you're just some mop-up guy. And dammit, these women weren't bad. Like Zeke had said, why should I lose out on this happiness? Tomorrow, if I got shelled, and Skip pulled me early, I could still shower and have a couple hours to go scout for them. Just outside the ballpark I could probably nab two or three before Skip even got to his machine.

And then once he did, my chippie quickies wouldn't have happened, and I could say I'd stayed true to Dorothy.

I could say it.

Zeke, I thought, your whole Einstein notion is crap. Guy gets a time machine, he's not gonna waste it on baseball. He's gonna go back and score with that Helen of Troy chick, buy stocks in computers around 1978, tell Kennedy to get out of Vietnam or Dallas. Something.

Unless he can only go back for a day. Those first few computers couldn't do much, either, and my dad always said the early TVs hurt his eyes. Well, this was the best toy Feinbrusser's flunkies could come up with: a machine that went one day back. Might be a while before they could do better.

Might be just as well if they never did. Because then if he got found out, the league office could go all the way back and undo our whole season.

Doing sprints in the outfield the next afternoon, this afternoon, I could almost feel the heat beating hard on my neck, the wind making the flags flap toward right field, the cruddy organ music playing the same tune, over and over . . . I could almost feel how pretty soon all of it might happen again, and again and again, and these moments now would never have been.

By the time I was on the mound warming up, I felt like guys in the Series must feel when they win the first three and can stand to let up. Margin of error, Zeke calls it.

By thinking about that, and not the damn game, I walked Hamish on five pitches and gave up a line single to Patokek.

Come on, I decided. A little professional pride.

Next up was Sam Cuppers. Slow-footed Sammy. Birdsall trotted out from back of the plate to tell me what I already knew: that you throw Sammy three curveballs low and away, and then watch him slam his bat on the way back to the dugout.

Except my first two curveballs were both in the dirt. And the third banged off the wall in deep center. By the time Wallace got the relay, two runs were in and Sammy, Slow-footed Sammy, had huffed and puffed his way to a triple.

Was I always this bad? I looked in at Skip on the bench for some clue. He had tobacco juice on his shirt and a finger up each nostril. No help there; the son-of-a-bitch always looks the same, whether he's checking for blondes or eating a pizza or sending some rookie back down to Buffalo.

I was always this bad. I hated Skip now, for making me ever think I wasn't. Them smug words he gave reporters after a win. "Lefty, righty, Christ almighty; any pitcher can get any guy out, long as his balls are on fire that day."

He'd be saying it again, or other dumb stuff just like it, in three hours or so. Or six, or nine. Depending on if you counted time by the way he lived it, or by what the rest of us could recall of it. But for now we were down by two, there was a runner on third, and some dick in back of the visitors' dugout was yelling how I was all out of gas. One bad game and they're on you like dogshit on a snowbank.

And Zeke was up next.

Dammit, I would not be this bad.

He stepped in, kicking up dirt, letting the bat rest for a full second on top of home plate just like always. He shook his head at me, real faint like. I didn't know what it meant and maybe I wasn't supposed to: Don't think about what he'd told me last night? Or he'd looked into things somehow and we were winning fair and square after all? Or don't go easy on him just 'cause he was one for his last fourteen, with five punch-outs?

Don't worry, I thought, I ain't gonna go easy on you. Not when you're the one making me think my sweet season ain't honest.

Birdsall called for a fastball down and in, and I almost okayed him: It was never learning how to hit fastballs down and in that had kept Zeke from making the All-Star team every year. Well, no god-damn sympathy. But then I remembered how if I'd ever learned how to throw fastballs down and in, I'd have been winning the Cy Young every year, too. Let's not go weakness against weakness.

So I shook off Birdsall's sign, and the phony genius behind it. This once, I would be smarter than Skip. Two shakes and Birdsall gave me the sign I wanted. Slider at the letters. Zeke could still kill a slider, but I could still throw one. Strength against strength. Even if this at-bat got time-traveled away.

I went into my stretch. Even before the ball left my hand, I knew the damn slider was gonna hang. As it got near the plate, Zeke's eyes went big as watermelons. He reached out and the crack of the bat rung in my ears as the ball went way up, way up, over the bleachers in left and clear to the highway. Four fucking runs. He stayed at the plate, with his arms folded, before he started his trot round the bases. Glared at me the whole way. He thought I'd served him that meatball on purpose.

"You earned it, you bastard," I yelled at him, as he crossed home plate. "You earned every foot of it."

But he wouldn't look back or listen. I couldn't blame him. Pretty soon his dinger would never have happened. He jogged into their dugout, took a dozen slaps to the hand and a dozen more pats on the ass, and I could guess how he felt, seeing his teammates full of the grins he knew the machine would wipe off.

Old Skip was on his way out to fetch me, four batters too late. He got in three good picks of his nose before he reached the first-base line.

And then I started wondering. Hoping. That this was already my second time out here today, my third or my fourth, and I'd got rocked each time. That Skip would get tired and let Zeke's homer count. That these weren't the first moments I'd ever spent on this particular hot afternoon with the sun right overhead; they were the last.

But then ten steps from the mound, Skip tapped his left arm for Torres to relieve me. Torres: this spring all the experts had said he was done, just another young hotshot who'd never reach his potential. His fastball was too wild and his curve was too hittable. Torres, who as he sprinted in from the bullpen had a nice, shiny record of three wins and one loss, ERA of 1.87. Torres, who with any other club would have a record plunging him back to the bushes. Skip took the ball from me, patted my ass, and said, "You'll get 'em next time."

'Cause he knew I would.

Baseball Memories

EDO VAN BELKOM

There was nothing wrong with Sam Goldman's memory. Not really.

He forgot the odd birthday or anniversary but no one ever thought him more than slightly absent-minded.

Sam remembered what he wanted to remember. His wife Bea could tell him a hundred times to take out the garbage but he never took notice of her, especially when he was doing something important — like watching a baseball game on television.

Sam liked baseball, not just watching it, but everything about the game. He was a fan in the truest sense of the word — he was a fanatic. He was also a student of the game and as a student he studied it with a peculiar passion that made everything else in his life sometimes seem secondary. Sam was never absent-minded when it came to baseball. Where baseball was concerned, Sam's memory was an informational steel-trap, a vault containing all sorts of trivial information. Inside Sam's head were the numbers for hitting averages, home runs, stolen bases, RBIs, and ERAs for just about anybody who was or had been anything in the sport.

Sam's head for figures made him a great conversationalist at parties; as long as the talk centered around his favorite subject he was fine. Once he got his hands on somebody who was willing to quiz him or be quizzed on baseball trivia, he never let them out of his sight. The only way to get rid of Sam at a party was to ask him how much he knew about hockey — which was nothing at all.

Some of Sam's friends began calling him "Psychlo" because he was a walking, talking encyclopedia of baseball to which they could refer to at any time to clear up some finer point of the game. His friends would be sitting in a circle on the deck in Sam's back yard talking baseball over a few beers when some statistic would come under question and the discussion's decibel level would get turned up a few notches. It was up to Sam to turn the volume back down and restore order with the right answer.

"Sammy, what did George Bell hit on the road in 1986?"

".293," Sam would say without hesitation.

"And how many homers?"

"Sixteen of his thirty-one were hit on the road."

"See I told you . . ." one friend would say to another, proved correct by the circle's supreme authority.

Sam considered himself gifted. He thought that what he had was a natural talent for numbers, something that might, at the very least, get him on the cover of a magazine or onto some local talk show.

It had begun as a hobby, something he liked to do with a cup of coffee and a book late at night after the rest of the family had gone to bed. Lately, however, it had become something more, something abnormal, if you asked Bea.

But even though Bea wasn't crazy about baseball or her husband's love affair with the game, she put up with it as most wives do with their husband's vices. She thought it was better for their marriage if Sam spent his nights at home with his nose buried in a baseball fact book instead of in a bar flirting with some woman with an "x" in her first name.

"As long as he sticks to baseball it's pretty harmless," she always said.

And then one day she began to wonder.

The two were sitting at the breakfast table one Saturday morning when Sam said something that put a doubt in her mind about her husband's mental well-being.

"Why don't we take a drive up north today and visit your cousin Ralph?" he said.

Bea was shocked. She looked at Sam for several seconds as if trying to find some visible proof that he was losing his mind.

"Ralph died last winter, don't you remember? We went to the funeral, there was six inches of snow on the ground and you bumped into my mother's car in the church parking lot. She still hasn't forgiven you for it."

Sam was shocked too. He could remember how many triples Dave Winfield hit the last three seasons but the death of his wife's cousin had somehow slipped his mind.

"Oh yeah, that's right. What the hell am I thinking about?" he said and then added after a brief silence. "I better go out and wash the car."

Things were fairly normal the next few weeks. Sam was still able to wow his friends with his lightning-fast answers and astounding memory. As long as baseball was in season Sam was one of the most popular guys around.

A co-worker of Sam's even figured out a way to make money with his head for figures. Armed with *The Sports Encyclopedia of Baseball,* they'd go out to some bar where nobody knew about Sam and bet some sucker he couldn't stump Sam with a question.

"Who led the Cleveland Indians in on-base percentage in 1952?" the sucker would ask, placing a ten-dollar bill on top of the bar.

"Larry Doby, .541, good enough to lead the American League that year," Sam would answer. After a quick check in the encyclo-pedia, the two had some pocket change for the week.

Sam was astonished at the financial rewards his talent had brought him. He had always thought himself something of an odd-ball, but if he could make some money at it — tax free to boot — then why the hell not. The prospect of riches made him study the stats even harder, always looking to increasingly older baseball publications to make sure he knew even the most trivial statistic.

"Well would you look at that," he would say as his eyes bore down on the page and his brain went through the almost com-puter-like process of defining, processing and filing another little-known fact. It took less than ten seconds for him to remember forever that a guy by the name of Noodles Hahn led the Cincinnati Reds pitching staff in 1901 with a 22-19 record. Hahn pitched 41 complete games that year and had two-hundred and thirty-nine strikeouts to lead the league in both categories. No mean feat considering the Reds finished last that season with a 52-87 record.

The information was stored in a little cubbyhole deep within Sam's brain and could be recalled anytime like a book shelved in a library picked up for the first time in fifty years. The book, a little dusty perhaps, would always tell the same story.

Bea went to see Manny Doubleday, their family physician, the morning after Sam did another all-nighter with his books.

While it was true Sam had bought her some fine things since he'd been making money in bars, Bea felt the items were bought with tainted money. The fur coat had been hanging in the hall closet since the day Sam had bought it for her, not because it was the middle of summer, but because she was ashamed of it. She never showed it to guests, even those who might have thought Bea the luckiest girl in the world — and Sam the greatest husband.

Bea sat quietly in Doctor Doubleday's private office, waiting. The office was decorated like a tiny corner of Cooperstown. On the walls hung various team photos and framed press clippings about Manny Doubleday in his heyday. On the desk were baseballs signed by Mickey Mantle and Hank Aaron, even one signed by Babe Ruth, although the authenticity of it came under suspicion since the "Bambino" signed his name in crayon.

From down the hall the doctor's melodic whistling of "Take Me Out To The Ball Game" pierced through the space made by the slightly ajar door. Moments later the door burst open and in strode the portly doctor. Doctor Doubleday had been the Goldman's family physician for what seemed like forever. He delivered both Sam and Bea into the world and always looked upon the couple's marriage as a match made by his own hands. He was also a former minor league pitcher and big baseball fan, something that had cemented a friendship between the doctor and Sam since Sam was a teenager. The doctor knew of Sam's ability to remember statistics and thought it was simply wonderful.

"What seems to be the problem, Bea?" he asked, picking up a dormant baseball from his desk and wrapping his fingers around it as if to throw a split-fingered fastball right over the plate.

"It's Sam, I think he's —"

"How is the old dodger?" the doctor interrupted as he took a batter's stance and pretended to swing through on a tape-measure home run. "You know I've never seen anyone with a memory like his. It's uncanny the way he can tell you anything you want to know at the drop of a hat."

"Yes, that's what I mean. I think he's overdoing it a bit," Bea said, sitting up on the edge of her chair anxious to hear some words of support.

"Nonsense," replied the doctor.

Bea slumped back in her chair.

"What your husband has is a gift. He has a photographic memory that he's chosen to use for recording baseball statistics. It's harmless."

"It used to be harmless. He used to do it in his spare time but now he's obsessed with it. He lets other things slide just so he can cram his head with more numbers. He's beginning to forget things."

"Bea," the doctor said, putting down his invisible bat. "Forget for a minute that I'm your doctor and consider this a discussion between two friends.

"Most people are able to use about ten percent of the brain's full capacity. Your husband has somehow been able to tap in and exceed that ten percent. Maybe he's using twelve or thirteen percent, I don't know, but it happens. He could be making millions at the black jack tables in Atlantic City but he chose to use his gift for baseball. Just be happy it's occupying him instead of something more dangerous. I'll talk to him the next time he's in. How are the kids?"

Bea was brought sharply out of her lull and answered in knee-jerk fashion. "Fine, and yours?"

She was satisfied, but marginally. It was one thing for the doctor to talk about Sam's mind in the comfort of the office, it was another thing entirely to sit at the dinner table and watch Sam try to eat his soup with a fork.

"Honey," she'd say. "Why don't you try using your spoon? You'll finish the soup before it gets cold."

"Yeah, I guess your *right-handed batters versus lefties,*" Sam would reply and then sit silently for a few moments. "Did I say that? Sorry Bea, I don't know where my head is."

Sam knew he was spending a little too much time with his baseball books. He was weary of the numbers and after a couple hours study, some nights the inside of his skull pounded incessantly and felt as if it might explode under the growing pressure. But he loved the game too much to give it up.

Anyway, the money he earned on the bar circuit was too good to give up. It was so good in fact that he could probably put the kids through college with his winnings; something he could never do just working at his regular job.

Sam worked as an airplane mechanic in the machine shop at the local airport. He was good at his job and always took the time to make sure it was done right.

One day he was drilling holes in a piece of aluminum to cover a wing section they had been working on. The work was monotonous so Sam occupied his time thinking about the previous night's study.

Pete Rose hit .273 his rookie year, .269 his second, .312 his third . . .

The drill bit broke and Sam was brought back into the machine shop. He stopped the press, replaced the bit, tightening it with the key.

Lou Gehrig hit .423 in thirteen games for New York in 1923, .500 in ten games in 1924, .312 in his first full season in 1925 . . .

Sam started the drill press and the key broke free of its chain, flew across the shop and hit another mechanic squarely on the back of the head.

He was once again brought into reality. He shut the drill off and rushed over to see if his co-worker was still alive. A crowd had gathered around the prone man and all eyes were on Sam as he neared the scene.

"What the hell were you thinking of?"

"You gotta be more careful."

"That was pretty stupid."

The other mechanics were crowing at him in unison and Sam felt like a baseball that had been used too long after its prime. His insides felt chopped up and unraveled as he looked at the man lying on the floor.

A groan escaped the downed man's lips. "What the hell was that?" he asked. The crowd around him let out a collective sigh. Sam felt better too, but just slightly. The shop foreman walked up to him, placed a comforting hand on his shoulder and told him to go home.

"Why don't you take the rest of the day off, before he gets up off the floor and these guys turn into a lynch mob."

"Sure boss. I'll go *home run leaders for the past twenty years.*"

"What?"

"Nothing, nothing. I don't know what I was thinking of."

On the way home, Sam stopped by The Last Resort, a local sports bar with big-screen TV and two-dollar draughts. He needed a drink.

After what happened at the shop, Sam thought he might be going crazy. Baseball trivia was fun but if it turned him into an accident waiting to happen, he might as well forget all about his baseball memory.

He sat on a stool in front of the bartender and eased his feet onto the brass foot-rail. Comfortable, he ordered the biggest draught they had.

As he sipped the foam off the top of the frosted glass, he overheard a conversation going on down at the other end of the bar.

"Willie Mays was the best player ever to play the game, and believe me, I know . . . I know everything there is to know about the greatest game ever invented."

Sam watched the man speak for a long time. He stared at him, trying to see right through his skull and into the folds of his brain. Sam wanted to know just how much this blow-hard really knew.

"Go ahead, ask me anything about the game of baseball, anything at all. I'll tell you the answer. Heck, I'll even put ten dollars on the bar here — if you stump me it's yours."

"How many home runs did Hank Aaron hit in his first major league season?" asked Sam as he carried his beer down the bar toward the man.

"Awe, that's easy, thirteen, Milwaukee, 1954. I want some kind of challenge."

"All right, then. In what year did Nolan Ryan pitch two no hitters and who did he pitch them against?"

"Another easy one. Nolan Ryan was pitching for the California Angels and beat Kansas City 3-0, May 15 and Detroit 6-0, July 15, 1973."

Sam was startled. No hitters were something he'd studied just the night before. This guy was talking about them like they were old news.

"Okay, now it's my turn," the man said, massaging his cheeks between his thumb and forefinger. "But first, would you care to put a little money on the table?"

"Take your best shot," Sam answered, slamming a fifty-dollar bill down on the bar.

"Well, fifty bucks," the man said impressed. "That deserves a fifty-buck question!"

The man looked into Sam's eyes. A little sweat began to bead on Sam's forehead but he was still confident the bozo had nothing on him.

"Okay, then. Who was the Toronto Blue Jays winning pitcher in their opening game 1977, and what was the score?"

Sam smiled, he knew that one. But suddenly something about the way the other man looked into his eyes made his mind draw a blank. It was as if the man had reached inside and pulled the information out of Sam's head before Sam had gotten to it. The beads of sweat on Sam's forehead grew bigger.

"I'm waiting," said the man, enjoying the tension. "Awe, c'mon, you know that one. I only asked it so you'd give me a chance to win my money back."

Sam closed his eyes and concentrated. Inside his brain, pulses of electricity scrambled through the files searching for the information, but all pulses came back with the same answer.

"I don't know," said Sam finally.

"Too bad. It was Bill Singer, April 7, 1977, 9-5 over Chicago. Fifty bucks riding on it too. Better luck next time, pal."

The man picked up the money and walked out of the bar. Sam stood in silence. He'd never missed a question like that before — never! He finished his draught in one big gulp and ordered another.

Sam said nothing about the incident to Bea over dinner. He ate in silence, helped his wife with the dishes and told her to enjoy herself bowling with the girls.

When she was safely out of the driveway, Sam dove in his books. He vowed never to be made fool of again and intensified his study. He looked up Bill Singer and put the information about him back on file in his head. He studied hundreds of pitchers and after a few hours their names became a blur.

Noodles Hahn, Cy Young, Ambrose Putnam, Three Finger Brown, Brickyard Kennedy, Kaiser Wilhelm, Smokey Joe Wood, Wild Bill Donovan, Twink Twining, Mule Watson, Homer Blankenship, Chief Youngblood, Clyde Barfoot, Buckshot May, Dazzy Vance, Garland Buckeye, Bullet Joe Bush, Boom Boom Beck, Bots Nickola,

Jumbo Jim Elliot, George Pipgrass, Schoolboy Rowe, Pretzels Puzzullo, General Crowder, Marshall Bridges, Van Lingle Mungo, Boots Poffenberger, Johnny Gee, Dizzy Dean, Prince Oana, Cookie Cuccurullo, Blackie Schwamb, Stubby Overmire, Webbo Clarke, Lynn Lovenguth, Hal Woodeshick, Whammy Douglas, Vinegar Bend Mizell, Riverboat Smith, Mudcat Grant, John Boozer, Tug McGraw, Blue Moon Odom, Rollie Fingers, Billy McCool, Woody Fryman, Catfish Hunter, Vida Blue, Goose Gossage, Rich Folkers, Gary Wheelock.

Sam slammed the book shut. His head was spinning.

He felt like he couldn't remember another thing, not even if the survival of baseball itself depended on it.

But then a strange thing happened.

Sam swore he heard a clicking sound inside his head. His brain felt as if it buzzed and whirred and was suddenly lighter.

He reopened the book and looked at a few more numbers. He took them in, closed the book once more and recited what he had learned.

"We're back in business," Sam said out loud and returned, strangely refreshed, to the world of statistical baseball.

Bea came home around eleven o'clock and found Sam in the den asleep with his face resting on a stack of books.

"Doesn't he ever get enough?" she muttered under her breath and poked a finger into his shoulder, trying to wake him.

"Huh, what . . . *Phil Niekro, Atlanta Braves 1979, 21-20 at the age of 40. Gaylord Perry, San Diego Padres 1979, also 40, 12-11 . . .*"

"Sam, wake up! Isn't it time you gave it a rest and went to bed?" Bea said, pulling on his sleeve, hoping to get him out of his chair.

"Who are you?" asked Sam, looking at Bea as if they were meeting in a long narrow alleyway somewhere late at night.

"Well, I'll say one thing for you, Sam, you still have your sense of humor. C'mon, time for bed."

"Which way is the bedroom?" Sam asked. He thought his surroundings familiar but wasn't too clear about their details.

"Into the dugout with you," Bea said, caught up in the spirit of the moment. "Eight innings is more than we can ask from a man your age!"

After the two were finally under the covers, Sam lay awake for a few minutes looking the bedroom over. The pictures on the wall looked familiar to him and he thought he might be in some of them. Comfortable and exhausted, he finally dozed off.

Sam's brain was hard at work while the rest of his body rested in sleep.

It had started with a faint click but now his brain hummed and buzzed with activity. After being bombarded with information over the past months, every available cubbyhole in Sam's brain had been filled. There wasn't room for one more ERA, one more home run, not even one more measly single.

But like an animal that has adapted to its environment over the course of generations, Sam's brain was evolving too, and decided it was time to clean house.

The torrent of information it had been receiving must be essential to the survival of the species, the brain reasoned. Why else would so many names and numbers be needed to be filed away? So the brain began a systematic search of every piece of information previously stored, from birth to present, and if it did not resemble the bits of information the brain was receiving on a daily basis, out the window it would go.

Sam's brain decided it wasn't essential that he remember how to use the blow-torch at work so the information was erased to open up new space for those supremely important numbers.

By the time Sam awoke, a billion cubbyholes had been swept clean.

Sam walked sleepily toward the kitchen where Bea already had breakfast on the table.

"What's that?" Sam asked, pointing at a yellow semi-sphere sitting on a perfect white disk.

"Are you still goofing around?" Bea answered. "Hurry up and eat your grapefruit or you'll be late for work."

Sam watched Bea closely, copying her movements exactly. He decided he liked the yellow semi-sphere called grapefruit and every bite provided a brand new taste sensation on his tongue. Sam's brain couldn't be bothered to remember what grapefruit tasted like, not even for a second.

Bea helped Sam get dressed for work because he said he couldn't remember which items on the bed were the ones called pants and which were the ones called shirts.

Bea decided she'd speak to Dr. Doubleday the moment she got Sam out of the house and insist he come by and give Sam a check up. She nearly threw Sam out the door in her rush to call the doctor.

As the door of the house closed behind him, Sam tried to remember just exactly where he worked and what it was he did for a living.

He also wanted to go back to The Last Resort and show that joker at the bar that Sam Goldman was no fool.

If only he could remember how to get there.

The Winning Spirit

ROBERT H. BEER

Mick Garcia knew that millions would have killed for his job, but right now he wasn't at all sure he wanted to keep it. A pink slip might have been a relief.

He also knew that the only way they'd get him out would be bound and gagged, and he'd kick and scream the whole way.

Such is the paradox of a major league manager.

If ever a team could turn a good man bad, it would be the 2019 Seattle Mariners. After a promising start (twelve and eight in April), his team had staggered through June, completing a dive from second place to the basement, where they were now mired. Because of a sick bullpen, he had been forced to overuse his starters early in the year, and as a result two of them were on the disabled list, and a third had just come back this week.

It sure looked like another gloomy year, Garcia reflected as he dodged a hoverboarder on the way to the tube. In the twenty years since all private motorized vehicles were banned from the greater metropolitan area, air quality had improved dramatically. Normally, Garcia applauded the decision that had removed the smog-belchers, but lately he found public transportation more and more disturbing. Too many people in Seattle knew his face from the vid and the papers, and the fans were always happy to blame the manager for the team's troubles.

Outside the tube station, he paused to pick up a newspaper. Sometimes they would leave him alone if he looked busy reading. Every morning he hoped for an empty pellet, and he never got one. Always there was a cub scout troop, or three housewives off shopping, or, worse, a couple of young pseudo-jocks just brimming with helpful suggestions on how he could turn his team into a winner, if he'd only change the batting order a bit.

He settled into the form-fitting seat and opened the paper to the comics. If only the fans had some idea of what they were asking. His lead off batter, Ramirez, was a popular topic for discussion on these morning trips. He hadn't been getting on base lately, which sort of defeated the purpose of batting first. Everyone thought that Garcia should move him down in the lineup, maybe to ninth. What the fans didn't know was that Ramirez had told Garcia that he'd be on the next plane back to the Dominican if he was moved down. Lacking another shortstop who could both catch and throw on the same play, Garcia had little choice but to leave Ramirez where he was.

"Who's running this team, anyway?" demanded a voice beside him. Startled by the parallel with his own thoughts, Garcia didn't answer right away. He peered over the top of the paper at the man next to him. *Oh, no. A pseudo-jock.*

"Who makes the decisions?" the man repeated, nodding at the newspaper. Appalled, Garcia realized that in opening the paper to the funnies, he had inadvertently left the front page of the sports page facing out. Looking at it now, he saw with horror that it featured a large picture of himself, hands in pockets, slouched on the dugout bench. The caption read: *Back to the Mud Hens?,* a reference to his previous job as manager of the minor league Toledo Mud Hens. He might as well have worn a sweater with the words "Kick Me" on it.

With a groan, he turned the paper around and pulled it higher to block the view. The front page was covered, as it had been for weeks, with commentaries on the recent successes in time travel at USC. Obviously, not much concrete was being released. The experiments were being carried out by a Doctor Karen Fitzroy, who just happened to be a good friend of Garcia and his wife. *Damn,* he thought. *She never even mentioned any of this last weekend when she was up.* Talk about secrecy. Reading the article gave Garcia a good excuse to ignore the boor next to him all the way into the city.

Assistant General Manager George Dunstan was waiting for Garcia when he got to Safeco Field. Garcia almost wanted to leave before anyone saw him — there was only one reason why Dunstan would be down here — but, with a sigh, he resigned himself to bad news.

"Hey, George," he called, waving a finger. "Looking for me?"

Dunstan brightened considerably when he saw the manager. A repository of baseball knowledge, and an excellent judge of talent, the assistant GM just couldn't relate to modern pro ball players, and seldom came down into the clubhouse area. That he was here at all meant that the news must be important.

"The Phillies signed MacIvor," he said without preamble after they closed the door to Garcia's office.

Garcia sank into his ancient swivel chair and let out a sigh. His pulse was racing, and he saw a couple of baseball-sized black spots drift across his vision. *Is this what a heart attack feels like?* he wondered idly, more curious than anything.

Dunstan was not curious. He was alarmed.

"Mick!" Dunstan said quickly. "Are you okay? You look kind of peaked. You said your blood pressure was okay at your spring physical."

Garcia waved a hand in a back and forth motion. "It was, and it is. Just felt a bit woozy for a second. I'm fine, really." He forced a thin grin to prove it. "The Phillies, you said?" he asked, to change the subject.

Dunstan gave him a wary look, but obviously didn't want to make an issue of it. "Yeah, Philadelphia. At least he won't be in the American League, so he can't rub our noses in it so bad."

He sounded bitter, Garcia thought. "You can't really blame the guy, George," he told him. "He only wants to get what other players of his caliber are getting. And he wants a chance at a pennant, which it doesn't look like he'd get here." He stared at the faded green blotter in front of him.

"I really thought this year might be different," he said quietly.

The assistant GM nodded sadly. "We started well this year, even with MacIvor holding out. With him and even one more really good player, we'd have a shot at the division. One good left-handed bat could make all the difference."

All Garcia could do was nod.

That night Karen Fitzroy called.

Garcia's wife, Kitty, was in the shower when she called, so Garcia answered the phone. She had called to thank them for their hospitality the previous weekend. Karen was an old friend of both

Garcias from college. Mick Garcia had even dated her a couple of times casually, before she had introduced him to Kitty. Somehow Karen had known that he and Kitty were a much better match, but the three had remained close friends.

She also happened to be the world's biggest Mariners' fan.

"So why didn't you tell us about this time travel business?" he demanded once the pleasantries had been exchanged.

The phone was silent for a moment. Then Karen laughed. "But I did!" she insisted. "I told you all about my work with the tachyon field continuum we've established."

Garcia stared at the receiver for a moment, banged it once on the desk, then put it back to his ear. "That's what you were talking about? Time travel?"

"Of course! What did you think I was talking about?"

Garcia looked around the bedroom uncomfortably. Why didn't Kitty get out of the shower and take over this conversation while he still had a bit of self respect? "Uh, I really didn't know. I took Phys Ed, you remember. Physics wasn't required reading."

"It doesn't matter," Karen replied, graciously letting him off the hook. "I spend all my time talking to other temporal physicists, and unfortunately it's sometimes hard to talk normally. I'm sorry if I overdid it with you guys."

"Oh, you didn't," Garcia replied. From the bathroom, his wife called, asking who was on the phone. He covered the mouthpiece and told her it was Karen. "I've been pretty preoccupied lately," he continued.

"I've heard. I still get *Baseball News,* you know. You're not responsible for the mistakes of your predecessors, Mick, so don't be too hard on yourself. If your scouts and the previous administration had made better draft choices, you'd have more to work with. You're the best manager the Mariners have had in twenty years, so don't let it get you down."

"Next subject, please. Can you actually go back in time?"

"It seems so," she replied. He thought he heard some pride in his friend's voice. *Good for you, Karen. You've worked hard.* "Even forward, in theory, but we haven't worked that out, yet. We can go back about twenty years, right now, before the uncertainty principle comes into play. There have been seven trips back so far, all successful within limits."

"Meaning . . . ?"

"Meaning, everyone survived with no ill effects. They didn't always reach the time that we were trying for, but it's usually close."

"That's tremendous! Have you —?"

"— Gone myself? No, not yet. But I have a trip myself scheduled in about three weeks."

Garcia shook his head. "That's incredible. Where, uh, *when* are you going?"

She chuckled at his confusion. "It really doesn't matter. I need to decide in a week or so."

Kitty came into the room, looking like a ball of candy floss in a pink housecoat, with a pink towel wrapped around her hair. She kissed him on the head and slipped the phone from his hand.

"My turn," she said.

Two days later — two losses later — Garcia was packing up for a road trip to Anaheim, Oakland, and San Jose. Truth be told, he was looking forward to a break from the incessant media crush of Seattle. George Dunstan had dropped by to tell him about the commissioner's decision on the MacIvor free agent signing. The Mariners, under the current rules, were entitled to one first round draft choice as compensation from the Phillies. The Mariners also got to choose the year, within a ten year span. That was to allow for variations in the talent available from year to year in the draft.

One of the things Dunstan wanted to talk with Garcia about was what year to pick for their draft choice, since they only had a week to notify the commissioner's office of their decision. The idea burned at Garcia, since he was sure to be long fired by the time this draft choice ever made it to the big club, if he ever did. After Dunstan left, Garcia began loading his uniforms into the ancient army duffle bag he used on these road trips.

Suddenly the bag slipped to the concrete floor, forgotten. A small smile appeared on Garcia's lips.

"*Son of a bitch,*" he whispered in the silent office. "*Son of a bitch!*"

He reached for the phone. "Get me Dunstan!"

The first night against the Angels, Garcia's pitcher just didn't have it. Garcia had been around baseball long enough to know that some nights a pitcher wouldn't have his good stuff — or any stuff at all — and he got the poor rookie out before the game was totally out of reach. The offence came back with three runs in the sixth and one in the seventh to tie the game at five, though, and Garcia thought that, just perhaps, they might win one.

Fat chance. In the bottom of the eighth the Mariners' reliever, Steve Jones, gave up a chopper off the plate to the leadoff hitter. He then promptly walked the next man, and followed that up by hitting the third batter between the shoulder blades to load the bases. But Jones struck out the next man, and Garcia started to breathe again. A double play ball could get them out of the inning, with still a chance to win it in the ninth.

Jones ran the count to three and one, and everyone in the park knew the next pitch would be a fastball. So did the batter, and he turned on it, ripping a grounder to first which the Mariners' first baseman bobbled once before getting a handle on it. The bobble had removed the chance of a double play, so the only play was to home for the force out, but Morrison at first seemed to have a sudden bout of confusion. He hesitated a moment, then took two steps and touched first base before throwing home. With the force play at home removed, the runner was safe in a slide.

The Mariners got the next out, but went down one, two, three in the ninth for the loss. Garcia barred reporters from the clubhouse after the game, and slipped out the back door and back to the hotel. The Mariners, he thought, were well on their way to setting a record for one-run losses.

The next day he met Karen Fitzroy for lunch.

"You want me to *what*?" she demanded over dessert. "Mick, do you have any idea how dangerous that could be?"

"No, I don't. You're the expert, and if you say it's impossible, then that's good enough for me, but I had to ask."

Fitzroy shook her head. "I didn't say it was impossible. I have no idea if it could be done. Some people think that there could be a lot of changes as a result of mucking around with the past. I don't know if that's true; personally, I have an idea that we're not really going back in time, that perhaps we're jumping to other time lines, and if that's the case, nothing I did would have *any* effect on *our* present.

We're going to have to test it sometime soon. But we just don't know."

"Yeah, I can see that. Just leave my grandfather alone." Garcia looked earnestly at his friend. "But this is such an opportunity. The commissioner's office has agreed that it's our right."

"Meaning there was a loophole?"

Garcia smiled thinly. "You bet, but they'll plug it by week's end, I'm sure. Too late to stop us, though. We're entitled to a draft pick as compensation for the Phillies signing MacIvor, and the wording doesn't specify that the time limit is only in the future. It can be read as meaning any year within ten years of this one, *in either direction*. It never came up before. I just want their first round draft pick from *seven years ago*. Guy named Jackson."

"Mick, Lord knows I'm the biggest Seattle fan in the world — I think it has something to do with rooting for the underdog — and I want to see you succeed, but this could be dangerous. There's no way to totally predict the outcome."

"So, it should be an interesting experiment, right?" He leaned forward so his face was only six inches from that of his friend. "Karen, this team is going nowhere. I'm going to be fired at the end of the season, if I last that long. There's nothing I can do about it — you can't fire the whole team. This is my last chance to make this team a winner."

He sat back and waited for her objections to resume. When she said nothing, Garcia continued softly. "I really thought last year we had a chance. But, with a few key injuries, a damn feud between our catcher and half the pitching staff, and a few tough losses, things fell apart. MacIvor was so disgusted that he wouldn't even talk contract with us, he just went free agent, and he was the franchise. But could you blame him . . ."

He couldn't go on. It just hurt too damn much. He'd rather win than almost anything in the world, but he wouldn't badger his friend any more. If she couldn't help, so be it.

Garcia's reverie was interrupted by the touch of a hand on his forearm. "If I tried this, how would I convince the Mariner's draft people that this is legitimate?" Fitzroy asked. "You weren't even the manager then."

"We still have the same commissioner," he replied. He reached into his jacket pocket. "I have a letter . . ."

Karen Fitzroy had called the night before, chatted with Kitty for a while, then asked to speak to Mick. When he picked up the phone, she had said only, "I go tomorrow. I'm going to try it." Then she had hung up.

Garcia got almost no sleep during the night. Several times he thought of calling Fitzroy and telling her to forget the whole thing. He wasn't sure exactly what the dangers were, but if they worried Karen, then he should be worried as well. He had a vague idea that changing something in the past might have more severe consequences in the present than he realized. Did he have the right to risk other people's lives just to turn a baseball team into a contender? And what guarantee did he have that one draft choice could do that? Sure, he had often felt that they were just one good player away, and Terry Jackson, the man he wanted, was a star with the Phillies now, so it *should* just be a simple switch. Jackson would be playing in Seattle instead of Philadelphia.

What could be so dangerous about that?

The team had gone two-and-eight on the California trip, and the bats were so anemic that he had the team in for extra batting practice this morning. He had a difficult time concentrating on the workout, though, between the lack of sleep and his continuing worries about Fitzroy's "trip". Why hadn't he asked what time she was going to make the attempt?

All through the morning session, his eyes kept straying up to the right field deck of Safeco Field, up to where the Mariners' pennants should be hanging, if there had been any. Tomorrow there might be banners hanging there, who knew?

He called the practice off early, much to the relief of his players, and retired to his office. Catching himself pacing and looking at the clock five times a minute, Garcia shook his head and grinned. *Got to relax*, he thought. *Not a damn thing I can do about it now.* He settled into his well-worn leather chair and picked up some scouting reports he had been putting off. He was exhausted. His eyes kept wanting to close of their own accord.

With a start, Garcia realized that he had dozed off. He looked up bleari-ly and saw a shadow outside the glass window of his door. Something felt vaguely wrong, but he couldn't pinpoint it. Someone must have knocked on the door — that must be what had wakened him.

"Come," he called.

His secretary, Bonnie, bustled in, all energy. "I see you woke up, sleepyhead. You really should go to bed earlier, if you're going to fall asleep during the day." She smiled fondly. "Maybe that's your secret. There isn't a manager in the league who wouldn't like to know how you pulled this team up from nowhere. Anyways, sleepyhead, here's your paper. Remember, you have a news conference in forty-five minutes, so at least comb your hair."

She left, but the feeling of out-of-sync didn't. *I shouldn't sleep in the middle of the day*, he mused, opening the paper to the sports sec-tion, where he always started. The opening article was on a pre-Olympic swim meet that the city was hosting. Mentally promising to read it later, he flipped the page to the baseball coverage. "Mariners Presented With World Series Rings" the headline proclaimed, over a picture of MacIvor and Jackson mugging for the camera.

Who couldn't win with those two batting third and fourth? he thought with a smile. Buck Slinghammer was one lucky guy to be managing *that* team, Garcia thought, but more power to him. He shook his head. Since when did I become a Seattle fan?

Oh well, maybe there was still a chance that Detroit would give him an opportunity some day. For now, though, the Toledo media was waiting for him, wanting to know how he got the team to per-form night after night.

They never understood what he told them. Or maybe it just didn't make good enough copy. All you had to do to build a winner was to dedicate yourself. Nothing else mattered. It was just that simple.

Drayton's Ace

L. K. ROGERS

I love the game, I admit it. I'm a true-blue fan. Makes no difference to me how many strikes these people have. Players, umpires, I don't care. It's not them that really matters, anyhow — it's the game.

Don't get me wrong. I'll hang out at the ballpark and try for a famous autograph same as the next guy. But it's the game that really counts, seeing it all happen right there in front of you. When you see that great circus catch in left field or a pick-off play at first base or a tape measure job over the center field wall, well, it doesn't matter who did it, just that you were there to see it. Those kind of thrills are what you pay your money for.

But I don't get out to see very many games. I'm on the road a lot, traveling through these one-horse places with names like Redtop and Clancy and Benevolence and Indian Springs. And most of them are too small even to field a minor league team. I'm a salesman — restaurant equipment — and this just comes with the territory, don't you know.

Still, now and again I do get to enjoy some good baseball talk, whenever I happen to stop at a bar or diner or some such place where the locals come in to chew the fat about hitters and pitchers.

A few weeks back, though, I guess I got more than I bargained for in that respect. It really did turn into an adventure, to say the least, and I hope I don't ever get caught up in anything like it again.

I was coming up on this little community called Drayton, where I'd never bothered to stop before, because there wasn't a single restaurant or watering hole anywhere around. But sometimes you like to look in on these places, even so. The status can change overnight. It's happened. And a good salesman doesn't let the competition get there first. So I got a notion that day that I might just drive through Drayton, instead of bypassing it, and see what was new, if anything. You never know.

Well, I don't know if it was just luck or my salesman's gut instinct or what, but there in the middle of that block-long burg was a spiffy new sports bar called Game Time, open for business and just waiting to be added to my customer list.

I pulled up in front of the place and got out. It was about six o'clock in the evening. There were a couple of other cars parked nearby.

I went in and looked around. There weren't too many customers yet. The bartender came over to greet me. "Yessir, what can I get you?" he said.

I handed him one of my cards. "Wakely's the name, Dale Wakely," I told him. "I was just passing through and noticed your place here — I do a lot of business with bars. Is the boss around?"

He told me no, but if I wanted to stay awhile, he'd probably be in within the hour. I decided to take him up on the suggestion.

I ordered a beer and settled down to wait.

About five minutes later, an old man, lean and leathery and nearly toothless, came in and sat down next to me. He was wearing overalls and I guessed he was a farmer, but I didn't ask. Right away, he began to jaw about the Braves, so I knew he was a baseball fan.

"You get out to see the games much?" I asked him.

"Naw," he said. "Hardly ever."

"Me neither," I said. "Seems like I'm on the road all the time."

He ordered a beer and had a few laughs with the bartender. Then he turned back to me. "I'll tell you what, though. If I want to see some real big-league pitching, all I have to do is look right out my front window."

I kind of smiled. "Oh yeah?" I thought maybe he was gonna tell me he had one of those trick cornfields where the old-time players come out from between the stalks to play baseball just for him. But he didn't.

He lowered his voice like he was telling me some kind of secret. "There's this kid who can whistle a baseball to the plate like nothing you've ever seen," he said. "I watch him throw all the time, and I'll bet you anything he's faster than anybody that's ever pitched in the majors."

"That so?" I took a sip of my beer.

"Damn right. Ball moves so fast when he throws it you don't see it till it's in the mitt."

"What's his name?" I asked, out of curiosity.

He squinted his eyes. "Don't know exactly. These folks moved here in the fall, just a man and a boy. Moved into the old Cullen place. They don't come into town much. Nobody's really gotten to know them." Then he chuckled. "That kid, though, well, I've sure got a name picked out for him."

"Oh yeah?"

"Drayton's Ace — that's what I'm calling him. Drayton's Ace, yes sir. Someday, when he gets to the big leagues, I guess we'll all find out what his real name is, but I'm still gonna call him Drayton's Ace."

There's nothing like the boast of ownership to tell you how deep the feeling runs, and this old geezer had already put a hometown claim on the kid pitcher, so I knew he was dead earnest about him.

I thought I might as well get all the information I could. "What is he, then, a high schooler? Does he play American Legion ball or what?" I asked.

The old man rubbed the stubble on his chin. "Tell you the truth, he don't seem to go to school." Then he broke off a high-pitched laugh. "Course, that ain't nothing unusual — lots of kids around here don't go to school. They just quit when they get old enough to go to work somewhere."

I shrugged. "Well, he must play on some kind of a team."

He took a swallow of his beer. "Not necessarily," he said. "The way I got it figured, his daddy moved him here to Drayton to keep him and his pitching arm under wraps for awhile — till he's ready for one of them try-out camps, you know."

I nodded. "Makes sense, I guess."

"And who can blame the man? I mean, here's his kid with a talent that's gonna be worth millions pretty soon. Why let some two-bit high school coach burn him out? Why run the risk of getting his arm hurt in games that don't really matter?"

I couldn't argue with the logic of his explanation. "How old do you reckon the boy is?" I asked him then.

He mulled it over. "Oh, sixteen, seventeen, eighteen — somewhere along there. It's hard to tell, looking at him from a distance."

"And where'd you say you watch him throw?" I asked. I didn't remember passing any baseball fields on my way in.

"There's an old field on the other side of the road that runs past my place," he explained. "Nobody's played ball on it in years. Backstop's nearly rusted through. They're out there just about every night, the old man, with catcher's gear on, and the kid, throwing to him from the mound."

I remembered then what he'd said about watching from his front window, and I wondered why, if the young pitcher was as good as he claimed, he hadn't gone across the road to get a better look. "If it was me," I said, "I think I would've tried to get a little closer to the action."

"Oh, I did try," he said, with a look of regret. "I did try that once. I went out and stood at the edge of the field, not interfering or anything, just stood there with my hands in my pockets."

"What happened?"

"They left," he said. "Father stood up and motioned for the boy to stop and they just walked away."

"Not too friendly, huh," I remarked.

"Well, I guess it's just part of the caution they're taking," he said, rationalizing. "I reckon if I was sitting on a gold mine like that, I wouldn't want anybody snooping around either."

I finished my beer and glanced around. I thought I'd better visit the men's room before I took to the road again. It looked like the owner wasn't going to show. I figured I could stop in another time and talk business with him. "I'd sure like to see that kid throw one of these days," I said to the farmer.

"You got time to stop by my place?" he asked hopefully. "It ain't dark yet. I know they'll still be out there."

I looked at the clock on the wall. I was already behind schedule. "I don't think so this time," I said. "I've got to be in Carsonville by morning."

He took a napkin from the holder and pulled out a pencil. "Well, I'll write down the directions anyway. If you can find the road, you'll be able to see the field clear enough. They might just be out there the next time you pass through. Then you can go home and tell everybody you saw Drayton's Ace."

He drew everything out for me and labeled it all, so I'd know exactly how to find the field. "But remember," he cautioned, "you'll have to do your watching on the sly. You don't want to scare them off."

I put the napkin in my pocket and thanked him, but by the time

I got to Carsonville I'd practically forgot all about this kid with the golden pitching arm.

On the return trip, though, a couple of days later, as I was coming up on Drayton from the opposite direction, I remembered what the farmer had told me and pulled out the map he'd given me.

It seemed like it would be easy enough to find the place. It was around six o'clock, same as it was when I came through the other time. I figured maybe the kid and his old man would be out there practicing.

I made a few turns and soon found myself on a dirt road. The weather had been dry and the car was really tossing up the dust. I was afraid there wouldn't be any way of sneaking up on Drayton's Ace under these conditions. They'd no doubt see the car coming.

Then I spotted the ball field up ahead, over on the right. It wasn't next to the road but was set off a little way. And there was a pair of people out there too. I realized if I stopped the car right then and there I would be a pretty good distance from the field, but I figured I could thread my way through the bushes that lined the road and get close enough to see what I wanted to see.

I pulled over and cut the engine and got out. I looked down the road and saw what must have been the farmer's house, across on the left. I didn't see any car or truck around, so I guessed he wasn't home.

I made my way into the bushes, hoping I wouldn't pick up redbugs. I inched along, getting closer and closer to the field, trying not to make any noise.

I stopped finally and pulled the bushes back so I could have a look. And there he was, Drayton's Ace, the boy with the golden arm.

He was a well-built kid, six-three, six-four, maybe. A good size for a pitcher. I couldn't see his face yet — he was a righty, and I was on the first base side of him, so it was mostly his back I was seeing.

I watched him hurl a couple of fastballs.

Shoot! He wasn't that good. Maybe a little late movement on the ball but I'd seen lots of pitchers who could throw like that. Better than that.

Then his old man stood up from the crouch and pushed back the catcher's mask and said to him, "All right, that's enough warm-up — let's do it for real."

So he'd just been warming up — well!

The boy adjusted his cap, paused while his dad got back down, then went into a full wind-up. Bam! The ball hit the mitt all of a sudden.

I blinked, surprised, and stuck my face a little farther through the bushes. Had I missed it? It didn't seem like the ball could have left his hand that fast.

The kid wound up and fired off another pitch. I still couldn't see it. All I could pick up was the whomp! and then that little rise of dust when it hit the pocket of the mitt.

It was incredible. Pitch after pitch, inside, outside, up high and down low, off the plate, on the corners, anywhere and everywhere. The old man would just put the mitt down and the boy would hit it every time. Fantastic control. And at that blinding speed, too — impossible!

I took out my handkerchief and mopped my face. That old farmer was right. This kid was something special. No wonder his father was guarding him like a hawk. He'd be worth his weight in gold, this kid, with an arm like that.

And not only was he going to make a ton of money, he was probably going to rewrite the record books as well. I could already see it in my mind. He'd be a perpetual Cy Young winner. He'd end up with all the superlatives you could name — most strike-outs, lowest ERA's, fewest base-on-balls, everything. He'd be an overnight sensation, a superstar. He'd be every Little Leaguer's idol. His autograph on a baseball would fetch thousands. He'd be everybody's darling, everybody's dream come true. Even people who didn't follow sports would be smitten by him. He was that phenomenal. If he'd been a writer instead of a pitcher, his name would've been Shakespeare; if music was his thing, you'd have called him Mozart.

And there I was getting a sneak preview of this prodigy at work, probably the greatest pitcher to come along in the history of the game. It was awesome. It gave me goosebumps. It made my legs go weak.

But the excitement of watching him pitch caused me to forget where I was, caused me to forget that I was in hiding, and I made a kind of an awkward, sideways step in the midst of the thicket. And something suddenly ran across my foot and kept right on going, into the field. It was a small animal of some kind, but I couldn't make out what it was. I must have set my foot down almost on top of the thing.

But the kid spotted the animal — it turned out to be a young rabbit — just as it darted across in front of him, and he hurled the baseball at it, hard. Well, it must have hit in a vital spot because the rabbit toppled right over and didn't move once, didn't make any kind of sound.

The kid threw down his glove and ran over to the lump of fur and picked it up. "Hey, look at this!" he shouted, laughing, holding up his prize.

His father seemed a little bit annoyed at the interruption. "Yeah, all right. So you got him — good shot. Now put him down and let's get back to business."

But the boy was just so tickled he'd hit that rabbit he could hardly stand it. He just kept holding it out there, turning it one way and another, admiring it.

Meanwhile, the old man was losing patience. He stood up, pushing back the catcher's cage on top of his head. "Come on, now," he grumbled. "We don't have time for this kind of stuff."

Frankly, I was on the kid's side. All work and no play, that's not my idea of any kind of life.

"Just give me a minute," the boy begged.

His old man turned away and stared off in the distance. "This what you gonna do when you get up to the majors?" he asked. "Just let any little thing break your concentration?"

"I can handle it — you know I can," the boy said. "Just one minute — that's all I'm asking for."

I was thinking to myself, Go on, Pop, give the kid a break. He's going to be a multimillionaire pretty soon and then you can retire and go live on Easy Street.

It was almost like the guy heard what I was thinking. He turned back to the boy and said, "Okay, do it — but you make it quick."

He hadn't even got all the words out before the kid had the rabbit up to his mouth and was tearing through the fur with his teeth, ripping it away in some kind of frenzy. I couldn't believe my eyes. He was behaving like an animal himself. He held the carcass up over his head and squeezed it like an orange, letting the fresh blood drip down his throat, making a grisly, gurgling sound as he swallowed it.

He drained it dry like that. There wasn't an ounce of blood left in the poor animal. When he was through, he wiped his mouth off on the tail of his shirt and grinned. I could see the actual bloodstains on his teeth. It was awful. I knew what he was then. Drayton's Ace wasn't just the world's greatest pitcher.

I stood there like I'd put down roots. I was too numb to move. Sweat was popping out all over my face. I thought I was going to heave.

They got back to throwing then, with the kid pitching like an all-fired machine. But I didn't watch too much more of it. I shut my eyes after awhile and tried to forget what was going on.

They threw till it was too dark to see the baseball, and then they packed up and left, walking off toward a little strip of woods at the other end of the field.

I left the bushes and headed for the car. But after I was inside, I realized my hands weren't steady enough to drive. I just couldn't grip the wheel good enough.

I lay down across the seat and cried. It was the most agonizing feeling in the world, knowing what I knew, and knowing there wasn't a thing I could do about it.

I could see what his future was going to be like, this gifted kid. Sure enough he'd be the big sports hero, but when he wasn't on the mound pitching, when he wasn't at the ballpark, when he wasn't being interviewed on talk shows or signing autographs, he'd be out there somewhere doing this other thing, indulging this other passion. Pretty soon he'd get a reputation for fighting and carousing. There'd be a little bloodshed here and there, naturally. But people would shrug it off. They'd say, Oh, well, he's just like all them other high-paid, high-profile athletes — what do you expect? And then sooner or later he'd bloody up some nice young woman, leave bad marks on her body — maybe even kill her — but nothing would ever come of it, because he's the big sports hero, you see, and we can always sacrifice a few virgins for a man like that, right? So he's got this taste for blood — so what? The world forgives that sort of thing if you're big enough to be idolized. It's a terrible truth, but it's a truth all the same.

I decided not to drive through that hayseed town anymore or stop in at the sports bar again. I didn't want to run into the old farmer and have to tell him what I'd seen.

As for Drayton's Ace, I hoped I'd never see him throw another baseball again as long as I lived, but I knew I was probably destined to. It would be crazy to think I wasn't.

After all, how you gonna tell your grandchildren you don't want to go out with them to see a ball game? Or your boss, or your brother, or your best friend? And especially when it's going to be the game's most celebrated pitcher on the hill. You going to tell them the truth? You going to tell them what you know about this guy, what you've seen with your own eyes? You going to tell them what Drayton's Ace really is? You going to spoil that dream for them?

You know you won't.

Maxie Silas

AUGUSTINE FUNNELL

I got the card in a trade one winter with some kid who'd inherited his older brother's collection, and the first time I looked at it I knew something was wrong. For one thing, I couldn't remember anybody in the game named Maxie Silas. Not for my Pirates, and certainly not as recently as the 1971 issue. I had a complete set of that year, so I flipped the card over to check on the number, and that was when I *really* knew something was wrong. Card #753. Seven five three. Impossible, because there were only 752 cards issued that year. But there he was, Maxie Silas, in the familiar black and gold trim, grinning at the photographer like he'd just won a hundred bucks on Stargell's last at bat.

I ended up with a couple hundred cards from the late sixties and early seventies, and gave up about twice that from the early and mid-eighties. The kid wasn't interested in 1970 players, couldn't have cared less about Roberto Clemente or Manny Sanguillen or José Pagan. Danny Murtaugh was just another name he couldn't pronounce. He wanted Dave Parker and Dwight Gooden and Gary Carter and Pete Rose. He didn't believe me when I told him Rose hit .273 for the Reds in 1963. Nineteen sixty-three, for Chrissakes! Wasn't that before the Flood?

At home I emptied the brown paper bag in which the kid had stacked the cards, and rechecked those I needed to fill gaps in my collection. There were only a couple dozen, but the others would be worthwhile as replacements for cards in poor condition, or traders.

I'd never really planned on growing up.

Maxie Silas was the only oddball card in the lot. On the front he gripped a bat poised over his left shoulder, his toothy smile as exuberant as all the bubbles in a seltzer tablet. *Pirates* the card read in yellow caps above him; below, in lowercase orange letters, *maxie silas.* An orange dot to separate name and position, and the position, in blue, lb-2b. What? According to the card, Silas was a southpaw. Second base? Notwithstanding Mike Squires, there aren't a whole lot of southpaws playing infield positions other than first.

The back listed his Major League Batting Record for one year, 1970. He appeared in 111 games, had 333 at bats, and hit .222. Wonderful. Eleven homers. Forty-four RBI's. If nothing else, Silas was neat about his numbers. I wished they'd listed errors.

I checked his personal information, and learned he was five feet eight, weighed 165, and was born June 16th, 1952 (how could I *not* have known about somebody so young playing for the Bucs!?), and made his home in Gananoque, Ontario. A *Canadian* besides? This was getting weirder all the time. The only normal thing about him? With both the stick and the leather, he was a lefty.

Briefly, I considered the possibility the card was from a Canadian set. Those were sometimes issued with different numbers and fewer cards in the set, but in both countries the 1971 issue had identical card numbers and 752 cards. Canadian cards had information printed in both French and English, and they were printed in Canada. This was in English only, and printed in the States. It said so. *PRINTED IN U.S.A.* And most of their cards were yellow-backed for 1971. This was green, like all the American ones. I also considered it might be a novelty item, produced by one of the companies specializing in such things, but it had the Topps copyright.

What convinced me the card was real was that it looked and *felt* real, even with Silas's longish blond hair protruding from under his cap. It fit with my other 1971-issue Pirate cards just as if it belonged. I think the blurb had a lot to do with my final acceptance: *Maxie never played in the minor leagues. A lifelong Bucs fan, he says his biggest thrill was starting his first game in a Pirate uniform.* It sent shivers up my spine, and jealousy through my heart. It was exactly the way, I'd feel if I'd ever gotten that chance. Younger, I'd lived and dreamed baseball, lusting after that one break that would open the doors. The dream faded as I grew older, its disintegration aided by four piddly little facts: I couldn't run, hit, field, or throw. The hand of reality closed its grim fingers around me, and I gave up.

I never gave up the game, though. The energy and interest expended in trying to play was channeled into enjoyment, and a large part of that enjoyment came from collecting baseball cards. How many times had I riffling through them brought back fragments of the dream, unexpected, to fill that void caused by my inability to play? How many times had I wanted to see *my* name and picture on one of those silly little cards?

So the card was genuine; I didn't doubt it for a minute. It was an oddity, but genuine. So who in the name of Stargell was Maxie Silas? I checked my record and stat books, but found no mention of him anywhere. And yet the card proved he existed, and that he'd played, if only for a year. The more I thought about it, the more puzzled I was, until finally I had no option: I'd have to call my walking, talking, baseball information encyclopedia, Donnie MacBeth, who collected cards as avidly as I, who had a larger collection, and whose knowledge of the sport — especially the cards — seemed inexhaustible.

"Have you ever heard of Maxie Silas?"

"Certainly no threat to the memory of Gabby Hartnett," he told me, which meant no. "Who'd he play for?" From him to me, the question was like the Pope clarifying a tricky theological point with the newly professed Sister Mary Ferocious.

I hesitated. Swallowed. He was going to laugh at me a whole lot when I told him. But dammit, I had the card! "The 1970 Pirates," I said miserably.

He laughed at me a whole lot. I let it slide, and when he made some smart remark I laughed with him, and dropped the subject. We set a date to get together and check out new acquisitions, then he ended the conversation with a trivia question.

"Quick, who was the thirty-ninth player to hit a homer in his first big-league at bat?"

"Gene Lamont." He always gave me easy ones so I'd be sure to get them.

But the real question was: Who was Maxie Silas?

Summer was on its way; I knew, because the Pirates had opened training camp in Bradenton. I got a copy of their roster from *The Sporting News* and checked to see which rookie names rang bells from AAA or AA ball of the year before, and how many sophomore players were on hand. But it wasn't until I realized I'd spent a long time looking for "Silas" that I recalled the card safe in its polyethylene pocket with the other 1971 issue Pirates. All the curiosity that had somehow dribbled away over the past couple months of snow and ice came surging back: Who the hell was Maxie Silas?

I took the card out and studied it one night after checking the box score from the Bucs' first Grapefruit League game, and the more I looked at it the more annoyed I became, until it finally dawned on me that I couldn't sit around forever, wondering about this southpaw Canuck I'd never heard of. The card proved he existed; I was going to find him.

Ontario was only two or three hours from my home in upstate New York. But I'd never heard of Gananoque, so I found a map of the province and located the town on the St. Lawrence River, about halfway between Toronto and Montreal, both cities with big-league teams. It might not be such a bad idea after all. I had a couple weeks holidays coming, so I arranged to take one of them the week the season opened; maybe I'd be able to catch a game or two in Canada.

Donnie and his wife invited me to supper a couple nights before I left, and afterward, while Donnie and I settled down to watch a highlight film of the previous year's Series, I told him what I planned to do. He still hadn't seen the card — for some reason I'd neglected to show it to him when we got together to check out new acquisitions, and by that time he'd forgotten about it — and he was understandably puzzled by my obsession with what seemed, to him, a novelty card. He debated the merits of coming with me to catch a game at Exhibition Stadium in Toronto or the Big "O" in Montreal, but his wife put the kibosh on that by reminding him he was still six months from vacation, and he'd used up all his sick time for the coming year by dint of a week-long trip to Minneapolis to see the Twins play the Angels. She told him he was nuts to even think about it. She told me I was just plain nuts.

It was the kind of day that's incomplete without the crack of a bat and the slap of leather, and although I couldn't get any second-day-of-the-season games on the car radio, it was satisfying to know that a new season had begun and they were playing baseball again.

I wondered if Maxie Silas would be listening. Or was he one of those who could enter the game and leave it without either leaving a mark on the other? I doubted that. His smile on the card was too wide, too full of the joy of the game and the thrill of being at bat in the bigs.

A twinge of ancient regret surfaced, and I had to fight it back into its cage. I'd stopped resenting the fringe players a long time ago — or thought I had — no longer seeing my face under their ball caps, and *my* name on the backs of their cards. Why resent the fringe players? Because *they* were the lucky ones; they got to play with Stargell and Clemente and Rose and Carter and Parker and Winfield. Never mind that they weren't those guys, and could never dream of accomplishing the things the stars did. It was the dream of making it to the bigs, realizing the dream, then staying there long enough to face the three-and-two fastball in the bottom of the ninth with two out and two on and your team down a pair that made the lack of star talent unimportant. For as long as he lived, Maxie Silas could say he played on the same team as Roberto Clemente. Didn't matter if Clemente forgot him ten minutes after the season ended: Maxie Silas had *been* there!

The distance passed quickly, mainly because my thoughts prevented me from noticing its passage. When I pulled up to the toll booth and paid the fare to cross the Thousand Islands Bridge, it was as if I'd merely driven down the street. At Canadian Customs the officer asked me a few cursory questions about my destination and what I was bringing across with me, then let me through and turned his attention to the next car.

I stopped at a service station and filled the tank; they sell gas in liters up there, so my plan to keep track of the mileage went out the window. I did, though, after bringing a smile to the attendant's face with my awkward pronunciation, learn the two correct ways to pronounce Gananoque: Gan-an-*ock*-way, or Gan-an-*ock*-kwee. He told me it was an Indian name meaning Rocks Rising Out of the Water. I took his word for it.

Gananoque was situated on the St. Lawrence River, thus suited for tourist traffic bound for the Thousand Islands area, and the minute I hit the town limits I could see they were trying damn hard to squeeze every nickel they could from the trade. Gaudy signs advertised boat tours and tourist facilities, and half a dozen hucksters at the side of the road waved their arms and flashed boat tickets, attempting to lure me to their booths. I ignored them.

The town resembled every tourist trap I'd ever seen in either country, with virtually nothing to distinguish it. But then, I wasn't looking for social individuality; I was looking for the man who'd achieved my dream.

I bought a paper and grabbed a bite to eat in one of the several Chinese restaurants, and afterward I scanned the paper. The news was what you'd read in any small-town paper: births, deaths, local issues poorly expressed, local sports inadequately covered, a limited classifieds section, and advertisements for virtually every store in town, including one for a bookstore. Advertising a *Season Opening Special. Prop: Max Silas.* I damn near choked on my egg roll.

Somehow I couldn't leave for the bookstore right away. The mystery of Maxie Silas had driven me to this little town, and thoughts of him had intruded into virtually every other thought I had had about baseball; now, with the riddle virtually solved, I couldn't quite finish it.

He owned a bookstore. Somehow I'd pictured him in another environment; but just what, I didn't know. Did he manage a Little League team? Play for a group of old-timers? After the bigs it must have been quite a comedown.

After a second coffee I noted the address, got directions in garbled English from my waiter, and returned to the car for the ball card. When I took it from my suitcase, sunlight on the plastic envelope I kept it in for safekeeping made it seem to waver momentarily. I blinked several times, stared into that country boy's face, and the image was as clear as ever. He owned a bookstore now, and he was offering a *Season Opening Special.* Right then I hurt for him as much as I hurt for me.

The bookstore was on a pleasant tree-lined side street paralleling the main drag. A plain, black-on-white hand-painted sign read, Maxie's Books. The *o's* in Books were baseballs. A neatly lettered poster decorated the window — *Season Opening Special on All Sports Editions.* Beyond the glare of sunlight on glass, I could see rows of books. I swallowed a little lump in my throat and walked up the pavement leading in. The sign on the door read, *Open.* It seemed like an order.

When I opened the door, the chime played the first few bars of "Take Me Out to the Ball Game," and Maxie Silas looked up from where he was reading behind the counter. The hair was over his shoulders now and his upper lip sported a mustache, but this was definitely an older version of the joystruck kid on the ball card. He returned my smile, and I walked to the counter just barely noticing the smell of books, both new and used, like a cloud all around us.

"Something I can help you with?"

"Maxie Silas?"

He nodded, and I introduced myself. "I just drove up from New York." When he nodded again, his eyes were still full of wondering what I wanted, and I started to get nervous. "I've got something I'd like you to autograph for me." I saw an opal earring in his right ear; what a hit *that* would have been in the 1970 big leagues!

Puzzled, he smiled, and again I saw behind the years and lines in his face to the face on the card. I pulled the plastic envelope out of my shirt pocket and handed it across the counter.

Any youthfulness I thought I'd seen in his eyes disappeared at once, and his expression changed to something hard and sad and old. When his gaze met mine, something on the edge of fury was straining hard to get out.

"This isn't very funny," he said, and tossed the plastic back across the counter. There was perfect stillness in the bookstore, as if time had stopped all around us. I would have bet money nobody would open the door while we spoke. Even as we stared at each other, I could see the fury dying, replaced by a yearning so full of hurt it was almost a physical thing between us.

"Go on," he said, and his voice was very soft, "get out."

"But —" I groped for something to say. I didn't know what I'd expected, but this infinite anguish wasn't it. I picked up the plastic and stared through it at the face grinning back at me. "Look, if I've insulted you, I'm sorry. But I came a long way to meet you, and I'm not going to just walk out without knowing a few things first."

He looked disappointed — in me, in life . . . in himself. He didn't strike me as the kind of man who'd try to make me leave if I didn't go of my own accord, so while I waited for his anger to disappear I slipped the envelope back into my shirt pocket and waited.

"What do you want?" he asked finally; he was very calm.

"I want to know why your name is on Topps card #753 when there were only 752 cards issued that year. I want to know how you got to play for the Bucs when I never even heard of you, and I'm the biggest Bucs fan I know. I want to know how you got to play second base when you're a southpaw." The words were coming out in bursts, like machine-gun fire on a quiet night, and the faster I spoke the more I could feel my control slipping. "I want to know how an eighteen-year-old Canadian got to the bigs in the first place. I want to know why all your stats are the same numbers. I want to know —"

"Let me see that card," he interrupted softly. He held out his hand, but his eyes were still on my face. "Come on, let me see it."

I got hold of myself and fished the card out of my pocket. When he took it, he dropped his gaze to the front and stared at himself for almost half a minute. When he looked up, his face was devoid of expression and his eyes emotionless.

"You collect ball cards?"

I told him I did.

He smiled thinly, and a trace of the youngster on the card returned. "So do I." He returned his attention to the card, then turned it to study the stats and other information. He inhaled sharply when he read something there, and bit at the corner of his mustache. The longing that had disappeared a few minutes earlier returned, and this time I thought his eyes were a little misty. Maybe not: my pulse was pounding; I might have imagined it.

"Where did you get this?" he asked finally.

"A trade with some kid last winter."

He studied me with eyes so vulnerable and full of hope, I knew if I snatched the card out of his hand and laughed at him or told him it was all a joke, he'd fold into an envelope of flesh and blood right before my eyes, with nothing of his soul left.

"I got it in a trade," I repeated softly, as earnestly as I could manage.

He sat and turned the card over to stare again at his face. "Jesus God," he whispered, and there was more reverence in the oath than I'd heard from most pulpits.

"Look," I told him, knowing now he didn't want me to leave, "I'd like you to autograph it for me if you would. And I'd like to talk to you."

"You say you're a Bucs fan?"

"Number One."

"Number Two," he said, and we smiled together. As he came out from around the counter, I saw that he moved with difficulty, "Business is pretty slow today anyway," he said and flipped the sign on the door to read *Closed*.

He led me through rows of books to the office at the back, and I marveled at the number of volumes he had. The store wasn't that large, but the selection seemed endless. There was a sports section, and his *Season Opening Specials* were marked with black and gold stickers. I saw he had last year's Green Book for a buck (a Buc? I wondered), and decided I'd get it before I left.

The office was small, and had the smell of a million musty books. Over the desk a dim bulb hung from a black cord, spilling light on riles and stacks of books and folders and binders and papers and a hundred other things. But what caught my eye right away were the distinctive long and rectangular card boxes stacked neatly in one corner, labeled in black; he'd said he collected, and from the looks of it he had a lot of complete sets. Donnie MacBeth was going to drool when I told him about Maxie Silas. He sat behind the cluttered desk and indicated the room's only other chair. I sat, but my eyes were on the boxes of ball cards.

"I'm a joke in this town," he said when I finally looked at him. He held up the plastic envelope. "And this is just the sort of thing the local assholes would do; they'd get a helluva kick out of it." He looked again at the ball card, and shook his head in awed disbelief and I knew it was not time to speak; Maxie Silas was going to talk.

He was still looking at the card when he started. "When I was a kid, I loved baseball. Couldn't wait for the snow to melt and the weather to warm up." He was back there now; I could tell it from the sound of distance in his voice. "The other kids liked it, too, of course — all kids do — but around here hockey's the big thing. The Bruins found Bobby Orr at a tournament right here in Gananoque, as a matter of fact. Anyway, as the other kids got more and more involved in hockey, I got more and more involved in ball. I lived for it. I could quote every Pirate batting average since the forties, and I went to sleep at night dreaming of Maxie Silas in black and gold trim, playing first base, and sometimes second just because it was different to put a lefty there. I don't think I ever wanted anything so much as to wear a Pirate uniform, even if it was only to start one lousy game. A defensive replacement in the bottom of the ninth would've been O.K. A stinkin' pinch-hit appearance, for Chrissakes! Even now I'd trade everything for that one chance."

He paused and turned the card over to his stats again. "I like eleven," he said, "and repeating numbers." He smiled, but it was the haunted, hunted kind. "Two twenty-two," he said, reading his average. "If nothing else, I wasn't greedy. I just wanted to play."

He looked up at me suddenly, his eyes boring holes through mine. But his voice was soft, very soft, and I had to strain to catch it. "Did you ever want something so much it hurt, right in your guts?

Ever watch your dreams wither, not because someone changed them on you, but because you just weren't good enough to make them real?"

I nodded, because I knew exactly what he meant, and because I still had that feeling.

"Even before I hurt my knees playing hockey, I knew the dream was dying," he went on, "and I knew I couldn't make it live again. There were no opportunities up here, and I didn't have the talent anyway. But that dream died hard. All my life I wanted to play in the bigs, and when I was a kid I dreamed of seeing my ball card. When I was a *teenager*, I dreamed about it! Do you *believe* that?"

I believed it. God, I believed it . . .

"But I just wasn't good enough," he said again, very softly, "and finally I had to admit I was never going to play, never going to hold a real ball card with *Maxie Silas* printed across the top of it." He looked up from the card again. "Then you walked in," he whispered, "and showed me this." And he turned it over yet again. His hands shook just a little. This time I *knew* I didn't imagine misty eyes.

Something with frigid claws scratched its way up my spine, and I shivered when it reached the base of my neck. An adage I'd read somewhere came back to me: *If wishes were horses, then beggars could ride.* I was watching a beggar ride. What made the journey more remarkable was that I knew how many kids lost their cards, ripped them up, threw them away or had mothers with a fetish for cleanliness and an intolerance for a kid's "junk." God, the odds!

"What else do you want to know?" he asked suddenly, without looking up.

I had a thousand questions, but only one of them mattered now. "Why did you say you're a joke here?"

He didn't even look up. "People with dreams always are, aren't they? I just spent too much time talking about mine when I got too old to be dreaming anymore. But it's funny . . . it was part of that dream that convinced me the card is real: I had this fantasy of playing without paying my dues . . . if you remember, the card says I never played in the minors." He said it with pride, as if the saying of it made it so. Maybe it did.

It took a long time, but he gradually found the courage to let go of the card, and he put it on the desk and talked with me. Even so, he couldn't keep from glancing at it now and again. We talked about the Pirates' prospects for the coming season, their past accomplishments and disappointments, and the state of baseball in general.

When it was over and I got up to leave, I knew I really didn't have any choice. I picked up the card, slipped it out of its plastic envelope, and stared at it with something of that disbelief with which Silas himself had first regarded it. It was real. Real! I read the stats and information again, and marveled at the power of dreams. Then I slid it back into the envelope and placed it carefully in front of him.

"Trade you even for the Green Book."

I left right away; I can't stand to see grown men cry.

All of which is prelude. I can still see the card. And I think about Maxie Silas a lot. He dreamed so hard he hurt, wanted to play ball and see himself on a ball card so much that he made it real. Or part of it. He said he'd trade everything, even now, for that one chance to play.

Me too. God, me too.

It's out there, I know it is; Maxie Silas couldn't possibly dream any harder than I did. Do. So it's out there. If you've got it, I'd give anything to see it just once, I'd give anything . . . .

The Franchise

JOHN KESSEL

"Whoever wants to know the heart and mind of America had better learn baseball."

— Jacques Barzun

When George Herbert Walker Bush strode into the batter's box to face the pitcher they called the Franchise, it was the bottom of the second, and the Senators were already a run behind.

But Killebrew had managed a bloop double down the rightfield line and two outs later still stood on second in the bright October sunlight, waiting to be driven in. The bleachers were crammed full of restless fans in colorful shirts. Far behind Killebrew, Griffith Stadium's green center-field wall zigzagged to avoid the towering oak in Mrs. Mahan's backyard, lending the stadium its crazy dimensions. They said the only players ever to homer into that tree were Mantle and Ruth. George imagined how the stadium would erupt if he did it, drove the first pitch right out of the old ball yard, putting the Senators ahead in the first game of the 1959 World Series. If wishes were horses, his father had told him more than once, then beggars would ride.

George stepped into the box, ground in his back foot, squinted at the pitcher. The first pitch, a fastball, so surprised him that he didn't get his bat off his shoulder. Belt high, it split the middle of the plate, but the umpire called, "Ball!"

"Ball?" Schmidt, the Giants' catcher, grumbled.

"You got a problem?" the umpire said.

"Me? I got no problem." Schmidt tossed the ball back to the pitcher, who shook his head in histrionic Latin American dismay, as if bemoaning the sins of the world that he'd seen only too much of since he'd left Havana eleven years before. "But the Franchise, he no like."

George ignored them and set himself for the next pitch. The big

Cuban went into his herky-jerky windup, deceptively slow, then kicked and threw. George was barely into his swing when the ball thwacked into the catcher's glove. "Steerike one!" the umpire called.

He was going to have to get around faster. The next pitch was another fastball, outside and high, but George had already triggered before the release and missed it by a foot, twisting himself around so that he almost fell over.

Schmidt took the ball out of his glove, showed it to George, and threw it back to the mound.

The next was a curve, outside by an inch. Ball two.

The next, a fastball that somehow George managed to foul into the dirt.

The next, a fastball up under his chin that had him diving into the dirt himself. Ball three. Full count.

An expectant murmur rose in the crowd, then fell to a profound silence, the silence of a church, of heaven, of a lover's secret heart. Was his father among them, breathless, hoping? Thousands awaited the next pitch. Millions more watched on television. Killebrew took a three-step lead off second. The Giants made no attempt to hold him on. The chatter from the Senators' dugout lit up. "Come on, George Herbert Walker Bush, bear down! Come on, Professor, grit up!"

George set himself, weight on his back foot. He cocked his bat, squinted out at the pitcher. The vainglorious Latino gave him a piratical grin, shook off Schmidt's sign. George felt his shoulders tense. Calm, boy, calm, he told himself. You've been shot at, you've faced Prescott Bush across a dining-room table — this is nothing but baseball. But instead of calm he felt panic, and as the Franchise went into his windup his mind stood blank as a stone.

The ball started out right for his head. George jerked back in a desperate effort to get out of the way as the pitch, a curve of prodigious sweep, dropped through the heart of the plate. "Steerike!" the umpire called.

Instantly the scene changed from hushed expectation to sudden movement. The crowd groaned. The players relaxed and began jogging off the field. Killebrew kicked the dirt and walked back to the dugout to get his glove. The organist started up. Behind the big Chesterfield sign in right, the scorekeeper slid another goose egg onto the board for the Senators. Though the whole thing was similar to moments he had experienced more times than he would care to admit during his ten years in the minors, the simple volume of thirty thousand voices sighing in disappointment because he, George Herbert Walker Bush, had failed, left him standing stunned at the plate with the bat limp in his clammy hands. They didn't get thirty thousand fans in Chattanooga.

Schmidt flipped the ball toward the mound. As the Franchise jogged past him, he flashed George that superior smile. "A magnificent swing," he said.

George stumbled back to the dugout. Lemon, heading out to left, shook his head. "Nice try, Professor," the shortstop Consolo said.

"Pull your jock up and get out to first," said Lavagetto, the manager. He spat a stream of tobacco juice onto the sod next to the end of the dugout. "Señor Fidel Castro welcomes you to the bigs."

2

The Senators lost 7-1. Castro pitched nine innings, allowed four hits, struck out ten. George fanned three times. In the sixth, he let a low throw get by him; the runner ended up on third, and the Giants followed with four unearned runs.

In the locker room, his teammates avoided him. Nobody had played well, but George knew they had him pegged as a choker. Lavagetto came through with a few words of encouragement. "We'll get 'em tomorrow," he said. George expected the manager to yank him for somebody who at least wouldn't cost them runs on defense. When he left without saying anything, George was grateful to him for at least letting him go another night before benching him.

Barbara and the boys had been in the stands, but had gone home. They would be waiting for him. He didn't want to go. The place was empty by the time he walked out through the tunnels to the street. His head was filled with images from the game. Castro had toyed with him; he no doubt enjoyed humiliating the son of a U.S. senator. The Cuban's look of heavy-lidded disdain sparked an unaccustomed rage in George. It wasn't good sportsmanship. You played hard, and you won or lost, but you didn't rub the other guy's nose in it. That was bush league, and George, despite his unfortunate name, was anything but bush.

That George Bush should end up playing first base for the Washington Senators in the 1959 World Series was the result of as improbable a sequence of events as had ever conspired to make a man of a rich boy. The key moment had come on a May Saturday in 1948 when he had shaken the hand of Babe Ruth.

That May morning the Yale baseball team was to play Brown, but before the game a ceremony was held to honor Ruth, donating the manuscript of his autobiography to the university library. George, captain of the Yale squad, would accept the manuscript. As he stood before the microphone set up between the pitcher's mound and second base, he was stunned by the gulf between the pale hulk standing before him and the legend he represented. Ruth, only fifty-three on that spring morning, could hardly speak for the throat cancer that was killing him. He gasped out a few words, stooped over, rail thin, no longer the giant he had been in the twenties. George took his hand. It was dry and papery and brown as a leaf in fall. Through his grip George felt the contact with glorious history, with feats of heroism that would never be matched, with 714 home runs and 1,356 extra-base hits, with a lifetime slugging percentage of .690, with the called shot and the sixty-homer season and the 1927 Yankees and the curse of the Red Sox. An electricity surged up his arm and directly into his soul. Ruth had accomplished as much, in his way, as a man could accomplish in a life, more, even, George realized to his astonishment, than had his father, Prescott Bush. He stood there stunned, charged with an unexpected, unasked-for purpose.

He had seen death in the war, had tasted it in the blood that streamed from his forehead when he'd struck it against the tail of the TBM Avenger as he parachuted out of the flaming bomber over the Pacific in 1943. He had felt death's hot breath on his back as he frantically paddled the yellow rubber raft away from Chichi Jima against waves pushing him back into the arms of the Japanese, had felt death draw away and offered up a silent prayer when the conning tower of the U.S.S. *Finback* broke through the agitated seas to save him from a savage fate — to, he always knew, some higher purpose. He had imagined that purpose to be business or public service. Now he recognized that he had been seeing it through his father's eyes, that in fact his fate lay elsewhere. It lay between the chalk lines of a playing field, on the greensward of the infield, within the smells of pine tar and sawdust and chewing tobacco and liniment. He could feel it through the tendons of the fleshless hand of Babe Ruth that he held in his own at that very instant.

The day after he graduated from Yale he signed, for no bonus, with the Cleveland Indians. Ten years later, George had little to show for his bold choice. He wasn't the best first baseman you ever saw. Nobody ever stopped him on the street to ask for his autograph. He never made the Indians, got traded to the Browns. He hung on, bouncing up and down the farm systems of seventh and eighth-place teams. Every spring he went to Florida with high expectations, every April he started the season in Richmond, in Rochester, in Chattanooga. Just two months earlier he had considered packing it in and looking for another career. Then a series of miracles happened.

Chattanooga was the farm team for the Senators, who hadn't won a pennant since 1933. For fifteen years, under their notoriously cheap owner Clark Griffith, they'd been as bad as you could get. But in 1959 their young third baseman, Harmon Killebrew, hit forty-two home runs. Sluggers Jim Lemon and Roy Sievers had career years. A big Kansas boy named Bob Allison won rookie of the year in center field. Camilo Pascual won twenty-two games, struck out 215 men. A kid named Jim Kaat won seventeen. Everything broke right, including Mickey Mantle's leg. After hovering a couple of games over .500 through the All-Star break, the Senators got hot in August, won ninety games, and finished one ahead of the Yankees.

When, late in August, right fielder Albie Pearson got hurt, Lavagetto switched Sievers to right, and there was George Bush, thirty-five years old, starting at first base for the American League champions in the 1959 World Series against the New York Giants.

The Giants were heavy favorites. Who would bet against a team that fielded Willie Mays, Orlando Cepeda, Willie McCovey, Felipe Alou, and pitchers like Johnny Antonelli, the fireballer Toothpick Sam Jones, and the Franchise, Fidel Castro? If, prior to the series, you'd told George Herbert Walker Bush the Senators were doomed, he would not have disagreed with you. After game one he had no reason to think otherwise.

He stood outside the stadium looking for a cab, contemplating his series record — one game, 0 for 4, one error — when a pale old man in a loud sports coat spoke to him. "Just be glad you're here," the man said.

The man had watery blue eyes, a sharp face. He was thin enough to look ill. "I beg your pardon?"

"You're the fellow the Nats called up in September, right?

Remember, even if you never play another inning, at least you were there. You felt the sun on your back, got dirt on your hands, saw the stands full of people from down on the field. Not many get even that much."

"The Franchise made me look pretty sick."

"You have to face him down."

"Easier said than done."

"Don't say — do."

"Who are you, old man?"

The man hesitated. "Name's Weaver. I'm a — a fan. Yes, I'm a baseball fan." He touched the brim of his hat and walked away.

George thought about it on the cab ride home. It did not make him feel much better. When he got back to the cheap furnished apartment they were renting, Barbara tried to console him.

"My father wasn't there, was he?" George said.

"No. But he called after the game. He wants to see you."

"Probably wants to give me a few tips on how to comport myself. Or maybe just gloat."

Bar came around behind his chair, rubbed his tired shoulders. George got up and switched on the television. While he waited for it to warm up, the silence stretched. He faced Barbara. She had put on a few pounds over the years, but he remembered the first time he'd seen her across the dance floor in the red dress. He was seventeen.

"What do you think he wants?"

"I don't know, George."

"I haven't seen him around in the last ten years. Have you?"

The TV had warmed up, and Prescott Bush's voice blared out from behind George. "I hope the baseball Senators win," he was saying. "They've had a better year than the Democratic ones."

George twisted down the volume, stared for a moment at his father's handsome face, then snapped it off. "Give me a drink," he told Barbara. He noticed the boys standing in the doorway, afraid. Barbara hesitated, poured a scotch and water.

"And don't stint on the scotch!" George yelled. He turned to Neil. "What are you looking at, you little weasel! Go to bed."

Barbara slammed down the glass so hard the scotch splashed the counter. "What's got into you, George? You're acting like a crazy man."

George took the half-empty glass from her hand. "My father's got into me, that's what. He got into me thirty years ago, and I can't get him out."

Barbara shot him a look in which disgust outweighed pity and went back to the boys' room. George slumped in the armchair, picked up a copy of *Look* and leafed through the pages. He stopped on a Gillette razor ad. Castro smiled out from the page, dark hair slicked back, chin sleek as a curveball, a devastating blonde leaning on his shoulder. "Look Sharp, Feel Sharp, *Be* Sharp," the ad told George.

Castro. What did he know about struggle? Yet that egomaniac lout was considered a hero, while he, George Herbert Walker Bush, who at twenty-four had been at the head of every list of the young men most likely to succeed, had accomplished precisely nothing.

People who didn't know any better had assumed that because of his background, money, and education he would grow to be one of the ones who told others what it was necessary for them to do, but George was coming to realize, with a surge of panic, that he was not special. His moment of communion with Babe Ruth had been a delusion, because Ruth was another type of man. Perhaps Ruth was used by the teams that bought and sold him, but inside Ruth was some compulsion that drove him to be larger than the uses to which he was put, so that in the end he deformed those uses, remade the game itself.

George, talented though he had seemed, had no such size. The vital force that had animated his grandfather George Herbert Walker, after whom he was named, the longing after mystery that had impelled the metaphysical poet George Herbert, after whom that grandfather had been named, had diminished into a trickle in George Herbert Walker Bush. No volcanic forces surged inside him. When he listened late in the night, all he could hear of his soul was a thin keening, a buzz like a bug trapped in a jar. *Let me go, let me go,* it whispered.

That old man at the ballpark was wrong. It was not enough, not nearly enough, just to be there. He wanted to be somebody. What good was it just to stand on first base in the World Series if you came away from it a laughingstock? To have your father call you not because you were a hero, but only to remind you once again what a failure you are.

"I'll be damned if I go see him," George muttered to the empty room.

3

President Nixon called Lavagetto in the middle of the night with a suggestion for the batting order in the second game. "Put Bush in the number-five slot," Nixon said.

Lavagetto wondered how he was supposed to tell the President of the United States that he was out of his mind. "Yessir, Mr. President."

"See, that way you get another right-handed batter at the top of the order."

Lavagetto considered pointing out to the president that the Giants were pitching a right-hander in game two. "Yessir, Mr. President," Lavagetto said. His wife was awake now, looking at him with irritation from her side of the bed. He put his hand over the mouthpiece and said, "Go to sleep."

"Who is it at this hour?"

"The President of the United States."

"Uh-huh."

Nixon had some observations about one-run strategies. Lavagetto agreed with him until he could get him off the line. He looked at his alarm clock. It was half past two.

Nixon had sounded full of manic energy. His voice dripped dogmatic assurance. He wondered if Nixon was a drinking man. Walter Winchell said that Eisenhower's death had shoved the veep into an office he was unprepared to hold.

Lavagetto shut off the light and lay back down, but he couldn't sleep. What about Bush? Damn Pearson for getting himself hurt. Bush should be down in the minors where he belonged. He looked to be cracking under the pressure like a ripe melon.

But maybe the guy could come through, prove himself. He was no kid. Lavagetto knew from personal experience the pressures of the Series, how the unexpected could turn on the swing of the bat. He recalled that fourth game of the '47 series, his double to right field that cost Floyd Bevens his no-hitter, and the game. Lavagetto had been a thirty-four-year-old utility infielder for the luckless Dodgers, an aging substitute playing out the string at the end of his career. In that whole season he'd hit only one other double. When he'd seen that ball twist past the right fielder, the joy had shot through his chest like lightning. The Dodger fans had gone crazy; his teammates had leapt all over him laughing and shouting and swearing like Durocher himself.

He remembered that, despite the miracle, the Dodgers had lost the Series to the Yankees in seven.

Lavagetto turned over. First in War, First in Peace, Last in the American League . . . that was the Washington Senators. He hoped young Kaat was getting more sleep than he was.

4

Tuesday afternoon, in front of a wild capacity crowd, young Jim Kaat pitched one of the best games by a rookie in the history of the Series. The twenty-year-old, left-hander battled Toothpick Sam Jones pitch for pitch, inning for inning. Jones struggled with his control, walking six in the first seven innings, throwing two wild pitches. If it weren't for the overeagerness of the Senators, swinging at balls a foot out of the strike zone, they would surely have scored; instead they squandered opportunity after opportunity. The fans grew restless. They could see it happening, in sour expectation of disaster built up over twenty-five frustrated years: Kaat would pitch brilliantly, and it would be wasted because the Giants would score on some bloop single.

Through seven, the game stayed a scoreless tie. By some fluke George could not fathom, Lavagetto, instead of benching him, had moved him up in the batting order. Though he was still without a hit, he had been playing superior defense. In the seventh he snuffed a Giant uprising when he dove to snag a screamer off the bat of Schmidt for the third out, leaving runners at second and third.

Then, with two down in the top of the eighth, Cepeda singled. George moved in to hold him on. Kaat threw over a couple of times to keep the runner honest, with Cepeda trying to judge Kaat's move. Mays took a strike, then a ball. Cepeda edged a couple of strides away from first.

Kaat went into his stretch, paused, and whipped the ball to first, catching Cepeda leaning the wrong way. Picked off! But Cepeda, instead of diving back, took off for second. George whirled and threw hurriedly. The ball sailed over Consolo's head into left field, and Cepeda went to third. E-3.

Kaat was shaken. Mays hit a screamer between first and second.

George dove, but it was by him, and Cepeda jogged home with the lead.

Kaat struck out McCovey, but the damage was done. "You bush-league clown!" a fan yelled. George's face burned. As he trotted off the field, from the Giants' dugout came Castro's shout: "A heroic play, Mr. Rabbit!"

George wanted to keep going through the dugout and into the clubhouse. On the bench his teammates were conspicuously silent. Consolo sat down next to him. "Shake it off," he said. "You're up this inning."

George grabbed his bat and moved to the end of the dugout. First up in the bottom of the eighth was Sievers. He got behind 0-2, battled back as Jones wasted a couple, then fouled off four straight strikes until he'd worked Jones for a walk. The organist played charge lines and the crowd started chanting. Lemon moved Sievers to second. Killebrew hit a drive that brought the people to their feet screaming before it curved just outside the left-field foul pole, then popped out to short. He threw down his bat and stalked back toward the dugout.

"C'mon, professor," Killebrew said as he passed Bush in the on-deck circle. "Give yourself a reason for being here."

Jones was a scary right-hander with one pitch: the heater. In his first three at-bats George had been overpowered; by the last, he'd managed a walk. This time he went up with a plan: he was going to take the first pitch, get ahead in the count, then drive the ball.

The first pitch was a fastball just high.

Make contact. Don't force it. Go with the pitch. The next was another fastball; George swung as soon as Jones let it go and sent a screaming line drive over the third baseman's head. The crowd roared, and he was halfway down the firstbase line when the third-base umpire threw up his hands and yelled, "Foul ball!"

He caught his breath, picked up his bat, and returned to the box. Sievers jogged back to second. Schmidt, standing with his hands on his hips, didn't look at George. From the Giants' dugout George heard, "Kiss your luck good-bye, you effeminate rabbit! You rich man's table leavings! You are devoid of even the makings of guts!"

George stepped out of the box. Castro had come down the dugout to the near end and was leaning out, arms braced on the field, hurling his abuse purple faced. Rigney and the pitching coach had him by the shoulders, tugging him back. George turned away, feeling a cold fury in his belly.

He would show them all. He forgot to calculate, swept by rage. He set himself as far back in the box as possible. Jones took off his cap, wiped his forearm across his brow, and leaned over to check the signs. He shook off the first, then nodded and went into his windup.

As soon as he released George swung, and was caught completely off balance by a change-up. "Strike two, you shadow of a man!" Castro shouted. "Unnatural offspring of a snail and a worm! Strike two!"

Jones tempted him with an outside pitch; George didn't bite. The next was another high fastball; George started, then checked his swing. "Ball!" the home-plate ump called. Fidel booed. Schmidt argued, the ump shook his head. Full count.

George knew he should look for a particular pitch, in a particular part of the plate. After ten years of professional ball, this ought to be second nature, but Jones was so wild he didn't have a clue. George stepped out of the box, rubbed his hands on his pants. "Yes, wipe your sweaty hands, mama's boy! You have all the machismo of a bankbook!"

The rage came to his defense. He picked a decision out of the air, arbitrary as the breeze: fastball, outside.

Jones went into his windup. He threw his body forward, whipped his arm high over his shoulder. Fastball, outside. George swiveled his hips through the box, kept his head down, extended his arms. The contact of the bat with the ball was so slight he wasn't sure he'd hit it at all. A line drive down the right-field line, hooking as it rose, hooking, hooking . . . curling just inside the foul pole into the stands 320 feet away.

The fans exploded. George, feeling rubbery, jogged around first, toward second. Sievers pumped his fist as he rounded third; the Senators were up on their feet in the dugout shouting and slapping each other. Jones had his hands on his hips, head down and back to the plate. George rounded third and jogged across home, where he was met by Sievers, who slugged him in the shoulder, and the rest of his teammates in the dugout, who laughed and slapped his butt.

The crowd began to chant, "SEN-a-TOR, SEN-a-TOR." After a moment George realized they were chanting for him. He climbed out of the dugout again and tipped his hat, scanning the stands for Barbara and the boys. As he did he saw his father in the presidential box, lean-ing over to speak into the ear of the cheering President Nixon. He felt a rush of hope, ducked his head, and got back into the dugout.

Kaat held the Giants in the ninth, and the Senators won, 2-1.

In the locker room after the game, George's teammates whooped and slapped him on the back. Chuck Stobbs, the clubhouse comic, called him "the Bambino." For a while George hoped that his father might come down to congratulate him. Instead, for the first time in his career, reporters swarmed around him. They fired flashbulbs in salvoes. They pushed back their hats, flipped open their notebooks, and asked him questions.

"What's it feel like to win a big game like this?"

"I'm just glad to be here. I'm not one of these winning-is-every-thing guys."

"They're calling you the senator. Your father is a senator. How do you feel about that?"

"I guess we're both senators," George said. "He just got to Washington a little sooner than I did."

They liked that a lot. George felt the smile on his face like a frozen mask. For the first time in his life he was aware of the muscles it took to smile, as tense as if they were lifting a weight.

After the reporters left he showered. George wondered what his father had been whispering into the president's ear, while everyone around him cheered. Some sarcastic comment? Some irrelevant polit-ical advice?

When he got back to his locker, toweling himself dry, he found a note lying on the bench. He opened it eagerly. It read:

To the Effeminate Rabbit:
Even the rodent has his day. But not when the eagle pitches.
Sincerely,
Fidel Alejandro Castro Ruz

5

That Fidel Castro would go so far out of his way to insult George Herbert Walker Bush would come as no surprise to anyone who knew him. Early in Castro's first season in the majors, a veteran Phillies reliever, after watching Fidel warm up, approached the young

Cuban. "Where did you get that curve?" he asked incredulously.

"From you," said Fidel. "That's why you don't have one."

But sparking his reaction to Bush was more than simple egotism. Fidel's antipathy grew from circumstances of background and character that made such animosity as inevitable as the rising of the sun in the east of Oriente province where he had been born thirty-two years before.

Like George Herbert Walker Bush, Fidel was the son of privilege, but a peculiarly Cuban form of privilege, as different from the blue-blooded Bush variety as the hot and breathless climate of Oriente was from chilly New England. Like Bush, Fidel endured a father as parsimonious with his warmth as those New England winters. Young Fidelito grew up well acquainted with the back of Angel Castro's hand, the jeers of classmates who tormented him and his brother Raul for their illegitimacy. Though Angel Castro owned two thousand acres and had risen from common sugarcane laborer to local caudillo, he did not possess the easy assurance of the rich of Havana, for whom Oriente was the Cuban equivalent of Alabama. The Castros were peasants. Fidel's father was illiterate, his mother a maid. No amount of money could erase Fidel's bastardy.

This history raged in Fidelito. Always in a fight, alternating boasts with moody silences, he longed for accomplishment in a fiery way that cast the longing of Bush to impress his own father into a sickly shadow. At boarding school in Santiago, he sought the praise of his teachers and admiration of his schoolmates. At Belén, Havana's exclusive Jesuit preparatory school, he became the champion athlete of all of Cuba. "El Loco Fidel" his classmates called him as, late into the night, at an outdoor court under a light swarming with insects, he would practice basketball shots until his feet were torn bloody and his head swam with forlorn images of the ball glancing off the iron rim.

At the University of Havana, between the scorching expanses of the baseball and basketball seasons, Fidel tolled over the scorching expanse of the law books. He sought triumph in student politics as he did in sports. In the evenings he met in tiny rooms with his comrades and talked about junk pitches and electoral strategy, about the reforms that were only a matter of time because the people's will could not be forever thwarted. They were on the side of history. Larger than even the largest of men, history would overpower anyone unless, like Fidel, he aligned himself with it so as not to be swept under by the tidal force of its inescapable currents.

In the spring of 1948, at the same time George Herbert Walker Bush was shaking the hand of Babe Ruth, these currents transformed Fidel's life. He was being scouted by several major league teams. In the university, he had gained control of his fastball and given birth to a curve of so monstrous an arc that Alex Pompez, the Giants' scout, reported that the well-spoken law student owned "a hook like Bo-Peep." More significantly, Pirates scout Howie Haak observed that Fidel "could throw and think at the same time."

Indeed Fidel could think, though no one could come close to guessing the content of his furious thought. A war between glory and doom raged within him. Fidel's fury to accomplish things threatened to keep him from accomplishing anything at all. He had made enemies. In the late forties, student groups punctuated elections for head of the law-school class with assassinations. Rival political gangs fought in the streets. Events conspired to drive Fidel toward a crisis. And so, on a single day in 1948, he abandoned his political aspirations, quit school, married his lover, the fair Mirta Diaz Balart, and signed a contract with the New York Giants.

It seemed a fortunate choice. In his rookie year he won fifteen games. After he took the Cy Young Award and was named MVP of the 1951 Series, the sportswriters dubbed him "the Franchise." This past season he had won twenty-nine. He earned, and squandered, a fortune. Controversy dogged him, politics would not let him go, the uniform of a baseball player at times felt much too small. His brother Raul was imprisoned when Batista overthrew the government to avoid defeat in the election of 1952. Fidel made friends among the expatriates in Miami. He protested U.S. policies. His alternative nickname became "the Mouth."

But all along Fidel knew his politics was mere pose. His spouting off to sports reporters did nothing compared to what money might do to help the guerrillas in the Sierra Maestra. Yet he had no money.

After the second game of the Series, instead of returning to the hotel Fidel took a cab down to the Mall. He needed to be alone. It was early evening when he got out at the Washington Monument. The sky beyond the Lincoln Memorial shone orange and purple. The air still held some of the sultry heat of summer, like an evening in Havana. But this was a different sort of capital. These North Americans liked to think of themselves as clean, rational men of law instead of passionate, a land of Washingtons and Lincolns, but away from the public buildings it was still a southern city full of ex-slaves. Fidel looked down the Mall toward the bright Capitol, white and towering as a wedding cake, wondered what he might have become had he continued law school. At one time he had imagined himself the Washington of his own country, a liberating warrior. The true heir of José Martí, scholar, poet, and revolutionary. Like Martí, he admired the idealism of the United States, but like him he saw its dark side. Here at the Mall, however, you could almost forget about that in an atmosphere of bogus Greek democracy, of liberty and justice for all. You might even forget that this liberty could be bought and sold, a franchise purchasable for cold cash.

Fidel walked along the pool toward the Lincoln Memorial. The floodlights lit up the white columns, and inside shone upon the brooding figure of Lincoln. Despite his cynicism, Fidel was caught by the sight of it. He had been to Washington only once before, for the All-Star Game in 1956. He remembered walking through Georgetown with Mirta on his arm, feeling tall and handsome, ignoring the scowl of the maître d' in the restaurant who clearly disapproved of two such dark ones in his establishment.

He'd triumphed but was not satisfied. He had forced others to admit his primacy through the power of his will. He had shown them, with his strong arm, the difference between right and wrong. He was the Franchise. He climbed up the steps into the Memorial, read the words of Lincoln's Second Inaugural address engraved on the wall. THE PROGRESS OF OUR ARMS UPON WHICH ALL ELSE CHIEFLY DEPENDS IS AS WELL KNOWN TO THE PUBLIC AS TO MYSELF ... But he was still the crazy Cuban, taken little more seriously than Desi Arnaz, and the minute that *arm* that made him a useful commodity should begin to show signs of weakening — in that same minute he would be undone. IT MAY SEEM STRANGE THAT ANY MEN SHOULD DARE TO ASK A JUST GOD'S ASSISTANCE IN WRINGING THEIR BREAD FROM THE SIN OF OTHER MEN'S FACES BUT LET US JUDGE NOT THAT WE BE JUDGED.

Judge not? Perhaps Lincoln could manage it, but Fidel was a different sort of man.

In the secrecy of his mind Fidel could picture another world than the one he lived in. The marriage of love to Mirta had long since gone sour, torn apart by Fidel's lust for renown on the ball field and his lust for the astonishing women who fell like fruit from the trees into the laps of players such as he. More than *once* he felt grief over his faithlessness. He knew his solitude to be just punishment. That was the price of greatness, for, after all, greatness was a crime and deserved punishment.

Mirta was gone now, and their son with her. She worked for the hated Batista. He thought of Raul languishing in Batista's prison on the Isle of Pines. Batista, embraced by this United States that ran Latin America like a company store. Raul suffered for the people, while Fidel ate in four-star restaurants and slept with a different woman in every city, throwing away his youth, and the money he earned with it, on excrement.

He looked up into the great sad face of Lincoln. He turned from the monument to stare out across the Mall toward the gleaming white shaft of the Washington obelisk. It was full night now. Time to amend his life.

6

The headline in the *Post* the next morning read, SENATOR BUSH EVENS SERIES. The story mentioned that Prescott Bush had shown up in the sixth inning and sat beside Nixon in the presidential box. But nothing more.

Bar decided not to go up to New York for the middle games of the Series. George traveled with the team to the Roosevelt Hotel. The home run had done something for him. He felt a new confidence.

The game-three starters were the veteran southpaw Johnny Antonelli for the Giants and Pedro Ramos for the Senators. The echoes of the national anthem had hardly faded when Allison led off for the Senators with a home run into the short porch in left field. The Polo Grounds fell dead silent. The Senators scored three runs in the first; George did his part, hitting a change-up to right center for a double, scoring the third run of the inning.

In the bottom half of the first the Giants came right back, tying it up on May's three-run homer.

After that the Giants gradually wore Ramos down, scoring a single run in the third and two in the fifth. Lavagetto pulled him for a pinch hitter in the sixth with George on third and Consolo at first, two outs. But Aspromonte struck out, ending the inning.

Though Castro heckled George mercilessly throughout the game and the brash New York fans joined in, he played above himself. The Giants eventually won, 8-3, but George went three for five. Despite his miserable first game he was batting .307 for the Series. Down two games to one, the Washington players felt the loss, but had stopped calling him "George Herbert Walker Bush" and started calling him "the Senator."

7

Lavagetto had set an eleven o'clock curfew, but Billy Consolo persuaded George to go out on the town. The Hot Corner was a dive on Seventh Avenue with decent Italian food and cheap drinks. George ordered a club soda and tried to get into the mood. Ramos moaned about the plate umpire's strike zone, and Consolo changed the subject.

Consolo had been a bonus boy; in 1953 the Red Sox had signed him right out of high school for $50,000. He had never panned out. George wondered if Consolo's career had been any easier to take than his own. At least nobody had hung enough expectations on George for him to be called a flop.

Stobbs was telling a story. "So the Baseball Annie says to him, 'But will you respect me in the morning?' and the shortstop says, 'Oh baby, I'll respect you like crazy!' "

While the others were laughing, George headed for the men's room. Passing the bar, he saw, a corner booth, Fidel Castro talking to a couple of men in slick suits. Castro's eyes flicked over him but registered no recognition.

When George came out, the men in suits were in heated conversation with Castro. In the back of the room someone dropped a quarter into the jukebox, and Elvis Presley's silky "Money Honey" blared out. Bush had no use for rock and roll. He sat at the table, ignored his teammates' conversation and kept an eye on Castro. The Cuban was strenuously making some point, stabbing the tabletop with his index finger. After a minute George noticed that someone at the bar was watching them, too. It was the pale old man he had seen at Griffith Stadium.

On impulse, George went up to him. "Hello, old-timer. You

really must be a fan, if you followed the Series up here. Can I buy you a drink?"

The man turned decisively from watching Castro, as if deliberately putting aside some thought. He seemed about to smile but did not. Small red splotches colored his face. "Buy me a ginger ale."

George ordered a ginger ale and another club soda and sat on the next stool. "Money honey, if you want to get along with me," Elvis sang.

The old man sipped his drink. "You had yourself a couple of good games," he said. "You're in the groove."

"I just got some lucky breaks."

"Don't kid me. I know how it feels when it's going right. You know just where the next pitch is going to be, and there it is. Somebody hits a line drive right at you, you throw out your glove and snag it without even thinking. You're in the groove."

"It comes from playing the game a long time."

The old man snorted. "Do you really believe this guff you spout? Or are you just trying to hide something?"

"What do you mean? I've spent ten years playing baseball."

"And you expect me to believe you still don't know anything about it? Experience doesn't explain the groove." The man looked as if he were watching something far away. "When you're in that groove you're not playing the game, the game is playing you."

"But you have to plan your moves."

The old man looked at him as if he were from Mars. "Do you plan your moves when you're making love to your wife?" He finished his ginger ale, took another look back at Castro, then left. Everyone, it seemed, knew what was wrong with him. George felt steamed. As if that wasn't enough, as soon as he returned to the table, Castro's pals left and the Cuban swaggered over to George, leaned into him, and blew cigar smoke into his face. "I know you, George Herbert Walker Bush," he said, "Sen-a-tor Rabbit. The rich man's son."

George pushed him away. "You know, I'm beginning to find your behavior darned unconscionable, compadre."

"I stand here quaking with fear," Castro said. He poked George in the chest. "Back home in Biran we had a pen for the pigs. The gate of this pen was in disrepair. But it is still a fact, Senator Rabbit, that the splintered wooden gate of that pigpen, squealing on its rusted hinges, swung better than you."

Consolo started to get up, but George put a hand on his arm. "Say, Billy, our Cuban friend here didn't by any chance help you pick out this restaurant tonight, did he?"

"What, are you crazy? Of course not."

"Too bad. I thought if he did, we could get some good Communist food here."

The guys laughed. Castro leaned over.

"Very funny, Machismo Zero." His breath reeked of cigar smoke, rum, and garlic. "I guarantee that after tomorrow's game you will be even funnier."

8

Fidel had never felt sharper than he did during his warmups the afternoon of the fourth game. It was a cool fall day, partial overcast with a threat of rain, a breeze blowing out to right. The chill air only invigorated him. Never had his curve had more bite, his screwball more movement. His arm felt supple, his legs strong. As he strode in from the bullpen to the dugout, squinting out at the apartment buildings on Coogan's Bluff towering over the stands, a great cheer rose from the crowd.

Before the echoes of the national anthem had died he walked the first two batters, on eight pitches. The fans murmured. Schmidt came out to talk with him. "What's wrong?"

"Nothing is wrong," Fidel said, sending him back.

He retired Lemon on a pop fly and Killebrew on a fielder's choice. Bush came to the plate with two outs and men on first and second. The few Washington fans who had braved the Polo Grounds set up a chant: "SEN-a-TOR, SEN-a-TOR!"

Fidel studied Bush. Beneath Bush's bravado he could see panic in every motion of the body he wore like an ill-fitting suit. Fidel struck him out on three pitches.

Kralick held the Giants scoreless through three innings.

As the game progressed, Fidel's own personal game, the game of pitcher and batter, settled into a pattern. Fidel mowed down the batters after Bush in the order with predictable dispatch, but fell into trouble each time he faced the top of the order, getting just enough outs to bring Bush up with men on base and the game in the balance. He did this four times in the first seven innings.

Each time Bush struck out.

In the middle of the seventh, after Bush fanned to end the inning, Mays sat down next to Fidel on the bench. "What the hell do you think you're doing?"

Mays was the only player on the Giants whose stature rivaled that of the Franchise. Fidel, whose success came as much from craft as physical prowess, could not but admit that Mays was the most beautiful ball player he had ever seen. "I'm shutting out the Washington Senators in the fourth game of the World Series," Fidel said.

"What's this mickey mouse with Bush? You trying to make him look bad?"

"One does not have to try very hard."

"Well, cut it out — before you make a mistake with Killebrew or Sievers."

Fidel looked him dead in the eyes. "I do not make mistakes."

The Giants entered the ninth with a 3-0 lead. Fidel got two quick outs, then gave up a single to Sievers and walked Lemon and Killebrew to load the bases. Bush, at bat, represented the lead run. Schmidt called time and came out again. Rigney hurried out from the dugout, and Mays, to the astonishment of the crowd, came all the way in from center. "Yank him," he told Rigney.

Rigney looked exasperated. "Who's managing this team, Willie?

"He's setting Bush up to be the goat."

Rigney looked at Fidel. Fidel looked at him. "Just strike him out," the manager said.

Fidel rubbed up the ball and threw three fastballs through the heart of the plate. Bush missed them all. By the last strike, the New York fans were screaming, rocking the Polo Grounds with a parody of the Washington chant: "Sen-a-TOR, Sen-a-TOR, BUSH, BUSH, BUSH!" and exploding into fits of laughter. The Giants led the series, 3-1.

9

George made the cabbie drop him off at the corner of Broadway and Pine, in front of the old Trinity Church. He walked down Wall Street through crowds of men in dark suits, past the Stock Exchange to the offices of Brown Brothers, Harriman. In the shadows of the buildings the fall air felt wintry. He had not been down here in more years than he cared to remember.

The secretary, Miss Goode, greeted him warmly; she still remembered him from his days at Yale. Despite Prescott Bush's move to the Senate, they still kept his inner office for him, and as George stood outside the door he heard a piano. His father was singing. He had a wonderful singing voice, of which he was too proud.

George entered. Prescott Bush sat at an upright piano, playing Gilbert and Sullivan:

"Go, ye heroes, go to glory
Though you die in combat gory.
Ye shall live in song and story.
Go to immortality!"

Still playing, he glanced over his shoulder at George, then turned back and finished the verse:

"Go to death, and go to slaughter,
Die, and every Cornish daughter
With her tears your grave shall water.
Go, ye heroes, go and die!"

George was all too familiar with his father's theatricality. Six feet, four inches tall, with thick salt-and-pepper hair and a handsome, craggy face, he carried off his Douglas Fairbanks imitation without any hint of self-consciousness. It was a quality George had tried to emulate his whole life.

Prescott adjusted the sheet music and swiveled his piano stool around. He waved at the sofa against the wall beneath his shelf of golfing trophies and photos of the Yale Glee Club. "Sit down, son. I'm glad you could make it. I know you must have a lot on your mind."

George remained standing. "What did you want to see me about?"

"Relax, George. This isn't the dentist's office."

"If it were, I would know what to expect."

"Well, one thing you can expect is to hear me tell you how proud I am."

"Proud? Did you see that game yesterday?"

Prescott Bush waved a hand. "Temporary setback. I'm sure

you'll get them back this afternoon."

"Isn't it a little late for compliments?"

Prescott looked at him as calmly as if he were appraising some stock portfolio. His bushy eyebrows quirked a little higher. "George, I want you to sit down and shut up."

Despite himself, George sat. Prescott got up and paced to the window, looked down at the street, then started pacing again, his big hands knotted behind his back. George began to dread what was coming.

"George, I have been indulgent of you. Your entire life, despite my misgivings, I have treated you with kid gloves. You are not a stupid boy; at least your grades in school suggested you weren't. You've got that Phi Beta Kappa key, too — which only goes to show you what they are worth." He held himself very erect. "How old are you now?"

"Thirty-five."

Prescott shook his head. "Thirty-five? Lord. At *thirty-five* you show no more sense than you did at seventeen, when you told me that you intended to enlist in the navy. Despite the fact that the secretary of war himself, God-forbid-me, *Franklin D. Roosevelt's* secretary of war, had just told the graduating class that you, the cream of the nation's youth, could best serve your country by going to college instead of getting shot up on some Pacific Island."

He strolled over to the piano, flipped pensively through the sheet music on top. "I remember saying to myself that day that maybe you knew something I didn't. You were young. I recalled my own recklessness in the first war. God knew we needed to lick the Japanese. But that didn't mean a boy of your parts and prospects should do the fighting. I prayed you'd survive and that by the time you came back you'd have grown some sense." Prescott closed the folder of music and faced him.

George, as he had many times before, instead of looking into his father's eyes looked at a point beyond his left ear. At the moment, just past that ear he could see half of a framed photograph of one of his father's singing groups. Probably the Silver Dollar Quartet. He could not make out the face of the man on the end of the photo. Some notable businessman, no doubt. A man who sat on four boards of directors making decisions that could topple the economies of six banana republics while he went to the club to shoot eight-handicap golf. Someone like Prescott Bush.

"When you chose this baseball career," his father said, "I finally realized you had serious problems facing reality. I would think the dismal history of your involvement in this sport might have taught you something. Now, by the grace of God and sheer luck you find yourself, on the verge of your middle years, in the spotlight. I can't imagine how it happened. But I know one thing: you must take advantage of this situation. You must seize the brass ring before the carousel stops. As soon as the Series is over, I want you to take up a career in politics."

George stopped looking at the photo. His father's eyes were on his. "Politics? But, Dad, I thought I could become a coach."

"A coach?"

"A coach. I don't know anything about politics. I'm a baseball player. Nobody is going to elect a baseball player."

Prescott Bush stepped closer. He made a fist, beginning to be carried away by his own rhetoric. "Twenty years ago, maybe, you would be right. But, George, times are changing. People want an attractive face. They want somebody famous. It doesn't matter so much on what they've done before. Look at Eisenhower. He had no experience of government. The only reason he got elected was because he was a war hero. Now you're a war hero, or at least we can dress you up into a reasonable facsimile of one. You're Yale educated, a brainy boy. You've got breeding and class. You're not bad looking. And thanks to this children's game, you're famous — for the next two weeks, anyway. So after the Series we strike while the iron's hot. You retire from baseball. File for Congress on the Republican ticket in the third Connecticut district."

"But I don't even live in Connecticut."

"Don't be contrary, George. You're a baseball player; you live on the road. Your last stable residence before you took up this, this — baseball — was New Haven. I've held an apartment there for years in your name. That's good enough for the people we're going to convince."

His father towered over him. George got up, retreated toward the window. "But I don't know anything about politics!"

"So? You'll learn. Despite the fact I've been against your playing baseball, I have to say that it will work well for you. It's the national game. Every kid in the country wants to be a ballplayer, most of the adults do, too. It's hard enough for people from our class to overcome the prejudice against money, George. Baseball gives you the common touch. Why, you'll probably be the only Republican in the Congress ever to have showered with a Negro. On a regular basis, I mean."

"I don't even like politics."

"George, there are only two kinds of people in the world, the employers and the employees. You were born and bred to the former. I will not allow you to persist in degrading yourself into one of the latter."

"Dad, really, I appreciate your trying to look out for me. Don't get me wrong, gratitude's my middle name. But I love baseball. There's some big opportunities there, I think. Down in Chattanooga I made some friends. I think I can be a good coach, and eventually I'll wear a manager's uniform."

Prescott Bush stared at him. George remembered that look when he'd forgotten to tie off the sailboat one summer up in Kennebunkport. He began to wilt. Eventually his father shook his head. "It comes to me at last that you do not possess the wits that God gave a Newfoundland retriever."

George felt his face flush. He looked away. "You're just jealous because I did what you never had the guts to do. What about you and your golf? You, you — dilettante! I'm going to be a manager!"

"George, if I want to I can step into that outer office, pick up the telephone, and in fifteen minutes set in motion a chain of events that will guarantee you won't get a job mopping toilets in the club-house."

George retreated to the window. "You think you can run my life? You just want me to be another appendage of Senator Bush. Well, you can forget it! I'm not your boy anymore."

"You'd rather spend the rest of your life letting men like this Communist Castro make a fool of you?"

George caught himself before he could completely lose his temper. Feeling hopeless, he drummed his knuckles on the window sill, staring down into the narrow street. Down below them brokers and bankers hustled from meeting to meeting trying to make a buck. He might have been one of them. Would his father have been any happier?

He turned. "Dad, you don't know anything. Try for once to understand. I've never been so alive as I've been for moments — just moments out of eleven years — on the ball field. It's truly American."

"I agree with you, George — it's as American as General Motors. Baseball is a product. You players are the assembly-line workers who make it. But you refuse to understand that, and that's your undoing. Time eats you up, and you end up in the dustbin, a wasted husk."

George felt the helpless fury again. "Dad, you've got to —"

"Are you going to tell me I *have to* do something, George?" Prescott Bush sat back down at the piano, tried a few notes. He peeked over his shoulder at George, unsmiling, and began again to sing:

"Go and do your best endeavor,
And before all links we sever,
We will say farewell for ever.
Go to glory and the grave!

"For your foes are fierce and ruthless,
False, unmerciful and truthless.
Young and tender, old and toothless,
All in vain their mercy crave."

George stalked out of the room, through the secretary's office, and down the corridor toward the elevators. It was all he could do to keep from punching his fist through the rosewood paneling. He felt his pulse thrumming in his temples, slowing as he waited for the dilatory elevator to arrive, rage turning to depression.

Riding down he remembered something his mother had said to him twenty years before. He'd been one of the best tennis players at the River Club in Kennebunkport. One summer, in front of the whole family, he lost a championship match. He knew he'd let them down, and tried to explain to his mother that he'd only been off his game.

"You don't have a game," she'd said.

The elevator let him out into the lobby. On Seventh Avenue, he stepped into a bar and ordered a beer. On the TV in the corner, sound turned low, an announcer was going over the highlights of the Series. The TV switched to an image of some play in the field. George heard a reference to "Senator Bush," but he couldn't tell which one of them they were talking about.

10

A few of the pitchers, including Camilo Pascual, the young right-hander who was to start game five, were the only others in the club-house when George showed up. The tone was grim. Nobody wanted to talk about how their season might be over in a few hours. Instead they talked fishing.

Pascual was nervous; George was keyed tighter than a Christmas toy. Ten years of obscurity, and now hero one day, goat the next. The memory of his teammates' hollow words of encouragement as he'd slumped back into the dugout each time Castro struck him out made George want to crawl into his locker and hide. The supercilious brown bastard. What kind of man would go out of his way to humiliate him?

Stobbs sauntered in, whistling. He crouched into a batting stance, swung an imaginary Louisville Slugger through Kralick's head, then watched it sail out into the imaginary bleachers. "Hey, guys, I got an idea," he said. "If we get the lead today, let's call time out."

But they didn't get the lead. By the top of the second, they were down 3-0. Pascual, on the verge of being yanked, settled down. The score stayed frozen through six. The Senators finally got to Jones in the seventh when Allison doubled and Killebrew hit a towering home run into the bullpen in left center: 3-2, Giants. Meanwhile the Senators' shaky relief pitching held as the Giants stranded runners in the sixth and eighth and hit three double plays.

By the top of the ninth the Giants still clung to the 3-2 lead, three outs away from winning the Series, and the rowdy New York fans were gearing up for a celebration. The Senator dugout was grim, but they had the heart of the order up: Sievers, Lemon, Killebrew. Between them they had hit ninety-four home runs that season. They had also struck out almost three hundred times.

Rigney went out to talk to Jones, then left him in, though he had Stu Miller up and throwing in the bullpen. Sievers took the first pitch for a strike, fouled off the second, and went down swinging at a high fastball. The crowd roared.

Lemon went into the hole 0-2, worked the count even, and grounded out to second.

The crowd, on their feet, chanted continuously now. Fans

pounded on the dugout roof, and the din was deafening. Killebrew stepped into the batter's box, and George moved up to the on-deck circle. On one knee in the dirt, he bowed his head and prayed that Killer would get on base.

"He's praying!" Castro shouted from the Giants' dugout. "Well might you pray, Sen-a-tor Bush!"

Killebrew called time and spat toward the Giants. The crowd screamed abuse at him. He stepped back into the box. Jones went into his windup. Killebrew took a tremendous cut and missed. The next pitch was a change-up that Killebrew mistimed and slammed five hundred feet down the left-field line into the upper deck — foul. The crowd quieted. Jones stepped off the mound, wiped his brow, shook off a couple of signs, and threw another fastball that Killebrew slapped into right for a single.

That was it for Jones. Rigney called in Miller. Lavagetto came out and spoke to George. "All right. He won't try anything tricky. Look for the fastball."

George nodded, and Lavagetto bounced back into the dugout. "Come on, George Herbert Walker Bush!" Consolo called. George tried to ignore the crowd and the Giants' heckling, while Miller warmed up. His stomach was tied into twelve knots. He avoided looking into the box seats where he knew his father sat. Politics. What the blazes did he want with politics?

Finally, Miller was ready. "Play ball!" the ump yelled. George stepped into the box.

He didn't wait. The first pitch was a fastball. He turned on it, made contact, but got too far under it. The ball soared out into left, a high, lazy fly. George slammed down his bat and, heart sinking, legged it out. The crowd cheered, and Alou circled back to make the catch. George was rounding first, his head down, when he heard a stunned groan from fifty thousand throats at once. He looked up to see Alou slam his glove to the ground. Miller, on the mound, did the same. The Senators' dugout was leaping insanity. Somehow, the ball had carried far enough to drop into the overhanging upper deck, 250 feet away. Home run. Senators lead, 4-3.

"Lucky bastard!" Castro shouted as Bush rounded third. Stobbs shut them down in the ninth, and the Senators won.

11

SENATOR BUSH SAVES WASHINGTON! the headlines screamed. MAKES CASTRO SEE RED. They were comparing it to the 1923 Series, held in these same Polo Grounds, where Casey Stengel, a thirty-two-year-old outfielder who'd spent twelve years in the majors without doing anything that might cause anyone to remember him, batted .417 and hit home runs to win two games.

Reporters stuck to him like flies on sugar. The pressure of released humiliation loosened George's tongue. "I know Castro's type," he said, snarling what he hoped was a good imitation of a manly snarl. "At the wedding he's the bride, at the funeral he's the dead person. You know, the corpse. That kind of poor sportsmanship just burns me up. But I've been around. He can't get my goat because of where I've got it in the guts department."

The papers ate it up. Smart money had said the Series would never go back to Washington. Now they were on the train to Griffith Stadium, and if the Senators were going to lose, at least the home fans would have the pleasure of going through the agony in person.

Game six was a slugfest. Five homers: McCovey, Mays, Cepeda for the Giants; Naragon and Lemon for the Senators. Kaat and Antonelli were both knocked out early. The lead changed back and forth three times.

George hit three singles, a sacrifice fly, and drew a walk. He scored twice. The Senators came from behind to win, 10-8. In the ninth, George sprained his ankle sliding into third. It was all he could do to hobble into the locker room after the game.

"It doesn't hurt," George told the reporters. "Bar always says, and she knows me better than anybody, go ahead and ask around, 'You're the game one, George.' Not the gamy one, mind you!" He laughed, smiled a crooked smile.

"A man's gotta do what a man's gotta do," he told them. "That strong but silent type of thing. My father said so."

12

Fonseca waited until Fidel emerged into the twilight outside the Fifth Street stadium exit. As Fonseca approached, his hand on the slick automatic in his overcoat pocket, his mind cast back to their political years in Havana, where young men such as they, determined to seek prominence, would be as likely to face the barrel of a pistol as an electoral challenge. Ah, nostalgia.

"Pretty funny, that *Sen*-a-TOR Bush," Fonseca said. He shoved Fidel back toward the exit. Nobody was around.

If Fidel was scared, a slight narrowing of his eyes was the only sign. "What is this about?"

"Not a thing. Raul says hello."

"Hello to Raul."

"Mirta says hello, too."

"You haven't spoken to her." Fidel took a cigar from his mohair jacket, fished a knife from a pocket, trimmed off the end, and lit it with a battered Zippo. "She doesn't speak with exiled radicals. Or mobsters."

Fonseca was impressed by the performance. "Are you going to do this job, finally?"

"I can only do my half. One cannot make a sow look like a ballet dancer."

"It is not apparent to our friends that you're doing your half."

"Tell them I am truly frightened, Luis." He blew a plume of smoke. It was dark now, almost full night. "Meanwhile, I am hungry. Let me buy you a Washington dinner."

The attitude was all too typical of Fidel, and Fonseca was sick of it. He had fallen under Fidel's spell back in the university, thought him some sort of great man. In 1948, his self-regard could be justified as necessary boldness. But when the head of the National Sports Directory was shot dead in the street, Fonseca had not been the only one to think Fidel was the killer. It was a gesture of suicidal machismo of the sort that Fidel admired. Gunmen scoured the streets for them. While Fonseca hid in a series of airless apartments, Fidel got a quick tryout with the Giants, married Mirta, and abandoned Havana, leaving Fonseca and their friends to deal with the consequences.

"If you don't take care, Fidel, our friends will buy you a Washington grave."

"They are not my friends — or yours."

"No, they aren't. But this was our choice, and you have to go through with it." Fonseca watched a beat cop stop at the corner, then turn away down the street. He moved closer, stuck the pistol into Fidel's ribs. "You know, Fidel, I have a strong desire to shoot you right now. Who cares about the World Series? It would be pleasant just to see you bleed."

The tip of Fidel's cigar glowed in the dark. "This Bush would be no hero then."

"But I would be."

"You would be a traitor."

Fonseca laughed. "Don't say that word again. It evokes too many memories." He plucked the cigar from Fidel's hand, threw it onto the sidewalk. "Athletes should not smoke."

He pulled the gun back, drew his hand from his overcoat, and crossed the street.

13

The night before, the Russians announced they had shot down U.S. spy plane over the Soviet Union. A pack of lies, President Nixon said. No such planes existed.

Meanwhile, on the clubhouse radio, a feverish announcer was discussing strategy for game seven. A flock of telegrams had arrived to urge the Senators on. Tacked on the bulletin board in the locker room, they gave pathetic glimpses into the hearts of the thousands who had for years tied their sense of well-being to the fate of a punk team like the Senators.

Show those racially polluted commie-symps what Americans stand for.

My eight year old son, crippled by polio, sits up in his wheelchair so that he can watch the games on TV.

Jesus Christ, creator of the heavens and earth, is with you.

As George laced up his spikes over his aching ankle in preparation for the game, thinking about facing Castro one last time, it came to him that he was terrified.

In the last week, he had entered an atmosphere he had not lived in since Yale. He was a hero. People had expectations of him. He was admired and courted. If he had received any respect before, it was the respect given to someone who refused to quit when every indication shouted he ought to try something else. He did not have the braggadocio of a Castro. Yet here, miraculously, he was shining.

Except he *knew* that Castro was better than he was, and he *knew* that anybody who really knew the game knew it, too. He knew that this week was a fluke, a strange conjunction of the stars that had knocked him into the "groove," as the old man in the bar had said. It could evaporate at any instant. It could already have evaporated.

Lavagetto and Mr. Griffith came in and turned off the radio. "Okay, boys," Lavagetto said. "People in this city been waiting a long time for this game. A lot of you been waiting your whole careers for it, and you younger ones might not get a lot of chances to play in the seventh game of the World Series. Nobody gave us a chance to be here today, but here we are. Let's make the most of it, go out there and kick the blazes out of them, then come back in and drink some champagne!"

The team whooped and headed out to the field. Coming up the tunnel, the sound of cleats scraping damp concrete, the smell of stale beer and mildew, Bush could see a sliver of the bright grass and white baselines, the outfield fence and crowds in the bleachers, sunlight so bright it hurt his eyes. When the team climbed the dugout steps onto the field, a great roar rose from the throats of the thirty thousand fans. He had never heard anything so beautiful, or frightening. The concentrated focus of their hope swelled George's chest with unnameable emotion, brought tears to his eyes, and he ducked his head and slammed his fist into his worn first baseman's glove.

The teams lined up on the first- and third-base lines for the National Anthem. The fans began cheering even before the last line of the song faded away, and George jogged to first, stepping on the bag for good luck. His ankle twinged; his whole leg felt hot. Ramos finished his warmups, the umpire yelled "Play ball!" and they began.

Ramos sent the Giants down in order in the top of the first. In the home half Castro gave up a single to Allison, who advanced to third on a single by Lemon. Killebrew walked. Bush came up with bases loaded, one out. He managed a fly ball to right, and Allison beat the throw to the plate. Castro struck out Bertoia to end the inning. 1-0, Senators.

Ramos retired the Giants in order in the second. In the third, Lemon homered to make it 2-0.

Castro had terrific stuff, but seemed to be struggling with his control. Or else he was playing games again. By the fourth inning he had seven strikeouts to go along with the two runs he'd given up. He shook off pitch after pitch, and Schmidt went out to argue with him. Rigney talked to him in the dugout, and the big Cuban waved his arms as if emphatically arguing his case.

Schmidt homered for the Giants in the fourth, but Ramos was able to get out of the inning without further damage. Senators, 2-1.

In the bottom of the fourth, George came up with a man on first. Castro struck him out on a high fastball that George missed by a foot.

In the Giants' fifth, Spencer doubled off the wall in right. Alou singled him home to tie the game, and one out later, Mays launched a triple over Allison's head into the deepest corner of center field, just shy of the crazy wall protecting Mrs. Mahan's backyard. Giants up, 3-2. The crowd groaned. As he walked out to the mound, Lavagetto was already calling for a left-hander to face McCovey. Ramos kicked the dirt, handed him the ball, and headed to the showers, and Stobbs came on to pitch to McCovey. He got McCovey on a grounder to George at first, and Davenport on a pop fly.

The Senators failed to score in the bottom of the fifth and sixth, but in the seventh George, limping for real now, doubled in Killer to tie the game, and was driven home, wincing as he forced weight down on his ankle, on a single by Naragon. Senators 4-3. The crowd roared.

Rigney came out to talk to Castro, but Castro convinced him to let him stay in. He'd struck out twelve already, and the Giants' bullpen was depleted after the free-for-all in game six.

The score stayed that way through the eighth. By the top of the ninth the crowd was going wild in the expectation of a world championship. Lavagetto had pulled Stobbs, who sat next to Bush in his warmup jacket, and put in the right-hander Hyde, who'd led the team in saves.

The Giants mounted another rally. On the first pitch, Spencer laid a bunt down the first-base line. Hyde stumbled coming off the mound, and George, taken completely by surprise, couldn't get to it on his bad foot. He got up limping, and the trainer came out to ask him if he could play. George was damned if he would let it end so pitifully, and shook him off. Alou grounded to first, Spencer advancing. Cepeda battled the count full, then walked.

Mays stepped into the box. Hyde picked up the rosin bag, walked off the mound, and rubbed up the ball. George could see he was sweating. He stepped back onto the rubber, took the sign, and threw a high fastball that Mays hit four hundred feet, high into the bleachers in left. The Giants leapt out of the dugout, slapping Mays on the back, congratulating each other. The fans tore their clothing in despair, slumped into their seats, cursed and moaned. The proper order had been restored to the universe. George looked over at Castro, who sat in the dugout impassively. Lavagetto came out to talk to Hyde; the crowd booed when the manager left him in, but Hyde managed to get them out of the inning without further damage. As the Senators left the field, the organist tried to stir the crowd, but despair had settled over them like a lead blanket. Giants, 6-4.

In the dugout, Lavagetto tried to get them up for the inning. "This is it, gentlemen. Time to prove we belong here."

Allison had his bat out and was ready to go to work before the umpire had finished sweeping off the plate. Castro threw three warmups and waved him into the box. When Allison lined a single between short and third, the crowd cheered and rose to their feet. Sievers, swinging for the fences, hit a nubbler to the mound, a sure double play. Castro pounced on it in good time, but fumbled the ball, double-clutched, and settled for the out at first. The fans cheered.

Rigney came out to talk it over. He and Schmidt stayed on the mound a long time, Castro gesturing wildly, insisting he wasn't tired. He had struck out the side in the eighth.

Rigney left him in, and Castro rewarded him by striking out Lemon for his seventeenth of the game, a new World Series record. Two down. Killebrew was up. The fans hovered on the brink of nervous collapse. The Senators were torturing them; they were going to drag this out to the last fatal out, not give them a clean killing or a swan-dive fade — no, they would hold out the chance of victory to the last moment, then crush them dead.

Castro rubbed up the ball, checked Allison over his shoulder, shook off a couple of Schmidt's signs, and threw. He got Killebrew in an 0-2 hole, then threw four straight balls to walk him. The crowd noise reached a frenzy.

And so, as he stepped to the plate in the bottom of the ninth, two outs, George Herbert Walker Bush represented the winning run, the potential end to twenty-seven years of Washington frustration, the apotheosis of his life in baseball, or the ignominious end of it. Castro had him set up again, to be the glorious goat for the entire Series. His ankle throbbed. "C'mon, Senator!" Lavagetto shouted. "Make me a genius!"

Castro leaned forward, shook off Schmidt's call, shook off another. He went into his windup, then paused, ball hidden in his glove, staring soberly at George — not mocking, not angry, certainly not intimidated — as if he were looking down from a reconnaissance plane flying high above the ballpark. George tried not to imagine what he was thinking.

Then Castro lifted his knee, strode forward, and threw a fat hanging curve, the sweetest, dopiest, laziest pitch he had thrown all day. George swung. As he did, he felt the last remaining strength of the dying Babe Ruth course down his arms. The ball kissed off the sweet spot of the bat and soared, pure and white as a six-year-old's prayer, into the left-field bleachers.

The stands exploded. Fans boiled onto the field even before George touched second. Allison did a kind of hopping balletic dance around the bases ahead of him, a cross between Nureyev and a man on a pogo stick. The Senators ran out of the dugout and bear-hugged George as he staggered around third; like a broken-field runner he struggled through the fans toward home. A weeping fat man in a plaid shirt, face contorted by ecstasy, blocked his way to the plate, and it was all he could do to keep from knocking him over.

As his teammates pulled him toward the dugout, he caught a glimpse over his shoulder of the Franchise standing on the mound, watching the melee and George at the center of it with an inscrutable expression on his face. Then George was pulled back into the maelstrom and surrendered to his bemused joy.

14

Long after everyone had left and the clubhouse was deserted, Fidel dressed, and instead of leaving walked back out to the field. The stadium was dark, but in the light of the moon he could make out the trampled infield and the obliterated base paths. He stood on the mound and looked around at the empty stands. He was about to leave when someone called him from the dugout. "Beautiful, isn't it?"

Fidel approached. It was a thin man in his sixties. He wore a sporty coat and a white dress shirt open at the collar. "Yes?" Fidel asked.

"The field is beautiful."

Fidel sat next to him on the bench. They stared across the diamond. The wind rustled the trees beyond the outfield walls. "Some people think so," Fidel said.

"I thought we might have a talk," the man said. "I've been waiting around the ballpark before the last few games trying to get hold of you."

"I don't think we have anything to talk about, Mr . . ."

"Weaver. Buck Weaver."

"Mr. Weaver. I don't know you, and you don't know me."

The man came close to smiling. "I know about winning the World Series. And losing it. I was on the winning team in 1917, and the losing one in 1919."

"You would not be kidding me, old man?"

"No. For a long time after the second one, I couldn't face a ballpark. Especially during the Series. I might have gone to quite a few, but I couldn't make myself do it. Now I go to the games every chance I get."

"You still enjoy baseball."

"I love the game. It reminds me of where my body is buried." As he said all of this the man kept smiling, as if it were a funny story he was telling, and a punch line waited in the near future.

"You should quit teasing me, old man," Fidel said. "You're still alive."

"To all outward indications I'm alive, most of the year now. For a long time I was dead the year round. Eventually I was dead only during the summer, and now it's come down to just the Series."

"You are the mysterious one. Why do you not simply tell me what you want with me?"

"I want to know why you did what you just did."

"What did I do?"

"You threw the game."

Fidel watched him. "You cannot prove that."

"I don't have to prove it. I know it, though."

"How do you know it?"

"Because I've seen it done before."

From somewhere in his boyhood, Fidel recalled the name now. Buck Weaver. The 1919 Series. "The Black Sox. You were one of them."

That appeared to be the punch line. The man smiled. His eyes were set in painful nets of wrinkles. "I was never one of them. But I knew about it, and that was enough for that bastard Landis to kick me out of the game."

"What does that have to do with me?"

"At first I wanted to stop you. Now I just want to know why you did it. Are you so blind to what you've got that you could throw it away? You're not a fool. Why?"

"I have my reasons, old man. Eighty thousand dollars, for one."

"You don't need the money."

"My brother in prison does. The people in my home do."

"Don't give me that. You don't really care about them."

Fidel let the moment stretch, listening to the rustling of the wind through the trees, the traffic in the distant street. "No? Well, perhaps. Perhaps I did it just because I could. Because the game betrayed me, because I wanted to show it is as corrupt as the *mierda* around it. It's not any different from the world. You know how it works. How every team has two black ballplayers — the star and the star's roommate." He laughed. "It's not a religion, and this place" — he gestured at Griffith Stadium looming in the night before them — "is not a cathedral."

"I thought that way, when I was angry," Weaver said. "I was a young man. I didn't know how much it meant to me until they took it away."

"Old man, you would have lost it regardless. How old were you? Twenty-five? Thirty? In ten years it would have been taken from you anyway, and you'd be in the same place you are now."

"But I'd have my honor. I wouldn't be a disgrace."

"That's only what other people say. Why should you let their ignorance affect who you are?"

"Brave words. But I've lived it. You haven't — yet." Plainly upset, Weaver walked out onto the field to stand at third base. He crouched; he looked in toward the plate. After a while he straightened, a frail old man, and called in toward Fidel: "When I was twenty-five, I stood out here; I thought I had hold of a baseball in my hand. It turned out it had hold of me."

He came back and stood at the top of the dugout steps. "Don't worry, I'm not going to tell. I didn't then, and I won't now."

Weaver left, and Fidel sat in the dugout.

15

They used the photo of George's painfully shy, crooked smile, a photograph taken in the locker room after he'd been named MVP of the 1959 World Series, on his first campaign poster.

In front of the photographers and reporters, George was greeted by Mr. Griffith. And his father. Prescott Bush wore a political smile as broad as his experience of what was necessary to impress the world. He put his arm around his son's shoulders, and although George was a tall man, it was apparent that his father was still a taller one.

"I'm proud of you, son," Prescott said, in a voice loud enough to be heard by everyone. "You've shown the power of decency and persistence in the face of hollow boasts."

Guys were spraying champagne, running around with their hair sticky and their shirts off, whooping and shouting and slapping each other on the back. Even his father's presence couldn't entirely deflect George's satisfaction. He had done it. Proved himself for once and for all. He wished Bar and the boys could be there. He wanted to shout in the streets, to stay up all night, be pursued by beautiful women. He sat in front of his locker and patiently answered the reporters' questions at length, repeatedly. Only gradually did the furor settle down. George glanced across the room to the brightly lit corner where Prescott was talking, oil camera, with a television reporter.

It was clear that his father was setting him up for this planned political career. It infuriated him that he assumed he could control George so easily, but at the same time George felt confused about what he really wanted for himself. As he sat there in the diminishing chaos, Lavagetto came over and sat down beside him. The manager was still high from the victory.

"I don't believe it!" Lavagetto said. "I thought he was crazy, but old Tricky Dick must have known something I didn't!"

"What do you mean?"

"Mean? — nothing. Just that the President called after the first game and told me to bat you behind Killebrew. I thought he was crazy. But it paid off."

George remembered Prescott Bush whispering into Nixon's ear. He felt a crushing weight on his chest. He stared over at his father in the TV lights, not hearing Lavagetto.

But as he watched, he wondered. If his father had indeed fixed the Series, then everything he'd accomplished came to nothing. But his father was an honorable man. Besides, Nixon was noted for his sports obsession, full of fantasies because he hadn't succeeded himself. His calling Lavagetto was the kind of thing he would do anyway. Winning had been too hard for it to be a setup. No, Castro had wanted to humiliate George, and George had stood up to him.

The reporter finished talking to his father; the TV lights snapped off. George thanked Lavagetto for the faith the manager had shown in him, and limped over to Prescott Bush.

"Feeling pretty good, George?"

"It was a miracle we won. I played above myself."

"Now, don't take what I said back in New York so much to heart. You proved yourself equal to the challenge, that's what." Prescott lowered his voice. "Have you thought any more about the proposition I put to you?"

George looked his father in the eye. If Prescott Bush felt any discomfort, there was no trace of it in his patrician's gaze.

"I guess maybe I've played enough baseball," George said.

His father put his hand on George's shoulder; it felt like a burden. George shrugged it off and headed for the showers.

Many years later, as he faced the Washington press corps in the East Room of the White House, George Herbert Walker Bush was to remember that distant afternoon, in the ninth inning of the seventh game of the World Series, when he'd stood in the batter's box against the Franchise. He had not known then what he now understood: that, like his father, he would do anything to win.

Sunny Billy Day

RON CARLSON

The very first time it happened with Sunny Billy Day was in Bradenton, Florida, spring training, a thick cloudy day on the Gulf, and I was there in the old wooden bleachers, having been released only the week before after going 0 for 4 in Winter Park against the Red Sox, and our manager, Ketchum, saw that my troubles were not over at all. So, not wanting to go back to Texas so soon and face my family, the disappointment and my father's expectation that I'd go to work in his Allstate office, and not wanting to leave Polly alone in Florida in March, a woman who tended toward ball players, I was hanging out, feeling bad, and I was there when it happened.

My own career had been derailed by what they called "stage fright." I was scared. Not in the field — I won a Golden Glove two years in college and in my rookie year with the Pirates. I love the field, but I had a little trouble at the plate. I could hit in the cage; in fact, there were times when batting practice stopped so all the guys playing pepper could come over and bet how many I was going to put in the seats. It wasn't the skill. In a game I'd walk from the on-deck circle to the batter's box and I could feel my heart go through my throat. All those people focusing on one person in the park: me. I could feel my heart drumming in my face. I was tighter than a ten-cent watch — all strikeouts and pop-ups. I went .102 for the season — the lowest official average of any starting-lineup player in the history of baseball.

Ketchum sent me to see the team psychiatrist, but that turned out to be no good, too. I saw him twice. His name was Krick and he was a small man who was losing hair, but his little office and plaid couch felt to me like the batter's box. What I'm saying is: Krick was no help — I was afraid of him, too.

Sometimes just watching others go to bat can start my heart jangling like a rock in a box, and that was how I felt that cloudy day in Bradenton as Sunny Billy Day went to the plate. We (once you play for a team, you say "we" ever after) were playing the White Sox, who were down from Sarasota, and it was a weird day, windy and dark, with those great loads of low clouds and the warm Gulf air rolling through. I mean it was a day that didn't feel like baseball.

Billy came up in the first inning, and the Chicago pitcher, a rookie named Gleason, had him 0 and 2, when the thing happened for the first time. Polly had a hold of my arm and was being extra sweet when Billy came up, to let me know that she didn't care for him at all and was with me now, but — everybody knows — when a woman acts that way it makes you nervous. The kid Gleason was a sharpshooter, a sidearm fastballer who could have struck me out with two pitches, and he had shaved Billy with two laser beams that cut the inside corner.

Gleason's third pitch was the smoking clone of the first two, and Sunny Billy Day, my old friend, my former roommate, lifted his elbows off the table just like he had done twice before and took the third strike.

It *was* a strike. We all knew this. We'd seen the two previous pitches and everybody who was paying attention knew that Gleason had nailed Billy to the barn door. There was no question. Eldon Finney was behind the plate, a major-league veteran, who was known as Yank because of the way he yanked a fistful of air to indicate a strike. His gesture was unmistakable, and on that dark day last March, I did not mistake it. But as soon as the ump straightened up, Sunny Billy, my old teammate, and the most promising rookie the Pirates had seen for thirty years, tapped his cleats one more time and stayed in the box.

"What's the big jerk doing?" Polly asked me. You hate to hear a girl use a phrase like that, "big jerk," when she could have said something like "rotten bastard," but when you're in the stands, instead of running wind sprints in the outfield, you take what you can get.

On the mound in Bradenton, Gleason was confused. Then I saw Billy shrug at the ump in a move I'd seen a hundred times as roommates when he was accused of anything or asked to pay his share of the check at the Castaway. A dust devil skated around the home dugout and out to first, carrying an ugly litter of old sno-cone papers and cigarette butts in its brown vortex, but when the wind died down and play resumed, there was Sunny Billy Day standing in the box. I checked the scoreboard and watched the count shift to 1 and 2.

Eldon "the Yank" Finney had changed his call.

So that was the beginning, and as I said, only a few people saw it and knew this season was going to be a little different. Billy and I weren't speaking — I mean, Polly was with me now, and so I couldn't ask him what was up — but I ran into Ketchum at the Castaway that night and he came over to our table. Polly had wanted to go back there for dinner — for old times' sake; it was in the Castaway where we'd met one year ago. She was having dinner with Billy that night, the Bushel o' Shrimp, and they asked me to join them. Billy had a lot of girls and he was always good about introducing them around. Come on, a guy like Billy had nothing to worry about from other guys, especially me. He could light up a whole room, no kidding, and by the end of an hour, there'd be ten people sitting at his table and every chair in the room would be turned his way. He was a guy, and anybody will back me up on this, who had the magic.

Billy loved the Castaway. "This is exotic," he'd say. "Right? Is this the South Sea island or what?" And he meant it. You had to love him. Some dim dive pins, an old fishing net on the wall and he'd be in paradise.

Anyway, Polly had ordered the Bushel o' Shrimp again and we were having a couple of Mutineers, the daiquiri deal that comes in a skull, when Ketchum came over and asked me — as he does every time we meet — "How you feeling, kid?" which meant have I still got the crippling heebie-jeebies. He has told me all winter that if I want another shot, just say so. Well, who doesn't want another shot? In baseball — no matter what you hear — there are no ex-players, just guys waiting for the right moment for a comeback.

I told Ketchum that if anything changed, he'd be the first to know. Then I asked him what he thought of today's game and he said, "The White Sox are young."

"Yeah," I said. "Especially that pitcher."

"I wouldn't make too much out of that mix-up at the plate today. You know Billy. He's a kind that can change the weather." Ketchum was referring to the gray pre-season game a year before. Billy came up in a light rain when a slice of sunlight opened on the field like a beacon, just long enough for everyone to see my roommate golf a low fastball into the right-field seats for a round trip. It was the at-bat that clinched his place on the roster, and that gave him his nickname.

"Billy Day is a guy who gets the breaks." Ketchum reached into the wicker bushel and sampled one of Polly's shrimp. "And you know what they say about guys who get a lot of breaks." Here he gave Polly a quick look. "They keep getting them." He stood up and started to walk off. "Call me if you want to hit a few. We don't head north until April Fools' Day."

"I don't like that guy," Polly said when he'd left. "I never liked him." She pushed her load of shrimp away. "Let's go." I was going to defend the coach there, a guy who was fair with his men and kept the signals (steal, take, hit-and-run) simple, but the evening had gone a little flat for me too. There we were out to celebrate, but as always the room was full of Billy Day. He was everywhere. He was in the car on the way back to the hotel; he was in the elevator; he was in the room; and — if you want to know it — he was in the bed too. I knew that he was in Polly's dreams and there he was in my head, turning back to the umpire, changing a strike to a ball.

The papers got a hold of what was going on during the last week of March. It was a home game against the Yankees and it was the kind of day that if there were no baseball, you'd invent it to go with the weather. The old Bradenton stands were packed and the whole place smelled of popcorn and coconut oil. Polly was wearing a yellow sundress covered with black polka dots, the kind of dress you wear in a crowded ballpark if you might want one of the players to pick you out while he played first. By this time I was writing a friendly little column for the *Pittsburgh Dispatch* twice a week on "Lifestyles at Spring Training," but I had not done much with Billy. He was getting plenty of legitimate ink, and besides — as I said — we weren't really talking. I liked the writing, even though this was a weird time all around. I kind of *had* to do it, just so I felt useful. I wasn't ready to go home.

It was a good game, two-two in the ninth. Then Billy made a mistake. With one down, he had walked and stolen second. That's a wonderful feeling being on second with one out. There's all that room and you can lead the extra two yards and generally you feel pretty free and cocky out there. I could see Billy was enjoying this feeling, leaving cleat marks in the clay, when they threw him out. The pitcher flipped the ball backhand to the shortstop, and they tagged Billy. Ralph "the Hammer" Fox was umping out there, and he jumped onto one knee in his famous out gesture and wheeled his arm around and he brought the hammer down: OUT! After the tag,

Billy stood up and went over and planted both feet on the base.

"What?" Polly took my arm.

Ralph Fox went over and I could see Billy smiling while he spoke. He patted Ralph's shoulder. Then Fox turned and gave the arms-out gesture for safe — twice — and hollered, "Play ball." It was strange, the kind of thing that makes you sure you're going to get an explanation later.

But the ballpark changed in a way I was to see twenty times during the season: a low quiet descended, not a silence, but an eerie even sound like two thousand people talking to themselves. And the field, too, was stunned, the players standing straight up, their gloves hanging down like their open mouths during the next pitch, which like everything else was now half-speed, a high hanging curve which Red Sorrows blasted over the scoreboard to win the game.

Well, it was no way to win a ballgame, but that wasn't exactly what the papers would say. Ralph Fox, of course, wasn't speaking to the press (none of the umpires would), and smiling Sunny Billy Day only said one thing that went out on the wire from coast to coast: "Hey guys, come on. You saw that Mickey Mouse move. I was safe." Most writers looked the other way, noting the magnitude of Red Sorrows' homer, a "lowering blast," and going on to speculate whether the hit signaled Sorrows' return from a two-year slump. So, the writers avoided it, and in a way I understand. Now I have become a kind of sportswriter and I know it is not always easy to say what you mean. Sometimes if the truth is hard, typing it can hurt again.

There were so many moments that summer when some poor ump would stand in the glare of Billy's smile and toe the dirt, adjust his cap, and change the call. Most of the scenes were blips, glitches: a last swing called a foul ticker; a close play called Billy's way; but some were big, bad, and ugly — so blatant that they had the fans looking at their shoes. Billy had poor judgment. In fact, as I think about it, he had no judgment at all. He was a guy with the gift who had spent his whole life going forward from one thing to the next. People liked him and things came his way. When you first met Billy, it clicked: who is this guy? Why do I want to talk to him? Ketchum assigned us to room together and in a season of hotel rooms, I found out that it had always been that way for him. He had come out of college with a major in American Studies, and he could not name a single president. "My teachers liked me," he said. "Everybody likes me."

He had that right. But he had no judgment. I'd seen him with women. They'd come along, one, two, three, and he'd take them as they came. He didn't have to choose. If he'd had any judgment, he never would have let any woman sit between him and Polly.

Oh, that season I saw him ground to short and get thrown out at first. He'd trot past, look back, and head for the dugout, taking it, but you got the impression it was simply easier to keep on going than stop to change the call. And those times he took it, lying there a foot from third dead out and then trotting off the field, or taking the third strike and then turning for the dugout, you could feel the waves of gratitude from the stands. Those times I know you could feel it, because there weren't many times when Billy Day took it, and as the season wore on, and the Pirates rose to first place, they became increasingly rare.

Sunny Billy Day made the All-Stars, of course. He played a fair first base and he was the guy you couldn't get out. But he was put on the five-day disabled list, "to rest a hamstring," the release said. But I think it was Ketchum being cagey. He wasn't going to gain anything by having a kid who was developing a reputation for spoiling ball games go in and ruin a nice July night in Fenway for fans of both leagues.

By August, it was all out: Billy Day could have his way. You never saw so much written about the state of umping. Billy was being walked most of the time now. Every once in a while some pitcher would throw to him, just to test the water. They were thinking Ketchum was going to pull the plug, tell Billy to face the music, to swallow it if he went down swinging, but it never happened. The best anybody got out of it was a flyout, Billy never contested a flyout. And Ketchum, who had thirty-four good years in the majors and the good reputation to go with them, didn't care. A good reputation is one thing; not having been in the Series is another. He would be seventy by Christmas and he wanted to win it all once, even if it meant letting Billy have his way. Ketchum, it was written, had lost his judgment, too.

I was writing my head off, learning how to do it and liking it a little more. It's something that requires a certain amount of care and it is done alone at a typewriter, not in the batting box in front of forty thousand citizens. And I found I was a hell of a typist; I liked typing. But I wasn't typing about my old roommate — at all. I missed him though; don't think I didn't miss him. I had plenty to say about the rest of the squad, how winning became them, made them into men after so many seasons of having to have their excuses ready before they took the field. Old Red Sorrows was hitting .390 and hadn't said the word "retirement" or the phrase "next season" in months. There was a lot to write about without dealing with Billy Day's behavior.

But, as September came along, I was getting a lot of pressure for interviews. I had been his roommate, hadn't I? What was he like? What happened to my career? Would I be back? Wasn't I dating Billy Day's girl? I soft-pedaled all this, saying "on the other hand" fifty times a week, and that's no good for athletes or writers. On the topic of Polly, I said that we were friends. What a word. The papers went away and came out with what they'd wanted to say anyway: that Billy Day's old roommate had stolen his girl and now he wouldn't write about him. They used an old file photograph of Billy and Polly in the Castaway and one of Billy and me leaning against the backstop in Pittsburgh, last year, the one year I played in the major leagues. Our caps are cocked back, and we are smiling.

During all this, Polly stopped coming to the games with me. She'd had enough of the Pirates for a while, she said, and she took a job as a travel agent and got real busy. We were having, according to the papers, "a relationship," and that term is fine with me, because I don't know what else to say. I was happy to have such a pretty girl to associate with, but I knew that her real ambition was to be with Billy Day.

The Pirates won their division by twenty-eight games, a record, and then they took the National League pennant by whipping the Cardinals four straight. With Billy talking the umps into anything he wanted, and the rest of the team back from the dead and flying in formation, the Pirates were a juggernaut.

It took the Indians seven games to quiet the Twins, and the Series was set. Pirate October, they called it.

The Cleveland Press was ready for Billy. They'd given him more column inches than the Indians total in those last weeks, cataloguing his "blatant disregard for the rules and the dignity of fair play." Some of those guys could write. Billy had pulled one stunt in the playoffs that really drew fire. In game four, with the Pirates ahead five-zip, he bunted foul on a third strike and smiled his way out of it.

As one writer put it, "We don't put up with that kind of thing in Cleveland. We don't like it and we don't need it. When we see disease, we inoculate." As I said, these guys, some of them, could write. Their form of inoculation was an approved cadre of foreign umpires. They brought in ten guys for the Series. They were from Iceland, Zambia, England, Ireland, Hungary, Japan (three), Venezuela, and Tonga. When they met the press, they struck me as the most serious group of men I'd ever seen assembled. It looked good: they knew the rules and they were grim. And the Tongan, who would be behind the plate for game one, looked fully capable of handling anything that could come up with one hand.

Polly didn't go out to Cleveland with me. She had booked a cruise, a month, through the Panama Canal and on to the islands far across the Pacific Ocean, and she was going along as liaison. She smiled when she left and kissed me sweetly, which is just what you don't want your girl to do. She kissed me like I was a writer.

So I went out alone and stayed in the old Hotel Barnard, where a lot of the writers stay. It was lonely out there in Ohio, and I thought about it. It was the end of a full season in which I had not played ball, and here I was in a hotel full of writers, which I had become, instead of over at the Hilton with my club.

I was closing down the bar the night before the Series opener when Billy Day walked in. I couldn't believe my eyes.

"I thought I'd find you here," he said.

"Billy," I said, waving the barman to bring down a couple of lagers. "I'm a writer now. This is where the writers stay. You're out after curfew."

He gestured back at the empty room. "Who's gonna write me up, you?" He smiled his terrific smile and I realized as much as I had avoided him for eight months, I missed him. I missed that smile.

"No," I said. "I don't think so." Our beers came and I asked him, "What's up?"

"It's been a rough season."

"Not from what I read. The Pirates won the pennant."

"Jesus," he said. "What is that, sarcasm? You gonna start talking like a writer too?"

"Billy, you've pulled some stunts."

He slid his beer from one hand to the other on the varnished bar of the Hotel Barnard. And then started to nod. "Yeah," he said. "I guess I did. You know, I didn't see it at first. It just kind of grew."

"And now you know."

"Yeah, now I know all about it. I know what I can do."

"So what brings you out on a night to the Hotel Barnard?" I pointed at his full glass of beer. "It's not the beer."

"You," he said, and he turned to me again and smiled. "You always knew what to do. I don't mean on the field. There was no rookie better. But I mean, what should I do? This is the Series."

"Yeah, it's the Series. If I were you, I'd play ball."

"You know what I mean. Ketchum wants me to use it all. He doesn't care if they tear down the stadium."

"And you?"

"I don't know. All my life, I played to win. It seems wrong not to do something that can help your team. But the people don't like it."

I looked at the clouds crossing the face of Sunny Billy Day, and I knew I was seeing something no man had ever seen there before: second thoughts.

"These new umps may not let you get away with anything."

"Kid," he said to me, touching my shoulder with his fist, his smile as wide and bright as the sun through a pop-up, "I've been missing you. But I thought you knew me better than that. I've lived my life knowing one thing: everybody let's me get away with everything. The only thing I ever lost, I lost to you. Polly. And I didn't even think about it until she was gone. How is she?"

"I'd get her back for you if I could," I said, lifting my glass in a toast to my old friend Billy Day. "Polly," I told him, "is headed for Tahiti."

Billy was right about the umps. They looked good; in fact, when they took the field and stood with their arms behind their backs along the first-base line, they looked like the Supreme Court. The people of Cleveland were ready for something too, because I noted in the article I wrote for the *Dispatch* that the squadron of umpires received a louder ovation when they took the field than the home team did. Everybody knew that without an iron heel from the umps, the Indians might as well take the winter off.

Okay, so it was baseball for several innings. Ohio in October smells sweet and old, and for a while I think we were all transported through the beautiful fall day, the stadium bathing in the yellow light and then patching steeply into the sepia shadow of the upper decks. See: I was learning to write like the other guys.

Sunny Billy Day hadn't been a factor, really, walking twice and grounding a base hit into left. It was just baseball, the score two to one, Cleveland in the top of the eighth. Now, I want to explain what happened carefully. There were seventy-four thousand people there and in the days since the Series I've heard almost that many versions. The thirty major papers disagreed in detail and the videotapes haven't got it all because of the angle and sequence. So let me go slow here. After all, it would be the last play of Sunny Billy Day.

I wasn't in the press box. The truth is that the season had been a little hard on me in terms of making friends with my fellow reporters. I'd had a hundred suppers in half-lit lounges and I don't think it came as a surprise that I didn't really care for the way they talked — not just about baseball, for which they had a curious but abiding disdain. And I'm not one of these guys who think you have to have played a sport — or really done anything — to be able to write about it well. Look at me — I was good in the field, but I can't write half as good as any of the guys I travel with. But sportswriters, when they are together at the end of the day, a group of them having drinks waiting for their Reuben sandwiches to arrive, are a fairly superior and hard-bitten bunch. You don't want to wander into one of these hotel lounges any summer evening if you want to hear anything about the joy of the sport. These guys don't celebrate baseball, and really, like me, they don't analyze it very well. But they have feelings about it; I never met a man who didn't. That's why it's called the major leagues.

Anyway, I don't want to get going on writers and all that stuff. And don't get me wrong. Some of them — hell, most of them — are nice guys and quick about the check or asking how's it going, but it was October and it was all getting to me. I could see myself in two years, flipping my ash into somebody's coffee cup offering a weary expert's opinion. So I waited to sit where someone might actually cheer or spill a little beer when they stood up on a third strike or a home run. Journalists are professionals, anyone will tell you this, and they don't spill their beer. I ended up ten rows behind third in a seat I paid for myself, and it turned out to be a lucky break given what was going to happen.

With one out in the top of the eighth, Billy Day doubled to right. It was a low fastball and he sliced it into the corner.

On the first pitch to Red Sorrows, Coach Ketchum had Billy steal. He's one run down with one out in the eighth, a runner in scoring position, and a fair hitter at the plate, and Ketchum flashes the steal sign — it's crazy. It means one thing: he's trading on Billy's magic all the way. When I saw Ketchum pinch his nose and then go to the bill of his cap, which has been the Pirate's steal sign for four years, I thought: Ketchum's going to use Billy any way he can. The pitch is a high strike which Sorrows fouls straight back against the screen, so now everybody knows. Billy walks back to second. I have trouble believing what I see next. Again Ketchum goes to his nose and his cap: steal. The Cleveland hurler, the old veteran Blade Medina, stretches and whirls to throw to second with Billy caught halfway down and throws the ball into center field. He must have been excited. Billy pulls into third standing.

Okay, I thought, Ketchum, you got what you wanted, now *stop screwing* around. In fact, I must have whispered that or said it aloud, because the guy next to me says to my face, "What'd I do?" These new fans. They don't want to fight you anymore, they want to know how they've offended you. Too much college for this country. I told him I was speaking to someone else, and he let it go, until I felt a tap on my shoulder and he'd bought me a beer. What did I tell you? But I didn't mind. A minute later I would need it.

Sorrow goes down swinging. Two outs.

It was then I got a funny feeling, on top of all the other funny feelings I'd been having in the strangest summer of my life, and it was a feeling about Ketchum, and I came to know as I sipped my beer and watched my old coach walk over to Billy on the bag at third that he was going to try to steal home. Coach Ketchum was the king of the fair shake, a guy known from Candlestick to Fenway as a square shooter, and as he patted Billy on the rump and walked back to the coach's box, I saw his grin. I was ten rows up and the bill of his cap was down, but I saw it clearly — the grin of a deranged miser about to make another two bucks.

Billy had never stolen home in his career.

Blade Medina was a tall guy and as he launched into his windup, kicking his long leg toward third, Billy took off. Billy Day was stealing home; you could feel every mouth in the stadium open. Blade Medina certainly opened his. Then he simply cocked and threw to the catcher, who tagged Billy out before he could decide to slide.

Ketchum was on them before the big Tongan umpire could put his thumb away. For a big guy he had a funny out call, flicking his thumb as if shooting a marble. I have to hand it to Billy. He was headed for the dugout. But Ketchum got him by the shirt and dragged him back out to the plate and made him speak to the umpire. You knew it was going to happen again — and in the World Series — because all the Indians just stood where they were on the field. And sure enough after a moment of Ketchum pushing Billy from the back, as if he was some big puppet in a baseball suit, and Billy speaking softly to the umpire, the large official stepped out in front of the plate and swept his hand out flat in the air as if calming the waters: "Safe!" he said. He said it quietly in his deep voice. Well, it was quiet in Cleveland, do you see? I sat there like everyone else looking at the bottom of my plastic glass of beer and wishing it wasn't so. Seventy-four thousand people sitting in a circle feeling sour in their hearts, not to mention all the sad multitudes watching the televised broadcast.

Then my old coach Ketchum made it worse by hauling Billy over to touch the plate; Billy hadn't even stepped on home base yet. Just typing this makes me feel the ugliness all over again.

But then the real stuff started to happen, and, as I said, there were no good reports of this next part because of everybody looking at their shoes, programs, or their knuckles the way people in a restaurant read the menu real hard when a couple is arguing at the next table. But I saw it, and it redeemed Sunny Billy Day forever to me, and it gave me something that has allowed me, made me really, get out my cleats again and become a baseball player. I'm not so bad a writer that I would call it courage, but it was definitely some big kick in the ass.

What happened was, halfway back to the dugout, Billy turned around. His head was down in what I called *shame* in my report to the *Pittsburgh Dispatch,* and he turned around and went back to home plate. Ketchum was back at third, smug as a jewel thief, and he caught the action too late to do anything about it. Billy took the ump by the sleeve and I saw Billy take off his cap and shake his head and point at the plate. We all knew what he was saying, everybody. The ballpark was back, everyone standing now, watching, and we all saw the big Tongan nod and smile that big smile at Ketchum, and then raise his fist and flick his thumb.

Oh god, the cheer. The cheer went up my spine like a chiropractor. There was joy in Ohio and it went out in waves around the world. I wrote that too. Not, joy at the out; joy at order restored. It was the greatest noise I've ever heard. I hope Billy recognized the sound.

Because what happened next, as the Cleveland Indians ran off the field like kids, and Ketchum's mouth dropped open like the old man he would become in two minutes, surprised everyone, even me.

When the Pirates took the field (and they ran out joyfully too — it was baseball again), there was something wrong. The Pirates pitcher threw his eight warm-up pitches and one of the Cleveland players stepped into the box. That is when the Irishman umping first came skittering onto the field wheeling his arms, stopping play before it had begun, and seventy-four thousand people looked over to where I'd been staring for five minutes: first base. There was no one at first base. Sunny Billy Day had not taken the field.

I wish to this day I'd been closer to the field because I would have hopped the rail and run through the dugout to the clubhouse and found what the batboy said he found: Billy's uniform hung in his locker, still swinging, on the hanger. I asked him later if he got a glimpse of a woman in a yellow dress, but he couldn't recall.

And now, this spring, I'm out again. I'd almost forgotten during my long season in the stands how much fun it was to play baseball. I still have a little trouble at the plate and I ride my heartbeat like a cowboy on a bad bull, but I want to play, and if I remember that and hum to myself a little while I'm in the box, it helps. The new manager is a good guy and if I can keep above .200, he'll start me.

Oh, the Indians won the series, but it went six games and wasn't as one-sided as you might think after such an event. Ketchum stayed in the dugout the whole time, under heavy sedation, though I never mentioned that in my stories. And I never mentioned the postcards I got later from the far island of Pago Pago. I still get them. Sometimes I'll carry one in my pocket when I go to the plate. It's a blue-and-green place mainly, and looks like a great place for a lucky guy and a woman who looks good in summer clothing.

Sunny Billy Day was a guy with a gift. You could see it a mile away. Things came his way. Me, I'm going to have to make my own breaks, but, hey, it's spring again and it feels like life is opening up. I'm a lot less nervous at the plate these days, and I have learned to type.

The Indestructible Hadrian Wilks

W.P. KINSELLA

I ache.

"Again, Liebowitz? You are the clumsiest man on the face of the earth, already," Dr. Harvey Sarner says to me.

I am at the hospital. It is 2:00 a.m.

"I need stitches. I would rather you sew me up than the intern here who looks twelve but must be all of sixteen. They don't let them operate on people until they turn sixteen, do they?"

I had, at first a small qualm at calling my friend Sarner at 2:00 a.m. Then I consider that over the years my injuries have paid for his condo in Key West. For me he should be delighted to get up at 2:00 a.m to suture above, and maybe below, my right eye. Also, Sarner is the only one I've talked to seriously about my being possibly possessed by a dybbuk. To my wife, Bernice, I have mentioned the possibility, which she dismisses as nonsense. Bernice is not much on either Hebrew mythology, or religion. She worships her Saks Fifth Avenue credit card, her charge at Tiffany's.

"Oy, Liebowitz, you should be clumsy in the middle of the day instead of always the dark of night?"

"I am occupied by a dybbuk. A dybbuk, a wandering soul, works at night. However, three hours I've been holding a handkerchief to my face at Emergency. Only now are my X-Rays back, I have a cracked cheekbone, a chipped tooth, a swollen lip, gravel embedded in my hands and knees, cuts above and below my right eye.

"You fell down again, yes? I have 90-year-olds who fall down less. You are in the prime of life, Liebowitz. Try to stay on your feet."

I am only thirty-eight, the same age as Hadrian Wilks, the famous baseball player. Geminis both of us. Wilks is eight days younger than me. My waist is thickening, there is a tinge of gray at the temples of my longish blue-black hair. Bernice, who is dark and tall, who looks stunning in green, says, "Yossi, you are handsome, sexy, virile." I am flattered. She has her sights set on a chestnut Mercedes the color of her eyes. She will get it.

"I fell down coming out of the ballpark. Tripped on a parking barrier, stumbled for twenty feet before I crash-landed on my face. My glasses are broken in half, the lenses gouged."

"And Hadrian Wilks?"

"Tonight I thought I had been spared. I'm listening on my radio to the Yankee game in Kansas City. Two hours earlier there. I sit in Shea Stadium watching them lose to Atlanta. On the radio, in the seventh inning, Hadrian Wilks gets hit in the face. 'Oy,' says the announcer, 'blood everywhere.' They drive an ambulance right onto the field to gobble up Hadrian Wilks and transport him to the hospital. At Shea Stadium, I'm sitting unharmed in my seat. I look above me, scan the dark sky in case something should fall on me. One of them damn planes, maybe, in and out of La Guardia all night like mechanized buzzards, every game.

"'Looks like for sure Hadrian Wilks' consecutive-game streak is over with. Only fifty-one games until he passes Cal Ripkin's all time record,' says the announcer. The Mets' game ends. I walk more carefully than you can imagine. Rude people everywhere, young thugs running, roughhousing. In Kansas City the game goes on; they await a bulletin on Wilks' condition.

"I make it to the parking lot. I dodge cars. I dodge people. I am careful you wouldn't believe. I see my car. I make a beeline for it. Suddenly, in front of me a parking barrier wasn't there five seconds ago. I trip, I stumble, I fall. Next thing, two guys are leaning over me. "'You alright, Mac?' one of them says.

"'Do I look alright?' I ask, groping for my glasses, blood dripping in my eyes. They help sit me up, wander away eyes downcast when I ask for further help. Everyone else ignores me. I look like a drunk who has fallen. Eventually, I make my way back to the stadium, to emergency medical, where a nurse wipes the dirt and blood off my face. 'You got some nasty bruises, scrapes.' She puts antiseptic on my hands, on my knees, right through the shredded cloth of my slacks, brand new, second time I wore them. 'You're gonna need stitches,' she says. Gives me directions to the hospital. Do they offer they should pay for a cab? Give to me a subway token? Neither."

"Sit tight. Twenty minutes I'll be there," says Dr. Sarner. "And

Wilks? You heard yet his condition?"

"The game just ended. Wouldn't you know, not so serious as first thought. A badly bruised cheekbone. Nothing broken. He'll at least be able to pinch hit tomorrow night. His streak's alive."

"And him not even Jewish."

"A Righteous Gentile, perhaps."

"So what's he done good for Jews, Yossi?"

"Is married to a Jewish girl. You should know that, Sarner."

"Is good for Jews he should marry a Jewish girl?"

"He refused to play golf at a country club that wouldn't admit Jews. He gives to good causes. To Israel some. I've seen the canceled checks. Sometimes is an advantage to be a partner in a multi-national accounting firm."

I was ten the first time it happened to me. Hadrian Wilks I knew from nothing. I was playing Little League. For a pudgy kid with glasses I was average. I could hit the ball. I ran with the speed of water finding its own level. In the second inning, as I batted, I took one right in the middle of the forehead. Next thing I am boots up in the dust, the umpire staring into my face. The stickiness when I touched my forehead I knew was blood. More stars than the planetarium. A night in hospital for observation. Five stitches. I am dizzy for days. My mother keeps me from baseball for two weeks.

It is only three years ago, after I become suspicious, that I read in a story about Hadrian Wilks that when he was ten he was hit in the forehead by a pitch, rushed to hospital. Doctors, even then, marvel that he needs only one stitch, a night for observation he spends, no dizziness, his eyes are fine. He plays ball the next day.

I have had more injuries than any accountant should suffer: every kind of sprain and muscle pull known to medicine. In high school I broke both ankles, one at a time, thankfully. Once, playing softball, when I slid into a home plate made of concrete, the other slipping on water as I took the two steps down from the cafeteria.

"Liebowitz, you are the clumsiest student on earth. Our medical insurance premiums rise simply because you are with us. They know about you," says Feldman, the principal.

On my honeymoon a rock falls from a cliff in Arizona, paralyzes my elbow. A bone spur. Surgery I need. "You'd think you were an athlete," Dr. Sarner said to me after the operation. "Such bone spurs come usually after pitching 200 innings a season."

That was my introduction to Harvey Sarner.

Who is Hadrian Wilks? Fifteen years ago he came to the major leagues. I'd heard his name a few times, touted by those in the know as a coming superstar. His streak started in his second season, he'll break Cal Ripkin's record for consecutive games in late September. He has been under a media spotlight for the last three years as he passes Lou Gerhig, closes in on Ripkin. It came on me like a biblical revelation, about two years ago, that my pattern of injuries coincided with those of Hadrian Wilks. The Indestructible Hadrian Wilks, as he has come to be called. He gives the sportswriters a thrill — a game. Wilks plays with total abandon, as if the approaching record never enters his mind. He doesn't like to come out of a game, though as long as he appears on the field in a game he inches toward the record.

"I don't want the record tainted," he says. "I want to play every inning possible."

He always plays like there is no tomorrow. He leaps into the stands behind first base after foul balls, topples into the dugout if a play calls for it. He still, at 38, steals an occasional base, sliding into second like a charging bull. No one knows better how to take out a second baseman in order to break up a double play than Wilks. He has had so many injuries. He plays through them. The sports writers love him, the fans love him. He is one of the most popular players ever to put on a uniform.

We are walking across the parking lot, me and Sarner, late as always — Harvey considers half an hour late, early. Doctors are used to keeping people waiting. Sarner is soft as a baby, lists forward, pulled that way by the extra weight he carries on his belly like a pregnancy.

"A fine example for your patients," I have chided him.

"A love affair with pie and ice cream," he says shrugging amiably. "Lori prefers I should be enamored of food rather than other women."

Sarner may well have married one of the world's most beautiful women. Doctors get all the breaks that way. While Sarner puffs up like he's snake-bitten, Lori not only fails to age, she becomes more beautiful as the years pass.

We are listening to the national anthem on Harvey's transistor radio. By the time we buy tickets and find our seats we will have missed Hadrian Wilks' first at-bat.

"Muddy Corcoran takes his final warm-up pitch and Hadrian Wilks steps into the batter's box," the announcer says while we shuffle toward the ticket window.

"Corcoran looks awfully sharp tonight," the announcer goes on. "It's not that he has such wonderful stuff, but the way he delivers. He hasn't been called the 'Octopus' all these years for nothing. Corcoran is all arms, legs, knees and elbows, making it almost impossible for the batter to pick up the ball as it leaves his hand. Corcoran has always had a tremendous advantage over the hitters, consider his 2.80 ERA over his seven-year career.

"Here's the first pitch, it's in on . . . Oh, it hit him. It hit Wilks in the face. He's down writhing in the dirt. The trainer and manager are at his side. Oh, it looks like he took it on the right cheek. There's blood everywhere. Wilks is still now, it appears he's lost consciousness."

We are still fifty yards from the front of the stadium.

"Damn," says Harvey Sarner, and steps up his pace.

"Slow down. I'm the one in danger here."

"They're bringing a stretcher out on the field, this looks bad. His teammates are gently lifting him onto the stretcher. Manager Schmidt is holding a towel against Hadrian's face. The towel is already soaked through with blood. It looks like this signals the end of Hadrian Wilks incredible string of consecutive games."

The announcer describes how Wilks is closing in on Cal Ripkin's record, and how before that Lou Gerhig held the record for fifty-some years, and once he passes Ripkin there will be only fifteen games to go to pass the all time record holder, Winslow Martinez, the white-eyed short stop from Courteguay, who was rumored to be bionic, or perhaps voodoo-induced. Martinez never in his career allowed himself to be examined by anyone in the medical profession. "It is my diet, mon, he told reporters thousands of times over the years, "high in guava, low in fat, my bones bend like a baby's, never break, my skin is thicker than a leather belt."

Proceeding quickly but cautiously, I keep my eyes on the entrance to the stadium, when from behind I'm taken out by a hoodlum on a Jetpower Board, the latest machination of evil manufactured specifically for teenagers. The rider bears so much armor he looks like something directly from the futuristic movie *Rollerball*, a movie, incidentally, whose time has come.

"Are you alright," Sarner asks stupidly, as he kneels beside me.

"I should know how I am?" The world spins dizzily. "Aren't you the doctor? Figure out how I am."

I lay with my right hand under the right side of my face, blood is oozing through my fingers, dripping on the grit-covered asphalt, a small pool forming.

"Today, for Hadrian Wilks was consecutive game number . . ." I miss the exact total as a horn honks behind us. "He's been called Indestructible for so long it's like a second name. The ambulance is pulling in from left field. Corcoran is walking along beside the stretcher. Off the field he and Hadrian Wilks are best friends. There was no ill intent. Just a curve ball that got away. In fact, I believe Hadrian was the best man at Corcoran's wedding a few years ago.

I lay perfectly still. My left eye is open. I see. Therefore, I must be conscious.

"Are you alright?" Sarner asks again.

"NO! Alright, I'm not," I say. I am one large bruise. I'm in shock.

A young couple, the girl in jeans and a pink halter top, stare at us.

"Would you run to the gate, have them send someone from first aid, or security? My friend is hurt," says Sarner.

"The Powerboarder went that way," the girl says as they hurry off. She has a nasty, nasal Bronx accent. Sarner probes.

"Anything broken?" I ask.

"Only your face as far as I can tell." Sarner blows grit away from in front of my mouth.

"The veteran, Bobby Monday runs for Wilks as Pokey Valdez the shortstop steps in to bat. Corcoran is obviously shaken up. The umpire has allowed him some warm-up pitches. I imagine the umpires are shaken up, too. I don't know anyone in the game who doesn't like the Indestructible Hadrian Wilks."

We can hear the roar of the crowd honoring Hadrian Wilks as the ambulance carries him off the playing field.

A security guard and a young man in a white shirt with a Red Cross arm band hurry toward us. The pool of blood under my head grows larger.

"Can you move?" asks the First Aid person. "Should we move him?" he says to Sarner, who has identified himself as a doctor. Sarner nods.

"I can move," I say. With the young man's help, Sarner rolls me onto my back, where I lay like a squashed bug.

"We better call for an ambulance," the First Aid person says to the Security Guard and Sarner.

"Give me a minute," I say. "I'll be able to walk." Wouldn't it be ironic if I ended up in the same vehicle as Hadrian Wilks, I think?

After my brief stint of flying through the air I landed palms first. Both hands are bleeding. The dizziness dissipates. I crawl a few feet to retrieve my glasses, one lens is scourged with deep grooves. One of the arms has been snapped off.

"That eye looks really bad," the First Aid person says. "Do you think you can stand up. We could help you to the First Aid Room under the grandstand."

With Sarner on one side, the First Aid person on the other, they manage to get me to my feet.

"I feel a little queasy," I say.

My right eye is already swelling shut.

In the first aid room, Sarner stops the blood flow, cleanses the abrasions with antiseptic, recommends that when I feel well enough, we should go to the nearest hospital for a tetanus shot, possibly sutures.

Sarner and the first aid people agree that I am in mild shock. "Just lay still for a while, and keep that blanket around you," they say.

We never did get to see the game. Ironically, we waited for hours in the emergency room of the hospital while inside Hadrian Wilks had his wounds cleaned and sutured, and received a tetanus booster.

Several reporters were milling around the Emergency Waiting Room, speculating on how long Hadrian Wilks would be out of action, and if the injury might possibly end his career.

It turned out that I had another fractured cheek bone, with

everything on the right side of my face displaced in some manner.

"What about Hadrian Wilks?" I asked a reporter as I was leaving.

"The guy is truly indestructible," the reporter said, shaking his head in wonder. "No breaks, just a bruised cheek bone and a one-stitch cut under his eye. No indication of any vision problems. The doctors say he should be able to bat in maybe three days. No reason he can't play a little defence tomorrow. I guess that's today," he added, looking at his watch. "And keep his string intact. Some guys sure have all the luck."

"They sure do," I said. I told him about the incident with the Powerboarder in the parking lot and sustaining a much worse injury to the same part of his face. "Some guys don't have any luck at all," I went on.

I was off work nearly two weeks, had to undergo two minor surgeries, a metal pin inserted in my cheek bone. Even after two weeks my eyes were still black and swollen. I looked like I'd gone ten rounds with a promising middleweight.

"Sarner," I asked, "how many injuries have I had in the past fourteen years?"

"More than I want to remember. You, Yossi, are the unluckiest, most accident prone son-of-a-bitch who ever lived."

"Would you guess one a year?" I persisted.

"At least."

"Okay, now listen to this, three weeks ago I fell and broke my cheekbone, got cuts and bruises and scrapes. When was the one before that?"

"Last August, I guess. You were golfing, stepped into a sand trap and broke your right ankle."

"And before that?"

"You fell down coming out of a restaurant. Before that you were playing catch with your son and took one on the right ring finger."

"It'll never be the same."

I waved my right hand in his face. The first joint of the ring finger appeared stiff and permanently swollen.

"Okay, so now we go back two years to the fall at the restaurant.

I was talking, wasn't looking where I was going. There was a small step down. I caught myself by grabbing a parked car but I strained a groin muscle. I limped for two months, those kind of injuries never heal."

"What are you getting at?" said Sarner. "You looking for a pattern?"

"Seriously, I think there might be. All my injuries have taken place during baseball season.

It is Sarner to whom I first mention the word dybbuk.

"Dybbuk is what?" says Sarner.

"Mythology mainly, touches sometimes religion. A dybbuk, I've heard, is a wandering soul, is someone who takes on the pain of others."

"You think you? All these accidents?"

"Would explain a lot. But I've come up with a theory. Not just in general do I take on pain. Specifically, Hadrian Wilks. Sarner, I've been doing homework. Thousands of sports pages over twenty years. Wilks plays like tomorrow don't exist. He's injured too many times to count, sprains, twists, muscle pulls. Looks bad at the time, a few hours later he's recovered enough to play the next day. Me, I ache. Terminal ache. Wilks is injured, I suffer the pain, the disablement."

"Such a thing I have never heard." We are playing dominoes.

We have become friends because of my sprains, my fractures. Twice a week I try to win back some of my money. Sarner is too good for me. He has designed a variation of the game, seven dominoes each. Sarner wins far too often for it to be luck. Thank heaven I am a good accountant, make a fine living.

"You don't know your religion?" I accuse Sarner.

"Who has time for obscurities?"

"I'm making time. I'm on to something. I'm going to take my story to the press, to TV, to magazines. I have proof. I have checked every injury suffered by Hadrian Wilks, each one corresponds with an accident by me, an injury, a fall."

"I'd be careful if I were you, Yossi. No good can come from this."

Sarner, as usual, is right.

I began to put two and two together and what it added up to was something irregular.

In winter, I sometimes resort to teaching a semester of Bonehead Accounting at a community college named for a woman who was murdered by a jealous husband, to students who shouldn't be allowed within five hundred yards of a college unless they're bussing tables in the cafeteria. Time on my hands, I began doing some genuine research.

I spent days in the newspaper morgue reading the sports pages, seeing how many times in his many-season streak Hadrian Wilks had suffered injuries of any kind, but especially injuries that looked like they might cause him to miss a game.

The research took weeks, but what emerged was a definite pattern. Except for years three, six, and nine, there had been at least one, sometimes several injuries to Hadrian Wilks that at first appeared serious, but faded quickly, almost always within twenty-four hours (except once he pulled a hamstring just before the All-Star break, managed to be a designated hitter for four games after the break before returning to first base), to a bruise, a strain, a slight sprain, a muscle pull, the kind of injuries a veteran like Hadrian Wilks plays through.

It wasn't until Wilks was nearly ten seasons into his Odyssey that the press took any interest. I mean Gerhig's record stood for over half a century, Ripkin's for seven years, Martinez' for only three. Hadrian played in the shadow of both, not a lot of pressure or press until recently.

I went back to my diaries for that teenage summer when the streak began. It was all girls and cars and my summer job at the bottling plant where my father was a partner. There were days of blank pages. But there it was. July 7: Broke my collarbone while goofing around at the park. My old man was really pissed at me, like I broke it on purpose. I was showing off for some girls by standing on the kid's swings and took a spill.

In spite of my research, the facts I've uncovered, I've been ignored, turned away, spurned, laughed at by everyone from *USA Today* to *The New York Times*, to *Larry King Live*.

"Fanciful," is the kindest critique I've received, that from *Sports*

Illustrated, who at least took time to write me a letter. The editor at *SI* was Jewish. "No indication a dybbuk takes on the pain of others" was scribbled at the bottom.

"Have some imagination," I faxed back. I received no response.

I called Hadrian Wilks' agent. He listened for about thirty seconds and hung up.

I called the editor at *SI*, spent my own money for the call, waited through ten minutes of "Honey" and "Wichita Lineman," while they tried to locate him.

"But there are individuals who take on the pain of others," I cried. I tried to remain rational, not let my voice rise. Don't destroy your credibility, I said under my breath.

"I'm sorry, Mr. Liebowitz, but there's no way to corroborate your thesis."

"But dates coincide . . . the injuries . . ."

"We'd need medical records, which we can't obtain without Mr., ah, Wilks' permission."

Even *Geraldo* turned me down. Intriguing was how they described my proposition in their letter.

"You're crazy," a cheerful production assistant told me, "but not crazy enough. Maybe if you stalked Hadrian Wilks, sent him threatening letters. Hey, you didn't hear it from me. Depends how badly you want on National Television."

"Harvey? It's Yossi." I am in Los Angeles on business.

"Who else?"

"We need to talk. You understand what's going on with Wilks."

"You are enjoying the convention. Three thousand accountants roaming the streets. I assume all of LAPD is standing by on a Polyester alert."

"This is serious."

"So, tell me. Not another accident?"

"You don't believe me?"

"I have an open mind. So, what goes?"

"You haven't heard? His plane's gone down."

"Wilks?"

"Final game before the All-Star break was in Texas. He's supposed to play in the All-Star game in Cincinnati. He gets a pulled muscle. Gets in his private plane for the short hop to Shreveport and home for three days with his family. He ain't got there yet. Twelve hours his plane is missing. Dead probably."

"I'll turn on the news channel. You think maybe this affects you?"

"I am hiding in my hotel room, ordering room service, in case I should be squashed flat by a taxi if I was to cross a street to a restaurant. Or, I might walk into an open manhole. Have a piano fall on my head."

"But if he's dead, what you have to worry."

"What if he's not dead? What if multiple injuries?"

"You should be careful," says Sarner.

"Such advice I don't need. I'm in bed. What can happen to me? Bernice is on the phone from Connecticut every ten minutes. I should take the train home, she says. Imagine me on a train. Head-on collision, or jumps the tracks, rolls down an embankment, bursts into flames."

"Keep in touch," says Sarner. "I'd visit longer but I got two engagements in surgery."

I ease out of bed, careful I shouldn't stub my toe. I put on a robe. I think of making coffee. Who wants to be scalded? I sit carefully on the sofa. Turn on the TV with the remote grounded flat on the table, it shouldn't electrocute me.

My worst fears come true. They have found Wilks' plane crashed in a bayou, torn apart by mangrove trees. CNN is everywhere. Probably Ted Turner himself is there. Cameras on the scene. Police cars, ambulances, flashers whirling. He's alive. Multiple injuries, they say. Oy! Burns, perhaps. Flap, flap, comes a medical helicopter to evacuate Wilks to a burn center, Dallas? Did they say, Atlanta? He's on a stretcher. Wrapped like a mummy. They transfer him to a gurney. Runs beside him a paramedic holding an IV. The helicopter swallows him. Flap, flap, and they're off.

"Enough with this dybbuk," I say to the ceiling. I step to the balcony. The sun shines. From the street thirty-two stories below I can smell flowers, the sweetness of camelias. I clutch the railing, make sure it is well anchored, check above me in case something might be falling. I breathe the perfumed air.

A tremor. A tingle in the bottoms of my feet. I grip the railing harder. From a distance comes a rumble, like a huge herd of invisible buffalo charging closer. Earthquake. I freeze. Glancing to the interior, I watch the chandelier swinging my way. The rumble envelops me. The balcony crumbles beneath my feet. I am airborne. Still clutching the railing, I am hurtling toward the camelias. Multiple injuries. Hadrian Wilks stepping into the batter's box first game after the All-Star break. Time changes confuse me. If I live, how many hours before Sarner will be able to reach me?

W.P. KINSELLA is the author of *Shoeless Joe*, the Great American Baseball Novel, upon which the feature film *Field of Dreams* is based, as well as several other novels and collections of baseball stories, including *The Iowa Baseball Confederacy, Box Socials, The Thrill of the Grass,* and *The Dixon Cornbelt League.*

RON CARLSON is the author of several books, including the novel *Betrayed by F. Scott Fitzgerald* and the short story collections *Hotel Eden* and *Plan B For the Middle Class.*

JOHN KESSEL is a professor of American Literature at North Carolina State and a winner of the Nebula Award from the Science Fiction and Fantasy Writers of America for his novella "Another Orphan." His novels include *Freedom Beach* (with James Patrick Kelly), *Good News From Outer Space,* and *Corrupting Dr. Nice.*

ANDREW WEINER's first short story was published in Harlan Ellison's ground-breaking anthology, *Again, Dangerous Visions.* He is the author of two collections, *Distant Signals* and *This Is the Year Zero*, and two of his stories, "Distant Signals" and "Going Native," were filmed for the TV show *Tales from the Darkside,* while "The News from D Street" appeared in the series *Welcome to Paradox.*

RICK WILBER is the son of former Major Leaguer Del Wilber, who was a catcher for the Cardinals, Phillies, and Red Sox in the late 1940s to mid 1950s, and a manager, coach, and scout for thirty years more. The author of ten books, including the novel *Bone Cold* and the collection of baseball stories and essays *Where Garagiola Waits*, Rick is a journalism professor at the University of South Florida in Tampa.

DAVID SANDNER teaches English at the University of Oregon. He has published a book of non-fiction called *The Fantastic Sublime*, and fiction and poetry in such magazines and anthologies as *Asimov's Science Fiction, Weird Tales,* and *Pulphouse.*

JACOB WEISMAN is the editor and publisher of the SF small press Tachyon Publication whose fiction has appeared in a wide variety of magazines and anthologies, including *Amazing Stories, Fantasy and Science Fiction, Universe 1, Night Cry, Year's Best Fantasy,* and *Year's Best Fantasy and Horror.*

GEORGE ALEC EFFINGER won the Nebula award in 1988 for his novelette, "Schröedinger's Kitten." He is the author of many acclaimed novels, including *What Entropy Means To Me* and *When Gravity Fails,* and several entertaining short story collections, including one featuring all science fiction sports stories called *Idle Pleasures.*

SCOTT NICHOLSON works as a newspaper reporter in the mountains of North Carolina. He has sold stories to such publications as *Aboriginal SF, More Monsters From Memphis,* and *Canadian Fiction Magazine.* In 1998, he was the grand prize winner in the annual *Writers of the Future* contest.

LOUIS PHILLIPS has published a full-length play, *The Envoi Messages,* as well as a collection of his comic one-acts. He is the author of the story collection *A Dream of Countries Where No One Dare Live* and *The Hot Corner,* a collection of baseball writings.

STEFANO DONATI has had short fiction appear in such publications as *Fantasy and Science Fiction, Talebones, Indigenous Fiction,* and *Writers of the Future.*

EDO VAN BELKOM won the 1997 Bram Stoker Award for the story "Rat Food" (co-written with David Nickle) and the 1999 Aurora Award for his alternate history of the 1972 hockey series between Canada and the Soviet Union, "Hockey's Night in Canada." He is the author of the collection, *Death Drives a Semi,* the novels *Lord Soth* and *Teeth,* and several books of non-fiction.

ROBERT H. BEER has published stories in a diverse number of publications, including *North of Infinity, On Spec, Spaceways Weekly, Jackhammer,* and *Tales of the Unanticipated.* He was also a finalist in the *Writers of the Future* contest.

L.K. ROGERS is a life-long baseball fan who lives in Summerville, South Carolina. Her fiction has appeared in many small press magazines, both literary and genre, including the recent anthology, *The Best of Palace Corbie,* which collected the best stories from the magazine of the same title.

AUGUSTINE FUNNELL lives in New Brunswick and has published stories in a wide variety of magazines and anthologies, including *Magazine of Fantasy and Science Fiction.*